GODS AND ENDS

ORDINARY MAGIC - BOOK THREE

DEVON MONK

DEDICATION

To the dreamers and mischief makers.
And to my family, who are often both.

CHAPTER 1

THERE WAS a vampire in my kitchen unpacking a box that had once contained Big-n-Tasty Bananas if the advertisement on the side was to be believed.

It was an unexpected sight—the box, not the vampire. The vampire, I'd known all my life. Old Rossi was the leader, the prime of all the vampires who lived here in the sleepy little coastal town of Ordinary, Oregon.

He was also an old friend of the family.

But I had no idea what that box was all about.

"Who let you in?" I didn't cross the threshold to the kitchen. A small knot of fear settled in my stomach, stalling my feet. I hated that seeing a friend in my house set off new warning bells in me just because he was a vampire.

It had only been a day since I'd been attacked by another of his kind, though comparing the ancient evil that was Lavius with Rossi was like comparing the plague to a field of poppies. Not that Rossi was harmless and sweet as flowers, but because I'd never seen an evil as horrific as his one-time brother-at-arms Lavius. Also because I wasn't all that great at clever comparisons.

Rossi turned to face me, a tea kettle in one hand, a small wooden box in the other. "Your door was open because you never lock it, Delancy Reed."

"Ryder let you in?" I guessed. Not a hard guess. Someone had been standing watch over me since I'd been attacked and bitten by Lavius yesterday, and I was pretty sure both my sisters, Jean and Myra, had only left me to either get some sleep, or deal with the actual job of policing that we all shared.

"He's going out for food. Pizza, I think he said." Rossi hadn't moved. He stood there as if he knew any sudden movement would startle me, the little teal teapot in one hand, the little wooden box in the other, waiting.

He could probably sense my fear.

I hated being afraid of him. Because I wasn't. Never had been. He was not Lavius. He would never hurt me. I took a deep breath and tried to get my wobbly emotions under control.

"Uh…what are you wearing?" I asked.

One eyebrow arched in faint amusement. "An apron."

"It has lace."

"Yes?"

"It's sort of a pineapple yellow."

"Pale daffodil," he corrected.

"And very fluffy. Is that chiffon? Tule?"

He sighed.

"I didn't know you went for that kind of thing, Rossi. It's like I'm suddenly seeing a side to you I wished I'd known to exploit."

"I look amazing in pale yellow. You aren't making judgements on assumptive stereotypes, are you?"

I grinned. "I think it's cute you have a lacy apron. Aww…there are little butterflies on the pocket. The more I look at it, the more I think it suits you. You should really wear it more. Maybe when you're teaching your yoga classes, or when you're busting heads at vamp meetings."

He gave me a long, tolerant look. "Are you done?"

I shrugged. And yes, this felt good, felt normal between us. Well, not that he was in my kitchen wearing a frilly apron, but that he was there and I was teasing him and we were okay.

"Where did you get it?"

"Maybe I bought it."

No way. "Who gave it to you?"

"A woman I knew, years ago." He turned back around and continued placing things on my countertop: cups, several tins, spoons, a delicate pot that might hold sugar, tiny silver tongs, and a little pitcher. "She had a wicked sense of humor and liked to make me uncomfortable at public events, like charity tea parties."

"Bertie?" Bertie was our resident Valkyrie and had a thing for organizing every community and charity event in town. I was sensing a story here, so I walked into the kitchen. Just like that, everything in me settled and I was here, home, where I was safe and warm and cared for by my friends and family.

"No. Nicole. Your mother."

Just hearing her name again after all these years gave it sort of a charged quality. As if the echo of it, said so many times here in the house where I'd grown up, suddenly hummed out from the walls like a struck chime.

"I don't remember charity tea parties."

He made a small *hmm* sound. "It was before you were born. Bertie was behind the organization of the event, but your mother took care of supplying the waitstaff, which I volunteered to be a part of, and the uniforms we would all wear." He plucked at the hem of the apron as if it were proof of the event.

"She had originally told me it would be black slacks and shirts with plain black bibbed aprons, which I told her was boring. Then when she found out I was going to be hers to boss around for a few hours, suddenly there was chiffon and lace and lemon yellow puffiness everywhere."

He smiled, a tiny flash of fang. "Since then, it just seems like the thing to wear when serving tea."

Which brought me to my next question.

"Why are you serving me tea? I thought we were getting together to talk about how to track down Lavius and save Ben, not to reminisce over oolong."

"For one thing, you don't like oolong," he said.

It was weird and nice that he knew that. He didn't stop with his preparation, his movements practiced and graceful as if he had unpacked tea parties from banana boxes on a regular basis.

"For another thing, we are going to talk about our plans at the meeting later today. And for the last thing…" He paused, turned to me. His glacial blue eyes warmed, carrying the pain, the apology, the deep patience that only hundreds of years could create. But there was more in his gaze. Something that looked like affection. "I don't think I've ever told you how much I care for you, Delaney. I've never had a child. A granddaughter." He stopped, swallowed. It didn't look like he knew how to go forward from there.

I nodded, unexpected tears prickling at the corners of my

eyes. I heard him. Heard his caring, his kindness, and so much fondness for me and my family and my mixed-up life spent policing this town filled with gods and creatures and mortals and monsters, that it almost seemed like love.

No, it was exactly that: love.

"Great, great, great granddaughter, at least," I said with a sort of croaky whisper.

He shook his head. "Well, yes. At least. So." He waved a hand toward the living room behind me. "Sit down and let me pour you some tea."

I smiled as he went back to his ritual, filling the pot with water, and doing something with the cups and saucers. Then I left the kitchen and curled up on the couch with the afghan my sister Myra had made for me. I waited for my tea.

I fell asleep instead.

"WHO'S WATCHING the shop?" I asked.

"Roy. Ryder," Jean, my youngest sister, said while she pretended to pay really close attention to driving. We were winding down Jetty, the street that paralleled the Pacific Ocean and gave us glimpses of the stunningly blue water and sky. "And we all have our radios. If there's police work that need to be done, we'll get it done."

"I don't have a radio," I complained.

She smiled sunnily. "No, you don't, do you? And do you know why?"

I mumbled under my breath.

"Say it louder for the class, Delaney."

"Because I got bit by a vampire. How many times do I have to say I'm sorry about that?"

"You don't have to say you're sorry. It wasn't your fault. But you *do* have to let your stunningly gorgeous little sister get you out of the house for some sunlight and fresh air. You also have to tell your stunningly gorgeous little sister thank you. And pay for her lunch."

"And I'm doing this because…?"

"Because you want ice cream?"

Thor had finally given up on his rain-a-thon protest. It

was warming up to the mid-seventies today, and was supposed to be ten degrees hotter tomorrow. Summer that had skipped the little beach town of Ordinary, Oregon was back on, full throttle.

Months and months of rain evaporated in rising columns of steam off the roads, roofs, and sidewalks, making the still air thick and sticky.

"I don't want ice cream."

"You only ate half of your lunch. You need ice cream, stat."

By the time Ryder had arrived with pizza, I hadn't had much of an appetite. The unproductive conversation we'd skirted around of how we might find Ben and what we might use to fight Lavius had ended any remaining desire for lunch.

We were running out of time, Ben was running out of time. We needed a plan.

"Taking me out for fresh air is really some kind of secret pact between you and Myra to babysit me, isn't it?"

"Wow," she said. "It's like you're a cop or something. Nice work, detective. You caught us. Your reward for breaking the case wide open is chocolate sprinkles and a waffle cone."

I grinned despite myself. She was a pain in the neck, but I knew she loved me. "I am your boss, Jean. I can take care of myself. Without ice cream."

"Weird. That didn't sound like 'thank-you, Jean, my stunningly gorgeous sister'."

"Listen to your bossy old sister, Jean. Take me home."

"No way. I want caramel corn."

"What happened to ice cream?"

"I changed my mind. Want something crunchy now because someone was harshing all over my ice cream buzz."

"I just want to go home."

"So you can pout in the dark? Nope."

"I don't pout."

She laughed. "Right. Hey, when we get the caramel corn, I'll let you ring the lucky bell."

She sure was set on keeping me away from my house. "Why aren't you taking me home, Jean?"

"How about some music?" She pressed a few buttons

and classic rock spilled out of her truck's speakers.

I turned the volume down. "That's not suspicious at all. What's really going on? What aren't you telling me?"

She turned the volume back up, but not as loud as before. "I have no idea what you're talking about."

"Nice dodge."

"Not a dodge. There's a lot going on, Delaney. Which thing are you talking about?"

"Whichever thing you're not telling me about." Okay, this was getting a little ridiculous. Maybe it was time for some leading questions. "Are you and Hogan okay?"

"Stop it."

"What?"

"Worrying." Jean's blue eyes seemed darker with the new hair color. She'd gone for white with pale orange tips this week. It was gorgeous and a little wild, just like her.

"Why can't I be home in my pajamas?"

"We agreed you needed fresh air."

"You agreed I needed fresh air, then bullied me into the truck before I even got a shower."

She flashed a gleeful smile. "The sun is shining, you big grouch. Enjoy it."

It was an order. Still, it made me smile. "I know you're up to something."

She laughed. "Always." Then she cranked up the radio so any chance at conversation was drown out by her clapping loudly about how "so fine" Mickey was.

Dork.

The ocean appeared and disappeared between scrubby pines as we followed the highway that was tacked along the edge of the world like some kind of unspooled ribbon.

I fought her for the radio control once, because I hated that song about the world ending with an earthquake, no matter how fine the singer felt fine about himself. She, having fast reflexes, won, and sang every word while she leaned toward me, which was super annoying.

Finally, she parked facing the sidewalk and a short, uneven stone wall. Beyond that were the craggy rocks of the jetty and the endless stretch of ocean. Waves shrugged up onto the rocks, sending white spray to hang in the non-existent wind. No fishing boats were coming in or out of the jetty, and the foot traffic was maybe half a dozen locals getting late afternoon coffee.

"Let's pop this shop." Jean was out of the truck and waiting for me on the sidewalk.

I got out and fell into step next to her, angling for the crosswalk. "I'm okay," I said as we waited for the signal. "I don't need you to cheer me up."

"Who said I'm trying to cheer you up? I'm in it for the free popcorn." She punched at the crosswalk button even though she knew it didn't really do anything.

"So there's really nothing wrong with you and Hogan?"

It wasn't the sunshine that put that blush on the top of her cheek bones. "No. We're…it's fine. And we are so not talking about him."

"Do I need to put on my uniform and threaten to tase him? Did he hurt you?"

I didn't know her eyes could get any wider. "You are not allowed to tase my boyfriends ever again."

"It was the one time. And it wasn't even a real TASER."

"He didn't know that."

I smiled. "I know."

She smacked my shoulder and I giggled.

"Still haven't heard that thank you for putting up with you today," she reminded me.

"Talk about your boyfriend and maybe you'll hear it. Wait." Something else occurred to me. "Did he propose to you?"

"No!"

"Did you propose to him?"

"Why would you even…no. It hasn't been…long enough." She pulled her fingers back through her hair, sending white and orange to swish and swirl like vanilla orange ice cream.

"You always get twitchy and bail before things get too serious. So is that it? Is it getting serious?" I waited. Put on the big sister eyes. The ones that made her think I could see what she was hiding from me.

Finally, she caved. "I didn't, haven't bailed. It's more the...opposite. I wanted to tell him. About. Everything."

Everything meant the supernatural creatures who lived in Ordinary and the gods who vacationed here. About our jobs as Reeds to keep the peace and see that mortal law and much, much older laws were observed.

It wasn't something a lot of mortals knew about. It was best kept that way.

Hogan had moved here when he was in middle school and his mom had decided to travel. He'd come back after finishing up his degree in business and opened the Puffin Muffin bakery.

His business was thriving, and apparently, so was their relationship.

"Telling him Ordinary's secrets is your call, Jean." I said. "If he's important to you, we'll support you no matter how it goes down."

"I know." That, with absolutely no conviction.

Was she that worried about his reaction? "Do you want Myra and me there with you?"

She bit her lip then lifted her chin like she wasn't bothered by any of this. Liar.

"I think, maybe I won't."

"Won't tell him about the gods?"

"About anything. Gods. Creatures. The whole thing. Just. Nothing."

"Why are you changing your mind?"

"I don't think it's a good time. I only wanted to tell him because I hate keeping secrets."

This was true. She was terrible with birthday gifts and surprise parties. If it meant keeping her mouth shut and her excitement locked away, she could only handle it for short periods of time.

"You like him. You want to keep him in your life." I made a rolling motion with my hand, trying to get a response out of her. She finally nodded. "You want to tell him all about your life, which includes...well, everything. I don't see the problem. You should tell him."

We were walking again, our reflections warped and wiggly

in the glass windows of the shops.

The Pop Shop was one of the last shops in a strip of touristy places on the bay. The smell of fresh caramel and salty popcorn mixed with the clean green overlays of the ocean and sunlight was all it needed to draw hungry visitors in through their door. Although the fact that a siren owned the shop didn't hurt either.

Jean stopped outside the door. "I...can't tell him. Not right now." Her gaze roamed over me like she had to make sure I was still in one piece, even though I hadn't been out of her sight for a second.

"I am fine." I put as much warmth and comfort into those words as I could. "And you should totally talk to Hogan about your life and about the secrets you don't want to keep from him. Whether I'm fine or not."

"It's not that easy." Yeah, I knew she was going to say that. The Reed stubbornness ran strong through our veins. "Let's just get popcorn, okay?"

"Sure," I said. A declaration of temporary ceasefire.

She opened the door and stepped inside.

The Pop Shop was one long counter of popcorn machines and popcorn-related mixes with nuts and chocolates. On the back wall sat candies, soda, and a slushy machine. There was floor space for maybe six people in the shop at one time, no chairs, no tables.

A mom and two little kids were inside, taking up half the available space. Gladys, the blonde-bombshell siren and co-owner of the shop, poured sample popcorn into the little outstretched hands. They clutched at it with sweaty fists before shoving it in their mouths.

Gladys loved working here on the edge of the bay during the day. During the night, she helped out at the bar just a few doors down.

She and her mortal husband, Cordova, had been together now for twelve years.

I wasn't sure if Cordova knew she was a siren. We left it up to each creature to decide if they wanted to tell a human companion who and what they were.

The default in Ordinary was secrecy. But when it became

clear that a few dates would slip into years of sharing a life, every creature had the right to share what they were with their loved one. Heck, they had the right to share before then too.

One would think we had droves of people spreading the word about all the supernaturals who lived in our town, but oddly, no.

I chalked it up to the nature of Ordinary. Created by the gods for the gods to put down their powers and vacation as mortals, and settled by creatures and humans alike, I had a theory that folks sort of…forgot about the unusual bits of the town when they moved out.

They remembered the good time they had here, the sand and sun and seashells. But they didn't remember buying popcorn from a siren, or living next door to a genie.

"Hey, officers," Gladys said as she handed the mom two little bags of popcorn. "What's your pleasure?"

The mom and kids left the store and the clang of the brass bell mounted on the side of the building rattled out twice, as each kid gave it a ring.

"I need an extra-large caramel and extra-large cheese, extra cheesy, and no comments on my love life." Jean dug in her back pocket for her card. "Oh, wait. You're paying, aren't you, Delaney?"

I rolled my eyes behind her back and then leaned in with my card.

Gladys fought a smile. "You got it. Do you want to sample the pumpkin and vanilla spice nut mix? I'm testing it on customers before the holidays. See if it's worth stocking up on."

"Sure." Jean said. Gladys scooped what appeared to be potpourri into two muffin liners.

Jean handed me mine. I eyed it a little warily. I still wasn't hungry.

"You okay, Chief?" Gladys started filling our popcorn order. "You look a little under the weather."

Oh, I'm fine. I've just been chomped on by an angry, ancient vampire who kidnapped my friend and wants to kill as many people as possible to force Old Rossi to give up a book of dark magic that could destroy the world. No big deal.

16

"I'm good, thanks."

She made a polite noise that really meant she didn't believe me and glanced over our shoulders at the door to make sure we were alone.

"I heard about Jame and Ben. Is Jame out of the hospital yet? Have you found Ben?"

News traveled fast in a small town. Staying up to the second on your neighbor's business was pretty much our Olympic sport and we took gold every year. It wasn't every day, or actually *ever* in our history, that a vampire was kidnapped right out from under Old Rossi's nose.

"Jame's recovering but isn't stable enough to go home," Jean said. "We haven't found Ben yet."

"Do you know what has him?" Gladys spun the extra-large clear bags of popcorn, deftly wrapping twist ties on the ends to keep them fresh.

"We're pretty sure we know." Jean said.

"Is it a human male?"

I knew what she was offering. She was a siren after all. Could lure men toward anything she wanted, from novelty snack foods to their deaths. But her special skills weren't going to work in this case.

"It's a vampire," Jean said. "So, no luck there."

Gladys swiped the back of her hand over her temple, pushing back thick gold waves of hair. "You're right. Vampires are a little out of my range. But if you think it would help, I'd be happy to try."

"Thanks," I said. "We'll call on you if it comes to that. Say hi to Cordova for us."

"Will do." She gave a finger wave, flashing what looked like a woven bracelet on her right wrist. It was blue and green, the colors of a summer ocean with little flecks of ragged beads caught here and there. It was pretty, and just unusual enough, I knew it was handmade. Maybe knitted.

A group of eight people laughed up to the door, and we did that crowded elevator thing to get out of the shop so they could squeeze in.

Which put us right in front of the brass bell. There was a little note on the wall beside it encouraging customers to ring it for luck.

And yes, the bell had been fashioned by a leprechaun who had lost a bet. The bell gave each person a tiny boost in the luck department. Maybe not enough to win the lottery, but enough to notice the glob of gum on the sidewalk before they stepped on it.

But we didn't need a little luck. We needed a damn miracle if we were going to kill the ancient vampire we still didn't have a good plan to find, much less stop, while somehow rescuing Ben.

If Ben was even still alive.

"Make a wish," Jean bumped me with her shoulder once we were on the other side. "Ring the bell."

I held my breath, made a wish, and rang the bell.

Let Ben be alive. Let us find him in time.

Jean closed her eyes a second and then rang the bell after me. I didn't have to ask what she wished for. I knew, even if she didn't, that her heart was full of Hogan.

CHAPTER 2

"TELL HIM."

The bench was positioned on a jut of sidewalk that curved out toward the ocean. A couple of sharp-eyed seagulls landed on the gray stone wall in front of us, laser-focused on the popcorn bags.

We stared down the birds as Jean carefully handed me the caramel corn. The kernels were warm. I popped several in my mouth, chewing slowly, letting the sweet and salt linger.

"Like you told Ryder?"

I made a face at her. "That's different."

"You've been in love with him for half your life and you didn't tell him about the monsters under the bed."

"I was not in love with him," I lied, "I was infatuated. It was a crush. I wasn't sure about him. About us. Not enough to risk the secrets of Ordinary."

"You are so full of shit." Hard words, but Jean laughed. "Dad told you not to tell Ryder when you were in fifth grade. I remember it. I remember how you stood there and cried, but nodded anyway and then never said a word. You were in love. It wasn't you who wasn't sure about Ryder, it was Dad."

I had mostly forgotten about that, but now the memory filled me, carrying the sorrow and crushing loss. I had told Dad that I really, really liked Ryder and would like him forever. He had dismissed it as a childish infatuation. I inhaled, exhaled, and released the ache of that long ago moment when my father's truth and my truth had not aligned.

"Then that's the question I should be asking. Are you sure that you love him?"

"It can't be love." Jean frowned. She leaned her head back and palmed a small pile of cheese popcorn into her mouth.

"Why not?"

She wiped her hand on her jeans, traded me cheese for caramel. "We haven't known each other long enough."

"There's a time requirement for love?"

The wind picked up, grudgingly stirring the heavy wet heat of the day.

"I don't know. It seems like...yes. You should know a person a...a long time before you say it's love. It takes time to grow. Years, maybe."

"Why can't years happen in a day? Or a month? Or several months? Where did you get the idea that you have to know someone all your life before you can love them?" As soon as it was out of my mouth, I knew. I knew why.

"Ryder and me. Jean, you know he and I have not handled our relationship very...we really haven't even *tried* to be a relationship until recently."

"You've known him all your life. He's known you." She said it with a sigh of longing. I kind of wanted to smack her out of it.

"You're ridiculous. Knowing him that long hasn't made it easier. And it doesn't make it the only way to fall in love."

Jean closed her eyes, soaking in the sun. "I missed summer. I'm glad we'll get a couple weeks of it. Did you make a deal with Thor?"

Total change of subject, the chicken. "Sort of. I told him we'd throw him a big welcome home party next year when he comes back if he'd lay off the water works. I think he got bored and decided to go start a hurricane in the south. Talk to me." I whacked her with the popcorn bag and the seagulls squawked, cheering for a kernel-spilling fight.

"No."

"Don't ignore Hogan. And you loving him. And him loving you and wanting to share his life with you."

She scowled out at the ocean. No easy feat with the wall of seagulls crowded in front of us, beady black eyes following our every potential popcorn dropping move.

"I've never thought of our town as dangerous." She winced. "That's so naive."

"Our town isn't any more dangerous than any other small town."

Jean chewed on a few kernels. "Lavius got across our border, Delaney. He found you alone on the beach and he attacked you. He could have killed you."

"He didn't kill me. You all got there in time."

"He didn't leave you alive because we showed up. If he thought he could have gotten his message across better with you dead, you'd have been dead, even with us standing there."

Wow. That was difficult to hear.

"It's...it reminds me too much of Dad," she said. "He was there, and then...then he was gone. Off a cliff he'd driven along all of his life. You and I both know he didn't lose control of the car accidentally."

"What are you saying?"

"Something killed Dad. Something that was here in Ordinary. Something we still haven't found. And now there's something that wants you dead too. A vampire of all things. Do you know the last time a vamp from the outside crossed over into Ordinary, challenged Old Rossi and attacked someone?"

"No."

"I do. Myra told me. It was never. Never, Delaney. This shit doesn't happen. Except that it did."

She drew her gaze away from the waves to take a good look at my face and make sure I was paying attention.

I was.

"Crow made a stupid mistake with his power and the god Mithra used that to get his grips on Ryder and make him a warden so that Mithra could have his...whatever...god hands in all our rules and laws and contracts. The newest vampire in town was murdered outside of a gas station. Heimdall, a god, was killed. Ben was attacked and dragged away from Jame, who was left for dead. You got bitten by a vampire.

"Is that enough? Oh, no, it is not enough. You also got shot by a crazy woman and Dad drove off a cliff and died. Dangerous things are piling up around here, Delaney. Lots of them. Way too many of them."

"The crazy woman was human. Nothing supernaturally dangerous about her." I was trying to lighten the mood a little because, yeah, that was a big list.

Jean didn't even smile.

"I thought some things would always be safe in Ordinary. That certain things couldn't reach us, hurt us. I mean, we have a heap of gods living here. That should count for something."

"Is that what a group of gods is called? A heap?"

"Shut up. Even though they walk around like mortals and have their powers in cold storage, they still have some influence over the place. Old Rossi has always kept things okay with the vamps because of all the rules he makes them follow. We have werewolves in most of our emergency response departments, a Valkyrie running the community center, and every Thaumas, Dictys and Hylaeus—"

"—those are all centaurs, so pretty much the same thing."

"—be quiet, I'm on a roll—all sorts of supernatural people, work everything from security to our burger joints."

"None of the centaurs work at the burger joints."

And, oh, the look she gave me. I grinned at her and crunched popcorn.

"What I'm saying is there have never been attacks like this, but now…."

I waited, letting her work it out.

"Now everything is different. Nothing is as safe as I thought it was. I don't want to drag Hogan into that. I like him and I think…keeping him safe, which means keeping him in the dark about stuff is the better thing to do. Until Ordinary is safe again. Until we make it safe again. Then maybe. Maybe then."

She slumped back against the bench, all out of steam.

"This isn't like you, Jean."

"Putting someone else's safety ahead of my wants? I can be selfless."

"No, I know that. Giving up on something you want. Someone you want." Jean was fearless, willing to jump into anything for the fun, for the joy, for the sheer experience no matter what the risks might be. I hated that I'd been a part of shutting down that wild joy inside her.

"Well, it's me now. It's me until we make sure this kind of crap doesn't hurt anyone again."

"We can do that and still live our lives on our own terms. Just because things go wrong once in a while doesn't mean we should stop doing and being what we love."

"I'm not ready to show Hogan how wrong things are yet, okay?"

What was I supposed to do? Force my sister into sharing a secret she didn't want to share?

Not this time.

She glanced at the bulky watch on her wrist. "Hey. It's time. Let's go back to your place." She shoved a handful of popcorn in her mouth, twisted the bag as she stood, and walked toward the truck.

I knew this whole popcorn and fresh air thing had been a cover to get me out of the house.

"What did you do?"

"Me?" She made big kitten eyes at me. That hadn't worked since she was five and told me Dad said she should take the carton of ice cream over to the neighbor kids who were sick with chicken pox.

Turned out Dad had not said that, there were no sick neighbor kids, and Jean could down an entire quart of mint chocolate chip ice cream before Myra and I could finish chasing her around the block.

"Why did you drag me out here?"

"For the sunlight. Fresh air. Popcorn."

"Jean."

"Just get in the truck. We can go back now."

"What did you do to my house? Oh, gods, you didn't move me out of it did you? Like take all my stuff to an underground bunker? Or some weird vampire proof yurt?"

She paused with the door open and squinted at me. "If we had either of those things, yeah, I'd probably lock you in one. But we don't. The yurt idea has merit. Tourist attraction? Vampire camping. Vamping?"

"What did you do?"

"Nothing big. We might have modified a couple teensy little things."

She ducked into the truck and started the engine.

"What things?" I slammed the door and buckled up. "What things, Jean? What did you modify on my house?"

That house meant a lot to me. It wasn't much, but it had been my family's before it became mine, and I didn't want anyone changing it just because I got attacked by a vampire.

"You hosed it down with garlic and holy water, didn't

you?" I groaned. "I will never get the stink out of the place."

Jean snorted and made a totally illegal U-turn to head north.

"You spread goofer dust on my roof?"

"Seriously? Goofer dust?"

"You sprinkled salt over the thresholds and window sills?"

"Would that even work?"

"Not on vampires."

"We didn't hose, spread, or sprinkle anything, you big baby. Your house is fine."

"Myra's behind this, isn't she? Because if she is, forget those other things, she's probably installing an electric fence around my property. Oh, gods. Think of the seagulls. So many dead beach chickens."

"Getting warmer."

I groaned again and leaned my head against the window. After some time, I muttered, "It's one bite. One little bite. I don't need to be wrapped in cotton."

The muscle at her jaw tightened and so did the corners of her eyes. "Yeah, we'll see. And you can stop whining now. We're here."

Myra's police cruiser was parked next to my Jeep in the gravel driveway. A van was also parked in front of the empty vacation house across the street. QUICK BROWN LOCKS was painted over the image of a fox with a key in its mouth jumping over a dog sleeping in a lock-shaped dog house.

Our local locksmith, who also happened to be both a reformed thief and an elf.

"You called Brown? You let him in my house? *Brown*? You do know I'm the police chief, right? And he has a record? And he's in my house?"

"'Thank you, my stunningly gorgeous little sister.' Besides, this has been a long time coming."

True. I'd put off getting better locks on my house because I never locked the house. It wasn't because I was stupid or thought the best of people. It was simply because before a few months ago, nothing bad had ever come near my house which sat at the top of about a hundred steps, and was pretty inaccessible by any other route.

It looked out over the bluff to a tumble of salal bushes and huckleberries, below which rolled sea grass and then sand that skiffed and humped all the way out to the sea.

When we were kids, we burrowed our way like rabbits through all those bushes to create a pine needle padded, root-riddled trail between the house and the sand. We'd been clever about where the trail spilled out onto the beach, so it was nearly invisible.

That trail had long since grown over and suffered a small rockslide, so there was no sneaking up on my house from any way except the front door.

Maybe Jean had a point. Ordinary had gotten dangerous lately. A small part of me wondered if it had always been this dangerous and I just hadn't noticed, or if, since Dad's death, something in our happy town had been broken and was now bleeding black.

I started up the stairs. "The original locks were fine."

"How would you know?" Jean said, behind me. "You never used them."

"I liked them the way they were."

"I know. But that had to change. You understand that, right? All bets are off. You've been attacked. Twice. What we're up against right now—Lavius—isn't something we can just assume won't happen again. I need you to tell me you know that."

"I know that." I did. I still hated that it was messing with my house.

"I need you to tell me like you mean it."

"Yeah, well."

She slapped my hip. "Stop being grumpy. We're going to keep you safe no matter what, you idiot. Accept our overly-protective, demanding love, or else we'll threaten you."

I threw her a finger over my shoulder and was so glad to hear her laugh.

Okay. Maybe things were still a little normal. Well, as normal as they ever were.

"Dee-laney Reed!" a male voice sang out. "Here you are!"

I stopped with three steps still ahead of me and looked up at the sneaky elf thief masquerading as a reliable business owner.

"Brown."

Gabriel Brown was a handsome man. Like, thin and graceful runway model handsome. He had bright, soft eyes that seemed to lean toward whatever color was in his immediate environment and blond hair that was shoulder-length, artfully tousled and just begging for fingers to be dragged through it.

His face was sharp at the jaw and cheekbones, but not too much at the chin. He had a tasteful amount of stubble over his jaw and the perfect symmetry of his face made his eyes bigger, his shoulders wider, his chest firmer, his hips narrower…no, it wasn't just his face that did all that.

His elfness did it. He was extraordinarily gorgeous. And boy-howdy did he know it and use it to his advantage.

That was the reason why he'd never served time for his string of burglaries. His victims took one look, got hit with his one-two punch—smile and dimples—and the charges, (and often panties) were dropped.

I didn't hate the guy, but I tired of his charm pretty quickly.

"You look lovely today, Dee."

"Still hate that nickname. What are you doing to my house, Brown?"

"Something that should have been done years ago. Making it safe. Do you have any idea how easy it would be to break into your house? I mean even blind, drunk and with one foot tied behind my back, it would have been child's play. No, what's easier than that? Baby play? Fetus play?"

"Go back to the part where you're tied up and blind," I said. "Because I was liking that."

Dimples: *pow, pow!*

Like that would work on me.

"You are a treat. Why aren't we besties?" He said it like he'd just run out of chocolate to lick off his fingers and wanted to try mine.

Like I'd ever let him.

"Hey, Delaney." Myra stepped out and pushed Brown to one side so she could give me a brief hug.

The scowl on Brown's face made me feel better immediately, though her sudden affection toward me was a little concerning. "You just saw me less than an hour ago. I'm okay, Mymy. Still okay."

Myra stepped back, her lined blue eyes light under the short blunt bang haircut which gave her that amazing rock-a-billy vibe. "Are you?"

"I was gone for an hour. For sunlight. And popcorn. With Jean."

"You looked pretty rough when you left. I told Jean I thought you needed more sleep, not popcorn." She didn't say it with any heat, just concern, but there was no way I was going to let her mother me.

"Stop worrying. And stop looking at me like that."

"Like what?" A crease pressed between her eyebrows.

"Like you're worried."

"I am worried. And if you aren't then I'm even more worried."

"Look! Popcorn!" Jean shoved at my shoulders, forcing me up the last few steps, and then corralled both Myra and me toward the house.

Brown was inside my living room, handsoming all over the place. "What kind of popcorn?"

Jean tossed both bags at him. "Sweet and salt. How goes the install, Brown boy?"

"Just about done." He turned the bags in his long, weirdly graceful fingers, but didn't help himself to the contents. Elves were strange about permissions and food. That kind of hesitance didn't seem to transfer to anything else though, like personal property, cars, safety deposit boxes, jewelry, or the town whale fountain. And seriously, did he have to leave it on the roof of the adult shop?

Elves were born to thieve and cause trouble.

Or maybe that was just Brown. We'd had a few other elves in town over the years. They all seemed to have an over-developed wanderlust and never stayed inside city limits for long. I'd wondered why Brown had settled here. But the more I got to know him, the more I was beginning to suspect it was because he delighted in annoying me.

"What installation? Locks?" I glanced at the door, which didn't seem all that different than when I had left it.

There was, however, a discreet box mounted on the wall beside the door with a muted gray digital display.

"Yes," Brown said. "But not just locks." He carried the bags of popcorn to the coffee table and set them down there before dusting his hands on the back of his slacks. "So, let me walk you through this."

"I blame you," I said to Myra.

"Don't care."

That was better. I liked that she wasn't looking at me like I might crumple at the first stir of a breeze.

"You refuse to lock the damn thing, so we decided to take that decision away from you."

"I can lock a door."

"Could have fooled us." Jean dropped down in one of the chairs and propped her high tops on the edge of the coffee table, away from the popcorn. "Carry on, my good man."

Brown gave her a double-dimple-dip and she winked at him.

"We wanted something simple but effective," Brown said. "Myra explained that you're not going to key in codes to disarm alarms or anything else complicated, so I made this as straightforward as possible."

"A key is straightforward."

"Exactly." He handed me a key ring. On it was a slim white plastic square. "Think of this as your key. It's digital. When you're right in front of the door, it will automatically unlock. When you are any distance from the door, it will automatically lock. Are you following me so far?"

"Right down to jail, if needed."

"Ha!" he laughed.

"What if I'm standing on one side of the door and I don't want it unlocked?"

"You'll attach this to your key chain. If your key chain isn't in your hand, the door stays locked. If the key chain is in your hand, just hold this." He pointed at a button on the white square. "It's an override." He pressed it and locks engaged with a weird electric hotel-door sound.

"To unlock the door, just press again." He did so, and the locks swished and chittered. "You can tell that it's locked by this little blue light. Open when it turns green." He flicked between the two settings, making sure I was paying attention. "That's it."

"I'm going to have to unlock it every time someone comes over," I grumped.

"The terrible inconvenience of living safely in the modern world. How you suffer," Jean said around a mouthful. "Does the lock have any special settings for our extraordinary citizens?"

Brown nodded. "I put in a few indicators, yes. If it's a god out there, you'll see this light flash yellow. Human won't make any lights go off, and since it's impossible to find something that is common among all our other kinds, I set it to flash red if something on the other side of the door is anything but human or god."

"Red supernatural, yellow gods, green open, blue locked, square white, pest brown. Got it."

He flashed me a smile. "I also set up some cameras."

"Please say you're joking."

"I am absolutely not joking. You can access the cameras on your phone, or it can pop on your TV like…so." I hadn't noticed he had stolen the remote from the side table and deposited it in his pocket until he pointed it at the small flat screen.

A split image of all four sides of my house appeared on the screen. Nothing out there right now but bushes and grass, shadow and sunlight.

"Think of the beach chickens," I said.

Jean snorted.

"What?" Myra asked.

"This is a little overkill, don't you think?"

"No, I don't," she said. "It is exactly the right amount of overkill. You're the police chief. You should have good security. And now you do."

"This feed doesn't go anywhere else does it?" I could just imagine Myra ordering Brown to send the camera feed to her phone, her house, and the station so she could Mom-eye me 24/7.

"We could do that," he said. "What a great idea!"

"No!" I said, before Myra could open her big mouth. "This is enough. More than. What do I owe you?"

"Taken care of," Myra said.

"It is. So." Brown laced his fingers together in front of him I noticed a thin bracelet on his left wrist. Crocheted out of copper wire and red thread and soft orange beads. Both delicate and strong, it was eye-catching in its simplicity. I wondered where he'd gotten it. "Are you going to tell me why your sisters suddenly went all Fort Knox on your house?"

"It's not all that sudden." Myra moved around to sit in one of the chairs. "We've been on her about this since she was twelve. She's never been a door-locker."

"Is it because of Ben?" he asked. "The attack? I heard about it. Was it a vampire?"

"Yes," I said. "And yes." I gave up hoping he'd leave since his toolbox was still open and propped against the wall.

The unusually serious look in his eyes caught me by surprise.

"I felt him enter Ordinary. The vampire." He nodded toward me, toward my neck and the twin black circles that were the only visible reminder of the bite, the attack. It was hidden under the collar of my shirt, but the elf knew it was there.

"How?" Jean asked.

He shrugged.

"Are you blushing?" she crowed. "I've never seen you blush before. Wow, the tops of your ears get really red."

He puffed out a burst of self-conscious breath. "You know, I could just leave instead of trying to be helpful."

"Leaving might do both, really." I gave him a sweet smile.

"I'm connected to the land where I live." He waved a hand dismissively. "It's an elf thing, when an elf, ah, settles down. So when that vampire...does it have a name?"

"Not one you need to know," I said.

He nodded. He knew names had power. "I felt the rot of it...the evil of it when it touched Ordinary."

"Anything else you could sense?" Myra had a pad in her hand and was taking notes.

"He was at the north side of town. Road's End, maybe?"

That was right. I'd been jogging up by Road's End when Lavius had appeared on the beach.

"How precise is your sense of vampires?" I asked.

"Vampires?" He shrugged. "I can tell they're in town, but it's not like I know where they are at all times. But that kind of evil is pretty easy to feel. He? It's a he, or was a he at one time, right?"

"Yes," Jean said.

"He radiates more darkness than Death does."

"Death's on vacation," I said.

"Yes, but he's still Death." When I didn't argue, Brown went on. "Death is...the grim reaper. Soul collector. Shepherd of the end days. That sort of power lingers like a shadow in him, rubs off on everything he touches, even while he's on vacation. My kind are of the light, so Death will always radiate a darkness that I can taste, feel."

"You think Death is evil just because it's dark?" Jean asked skeptically.

Death, or Than, as he'd taken to being called while he was vacationing as a human, was reserved, high-mannered and formal. But he was also the delighted owner of a rundown kite shack.

He'd named the place HAPPY KITES, and even though the font choice on his logo made it look more like HAPPY KILLS, it was clear he enjoyed running a business that was a lot more frivolous than his godly day job.

"Death is not exactly evil," Brown said "But the vampire that came into town? That's an ancient horror."

I felt the chill of his words and the truth that they carried.

"We don't like him," Jean said. "If you feel anything like that again, horror, darkness, evil, you need to give one of us a call immediately."

"I'll do that. If I can be of any help, you'll let me know."

I raised one eyebrow. I was pretty sure getting an elf involved in the fight against Lavius wasn't on the list of good ideas. Elves were creatures of light, and exposing him to that kind of horror, face-to-face might do him permanent damage.

"We will," Jean said with a lot more enthusiasm than I would have.

"Doors aren't the only thing I can put locks on." He crouched down to arrange his tools and closed the box.

"You don't mean the town do you?" I asked.

"Lock down Ordinary? Like keep a certain vampire out of it?" He shifted his gaze just over my shoulder and lost some of the humanness that he carried around himself like a shield.

Sometimes when the creatures in town let go of whatever they used to make them appear more human, a glimpse of the monster that lingered beneath the facade was revealed. But when Brown eased off on his control there was nothing but even more beauty that shone through, the kind of beauty that left his normal handsomeness in the dust.

Everything about him became sculpted and fluid, his skin luminous, his hair rich, his mouth soft and pliant, his muscles hard, lean, graceful and strong.

Despite myself, despite knowing he was a sneaky little thief who had an ego the size of a continent, I couldn't help but lean toward him a bit, moth yearning for that beautiful flame.

"There are too many laws set in place, at the very root of creating this town. To lock it down...." He frowned, then blinked and seemed to remember where he was. The gorgeousness dimmed bit by bit. "Well." His dimples made an appearance while all the rest of him faded back to that ridiculous, but tolerable, handsomeness. "I'd be willing to try it, but I'm pretty sure none of you would agree with what would have to be done to make it happen."

"Virgin sacrifices?" Jean asked.

"Something like that. Soul of the child of the blossom of the vine of the root of the land, etc., etc. Which, yes, would mean killing someone and using their life and blood to lock the town down. There would need to be a focus, something rare and solid, like a gem or stone, and it takes some searching to find something that won't break beneath the pressure of the task. Although..." He turned a little, his face shifting to the north, as if he had just noticed something. "Huh. Never mind."

"Nope. Back up and explain," Myra said.

Brown finished with the tool box and stood with it in his hand. "Naw. Let's not." He dazzled the shiners, but Myra didn't back down.

"You were talking about blood sacrifice and locking down Ordinary. I'd like to know what caught your attention in the middle of all that."

He inhaled, held it for a second, then, very carefully not looking at me, but holding Myra's gaze, answered. "I had the weirdest feeling that Chief Reed was here."

The chill that swept over my damp skin wasn't pleasant. "Dad?"

Brown still didn't look my way.

"Where?" Myra's question was far more useful than mine.

"In town. But it was a fleeting thing. Not…real. I know he's gone."

Dead. What he meant to say was that our dad was dead.

"Gabriel?" Myra asked.

"It was just a feeling. Nothing solid. I was thinking about the things that had protected this place, the people who had looked after it. Children of the blossom of the vine of the town—elf talk. You Reeds all fall under that title, chosen by gods to protect this place.

"He was a good man. I expected him to be around for many more years. Not that I think you all can't take over in his place, but he was good. Of the light."

"Yes he was," Myra said.

I couldn't blame Brown for thinking about Dad. He had left a big impression on this town, and I didn't think anyone who knew him was still comfortable with his absence.

Just a few months ago I'd thought I'd heard him haunting me. I hadn't felt him since then, but in that early morning after a restless night of sleep, it had felt real. He had felt real.

Then Dan Perkin had gone and blown up his rhubarb patch, a dead god had washed ashore, my childhood crush had dumped me, and I'd pretty much put that experience out of my mind.

"You sure you don't want me to go through the lock system again?"

"Walk to door, door unlocks. Walk away, door locks. Push button to override. I think I can handle that."

"Good! We like to supply simple solutions whenever we can."

"Thanks for doing this on short notice," I said. "Even though I still don't like it, I'm sure you pushed other business aside for me. I appreciate that."

"No problem, baby blossom."

"Excuse me?"

"Elf talk," he said with a serious nod. "Because I know you

wouldn't want to deny my elf traditions. It is also a part of my elf traditions to charge you double for rush jobs, baby blossom."

"Convenient," I drawled.

"Capitalism." He grinned.

"Con artist."

"Keep complimenting a man like that and I'll never want to leave."

"Want me to come up with some traditional names of my own I can call you?"

He laughed. "I do. But alas. The joy of parting is nothing to the pain of meeting again."

It was my turn to laugh. I think it was the first time he and I had ever agreed with each other.

He waved and was out the door that locked with a third-act swish behind him.

"Totally unnecessary," I said into the silence. "All of this. Even the popcorn."

"Don't hate on my salty love," Jean said.

Myra stood and stretched, then walked into the kitchen. "I made soup. Let's eat before we have to go see Old Rossi and make a plan to kill an ancient evil."

I would have argued for a nap instead, but I knew better than to pass up Myra's homemade soup or to head into today's meeting with an empty stomach.

CHAPTER 3

STANDING IN my little kitchen with my hands in sudsy water while my sisters talked quietly in the living room gave me time to take stock of myself.

I'd put up a pretty good face for both my sisters. They knew I was tired, they knew I was angry that we still hadn't found Ben, they knew I was irritated by the new lock and camera system on my house.

What they didn't know, what I was very careful not to show them, was my terror.

Lavius had bound me to him. Drank my blood. Claimed me. He hadn't turned me into a vampire. That took more than one bite, and honestly, I wasn't sure if my Reed blood would actually take to being undead. It was more likely I'd die before transitioning to vampirism.

I wasn't frightened, exactly, about the possibility of being turned.

I also wasn't frightened, exactly, about dying.

But belonging to Lavius, the ancient horror? Yeah, that was pretty much on the teetery top of my nightmare shelf.

And I knew, because I'd seen it before, that being claimed by a vampire meant being used against the people you loved.

Our ability to keep the people, gods, and creatures safe in Ordinary was not looking very strong right now.

"What would you do if you were here, Dad?" I asked too quietly to be heard over the sounds of the conversation in the other room.

I waited, hoping maybe I'd hear him, or feel him, warm and solid moving beside me. I could picture him drying the dishes in the drainer and placing them in the wrong cupboards like he used to when I was little. For a man who had run the police station with one hand behind his back, he had never been good at kitchen organization.

But he was not here. Not anymore. We were on our own

with this mess. And just because we'd taken a couple hits didn't mean we were out of the fight.

I let the water out of the sink and squared my shoulders. With all of the creatures, the gods, and the humans in this town, there had to be a way to save Ben.

There wasn't anything I wouldn't do to bring him back safe.

"Ready?" Jean called from the couch.

I dried my hands and walked into the living room. Myra and Jean waited by the open door, sunglasses propped on their heads.

"Where is the meeting?"

"We thought about having it here, but not enough room." Myra nodded at the door, and I grabbed my keys, let the lock do its thing, and walked out.

We headed down the stairs, Jean already almost at the bottom. "Any reason you and Jean have decided not to keep me in the loop on what's going on? Locks, cameras, and now this meeting relocation?"

"You can't blame us for wanting to protect you."

I could, actually, but I got her point.

"All right. Yes. You're worried, and you should be. Withholding information will backfire. It always does. I might be compromised, but I'm not sidelined. So from now on, you get information, I hear it. And I'll do the same with you. Right?"

We'd reached the gravel driveway, which was still wet in all the shaded places.

Myra ran her fingers back through her hair, tucking it behind one ear. I couldn't tell what she was thinking since her eyes were hidden behind her aviators.

"We'll tell you. We only kept you in the dark about the locks because we knew you'd hate it. But it's not the wrong decision."

"I'll give you that. But would have rather known you were doing it. I can argue. You can out-vote me."

Jean scoffed. "You'll veto."

I shrugged. "Get Ryder on your side. Or Roy, or Bertie. You know how to force me to see things your way."

"We're not letting you out of our sight," Myra said. "We all agreed on that."

"That's going to make showering and using the toilet unnecessarily weird."

"You know what I mean," Myra said.

"Just as long as you both understand I am still your boss."

The breeze picked up and ruffled across the tops of the twisted trees, buffering us with scented puffs of warmed pine and green.

"Like you'd ever let us forget." Myra started toward her cruiser and Jean did too.

"Carpool," Jean said.

"Shotgun," I called.

Jean paused with her hand on the passenger side door, then laughed. "You suck."

"Backseat, little sister."

"Stunningly gorgeous little sister, thank you."

Myra and I both snorted." If you kick my chair, I will hide your new Saruman action figure."

She made an offended sound then more noise as she threw a few elbows and knees at the back of it my seat.

"Hey!"

"Knees don't count!"

Myra ignored the whole thing as she settled in, started the engine and turned down the talk show about jazz on the radio.

"Which of you arranged this meeting and where are we going?" I asked.

"We left it up to Ryder." Myra headed down the gravel road.

Jean laughed. "You'll never guess where he chose."

"Is it a weird place?" I gave a moment's thought. "Too many weird places to choose from. Tell me it's not out in the middle of the Devil's Punchbowl or something."

A very small smile tucked up the corner of Myra's mouth. "It's indoors. I think he was going for neutral ground, out of the way, and private. He is such a rule follower now."

"Don't tell me he rented a boat."

"Better." Myra's smile had teeth. "The lighthouse."

"Really?"

"Yup." Jean said.

"Well, it is neutral ground," I said. "Like seriously set in stone from the moment Ordinary was established as neutral ground between gods, creatures and humans. How did he know that?"

"How do you think?" Myra asked.

Yeah, he knew it because my boyfriend was now tied to a god of contracts. Even if he hadn't been told, Ryder could probably sense the neutrality of the place.

"I'm thinking of bringing in a few more hands," Myra said.

The day was sliding into afternoon, the sky a dreamy blue. People wandered the sidewalks and businesses a little stunned and drunk on sunlight.

We were going to see a huge influx of tourists catching at the last straws of decent vacation weather.

"Tillamook?" I suggested.

"They didn't get the rains like us," Myra said. "Maybe Hatter and Shoe?"

Hatter and Shoe sounded like names out of a fairytale book, but they were actually humans who had been partners for the last eight years up in Tillamook about forty-five miles north of us. They were good cops and had sharp eyes. Sharp enough that they'd cornered Dad and he'd let them in on the secrets of our little town.

They'd both not only believed him, but had kept their mouths shut and offered to help when needed.

I hadn't called them in for anything since his death, hadn't seen them since his funeral. I guess I wanted to prove to myself and everyone else that my sisters and I were enough to take care of this town.

Not sure I'd stuck the landing on that yet.

"Stop scowling," Myra said. "We could use the help. Dad used to call them in at least once a summer. No reason why we can't do that too."

She was right.

"Are you going to put them up at your place?" I asked.

"It's Jean's turn."

"Damn straight it is," Jean said. "We're gonna party all night."

"You work nights," I reminded her.

"Party all *my* night."

"Do not corrupt them."

"Like I could. You ever done shots with those boys? I did. Once. Haven't touched tequila since."

The twisty single lane off the main road led us to the lighthouse built on a high jut of rock that overlooked the bay.

Long summer grass in the field surrounding it wouldn't go brown for weeks yet. A walkway wended along the edge of the bluff, the stone and cable fence standing as the only barrier between walkers and the ocean below.

The lighthouse should be open for tours explaining how far out to sea the light could be seen (twenty-two miles) and whether or not the place was haunted by the ghost of the lighthouse keeper's daughter, Harriett (probably).

We got out of the car, and I waited there on the sidewalk. I didn't see Ryder's truck among the dozen parked cars, and my heart caught with worry. He should be here. He set this up.

For one private, ridiculous moment, I let the terror of all the other things I was dealing with roll over into fear for Ryder's safety. Was he hurt? Kidnapped? Was he the next person in my life who I'd lose?

But as soon as I'd thought that, the growl of an engine grew louder and his truck came into view.

My stupid racing heart leveled down to a dull thud as he parked precisely two spaces over from where Myra's cruiser was slotted a little crookedly and over one line.

Ryder stepped out of the truck.

Sunlight caught in his dark hair, flickering against the random strands of copper and blond, and setting off the gold of his tanned skin. He wore a clean white T-shirt that clung to his chest and lean stomach and a dark green flannel rolled up at the elbows to show off his thick, muscled forearms. The jeans were worn down and faded where they curved over his strong thighs. His steel-toed boots were scuffed and practical since he spent a lot of his time either on build sites or as acting reserve officer for the force.

But it was his smile, soft and warm when he caught me staring at him, that lit up his face with so much relief and happiness, I wanted to push the sun out of the sky so I could soak up his light alone.

The way he walked, that comfortable rolling stride that was all confidence with a little challenge, drew my eyes to his hips, the twist of his waist, and his broad shoulders.

Everything in me went tight and warm and wanting.

Mercy me.

I couldn't stop staring at him, wanted the taste of him on my lips, the warmth of his skin pressed against mine, the weight of his hands touching me everywhere, holding me.

He'd been turning my head since before we were in middle school and now that we'd admitted we wanted each other, I couldn't look away from him. Didn't want to waste any more years trying to.

"Hey, Delaney." He reached out for me, and I drew forward easily, folding into his arms, pressing my face against his shoulder, breathing in the scents of him: spice and wood shavings and the under-sweetness of his cologne that mixed with a smell that was all his own.

His arms wrapped around my back. Thick, muscular fingers caught then slid into my back pocket. His other palm drifted up to cup the back of my head.

We'd just seen each other yesterday evening before Old Rossi had shown up. Even so, it had been far too long since we'd touched.

We had years to make up for.

"Hey, snuggle boo-boos!" Jean called out. "Smoochy-smoo later. Worky-work now."

Ryder grunted so softly, if my head hadn't been on his chest, I wouldn't have heard him. His arms tightened, then released.

I stepped back and grinned up at him. "Just like that? Are you gonna let her boss you around?"

"Yes. I know better than to argue with a Reed."

I didn't know I could smile any brighter. "Smart man."

We started toward the lighthouse. Jean stood waiting at the door—Myra hadn't been kidding they were going to keep an eye on me at all times. Then Ryder stopped as if a rope around his waist had just pulled him up short.

"Problem?"

He scowled at the police cruiser. Specifically at the tires.

"Ryder?"

"What?"

"Something wrong?"

He tightened his hands into fists, then relaxed them with what looked to be applied effort. "No."

"There's plenty of parking," I said. "It's okay if she's a little over the lines. The park is going to close pretty soon."

"I know. Closed an hour after sunset." He said it in monotone as if he were reading it off the back of a brochure.

"Yeah, that's right. So…you want to come inside?"

"I…." He wiped his palm over his mouth then dragged fingers across his jaw and scratched at the stubble there. "Yeah. I'm coming."

He couldn't seem to look away from the slightly crooked parking job.

And sure, things had been weird lately, but this was double-weird.

"Tell me." I closed the distance between us, crowding into him as if our contact would explain what his words could not.

He looked down at me, seemed surprised I was wrapped around him again.

"Now would be good."

"It's…no, it's not a big deal." He drew his arms around me as if he couldn't help himself, which I liked, and looked sort of embarrassed, which I didn't like.

"It's the cruiser? Something about the cruiser? About it being here?"

He hesitated a second, then exhaled. "It's outside the lines."

"I see. And that's…important?"

One jerky nod.

"I didn't know this would be a problem."

"It isn't. For you." This time his gaze locked on mine. I saw more than embarrassment there. I saw a deep stubbornness.

"Because?"

"It's…I notice all the breaks in contracts now. All of them."

"Contracts?"

41

"Going over the speed limit, spoon on the wrong side of the plate, jay-walking."

"Those are all things almost everyone does. Well, maybe not the speed limit breaking, but spoons and jay-walking? Not really contracts that have been broken. Just people making choices."

"I know that. You know *I* know that. But I can't ignore it. I can't *not* care about it."

"I told you being the snitch for a god of contracts came with some nasty side effects."

"I am not a snitch. I'm a warden."

"Mmm. Big difference." I rubbed my hand down his back, enjoying the rise and fall of muscles, the dip of his spine.

"Being a warden is a lot liked being a cop." He tightened his arms, shifted so our hips fit together better. I could feel one tension in his body sliding slowly into another.

"Not even a bit the same. You're more like a legal consultant. Deal with contracts. Which means something signed."

"'A written or spoken agreement that is intended to be enforceable by law,'" he quoted like he'd memorized the entry in the dictionary.

"You can't enforce cutlery placement, Miss Manners."

"Do not laugh at me."

"See me not laughing?"

"Oh, you're laughing." I liked how low and rumbly his voice had gotten.

"Is there some kind of rule against laughing? A contract enforceable by law, maybe?" I waggled my eyebrows.

He sighed and tipped his head up to the sky like he was looking for his patience to parachute in. "I don't want to be so…this isn't *me*."

The fact that he'd foolishly agreed to become tied to a god, to do that god's work here in Ordinary, must finally be soaking in.

"It's you now, Ryder. But just one part of you."

"That's how you see what you do? Guardian of Ordinary. It's just a job to you?"

No. But that was different.

42

I opened my mouth to tell him it wasn't the same thing. I was from a long bloodline chosen by gods to specifically not get foolishly tied to any one god. I was here to look after Ordinary and all those within it. To keep those who would do harm out of it.

I was born to this. I hadn't been tricked into it.

"Don't say it's not the same thing," he said.

"Some of it is the same. You're tied to a god, I'm tied to the town."

"But?"

"If I decide I don't want to be the bridge for god powers to be set down, that I don't want to be the guardian, I can step down. Someone else in the Reed line would show up to take over the job."

He was quiet. Jean, still at the door, was giving us this time. It was sweet of her.

"Would you ever leave Ordinary, Delaney?"

"I've thought of it." A lot. Especially before Dad died. "I watched Dad. Saw how this job drove him. Put shadows in his eyes and silence between his words. I know what it costs to keep Ordinary safe."

I didn't think I'd ever told anyone else all that before. I didn't think anyone had ever asked me.

"But you stayed. Why?" he asked softly.

"Dad. I wanted to make him proud. And Myra and Jean. I like looking after people. Making a difference. Maybe it's pride. I like being a bridge, a guardian, a cop. They're all me. That's all me."

"The pressure to follow his will is intense. I don't think that's me. That I'm someone who can follow like that." Ryder shook his head then gave me a look that said he was done talking about it. "It's new. I'll deal, or find a way to break it. Not today."

"Not today," I agreed, and I was pretty sure those two words said a lot more. Probably *I love you* and *I'm going to be okay*.

"Nice of you two to finally join us," Jean said as we walked past her into the building.

It was a small space, several degrees cooler than the outside and a little musty smelling over the very fresh scent of oranges. A wooden bench was tucked against the wall by the door and plastic pockets of brochures hung on the walls. The rest of the walls were covered by black and white historical photos and the glassed-in counter in the middle of the room held a few pictures and items, including the possible-ghost-daughter Harriett's handkerchief and locket.

Ryder and I followed Jean through to the next room.

It was just slightly larger than the first room, most of the extra space being taken up by the metal spiral staircase that spun up and up, a plain brown rope latched across the bottom of the railing to discourage unattended exploring.

Mason Rouge lounged against the banister, his Friends of the Park uniform pressed and official-looking. "Hey, Chief, Ryder."

Mason was half kelpie and a hell of a swimmer on the high school team. He'd been offered scholarships for colleges but had decided to stay here in Ordinary for a year. Other than wanting to be near the water he had grown up around, I wasn't sure why he was lingering.

"Mason," I said with a smile. "You decided on your college yet?"

He blushed a little, his already fair skin going red hot, and his slightly too-wide eyes narrowing as he crinkled his nose. "Maybe? I've narrowed it down to a couple, anyway. You trying to get rid of me?"

He tossed his head back and his nostrils widened. There was fire in those innocent eyes. He might only be half water-horse on his daddy Pat Rouge's side, but he got a double helping of his mama Leora's fire.

"Local boy does good only happens if local boy does something," I teased.

He laughed and pointed at the patches above his pocket. A thin weave of thread, blue like a heron's wing, wrapped his wrist and peeked out from under the right cuff of his shirt. "I am doing something. Spending my summer telling ghost stories and getting paid for it."

"That's gonna look good on a résumé."

"They're not looking at my résumé. They want me for my body." He winked, and I saw a lot of his daddy in that.

"Good body, but your brain's even better."

That earned me a smile that was kind of shy and blushy. And that, was all Mason. He'd been a cute kid. It was good to see that the cute kid wasn't lost under the wooing of sports scholarships and hints of the Olympics. "Yeah, okay. I'll get on that. Everyone's in the kitchen."

The kitchen was actually the remainder of the house attached to the lighthouse. It had been renovated to show off the vaulted ceilings with bare wooden beams, and the natural stone fireplace. The kitchen part of the space was to the left, which took up a portion of the ocean view and made good use of it via a bank of windows. To the right of that was the dining table with even more windows showing off the north view of the ocean and shore.

The far side of the space was broken up by a wall that jutted out, hiding a couple cots back there for visitors who might be ill, or for the caretaker of the place to stay overnight if needed. It used to be a closed-in bedroom, but the remodel had taken that out in favor of a more open space that could be used as a meeting place if needed.

And that's exactly what they were using it for.

Other than the kitchen, dining room table, bedroom, and the door to the bathroom, the rest of the place was a mix of couches and chairs. A few wooden tables gave extra sitting space against walls, one with a checkerboard, one with a stack of extra brochures, another with a box labeled: RAIN GEAR tucked beneath it.

The array of mismatched throw rugs on the wooden floor helped to soak up some of the voices and conversations going on in the room.

Looked like we were the last to arrive.

On one side of the room, lounging in a couple couches and chairs, were the vampires. Old Rossi, the prime of the vampire clan, looked dark and lean and uncharacteristically tight as a coil as he sat in a chair. Gone was the frilly apron and friendly smile.

Behind him stood Evan, who usually worked at the cat rescue shelter in town, but right now looked like the bodyguard he actually was. The light-haired twins Page and Senta who were part of the emergency response personnel, were crammed on the couch. Next to them were Keenan and Axel: the former part of the night-shift at the local lumber yard, the latter a mechanic who repaired cars and farm equipment and had the arms to prove it.

The couches and chairs opposite were covered in werewolves.

Small, deadly, the steely quiet Granny was the alpha of her pack. She sat in the middle of the couch, her saucer glasses adding weird light to her eyes. Behind her were either sons or nephews or cousins or nieces, about ten of them, all bulky, all silent, all a part of the family, the pack. Burly Rudy sat on one side of Granny and on her other, to my huge surprise, was Jame.

I quickly noted that Fawn, his cousin, sat next to him, her hand on the back of his neck in comfort as much as in protection. She was glaring daggers at the vampires.

Other than Myra, the only other person in the room was a god.

Thanatos, Death himself, was the only god who had come to this meeting, though I had no idea why he was interested in what was going on.

"Hello, everyone," I said. "Thanks for coming."

"Delaney," Old Rossi greeted me, his voice low, even, and cool. No tea and friendship there. No New Age peace and love either. Just wariness, and deadly focus.

Granny Wolfe nodded but did not take her eyes off Rossi and his crew. Neither did any of the other Wolfes, who were all staring at the vamps like they were food that wouldn't stop twitching.

"Rossi. Granny. Than. Good to see you all. This is neutral ground and there will be no blood shed here, no pain. We work together, we save Ben and kill Lavius. Understood?"

"Yes," Rossi said.

"Delaney, you come sit down and we can see what we can see." Granny pointed to her couch.

Myra stood across the room at parade rest. She gave me a look that probably mirrored my own. This tension between the two factions was going to catch fire. Sooner rather than later if we didn't do something about it.

"Benoni is not dead," Than said smoothly into the silence. *Crack, boom.* Tension busted.

Jame's swollen, red-rimmed eyes jerked to Death's face.

"Benoni lives," Than continued as if we were talking about upcoming movie times. "I would know if he did not. I believe you would too, Travail, is that not true?"

If Rossi was bothered by Death using his first name, he didn't show it. If anything, some of the tightness around his eyes eased slightly, though his jaw still twitched as he ground his teeth together.

"I would know," Rossi agreed softly.

"Yes, then. There is hope." Than smiled, as if he had never had the chance to say that before and liked the sound of it. "Is there also tea?"

Jean moved over to the kitchen. "I'll see what I can find. Anyone else want tea?"

Silence, then Ryder finished strolling into the room bringing that confidence and challenge that sat so well on him and did something to center the room, to ground the moment into the reality of people gathering together to find solutions.

"Coffee, if you have it," he said.

"Me too." I pulled a chair over so that I was settled between both factions, Than and Myra directly across the room from me. Once I sat, Myra did too.

"Do you know where Ben is?" I asked Than.

"No. He is between life and death, as all of his kind are. To sense his location I would have to either regain my power, or he would have to transition into a state I could perceive: death. He would have to die. I would feel him then, even without my power. The passing of vampires is a heated thing, and all too rare to be overlooked."

"You said you could find Lavius through the bite that ties me to him, right?" I asked Rossi. "We find him, we find Ben."

"It could be done," Rossi said. "But using that tie comes at a cost."

Of course it did. I resisted the urge to throw up my hands in frustration. Why couldn't anything be easy and why didn't anyone let me in on this stuff from the get-go?

"All right. Fine. What's the cost? Let's get paying."

The front door opened and we all paused while Mason welcomed what sounded like a dozen kids and a half dozen adults. He started into the tour spiel and I pitched my voice a little lower so the tourists wouldn't hear me.

"It's blood, right? I have to give up some blood to track him?"

Rossi's gaze was sharp and hungry. I raised one eyebrow, not falling for the deadly vampire routine. I'd hauled him in for indecent exposure for streaking down the beach and through the middle of town three times in the last couple years. I wasn't afraid of him.

"More than blood, Delaney."

I waited. We all waited.

Jame got tired of waiting first.

Jame growled, a low, painful sound that snagged and caught somewhere in his chest. "What. Price." His voice was gravel and sand, eyes glassy with fever, color too green and gray beneath the bruises. Sweat peppered his forehead and ran a thin line down his temples.

He looked like he'd been hit by a truck that had backed up, run him over again, and then pulled a trailer over his bones.

Fawn's hand on his upper arm held him stiffly propped against the couch. Granny radiated strength and power and protection at his other side.

"It is nothing you can pay, Jame," Rossi said with more kindness than I'd ever heard out of him.

"I'll pay it," I said. I was the one attached to the vampire, it only made sense I'd pay the price of being used as a human GPS unit.

"No," Myra and Jean both said at the same time Ryder said, "Not happening."

So, yeah, it was great to have a cheering squad, but I knew how this kind of paying-the-price stuff went down. I could deal with it. It was my *place* to deal with it.

"What price, if not blood, *strigoi*?" Granny's voice didn't carry kindness. Just flinty anger and more than a little hatred for Rossi's kind in general and Rossi himself in particular.

"Dark magic."

Okay, that was not what I expected him to say.

"Dark magic is what he wants," Rossi said. "It is what he has come to our land for, what he has killed for. To find him, we must give him what he will use to destroy Ben, this town, all of us. He will gut us on our own good intentions."

"We have dark magic?" Ryder asked. "It's a…thing? That we have here?"

Rossi's gaze didn't leave Jame's. "Yes. I have it here."

Jame's shallow breaths turned into a panting, frantic whine. "Pay. Pay it. Pay it pay it pay it."

It was heartbreaking.

Granny slipped her hand onto Jame's. She turned his hand over and drew her fingers across his bare wrist. Then she pressed her palm against his, linking their fingers tight enough it looked like it hurt.

"Hush now," she said so softly, so gently. "Hush. He is yours. He is always and only yours. We will find him. We will put him in your arms. You will feel his heart beat."

Jame swallowed, a thick, hard motion. Then he dropped his gaze from Rossi and slumped, his eyes closed, his shoulders hunched. Whatever energy it had taken for him to demand, to beg, was gone now, leaving him exhausted.

I wanted to reach out and comfort him, wanted to wipe away the tears running down his face. Fawn shifted on the couch so that her arm was across his back, and pulled his face into the curve between her shoulder and face, hiding him with her body from all eyes in the room. She held him, whispering comforting things.

"You have the magic that monster demands and you haven't given it to him?" Granny snarled. "You have refused? You have left one of mine to suffer?" Her words rumbled, the undertone a sound no little old lady should be capable of, a sub-audible growl that I felt in my spine, base of my skull, the shivers of fear.

"Peace," Rossi said. "I have reason to keep the book hidden from him all these years. Surrendering it to him would sign our end. Not just one of yours. Not just one of mine. All of us." Rossi's hands clenched so tightly on the arms of the chair, trying to hold him to his seat, I heard wood creak.

"Give the book of dark magic to me."

Her words were an order. A demand. A threat. Werewolves shifted, moving out from behind the couch, shoulders tipped, muscles bunched, ready. Ready to fight for their own, even if it meant killing people who had been, if not exactly friends, neighbors.

The vampires did not move at all. They went impossibly still, focused as arrows drawn home, taut and ready to fly.

In about half a second we were going to see the two biggest supernatural factions in our town broken and bleeding on the lighthouse floor. Ended not by the ancient enemy outside our border, but by the mistrust in each other.

Maybe that was why Than was here. There were about to be a lot of vampire deaths to not overlook.

"Who wants tea?" Jean stormed into the space between the vamps and weres with a tray of six steaming mugs in her hands, putting herself square in the middle of the battle zone.

Myra stood. I was half a second behind her. Ryder surged to his feet too, all of us clogging the space next to Jean, putting our mortal bodies in direct firing range of the other creatures.

No one spoke. There was only breathing, too loud, the rush of my heartbeat, also too loud, and the muted sound of feet walking up the metal spiral ladder to the lantern room.

There were civilians here. Innocents who had no part of the vampire werewolf war. People I was sworn to protect.

"Ease off," I said to Rossi. I turned my gaze to each vamp. "We have humans out there, and I will not have this historical landmark go down in the record books for mass murder."

Rossi twitched just one eyebrow as a fang slipped down to press into the soft mound of his lip. He otherwise didn't move or look away from me. Didn't challenge my authority.

Yet.

It was an acknowledgment. Not a big one, but enough to let me know he didn't want to fight the werewolves. Not over this.

Just enough to let me know he was furious that his old enemy, his one-time brother-at-arms had taken Ben, who Rossi thought of as a son. There was hunger in the killing gaze Rossi leveled at me. The hunger for revenge.

"If any of you draw werewolf blood I will kick you out of Ordinary. Permanently. We do not kill our own within this border. We do not kill each other."

I turned to Granny. She stood now, the illusion of age flung away so that all I could see was her strength, her power.

"You will not draw vampire blood on my soil. If you do, the Wolfe family will be exiled."

She narrowed her eyes, weighing the truth of my words against her need for violence.

"We will wipe Lavius off the face of this earth," I said. "That is our war. That is the fight we take on together."

"When?" It was still a challenge. Still an alpha wolf furious for one of her own enduring pain she could not end.

Jame pushed up to his feet, breath coming too fast and shallow, every fiber in his body, every beat of his battered heart unable to stay still, needing instead to rise, to stand, to fight.

To save his love.

"Two days," I said to Jame. "On the full moon we will kill Lavius and burn his bones. But tonight, tonight we will use this bite, my blood, and dark magic to find Ben." I could feel Rossi tense behind me.

No sound filled the space except for Jame's soft groan and the distant sound of Mason droning on about the lighthouse keeper's broken-hearted daughter who, having received word that her beloved sailor had perished at sea, threw herself to the rocks below.

"You must rest, Jame." I was close enough to him to press my fingers on his arm. "You are going to have to put Ben back together when we bring him home. You need to be as whole as possible for him. Strong for him."

Jame was a big man, built wide and thick like most of his family. He was as fit and hard-muscled as any firefighter in his prime. But under the stress of his internal and external wounds, he seemed smaller, more vulnerable. It was painful to see him working so hard just to stay on his feet.

His wounds had nearly put him in a coma. Lavius breaking the soul connection to Ben—Ben's bite freely given and freely taken by Jame—had nearly killed him.

I hadn't asked Rossi how long mates survived when that link between them was broken.

I could guess it wasn't very long.

"Isn't this wonderful?" Death cooed.

51

The tension between vamps and weres snapped, as every head jerked toward him.

The weres snarled, the vamps made that weird clicking sound at the back of their throats, all of them hunters locked on prey.

Than didn't seem to notice any of it. "Is it an oolong?" he asked. "I do enjoy a good oolong."

Of course he was more interested in his tea. These kinds of things, the very real struggle of the living trying to survive, was something he'd never been all that involved in.

"How?" Ryder asked into the weird silence.

"Hot with lemon usually," Than said.

"Not your tea." Ryder shifted, easing his stance so he wasn't squared off quite so hard toward the vamps. "How are we going to find Ben with the bite and blood—which still isn't happening, Delaney. What's the plan?"

"Blood will not work," Rossi said.

"I have a plan," Myra said, because of course she did. "We need to sit down. All of us. Jame? Could you sit down?"

He lifted his head and gave her a steady look. "No."

Okay, that was more like the old Jame. Fawn said something low and soothing, and after another moment, he returned to the couch.

And there went the rest of the tension in the room, whooshing away like someone had just opened the spill gates on a dam.

Jean got busy handing out tea and coffee, then placed herself with her back to the door toward the visitor's entrance. Myra stood near Death, facing Jean. That left Ryder and me between the supernaturals, shoulder-to-shoulder, Ryder on the vamp side, and me on the wolf.

Death sipped his tea, his dark eyes glittering over the chipped rim of the mug. He was enjoying every minute of this.

Jerk.

"We know Ben isn't in Ordinary," Myra began. "Outside of Ordinary becomes more of a problem for us to pin him down.

"They could have just driven him somewhere, or might still be on the move. Since vamps don't have to eat or sleep, we're not going to get the kind of hits off of bank accounts and purchases that we might if we were tracking a human.

"We have a few options, but we need to be careful not to tip our hands." She pulled the notebook out of her coat pocket and clicked a pen.

"If we are thinking of asking gods to enter this search, we might be able to bypass a lot of the standard kidnapping procedures and get some valuable information. I suggest we talk to a few gods, see if they would be willing to pick up their powers, leave Ordinary, and help us. If not, then we could contact the gods outside of Ordinary and see if they'll lend a hand. Possibilities for gods who might still feel generous toward us are Crow, Thor, Athena, Heimdall."

I winced a little at that last one. Heimdall was my ex-ex-ex-boyfriend. We hadn't left on great terms, but since he'd been chosen by Heimdall's god power and I'd made sure he could take on that power, maybe he didn't hate everyone in Ordinary.

But Myra was right about one thing. The longer a god stayed away from Ordinary, the less they seemed willing to go out of their way to help us.

Until they wanted to vacation again. Then it was like we were all long-lost friends who were finally meeting up.

"A few people in town might be able to give us information without relying on gods," Myra continued. "Jules is a witch and Yancey is a seer. We know Ben's scent can't be found, nor his blood, since neither the werewolves nor vampires had any luck tracking him.

"Tapping the possible information sources in town won't take more than a few hours. Maybe half a day. But if we want to do this fast and hard, we summon a demon or hellhound and bargain for their tracking services."

Death made a small humming sound in the back of his throat like that idea intrigued him.

"Demons?" Ryder said. "That's in our arsenal along with dark magic?" He shot a look my way and I sort of shrugged. "Okay," he said. "That's in our arsenal. I vote fast and hard."

"No demons," Granny Wolfe said.

Rossi grunted and I couldn't tell if it was an agreement or disagreement.

Death sighed, disappointed.

I was honestly a little impressed with Myra's thinking-outside-the-box. Of course it might also land us in dying-outside-the-box, which was usually the outcome when one summoned anything from the down below to the up above.

"We'll table demons for now." I glanced at Rossi, then at Granny. "We could use dark magic and this bite to find Lavius. Take the precautions available to us, then kill Lavius. What are the chances we'll find Ben if we kill Lavius first?"

"None." That rang out like a funeral bell from Rossi.

Granny grunted. She didn't want to agree, but I didn't think she knew more about dark magic or Lavius than Rossi. I hadn't expected Rossi to have some kind of book that could destroy the world, but if he said it was going to blow up in our face, I believed him.

"So our plan is first, find Ben," Myra said. "Second, kill Lavius. It's possible just finding Ben will put us in the right place and right time to take Lavius down. We will proceed quickly, and cautiously and stay in contact with information."

I spoke. "I want your word, Travail and Granny, that you'll give Myra, Jean, and I…"

Ryder cleared his throat.

"…and Ryder," I added, "until midnight to gather information for finding Ben. You will guarantee me that you will not fight our decisions, argue our actions, or kill each other. We'll find him. Without dark magic. Without demons. If we come up with nothing, we'll make a new plan with dark magic and demons and anything else we need."

"I will not stand in your way. Until midnight." Rossi's words carried the weight of a vow.

Granny sucked air through her teeth, then nodded once. "We want him back."

"That happens only if we work together. All of us. Promise me that."

"You have it," Granny said.

"Yes," Rossi agreed.

Myra took over. "I want to know how far outside of Ordinary you've searched. I don't want to waste time going over ground you've covered. Appoint someone in your clan and pack to stay in direct contact with me."

"Me," Rossi said. No surprise. He was a control freak under all that peace-and-love stuff.

"And me," Jame said.

That was a surprise.

"I don't think—"

But Granny cut me off. "You are wounded."

Yeah, that's what I was going to say.

"I will be there when he is found. I will be the first thing he sees. I will fight anyone who tells me otherwise."

The weres squirmed. Jame was hurt. If any of them wanted to take Jame down, now while he was vulnerable would be the time. But behind his pain was a rage, a kind of crazed focus that would have him fighting long after his body, or the body of his challenger, was broken.

He was a man who had nothing to lose.

"Jame," I said.

"No," Granny said. "He will be with you." Her lift of chin, her narrow gaze told me she expected me to take care of him, look after him.

Holy crap. Just what I needed, a wounded, heart-broken, claw happy werewolf on my team.

"Yes," I said without a second of hesitation. "He'll be with me."

A cold sweat washed over me. No pressure, right? I turned to Rossi. "Tell us everything you know about Lavius."

Rossi unclasped his hands and sat back, crossing one leg over the other, ankle resting on knee. "If I were to tell you everything I know about Lavius, we would be in this room for years."

Really? Work with me here, Travail.

Myra spoke up. "Narrow it down to the most pertinent details. Anything that would tell me who he has around him, where he might own property, what you think his next move might be. Why he's chosen to bring this fight to Ordinary now."

"He wants the book."

"You've said that. Why now?"

"This is an old promise between us."

"What promise?" Ryder asked.

"That of all the things on this earth, I will be the one to kill him."

Silence spread out slowly as Death exhaled a long breath. It was as if Death had been waiting to hear those words for decades and more, as if he craved Lavius's end.

"Why you?" Ryder asked.

"Because I vowed when he took what was mine, I would end him. Ben is mine. Delaney is mine…"

"…hey," I said.

"…Ordinary is mine." His words were dark and heavy as a gallows' drum beat.

Granny, who had been on her feet this entire time, finally sat back down on the couch beside Jame. Her anger was softened by something else. A hunger to see Rossi follow through with that promise. Two killers who spoke the language of vengeance.

"Can you?" I asked.

Rossi's shoulder lifted in a casual shrug. "Yes."

Okay, so it was good to know our vampire was just as much of a badass, maybe more, than the bastard who had crossed our boundaries, killed Sven, broken Jame and Ben's link, kidnapped Ben and bit me.

Suddenly, things were looking up.

"How?" Ryder asked.

"Brutally."

Jame growled and so did the other weres.

Look at that. Everybody on the same page like one big happy bloodthirsty family.

"He said he wants the book. Why challenge you for it now?"

Rossi's eyes tightened just slightly. He had an answer to that. An answer he didn't want to share with the class.

"Your father, perhaps?" Than offered.

"Rossi's father?" I stared at Rossi. "You have a father? Alive? Alive-ish? Why didn't I know that?"

"I was born once," Rossi said with an offended lift at the end of his words—almost, for a moment, the Rossi I had always known. "My father is long, long gone to dust."

"Ah," Than said. "I see I have misspoken. I did not mean your father, Travail. I meant your father, Delaney."

"My father is dead," I said.

Than took another sip of tea and watched me. "Yes," he agreed.

"What does he have to do with the insane murderer vampire who attacked, killed, and kidnapped?"

"And bit," Jean added, like I needed reminding.

"Perhaps Rossi could tell us?" Than suggested.

Rossi frowned as if he were trying to do the math. "I thought it was because I'd slipped up. Let Sven into my clan, missed that Lavius had his hooks in him, perhaps even eyes through him."

He was talking like no one else was in the room.

"But it isn't that. No. It isn't Ryder either."

"Me?" Ryder protested. "What do I have to do with any of this?"

"Or if it is Ryder, it isn't *just* Ryder. It isn't *just* Sven. What else? What am I missing?"

Death placed his tea cup down on the coffee table nearest him and was watching Rossi, looking for that moment of knowledge to ignite.

"You could save us all some time and just tell him what you meant," I said.

"It is not my place to affect such things. Even I have rules I must follow." Death placed his hands gracefully on his thighs, just the fingertips resting as if he were a pianist, ready to present a concert.

"Make it your place." Yes, it was an order. Yes, Than lifted an eyebrow before otherwise completely ignoring me.

"I'm sorry," Ryder cut in. "What does this have to do with me? How do I connect in any way to an ancient vampire I've never met?"

"He has ties to the government," Rossi said, still in the stare-down with Death.

"And?"

"What agency in the government do you think he would most want to keep an eye on?"

"I have no idea. The presidency?"

"The presidency is fleeting, capricious, and a victim to a much more specific machine of greed and power."

"Enlighten me then," Ryder said.

"If I were him, I would want to know where my enemies were at all times."

"All right," Ryder said.

"You think Lavius has people in the DoPP?" I asked.

"It was what I thought when Ryder first came back. But now? I don't know."

Ryder worked for the Department of Paranormal Protection as a freelance agent, charged with investigating if there were any paranormal creatures in Ordinary who needed to be contacted and offered whatever protection the secret government agency thought they could offer.

"Are you a part of the DoPP?" Ryder asked.

Myra made an approving sound. It wasn't the question I'd expected Ryder to ask either, but it was a damn good one.

"No." Rossi frowned. "What need do I have for spies? The vampires who search me out, find me. I'm not hiding. We come to an agreement about living in Ordinary. If they stay, they follow the rules or I kill them. I rule over the vampires here just as the Reed family rules over all the other supernatural creatures of the town."

"Sweet," Jean said. "I've always wanted to be royalty."

"We aren't royalty and we don't rule anyone," I said. "We guard. We police. We enforce the law, including for vampires. There is no ruling."

"There could be," Jean said. "Rossi said we could rule."

"No." I knew she was joking, trying to lighten the mood. But I wanted to crush that idea right now. There was no way our family would ever lord above the town. Uphold the law, yes. Control the lives of these people? Never.

"I'm not connected enough to the higher ups to know if Lavius has people in the agency or not," Ryder said. "But I'll ask around. See if there is anything anyone can tell me about where someone like Ben might be taken to."

"Good," I said. "Myra, you and I will check in with the witches and seers in town. Jean, you talk to the gods and see who will help us."

"Got it, Chief," they both said.

"We're bringing Hatter and Shoe in to take on the bulk of

the day-to-day policing in the town, and we'll brief them on the basics of the situation so they're not caught off guard. When are they arriving?"

"Tomorrow morning, bright and early," Myra said. "We're putting them up at the Winddrift cottage, I've cleared it with Hades."

I was, as ever, impressed with Myra's attention to detail and follow through. She was hands-down the most efficient of any of us.

"So," she said. "we all know what we need to do. Check in every hour. Delaney, do you want to be the contact point for information dispersal?"

"No, you're better at it. All information funnels through Myra. We'll grid out this search and make sure we're not double tracking over each other if we don't have to. We want to cover as much ground as possible as quickly as possible once we know where to start looking."

"Are demons still off the table for now?" Jean asked.

"No demons." After a quick silence, I added, "Last resort, we'll contact the underworld. But we're not at the last resort yet, and we're not going to let it get that far. Anything else?"

Ryder, of course, opened his mouth. "Why the full moon?"

"What?"

"Why do we have to wait until the full moon to kill Lavius? If we find him before then are we under a no stabbing rule?"

"Lavius can't be killed by a regular blade," Rossi said.

"Cutting off the head works though, right?" I asked.

Rossi rolled his shoulders, looking like he was trying to loosen muscles gone too tight. "In theory."

"That's not comforting. Tell me in application."

"He's old, Delaney."

"So you've said. You're old too. Tell me you know how to kill him."

"I know ways that will be the most effective. I am not convinced an average human has the strength of follow-through to do it."

"Well, we aren't average. Give us some ideas of how to slow him down."

Both the vampires on the couch and behind it shifted

slightly. Yeah, I could understand their discomfort. Who wanted the elder of their clan to offer up a paint-by-numbers vampire slaying guide to the local police in front of their racial enemies?

"Bullets won't injure, but if you can hit him in a close cluster through the brain, that might slow him. Aim for the eyes. Same with blades of any kind—aim for the eyes. TASER won't affect him. Neither will holy water, garlic, tear gas. I might have a few weapons I could loan you that would be more useful. Delaney, come to my place, and we'll see what I can pull together for your teams."

That was the most generous, open, and honest offer I'd ever heard from Rossi. He'd never invited me to take a stroll through his secret weapons stash before.

It terrified me how dire things were for him to allow me to have access to any of his weapons.

"Is there anything else?" When no one answered, Myra stood. "Okay, I want to hear from each team every hour on the hour. You all have my number?"

Nods all around.

Then Rossi's head lifted and his gaze locked on Death. "Oh. I see." It was a soft exhale, a sudden realization.

And then the room filled with screaming.

CHAPTER 4

EVERYONE RUSHED to their feet, the vampires so quickly, I couldn't track their movements; the wolves, except for Jame and Fawn, were barely a step behind them.

Ryder, Myra, Jean and I were already running out of the room into the smaller space, hands going for guns.

But half a step into that room, we all froze.

Before we humans even made it there, the vampires had surrounded the room, and the werewolves had surrounded the people in the room. Those people, the tourists, were ten children aged from six to sixteen, four sets of parents, and Mason. Everyone stood in the center of the room, huddled together as if they'd been frightened and pulled together for safety.

They weren't staring at the vampires. They weren't staring at the werewolves. They were staring at the spiral staircase to one side of the room. One kid, maybe about nine years old, was trembling and holding her hand out, pointing.

I looked at the stairs.

There was nothing there.

"Everything okay?" I asked in the tone that said I was listening, I would believe whatever they said, and hey, I was on their side.

"He was there." The girl's voice skated up too high. "The ghost. He was there. He pushed me."

I checked Mason, who winced and nodded.

Well then. Ghost. The girl must have thought Harriet, the lighthouse keeper's daughter was a man. Maybe she didn't get a good look at her face.

It was a little odd, in that Harriet didn't usually push people around. But sometimes she touched a shoulder, a cheek.

I could deal with this. Lots of people believed in ghosts, even pushy ones. As long as those ghosts didn't follow them home and insist on being believed in on a regular basis, it usually wasn't a problem.

I knew Harriet didn't want to live anywhere else but here. So what we had on our hands was a tourist group who was about to have a terrific story to tell about the haunted lighthouse they visited on the coast.

It was good for business, good for the town.

"We've had ghost sightings before," I soothed. "Are you all right?"

She nodded and her hand slowly lowered. "It felt so real. Solid."

I smiled. "Did anyone get a picture?"

Lots of heads shaking, shoulders dropping. Someone chuckled.

The tension was dissolving, falling away as I treated this like a successful whale watching tour. Which, I supposed it sort of was, only they'd been trolling to see a ghost. Being touched by one was even more rare than catching sight of one of the gray whales that pretty much lived right outside our bay.

Mason took over from there. "We don't usually get such terrific sightings during the day. Would you mind if we mentioned it in our tours?"

The vamps and the weres relaxed slightly, though I noticed several of the weres kept glancing at the stairs.

Mason deftly guided the group out into the entry room, and asked them to sign in, leave a comment, or to share with their social media. A lot of selfies were being taken.

And still the werewolves kept their gazes on the staircase.

"What?" I asked Granny.

"Something," she said.

"A ghost. Harriet."

"Not her."

I didn't think Granny could see the dead, but if she thought it was something other than our resident ghost girl, I was going to believe her.

The spiral staircase looked empty to me. I walked over to it, lifted the rope and started up.

"Hey, now." Ryder started up right behind me.

"I'm a cop, Ryder. I can go in the EMPLOYEES ONLY areas. It's not against the rules."

"This isn't about that," he groused. "This is about you

going after a ghost who just tried to push someone down the stairs."

I paused, glanced back at him over my shoulder. We'd been climbing so were now on the second flight, and hidden from the room below. "You really have no problem believing in any of this stuff, do you?"

"I'd have to be pretty stupid not to believe in what is right in front of my eyes, Delaney."

I grinned, and was about to tell him that it'd been in front of his eyes for pretty much all of his life and he hadn't believed in it, when a wave of icy air rolled over my skin as if the temperature had suddenly plummeted thirty degrees. That was followed by an instant blast of heat that was gone almost before I felt it.

Almost.

Also: ouch.

Also also: not normal.

Ryder's hand landed on my hip, and he stepped in closer behind me, protective. "You feel that?"

"Yes."

"Ghost?"

I was about to tell him the combination of Arctic blast and Death Valley summer wasn't like any ghost encounter that I'd ever had when a scent assaulted my senses.

Spicy, woodsy, I would know that cologne anywhere. It was my dad's.

He. The girl had said the ghost was a he, and that he had pushed her.

But the only ghost in this lighthouse was Harriet.

"Delaney?" Ryder's hand tightened on my hip.

"Dad?" I whispered.

The wash of cold and heat hit again. I closed my eyes briefly, straining to hear his voice, to feel his presence.

A fist punched my shoulder, right below the vampire bite. Hard enough I jerked backward, my eyes flying open. Ryder locked up behind me, solid as a concrete piling holding back the ocean, holding both of us steady so we didn't fall down the stairs.

For just a heartbeat, I saw my father standing in front of

me, his eyes familiar as my own, his hands reaching. Goose bumps broke out across my skin and it had nothing to do with the temperature.

The air around him twisted, went foggy. Something dark and burning reached out from behind him. A clawed hand wrapped around his throat and yanked him backward.

Dad's eyes widened, his mouth opened around words I could not hear.

Then Dad, the claw, the twisted fog disappeared.

"What the hell was that?" Ryder's voice was a growl in my ear. He'd pulled a gun out from somewhere and held it low to one side of me, aiming at the image, the phantoms that were no longer there. I could feel his heart beating against my back. It was as fast as mine.

The air was no longer hot or cold. But I shivered, glad for the heat rolling off of Ryder.

"A ghost." I swallowed and tried that again without the hesitance and crack in the middle of it. "My dad."

"What was with him?"

I reluctantly leaned forward so there was distance between us again. His hand fell from my hip to the stair railing. He did not holster his gun.

"That won't work on a ghost."

"Okay." He checked the safety, then tucked the gun away inside his overshirt. "You didn't answer me."

"What was the question?"

"The thing that grabbed your dad's ghost. What was that?"

"You two okay up there?" Myra called out.

"Fine. Just give us a couple seconds."

"Are you kissing?" Jean shouted.

"No!" I yelled just as Ryder said, "Maybe."

Jean laughed. "You better have your stories straight when you get back down here."

"We're checking the upper level," I called out. "Come on." I finished the climb, Ryder right behind me. I didn't know if there would be any more spook action up here on the landing below the lantern room, but there would be more room for the two of us to stand and face each other and less chance of us being pushed down the stairs.

Here, the wall of windows carved a massive and beautiful view of the ocean, the steep metal ladder that shot straight up through the hatch in the ceiling set against the wall behind us. The wood floor and ceiling were painted soft beige, the railing and metal work that protected the windows, a forest green.

If I hadn't just seen my dad's ghost, it would be stunning, maybe even romantic, to be standing here alone with Ryder above the rolling blue of the ocean, the softer blue of the sky glazed golden and rosy with the slowly setting sun.

"Talk." Ryder leaned against the window railing, his arms crossed over his chest.

"I heard Dad, or thought I heard him a few months ago right before the Rhubarb Rally. Once. After he was...after he died."

"Were you here?"

"No. At home."

"What did he say?"

"He called my name. Told me to wake up. Right after that, Dan blew up his own rhubarb patch."

"Did you see him then?"

I shook my head.

"Did you see that darkness and claw then?"

"No. I saw it this time though. Dad and...."

"And? What was it, Delaney?"

"I've never seen one, but I think.... I mean, Myra probably has a book that would tell us for sure...."

He pushed off the railing and stood in front of me, his hands rubbing down my arms and then stilling there below my shoulders, a solid, grounding warmth. "Just tell me what you think it was."

I didn't want to say it. Didn't want to give the knot of fear in my gut actual words.

Ryder waited, his head bent so he could meet my gaze.

"A demon."

He pulled his head back and blinked. "All right. We've established those are a thing. Seeing one isn't good?"

"Demons are never good."

"I thought they were on our list of allies?"

"You remember Crow?"

"Hard to forget him."

"Trickster god. At any given moment, he was lying, teasing, scheming, cheating. Just, seriously a pain in the butt twenty-four seven. If there was no trouble, he'd make trouble. For the gods, the creatures, the humans. He lived for chaos."

"Sure. But you handled him."

"I handled him because he's a god and that gives me some say over his behavior in town. Also, he's...nice. He's always been a sort of uncle to us. And even though I know he's a trickster, I trust him, trust who he's proven to be when things get bad, you know?"

Ryder nodded.

"I've never met a demon. None of us have. Dad talked about them. Warned us to never speak to one, to never summon one without the proper back up and protocols in place. Demons make deals with dangerous consequences and the price is almost always worse than the service you get from them. They like to possess people for kicks. We've never had a demon in Ordinary since before my dad was a bridge."

"And you think a demon was with your father's ghost?"

"Yes."

"So what's our move?"

"On what?"

"Your dad's ghost. Do we need to do something to help him? Put his spirit to rest? Do an exorcism?"

"I don't know. Ghosts don't stay in Ordinary unless they want to. The way the town is set up, it can't be used as a trap for spirits. It's against Ordinary's laws."

He waited, letting me try to wrap my brain around seeing Dad, seeing him distressed. Dad hadn't said anything, but I was sure it wasn't his hand that had punched me. That had to have been the demon, or ghost of a demon, or whatever that creature was behind him.

"We can talk to Jacques," I said. "He might know."

"Jacques Formton? Let me guess, ghost hunter?"

"Medium."

"He runs the bowling alley, Delaney."

"So?"

"Kind of hard to hear ghosts over all that racket."

"Why do you think he runs the bowling alley? He doesn't want to hear the ghosts all the time."

Ryder just shook his head. "This town…it's like I've been living with a blindfold over my eyes."

"Don't be hard on yourself. It's our job to keep it a secret. We're really good at it. Well, most of the time."

He closed the distance between us, his boots heavy on the painted wooden floor. His hands slipped up to my arms again, soothing. I'd wrapped my arms over my chest as if I were trying to protect myself.

"Shhh," he said before I could tell him I was fine. "Come here. Just for a second."

He tugged me gently toward him and I went. Pressed my face against his shoulder, let him hold me with my arms still wrapped around myself.

His wide, warm palms rubbed a slow circle in the center of my back. Comforting, soothing as he held me tight.

"I'm fine," I mumbled into his chest.

"You're shook up."

"I'm gonna be fine in a minute."

"I know. I'll keep track. You have fifty five seconds left."

I smiled, then relaxed into him. We didn't say anything. He didn't move other than to rub those relaxing, groundling circles across my back. I breathed in deep and blocked everything else out.

Right now there was no murdering vampire, no tortured ghost dad, no bite tying me to a horror I was going to have nightmares about for probably the rest of my life.

Right now there was Ryder, my childhood friend, my secret crush, my current lover. A man strong enough, clever enough, and good enough, he'd found his way into my heart despite all the things that should make doing so impossible.

A man I didn't want to risk with my crazy life, just like Jean didn't want to risk Hogan. But Ryder had taken that choice out of my hands. If he hadn't pushed, if he hadn't insisted that he was worth the chance, if he hadn't proved it, I never would have told him any of Ordinary's secrets.

Maybe that's what it took for one of us Reeds to really share our lives with the person we loved. That person had to be strong enough not to back down, smart enough to figure out all on their own that there was more to us, to our lives, to this town than it appeared.

So basically, we Reeds set nearly impossible goals for our partners.

So not fair.

Maybe Jean could change that. Maybe she would throw caution to the wind and tell Hogan because he deserved to be told, and she deserved to love him without secrets between them.

Maybe Myra, who hadn't dated since her last boyfriend left the country years ago, would finally stop trying to be the most responsible person on the planet and the mother of all of us. Maybe she'd let down those thick walls around her heart and fall for someone.

I worried about her. She'd been too serious and had thrown herself into work since Dad's death, going from dedicated to work-herself-to-death. I knew a lot of that was her way to grieve. We were all grieving, still, in our way.

But Myra seemed to be closing down, turning inward. She'd always been the quiet one but she was becoming even more quiet.

I should probably talk to her about it. Or give her a week vacation away from this place.

Which I knew she would never accept while we had a kidnapping, killer, and some kind of ghost problem on our hands.

"Five, four, three, two, one." Ryder squeezed me, his hand pressing flat against my back, his other hand, which had been still on my hip, rubbed up and down a little. "Time's up, beautiful."

Aw…that was sweet.

"You think I'm beautiful?" I couldn't help fishing for another compliment. This was still new between us and I liked hearing how he saw me.

I leaned back and unwound my arms, wrapping them around him.

He smiled down at me, the light from the setting sun casting his features in deep golds. "I have always thought you were beautiful."

"You told me I was dorky-looking in sixth grade."

"Yeah, I was stupid in sixth grade. Didn't want my friends to know how much I liked you."

"You liked me?"

"It was those ponytails you wore." His hand brushed my hair back from my face, tucking it behind my ear before he cupped my face. "They were always sort of crooked, and you were like, 'whatever, who cares? I like it like this.'"

"I obsessed over my ponytails. I could never get them straight."

"I was obsessed over wanting to straighten them for you."

"Latent OCD?"

"No. I just wanted to touch you, and it would have been a great excuse if I'd been brave enough to do it."

"Instead you went with the dorky comment? Lame, Bailey."

He brushed his hand over my hair again and smiled. "Yeah, well. I'm certainly not perfect."

I was about to open my mouth and tell him he was. He was perfect to me. That his flaws, his mistakes made him so. But before I could form the words, he bent, pressed his mouth to mine and kissed me, his fingers tangled in my hair so he could hold the angle of our mouths fitted together in the way he wanted.

I might have made soft sighing sounds as I kissed him back.

This thing that we'd had forever was still new to us. We'd spent so much of our time dancing around the idea of dating, then he'd left for years, and I'd moved on to other things that mattered to me. Training to become a police officer. Training to take care of Ordinary in particular.

When the kiss went from gentle to heated, we lingered, explored. There was a lot we needed to say to each other. A lot we had left to discover.

"You two done 'checking the upper level' yet?" Jean shouted. "Or should we just order you a breakfast delivery?"

I felt more than heard Ryder's chuckle against my chest, in my mouth.

Sisters.

"We have to go," I said as we pulled back to catch our breaths. "I have to talk to seers and witches…"

"…and the owner of the bowling alley…"

"…yeah, him too, but I'm going to see the seer first. And you have to shake the Department of Paranormal Protection and see what information falls out."

"I know." He kissed my forehead, then temple, cheek, and moved to my mouth, kissing just the corner. I should resist. But I wasn't really very good at doing what I should.

After another long kiss that had me panting, I took a step back. "We need to go. We need to find Ben."

His eyes were dilated, his hair a mess from me running my fingers through it. The last thing I wanted to do was to turn away from him and go back to work. A part of me was hoping he'd tell me we had time, that the others could start the search for Ben without us. A part of me wanted him to walk me back against one of the walls and pin me there so I could rub my hands all over him until I found skin.

"Yeah." He swallowed, his fingers tightening for a moment on my hips before he let them slide away. He took a step back too. He stood there breathing, just looking at me, as if he were committing the image of me to memory before he brushed his fingers back through his hair, taming it.

"So. Will I see you tonight?"

I pulled my hair back behind my ears and made sure my clothing was straightened. "If we have any luck at all, we'll find Ben before morning."

"We'll have luck," he said. "Or we'll make luck."

"I'm going to hold you to that, Mr. Bailey."

"Good."

He gestured toward the stairs and I started down, leaving the sunset, the ocean, and a perfect memory behind.

CHAPTER 5

"YANCY DOESN'T even like donuts," Jean complained as I drove us to Hogan's bakery.

"Have you met the man? He loves donuts."

"Don't do this."

"What?" I asked innocently.

"Get involved in my love life."

"Oh, it's about ten years too late for that, little miss make-my-older-sister-and-Ryder-fall-in-love." I turned into the Puffin Muffin parking lot.

"This isn't what we should be doing," she tried. I unhooked my seatbelt. "We don't have time to stop. We need to talk to the seer."

"This won't take long and we need a gift."

"Jame doesn't want to wait."

I looked into the rearview mirror at the werewolf in the back seat. His eyes were closed, his head resting on the top of the headrest behind him, arms crossed loosely over his chest. "Do it," he said without opening his eyes.

"Two against one," I said. "Stay here in the Jeep, Jean, you big baby. I'll get Yancy's bribe so he'll tell our future."

I got out, shut the door, and didn't look back. I hadn't expected her to stay in the Jeep, but I hadn't expected her to be so squirrely about possibly seeing Hogan at his bakery.

We both knew Hogan worked the early shift. There was no way he was there at closing.

A car door opened and then I heard boots on gravel as Jean jogged to catch up with me.

"I hate you."

"You don't. Hogan won't even be here. I don't know why you're so worried."

"It's...I just need some space."

"Wow. Did you say it to him like that?"

She chewed on her bottom lip.

"You did, didn't you? Why, Jean? Why are you pushing him away?"

"You know why." She squared her shoulders narrowed her eyes and was suddenly more a police officer than my goofy baby sister. "I'm done talking about this, Delaney. Let's just get the donuts."

We walked to the door and I glanced in. Only Gale, a retired teacher and human, was in the shop, wiping down the counter top in prep for closing in the next fifteen minutes.

We walked in and she looked up as the bell rang.

"Hey, Chief. Jean."

"Hi, Gale." I strolled up to the counter. "Hogan here?"

Jean tensed.

"No, just me. Do you need him for something? I could call."

"That's okay, we're just here for a dozen donuts if there are any left."

"You bet. Half off since we'll be selling them as day-olds tomorrow. Any particular kind?"

"One of each of the filled, then just a mix of whatever else you have."

She bent and retrieved a cute box with a puffin logo on the side, then turned and opened the glass case with tidy rows of donuts. I knew they rolled through hundreds of donuts a day, but somehow, even now at the end of a good-weather day that had probably doubled their regular business, the donuts were all neatly stacked and looked fresh and delicious.

Jean wandered the small shop, looking at the few items for sale on the shelves, glancing at the bulletin board. Her shoulders weren't quite so stiff, although I could tell she still wasn't happy to be here.

"Will that do it for you?" Gale asked, tucking in the ends of the box and sealing it with the puffin sticker.

"We'll take these too." Jean placed three lovely worry stones on top of the donut box. "And do you have anything you could wrap them in?"

"Um...let me see. Would tissue do?" The tissue was a soft blue and had lace on the corners. It was the same stuff they used on the inside of the more delicate pastries they delivered.

"Perfect."

Gale wrapped up the stones and used a little white silk ribbon to tie a bow at the top. "Anything else?"

I looked over at Jean. "That's it," she said.

Gale rang us up and I handed over my card. We said our goodbyes and were back out in the dusky evening having spent no more than a couple minutes in the shop.

"Told you it would be okay."

Jean sighed. "That's not what I'm upset about."

"Hogan?"

"You. Focusing on me. You need to let my decision go, Delaney. Let me and Hogan figure our stuff out."

"Weren't you the one telling me your worries about Hogan this morning?"

"I was sharing to share, not to have you take on another battle."

"What are sisters for, but sharing in each other's battles?"

"Don't you think you have enough on your plate?"

"We all have enough on our plates," I said. "That doesn't mean other things, life things, love things, aren't just as important."

She stopped, turned to me. "Thank you. I mean that. But Delaney, you're tied to a vampire who wants dark magic. A vampire who has proven he is willing to kill for what he wants. Ben has been gone for a day now…"

"…We're going to find Ben."

"…and we both know what the odds are of him being alive."

I blinked hard as a sort of sickening cold rolled over me. Jean was never the first to give up hope. Jean was always the one who was fearless, who knew that as long as we kept fighting we would come out the other side. If not victors, if not whole, then alive. We would survive. To hear her assume we were going to lose Ben was more shocking to me than being attacked by a vampire.

"He's going to be alive." My tone was even, low as if I were approaching a strange animal.

"You don't know that." Her eyes were a little bright, watery.

"Yes, I do. We're going to find Ben. Alive. And we're going to put him back in Jame's arms where he belongs so they can be bonded, as they deserve to be. Because they love each other, and they are in our town, and we're not going to let them down. Do you understand that? We're going to win this one, Jean. We are not going to let that bastard take us down. Any of us."

She sniffed and wiped under her eyes with her thumbs. "It's...I know. I know that." She sniffed again, and blinked back tears, her shoulders going strong again. "I just want to do that. End this. Kill Lavius so we can go back to the little stuff, like my love life."

I stepped forward and shifted the donut box so I could wrap my arm around her shoulders. "We will. And love is never the little stuff. It's always the biggest stuff. The stuff that makes us who we are. The stuff that saves us and builds the lives we want to live. The stuff that we risk everything else for."

"I know. But you being hurt like this is killing me, you know?"

"I know."

"So the quicker we can find Ben. Alive," she added with the kind of conviction I expected from her, "the quicker we can bring that bastard down. I don't want to waste any more time worrying about me and Hogan, okay? We can worry about all that after we take care of Ben. And you."

"Okay."

"Promise me."

"Pinky swear."

"Good." She patted my back and we strode back to the Jeep and got in.

Jame didn't open his eyes, move, or make a sound. I hoped he was sleeping, but from the ragged rhythm of his breathing, I knew he was conserving energy, resting and hopefully, healing.

He had also probably heard every word we'd said. Werewolves had incredible hearing.

I didn't like that he had insisted on following me around, nor that Granny had pushed it. I didn't want to second-guess myself if I got in a dangerous situation that might hurt him.

I didn't want to be the one who did him more damage.

But I knew exactly why he was staying by my side. I carried

Lavius's bite, the only concrete link we had to him. I was as close to Ben by one degree of separation, closer than anyone else in town.

It was both intelligence and instinct on Jame's part. And while I could admire that, it still made me uncomfortable to have his life, probably literally, under influence of my every action.

Even this love, one of friendship to Jame, of community, was the big stuff.

I knew we'd find Yancy in his office at the community college, which was built just across the road from the town's only six screen movie theater.

I parked and twisted in my seat so I could see Jame better. "We're going to go in and see if he can give us an idea about where Ben is, or when we will find him. Any glimpse of the future that will help us. You can stay here if you want."

Jame's eyes slit open. They were hot with pain and something else. Anger, I presumed. "Where you go, I go." He uncrossed his arms and opened the door.

It was hard to watch him pause, then hold his breath as he hauled himself out of the back of my Jeep. I wanted to help, but he wouldn't let me, and wouldn't appreciate me showing attention to his weakness.

"If you pass out, Jean and I are taking pictures so we can add it to our 'too stubborn for their own good' list on the station bulletin board."

He was walking toward the school, his steps slow but steady. "Bite me, Reed."

It was good to hear his growl, even if it was a bit breathy. Jean and I came up beside him and did our best not to look like we were making ourselves available to catch him if he fell.

Thankfully, the walk was short. Both door handles were covered in multi-colored yarn wraps. Someone had crocheted a cozy cover for the handles, with a little gold crocheted key hanging from the bottom of one. A bright red crocheted rooster, about the size of a walnut stood proud on the curve of the handle.

Art project? Class mascot?

I pulled the door open, the yarn soft under my palm. It was cooler inside and smelled a little of rain and honey.

I took over the lead, wending down the hall to Yancy's office, just a few doors over on the left. I paused for Jame and Jean to catch up, then knocked.

"Come on in."

I pushed on the door.

"Delaney, please sit down. Jame, perhaps you'd like the couch there? I've pulled out a blanket if you need it."

Yancy was exactly what I'd imagine a career advisor would look like. Friendly, thoughtful, earnest. His soft brown eyes and patient smile fit perfectly with the bright blue sweater he wore over a collared shirt. The tight black curls of his hair had just a few strands of silver running through them, and I knew once he went fully gray, it was going to look amazing against his deep brown skin.

He didn't look at all surprised to see the three of us. But then, I had never once surprised our resident seer.

Jame walked in and collapsed onto the couch, tugging the blanket over his chest, his eyes immediately closing. His breathing went heavy and slowed.

Yancy had known we were coming. It was nice of him to make sure Jame would be comfortable.

I put the donut box near his computer mouse and sat in one of the two swivel chairs across from his desk. "We brought you donuts."

"Wonderful!" He really did seem pleased. "I do love donuts," he said to Jean as if he'd heard our conversation at the bakery, which, maybe? He was a seer. I had never gotten a definitive answer as to the limits of his abilities. "Thank you."

"We brought you this too." Jean placed the wrapped package on the box.

His eyes lit up and laugh lines crept out from the corners of them. "A gift? Thank you. Is it for me?"

"It's for you, but I thought you might want to give it to students who need it?" Jean settled in the other chair.

He opened the little package and grinned in delight. "They're lovely. Worry stones. Certainly appropriate for my line of work." He placed them in a tidy row in front of him, the smooth thumb curves facing upward. One of them was a soft rose quartz that I was immediately drawn to.

Then he opened the donut box and shifted it sideways so the open lid wouldn't be in the way.

"Perfect. And I just so happen to have a carafe of fresh coffee. Would either of you care for a cup?"

"No thanks," I said. Jean shook her head.

He plucked a donut out of the box and placed it on the doily wrapper from Jean's gift.

"How can I be of help?" He took a bite of the powdered donut and then sat back in his chair, the cup of coffee in his hand.

Gift given, favor earned. Now all we had to do is ask for it.

"We need to find Ben. Quickly." I glanced over at Jame. I thought he might be sleeping. "We know who kidnapped him, and we know what he wants. We can walk that path, bring him here and offer him what he desires, but there is no guarantee Ben will be safe if we do that. We want to know where Ben is and if we can find him in the next twenty-four hours."

He sipped coffee, holding my gaze a moment. Then he glanced over at Jame.

"I didn't know." He leaned forward again, placing his coffee on the desk.

"Didn't know that Ben had been kidnapped?"

He nodded. "I've had some intense visions lately. Mostly about you, Delaney. Things I didn't want to see."

"Oh. This." I pulled the collar of my coat away so he could see the vampire bite.

He made a small *hmph* sound in agreement.

"This is not the future your father had hoped for."

I held my breath along with any reply. I didn't want to ask questions that would shift Yancy from the answer we needed: how to find Ben alive.

"I told him, but still, every decision creates a path. He created his path, and yours, I'm afraid. You will have to walk it to the end."

He paused, but I kept my lips firmly pressed together. I wouldn't ask. I knew I got one question here. I wasn't going to change it.

"Ben." He picked up one of the worry stones—a rich blue sodalite—and rubbed his thumb slowly over the smooth indent.

"He is alive."

Jame shifted on the couch, and I knew he was listening.

"He is alone, but watched. In pain. He is angry."

Yancy went silent, so that only the shush of his thumb across the stone and the muted footsteps of someone walking down the hall filled the room.

I wanted to ask where he was. Where we could find him. But I'd already asked my question. If Yancy could see where Ben was being held, he would tell me.

"Near to us but oceans away." Yancy's voice had gone soft, sonorous. His eyes were deep, spiraling with sparks of gold. The futures he saw swirled there like stars caught in time's dance, a million million possibilities, a million million futures all hinging on billions and billions of tiny choices.

"Darkness, cold. Time does not move, it rocks, it bleeds."

His thumb stilled and his eyes lost their stars and the lights, as futures winked out one by one.

Jame pushed up until he was sitting, but wisely did not say anything. Jean and I waited too. He'd come back to the present soon. It was best to give him a moment.

After two steady minutes, Yancy seemed to realize he had company in his office again. He offered us a small smile then took a bite of donut, chewed, and sipped coffee.

"What can you tell us?" I asked, hoping I had not chosen the wrong moment to nudge him.

"What I have already said. Ben is alive. Bound, in darkness and cold. There is a…timelessness about his capture. He cannot sense the movement of the world around him, yet everything is in motion.

"There are other impressions. If I tell you them, and I will, you must remember that these are not set truths. They are simply what I saw, possibilities, not probabilities. They are as likely to be metaphor as reality. Do you understand?"

Jean and I nodded, but Yancy's gaze fell on Jame.

"Do you understand me, Jame? You must survive this for him."

"I understand." Jame's voice was a little stronger than it had been. He was healing at a pace no human would be able to manage, his werewolf physiology repairing bone, organ, and skin.

He still looked exhausted, but his color was slowly returning to something that looked a little less cadaverous.

"Nothing of this world can free him. No dark magic or ancient text. No modern technology or intervention. If you are to ever see him again, he must be given as a gift, a terrible promise kept by that which does not walk our land. That is what I see. That is what I know. I'm sorry."

"What is a thing that doesn't walk our land?" Jame asked. "Everything comes to Ordinary."

Yancy shook his head. "I can't see more than that at this time. The future is flexible and distorts easily. Perhaps it is simply a person who isn't a part of Ordinary, perhaps it is something more. I would give you more if I had it. Believe me, Jame, I would."

I knew he was sincere. Yancy was a nice man, and he had chosen a profession, helping people find their career paths in life, that made use of his abilities and went a long way to helping others.

But Jame was a werewolf who had lost his mate. I didn't expect him to accept reason so easily.

"Thank you." I stood and moved over to Jame. Not that I'd be able to stop him if he decided to throttle Yancy. Or, well, maybe I would be able to since Jame was not fully recovered.

"We'll find him?" Jame asked, moving to the desk to scowl down at Yancy.

"If Delaney makes the right choice."

"What?" I said, and the same time Jean said, "The hell?"

Jean was standing shoulder-to-shoulder with Jame now, a matching scowl on her face. "You said something not of our land would find him. You didn't say Delaney. And she is the most of-our-land of all of us. What the hell are you talking about terrible promise?"

Yancy picked up his donut and took a bite. He shrugged. "It is what I see. Delaney will have to make a choice if Ben is to be saved. It is the truth, but isn't clear. Like a fortune cookie. Or a reality TV show."

"Not helping," I said. "Take it down a gear, Jean. You know he can't give us a map. He can give us the words and images that will hopefully help us make the right decisions we need to make. If he were able to spell everything out, he would be controlling the future directly, instead of observing it."

"Oh, you do not get to lecture me about metaphysical theory, Delaney."

She was angry. Angry that Ben was gone. Angry that Yancy had just put me firmly in the middle of saving him.

But I was already in the middle and more than willing to do so. To put myself on the line for him. For Jame.

"We got this," I said to her, holding her angry blue gaze. "Trust that we got this, Jean. We'll make the right choices, and I won't do anything stupid."

Yancy, wisely, said nothing, but instead finished his donut.

Jame took a deep breath, then reached over and pulled a maple bar out of the box.

Yancy smiled. "I have never been fond of maple. That one's yours."

Jame took a bite. "He's alive?"

"Yes."

"We'll find him alive?"

"If Delaney makes the right choice. That is what I see."

"Thank you."

That was more than I expected out of Jame.

Jean started out the door, Jame right behind her.

"Thank you," I said to Yancy. "I know you didn't have to give us that much for a box of donuts."

"I'm not sure you should thank me. I placed a very heavy decision on you, Delaney. A heavy decision on your soul that could change you permanently, change Ordinary permanently, change those you love permanently."

"If it means I can bring Ben back alive, I don't have any problem making that decision. I can do change. So can the people I love. As for Ordinary, well, we even have mostly reliable wireless service now, so we're full speed ahead with change."

He shook his head, his eyes fond, then held his hand out to me. "This should be yours."

I held my hand for his and he dropped the rose quartz worry stone into my palm.

"Hope is born from ashes. Love yields to no other power. Return, Delaney."

"Is that a vision speaking?"

He chuckled and settled back into his chair. "Always. It's a gift and a curse. Nothing I say is only my own words. The future, fate if you will, always has a hand in what I do and say."

"That would drive me mad."

"Oh, it's a job hazard, but I get by." He winked. "Donuts help. So does getting paid to tell people what they should do with their lives for ten hours a day. Cathartic."

"You know I'm going to go talk to a witch now?"

"I do."

"Any warnings you want to pass my way?"

He chuckled again. "Just because I can see the most possible futures doesn't mean I can see them all. Often the unexpected is as much a surprise to me as it is to anyone. Also, we should all have to suffer the joy of free will. It builds character."

"Now that is more like what I expect to hear out of you. Don't work too late, Yancy."

"I've been off for an hour. Just thought I'd hang around for the donuts."

He smiled again and chose a new pastry out of the box.

I tucked the worry stone in my pocket and left my hand there with it. It was still warm from Yancy's touch, and I hoped maybe a little bit of his magic and wisdom had rubbed off on it.

Jean and Jame waited for me in the lobby.

"That wasn't what I was hoping for," Jean said.

"Ben's alive. We're going to find him alive within twenty-four hours. That's good enough for me. Let's go talk to the witch."

"I'm not going to let this come down to you making some kind of decision," Jean said.

"Good. Yes. Fine." I started toward the door. "Do you think I want to make some kind of final call? No way. I want all hands on deck. That means you, and Myra, and Jame, and every witch, seer, or bowling alley medium we've got."

We walked out of the school and got into the Jeep. Jame folded into the back with a soft grunt. He crossed his arms and closed his eyes again.

I drove down the darkening street. It wasn't until we hit the main road that Jean spoke.

"Why did you mention Jacques?"

"What?"

"You said witch, seer, and bowling alley medium. Jacques is a medium who owns the bowling alley."

I could tell her I was just throwing out names, but she'd know I was lying. "After the ghost thing at the lighthouse, I thought visiting Jacques might clear that up."

"Clear up Harriet pushing that girl's shoulder?"

I took a deep breath. "I saw Dad there."

Beat.

"What?"

"I saw him on the stairs when Ryder and I went up them. I saw his ghost."

"Dad?"

"Yes."

It took her a couple blocks before she spoke again. "What did he say? What did he do? What did he look like?"

"He wasn't alone."

"Who else? Mom? Grandma?"

"No. Something else was behind him. It…all I saw was a…hand that grabbed him and pulled him backward. Then he disappeared."

"A hand."

"More like a claw."

"You saw a claw grab our dad's ghost and yank him away?"

"Yes."

"And you didn't think you should tell us this?"

"I didn't think it was the problem we needed to focus on at the moment. Dad's dead. So even though I saw him, there isn't anything I can do to change that. I thought after we got Ben back and took care of Lavius, I'd go talk to Jacques and ask if he had sensed Dad in town. If he could help me maybe talk to him. Make sure everything is okay with him."

"Or you could just ask Death," she suggested.

"I have asked him about Dad."

"When?" She seemed surprised.

"When he first came to town. He didn't give me a straight answer. Just one of those sort of vague things he likes to say, like he did back at the lighthouse."

"Did he say Dad was in trouble?"

"No, he told me he died peacefully. It wasn't what I asked, but it was good to hear that, anyway."

She nodded, staring straight ahead. It was still hard to think about Dad losing control of the car and driving off a cliff. It seemed like there had to be more to it than just operator error.

This was Ordinary. While we could and did have our share of accidental deaths, it was more common that our accidents were anything but.

"That's…good," Jean breathed, her voice a little choked. "Peaceful."

I reached over and put my hand on her arm.

Jame shifted in the backseat, his breath catching with the movement. But he remained silent. He had been one of the first responders who had rappelled down the cliff to retrieve Dad's body. I'd never talked to him about it, and didn't think getting into it now was a good idea.

"When you go talk to Jacques, I want to be there," Jean said.

"Of course. Myra too."

"Yes."

I stopped at the light to allow pedestrians to cross to the tavern on the other side of the street. The green city lamppost had been turned into a giant flower.

Well, not literally, but someone had knitted green petals and wrapped them around the middle of the lamp post. The top of the post was bent in a shepherd's crook style and the flared shade was draped in bright yellow petals.

It made the whole thing look like a sunflower.

"Is Bertie doing some kind of yarn decoration thing?"

Jean leaned forward to look up at the post as we drove past. "I don't think so. Maybe? It's hard to keep up with her community projects. Why yarn?"

"I have no idea."

I turned into the public parking lot and took a space near the back.

"You could stay in the Jeep, Jame." I knew he wouldn't, but I felt it was important to offer it to him.

He grunted. "I'm staying. *With* you." He pushed on the door. "So stop trying to get rid of me." He got out of the car and we followed.

Jules was our resident witch. She wasn't the only witch in town, but she was powerful and more than willing to help out the police department when we needed a witch on hand.

She wasn't a seer like Yancy, but there were things she could sense that could narrow down our search. Spells she might be willing to cast that would lead us quickly to wherever Ben was being held, bound, trapped.

"She's probably running a game," Jean said.

Jules worked in a coffee shop that was also a crystal store and wireless internet café. It held gaming nights a couple times a week. She was a big, joyful woman, and attracted people to her like a magnet pulled metal filings.

I'd always liked her, and so had Dad. When Mom died, she practically set up a daily ritual of coming by our house and making sure we had fresh flowers, baked goods, and small bits of good will, like tiny pillows and shiny stones and sticks wrapped in feathers and shells.

"This won't take long," I said.

Jean was already at the corner. She started across the crosswalk. Jame had lingered behind, catching his breath. No surprise. He was doing far more walking than any sane doctor or person would prescribe.

I slowed, giving him time to catch up, or me time to return to the sidewalk with him before the light changed. I glanced back at him just as he shouted, "Jean!"

Everything happened in slow motion.

I spun back toward Jean, too late to stop the car that was hurtling across three lanes. Too late to scream, though I did anyway, my own voice lost in the ragged grind of the engine roaring. Too late to reach Jean, to run to her, to push her out of the way.

Jean must have heard Jame's shout, my yell, the car's engine. She stopped, there in the middle of the street, and turned toward the sound.

Too late, too late, too late.

The sleek black sports car gunned straight for her. She threw herself to the side, trying to dodge, trying to minimize the damage.

But there was no dodging.

The sound of impact seemed far away as I ran toward her, already knowing she was hit, already knowing she was falling, fallen, broken on the ground. There was no license plate on the car and as it roared away, I couldn't see the driver through the blackened windows.

I reached for my phone, hit the speed dial on 911, and was talking to whoever picked up on the other side, demanding an ambulance, now, and giving my location.

I didn't hear them respond, didn't care. Our emergency services were top notch. They'd be here. They'd have to be here in time.

I skidded onto my knees next to Jean.

Already traffic was backing up. Already people were exiting their cars to rush over. They wanted to help.

Probably.

But someone had just run my sister down in the middle of the road and I was not about to let any stranger near her.

"Get back!"

Jean lay in a huddle, her head on an outstretched arm that was bent the wrong way at her forearm. There was blood, not a lot, but too much, too much. Too much blood. She wasn't moving. My sister was bleeding. She wasn't moving.

And I couldn't think. I couldn't move. All I could do was babble, "no, no, no," over and over again.

"I got her," a voice pushed through the drumming of my fear, my nightmare, pushed through the panic that filled my mind, my vision.

"Delaney, I got her. She's breathing. She's alive. We're going to wait for the ambulance. Just hold her hand, here. Hold her hand."

Her hand was in my hand and I was holding it and breathing too hard, and shaking and trying to focus on who was talking to me. My eyes finally registered that I was staring at Jame. That Jame had crouched down beside me and Jean, that he was telling the crowd to stay back in a firm and calm tone, while placing a coat which he seemed to have produced out of nowhere over Jean's torso.

She was on her back now, and her arm—the one that was bent the wrong way—was tucked up against her stomach. Her eyes were closed and her face was scraped, blood flowing from the rawness on her forehead, her cheek. There was bruising already forming along her cheek and that, seeing the wounds, seeing her chest rise and fall finally snapped me out of my panic.

Sounds came back to me, a lot of voices, someone telling people to move aside so there was room for the ambulance, someone dealing with traffic, clearing the lane we were in the middle of and directing cars around us to the other lanes.

Engines, seagulls, and Jame.

"You're okay, Jean," he said. "Hold still. You're going to be fine."

And then there was a new sound, a soft groan.

Her eyes fluttered, opened, fluttered again and stayed open, blurry and unfocused. "Shit. What hit me?"

I'd never been so happy to hear her.

"You got clipped by a car," Jame said, making it sound like an everyday happening. No big deal. Clipped. Just a scratch. You want the Band-Aid with Minions or Godzilla?

"Yeah? Did we get plate?"

"No," I said. "No plate. Blacked out windows. But we got the make and model. We'll track them down."

I hadn't even called it in yet. Which meant Myra would hear about this from the 911 call instead of straight from me.

Hell.

"You're okay, honey," I said, squeezing her hand gently and glancing up at Jame, who nodded. He still looked like he might fall over himself, but his hands were sure as he checked her skull for wounds, and did a quick pass over her body, checking limbs.

She groaned again as he shifted her leg. "Okay hurts."

"Broken arm," I said. "Just hang in there a little longer and we'll get you on the good meds."

"Yay." She said. "Morphine me, baby."

"Coming up," Jame said.

The siren that had been growing louder let off a few short bursts and then the ambulance was there, the crowd of curious onlookers parted and Mykal, a vampire EMT, and Steven, a human, strode over with the gurney which they expertly positioned beside us and lowered.

"Jame. Shouldn't you be warming a bed at Samaritan North?" Mykal asked.

Jame grunted. "Left this morning. Hit and run. Sports car, going about thirty. Right arm, right ankle."

"Concussion?"

"Probably."

"Whee," Jean said weakly.

"Just move to the side, Chief," Mykal said. "We're going to load her up."

I moved, but held on to her hand while the emergency technicians outfitted her with a neck brace, a soft brace for her arm and ankle, and did a quick wipe on her face to make sure the bleeding from the scrapes wasn't anything more serious.

They moved her swiftly and as gently as could be managed onto the gurney. She hissed in pain a lot anyway, and cursed a blue streak.

The cussing was good. The cussing was Jean. Cussing was better than screaming.

"Okay, let's do," Mykal said.

It had gotten darker, dusk slipping into the deepening shadows of night. I followed alongside the gurney.

"Keys, Delaney." Jame pressed his hand on my shoulder.

I dug in my pocket and tossed him my keys then crawled up into the back of the ambulance with her. I didn't care if he drove my Jeep, or locked it for the night. I wasn't leaving Jean.

"The witch…" Jean mumbled.

"Can wait." I held her hand all the way to the hospital.

CHAPTER 6

THE WITCH did not wait. We'd gotten Jean to the emergency room, and I'd been in the way enough, and yes, probably being scowly and pushy enough they'd finally stuck me in a corner out of the way where I could keep Jean in my line of vision.

A few minutes ticked by and then they were moving Jean to get X-rays.

"I'm going with her."

"You can't, Chief," a nurse, Peggy, said. "We'll be right down there in a room so small we have to synchronize our breathing to all fit in it at the same time."

"I'm going."

"'Sokay, Laney," Jean said. "Be right back. I'm goo."

She probably meant she was good, but goo might fit too.

She still was way too pale and in pain and it made me want to hit something. But she was being brave and rational, and the best thing I could do for her was to be brave and rational back.

"I'll be right here." I smiled. "Right here."

They wheeled her down the hall and I clenched my fists.

"Drink this." A cup was pressed into my clenched hand. I wrapped my fingers around it and looked into Jules' smart black eyes.

Jules was a woman who took up space in the world and filled it with her color, her laughter, her body, her voice, her joy. She was old enough to be my grandmother, but still looked young enough to be my sister. Her hair was an unexceptional brown, long, and currently being used as a backdrop for the silk and ribbon flowers braided into it.

Her face was round with a very sharp chin, and I'd never seen her without lipstick. Today's was lavender, and matched the lavender color she'd brushed through her eyebrows.

Her dress was layers of orange and yellows so bright, you could cook a frozen pizza with it.

"It's tea. You need it. Drink."

I lifted the cup and sniffed. Fragrant and probably her own mix, I caught vanilla, nutmeg and citrus. I sipped.

It was good. Warm.

It was also spiked.

I cleared my throat. "Rum? You know we're in a hospital, right?"

"Pah. There's less than a capful in there. Just enough to add heat to it. Along with the honey, it's medicinal. She's going to be just fine, Delaney, just fine."

"Her arm is broken. Her ankle. She might have a concussion. The car didn't even slow down. They sped up as they hit her. If Jame hadn't yelled, if she hadn't jumped…."

Jules produced a flask and unscrewed the top. "Need a little more heat?"

"No." I swung the cup out of her reach. "And put that away. There are police around here. You know we have open container laws."

She chuckled and it came from somewhere deep inside her, starting out low and grumbly and ending on a musical gurgle. "Haven't seen you girls in far too long."

"It's been a weird year."

"Thought you might be coming by my place soon, though. Cards said so."

"Which cards?"

She leaned against the wall next to me and I mimicked her stance.

"Eight of Wands and Judgment."

"I'm Judgment? I thought I was the Queen of Wands."

"Sometimes, yes. But not right now. Not since…well, with your father's death came some consequences. We're seeing the fruit of that. The darkness that's closing in has one hand on you, Delaney. Devil showed up in the spread, and while I don't usually counsel to take the cards literally, Devil is a strong image. The beast from below and the chains that bind us."

I knew the devil I was facing. Lavius. His chain, his claim on me was apparent in the bite on my neck. I shrugged a little deeper into my coat to hide the mark.

"What were you coming to me about?"

"Who said we were coming to you?"

89

She chuckled and took a sip of the flask. It didn't smell like hard alcohol. Maybe a berry wine. Cherry and sweet.

"Sweetheart. I know. Talk to me. Your sister's going to be here any second."

"Jean?"

"Myra."

Yeah, and I didn't need magic to know she'd be angry and worried.

"Ben's been kidnapped. We need to find him, soon. Before the full moon. Now would be better. The vamps can't find him. The weres can't find him. All Yancy could tell me was that he was cold, bound, in darkness and can't feel the passage of time."

"And what did you think you'd get out of a witch? I don't see the future, honey. You know that."

"The thing that has him wants dark magic. That's his demand. We hand over an item of dark magic, and he'll give us back Ben."

"When did you start allowing dark magic into our town, Delaney?"

"I've never allowed it. But it's here."

"Must be well warded. Or Old Rossi has it."

I might have winced a little.

"No," she breathed. "Really? He's dabbling in the darkness? He of all things should know better."

I sipped tea and didn't reply.

She sighed. "All right. Then we should do this. Had to pull the Two of Coins, didn't I? Come on. This should work in here."

She manhandled me into a tiny room with an empty bed. She turned on the light and shut the door at the same time.

"Hold on."

"No. Just sit, honey. It's what you need to hear from me. I wouldn't have come here if this wasn't supposed to happen. I mean, of course I would have come here to see Jean." She pointed at the chair on the opposite side of the bed. "Sit." She followed her own command and lowered into the chair on the close side of the bed, her dress floating out in blinding layers of sunshine, her perfume—soft and comforting—rising with the motion of the air.

"I need to be out there for Jean. For Myra."

"Everyone in this town has your phone number, and there's an intercom system. If you're needed–if there's an emergency– you'll be found."

She dug in the bag over her shoulder and pulled out a silk-wrapped deck of cards. "Let's see what we can see." She looked up as she unwrapped the cards, her gaze holding mine. "I'll need you to be in a receptive place to hear this, Delaney. Right now you're throwing off a mess of negative energy. That's going to screw with the cards. Sit. Drink the tea. Think Zen thoughts. You'll see Myra and Jean in just a minute. That handsome boy of yours too."

I sat, fiddled with my cup as she cut cards, shuffled, spread them in an arc on top of the silk, which she had smoothed out on the bed. She pulled three cards.

"The energy around you, your challenge, your assistance."

Nine of Swords, Death, and the Devil. I didn't know much about the Tarot, but the images were dark. A woman grieving in her bed, her hands over her face, and nine swords on the wall behind her; a skeleton in a knight's armor riding a pale horse; and the devil squatting on a throne behind two chained people.

"Neat." I said.

"Hush. You're humbugging my energy."

"I'm humbugging? Do you not see those cards?"

"Just because they look dire, doesn't mean they are. For goodness sake, you of all people should know never to judge a book by the cover. All right, let's see what we have. Nine of Swords. You've been worried, sleepless, sad. That's a no-brainer. As for your challenge, we have Death. Well. Hm."

"Hm, what?"

"Hm, Death doesn't usually represent a physical, actual death. It represents change. A caterpillar-to-butterfly energy. Your challenge is to accept a change. Possibly a difficult one. A change that will apply to you, personally. And your outcome is the Devil. Again. Not one of my favorite cards, but it's not usually a literal translation."

"So a devil isn't going to show up in town? That's a relief."

"Well, this is Ordinary. I wouldn't rule it out. But it wouldn't be my first inclination. The devil represents the chains that hold us back. Sometimes those chains are addictions, bad habits, behaviors, sometimes they are people or life circumstances. But for you…."

I waited. Jules was good at this kind of thing. I knew she'd be able to tell me what kind of chains and what kind of devil would be my outcome.

"Give me your hand, sweetheart."

I reached out and she took hold of my right hand. Then she picked up the first card, set it down, picked up the second card, frowned and put it down, then picked up the last.

"Oh, Delaney."

"Yes?" That didn't sound good. Didn't sound like I was going to be happy with the devil I'd have to deal with.

"This is…well, it feels like there is a clear literal bent to the reading. There may be a death in your near future. And a devil with chains."

Wow. Way to make me hate tarot readings.

"Is the, um, death something about my dad?"

She picked up the middle card again. "Yes. That resonates. It is connected with his death."

So that might mean his ghost showing up in my life was going to be a challenge. Fine. That was something I was pretty sure I could deal with.

"The chains, would that be the bite?"

"I wondered if you were going to tell me about that. Which vampire did you let mark you?"

"Not one of ours. Not one from inside Ordinary."

"And not willingly?"

I shook my head.

Without a word, she passed me the flask. I thought about taking a nice long drink, but decided to stick with my tea.

"Could that be it?" I asked. "The chains that bind me?"

She picked up the last card and held it for a long time. Then she returned all three cards to the deck and carefully folded the silk scarf around them.

"The bite could be the chains you need to break."

"But?"

"But it doesn't resonate. There's something else, new chains coming. Read very literally, the cards are saying you are afraid, but through a death you will bind yourself to a new devil."

"Well, now I'm so glad you pulled me aside to tell me this terrific news."

She grinned. "Your mother had the same kind of sarcasm."

"No she didn't."

"Not with you girls, but with her friends, oh, she very much did. So." She sat back and peered at me like I was a lake of muddy water and she was trying to track the fish swimming beneath.

"You needed this message. Enough that I let Marty run the game tonight. Marty." She shook her head, letting me know exactly what she thought of her nephew and his store-running capacity.

"I really did not need to hear that death and chains and darkness are in my future. You know what I needed to hear? How to find Ben. Think you can pull that out of your cards? Because if the answer is hazy, I'll try again later."

She barked out a laugh. "I miss my Magic 8 Ball."

"You have twelve."

"They all lie. I used to have this one that always told the truth. But someone worked a hex on the toy manufacturer and now the things spit out nonsense. All right, let's pull a card for Ben."

"No, I don't have time. Jean—"

"You have time." She unwrapped, shuffled, cut, cut again, let me cut, shuffled one more time then pulled a card.

"Huh."

My sentiments, exactly: Judgment.

"You said I was Judgment, right?"

"I did. You're going to be the one to find him, Delaney. No one else. Through you, and only through you will he be free."

Silence exploded between us from that truth bomb. I could feel it, we could probably both feel it: she'd just predicted the future, told the truth that went bone-deep.

I was going to save Ben. And from my reading of death and chains, I knew I was going to pay something for him to be free.

That lined up with what Yancy had told us. I was in the middle of this, or I *was* the middle of this.

It terrified me, but hey, that's what I was trained to do: make the hard decisions, do the right thing, keep the people of my town safe.

"You don't look surprised." She took a swig out of her flask before packing the cards away again and placing them in her bag.

"That's pretty much the same thing Yancy told us when we went to talk to him."

"He knows his stuff. But sometimes what he says can be misconstrued."

I laughed, one short huff of air. "Yeah, well, since every card you pulled did nothing but strengthen what he said, I'm going to go with the consensus."

"Free will, baby."

"I know I have it. I know I can use it. I know it can change the future. But I also know who I am and what I will give to save the people I care about."

"What will you give, Delaney?"

"My heart and soul and anything else that's necessary."

"Oh, honey. You sound just like your father, the stubborn old ass."

I choked on a sip of tea and she chuckled. "He used to say the exact same thing, and I don't know if you heard him, or if you're just cut from the same batch of dough. But I'm going to tell you what I told him. Do not give your heart or soul lightly. They are the most precious and valuable coin, and I will hunt you down and smack you in the back of the head if I find you running around here missing one of them. Do you understand me?"

"Don't sell my soul. Got it."

"I'm not kidding, Delaney."

"I know."

"You aren't listening to me."

"I really am."

"Stubborn. Just like your father."

"True."

"He didn't listen."

"You said that. See? Listening."

She sighed, then stood. "I love you, but you drive me crazy,

Delaney Reed."

"Love you too, Jules."

She motioned me forward and folded me into a big, soft, marshmallowy hug. Her perfume filled my nose and the jingle of her earrings and multiple bracelets brought back all the times she had hugged me when I was little and afraid.

"Whatever you get yourself into, know I'll be there doing what I can to pull you out."

"Thank you." I meant it from the bottom of my heart.

"Good. Now." She released me. "Myra's here."

The door swung open and Myra walked in. "What is going on?"

"Have you seen Jean?" I asked.

"They said she's getting X-rays. Are you okay? Jesus, Delancy."

We closed the distance without another word and wrapped arms around each other.

"You weren't hurt were you?" she asked.

"No. But Jean. She's conscious. She might have a concussion. Tell me you got a lead on the car."

"We have more than a lead. We found the car."

I pulled back to make room for Jules who shoved her way in between us to give Myra a hug.

"I'll let you girls talk for a moment. I'll be out there with Jean if she's brought back to her room." She swung out the door, and Myra glared at me.

"What?"

"How the hell does she get hit by a car?"

"That's what I want to know. She was ahead of us, crossing the street. Traffic was stopped. It was on purpose, Myra. I know she was run down on purpose."

"Yeah, she was."

"What? What do you know? Where was the car? Who was driving? Do you have a lead on who was driving?"

"He's dead. The driver is dead. He was a vampire who left Ordinary twenty years ago, or that's what Rossi told me. The car was down by Cape Foulweather. Smashed into a tree on the side of the cliff. Engine still running. Rossi found him before any tourists could stumble on him."

"And Rossi killed him?"

"No. He was already dead."

"I don't understand. The driver killed himself?"

"No. The crash didn't kill him. He was already dead."

"Vampire dead, or dead dead?"

"Dead dead. Had been for days, maybe months. But he was controlled like a puppet. Covered in blood and symbols."

"Are you kidding me? Lavius remote-controlled a vampire in a Corvette and ran over my sister? I am going to kick his ugly old ass."

"No. We're going to kill him. There is no negotiating. No trying to trade some book for Ben. We go in direct and we take Lavius out. Fast. Hard. Done."

"Do we know where he is? Where he will be?"

"Not yet."

"Then until we do, we keep all avenues open. Even negotiating on the full moon, if that's what it takes. We can't kill Lavius without knowing where Ben is. So we get hands on Ben first and then go after the bastard. Understand?"

Myra clenched her jaw but nodded.

"Where is the dead guy?"

"Rossi has him out at his place. He'd doing something to 'neutralize' the body. So it's not some kind of bomb, or spy, or zombie stowaway in town that can be reanimated and used by Lavius again."

"Well, shit. Reanimated vampire zombie. Is that a thing?"

"Rossi says that's what it might have been."

Might. That wasn't a definite.

I rubbed at the back of my neck, my hand sliding to the bite I couldn't feel on the outside. It felt cold on the inside though, as if a sliver of ice was lodged beneath my skin, that cold sliver pushing in deeper and deeper, aiming for my lungs, my heart.

"Okay, so Rossi has the body. We have the car?"

"Ryder's dealing with the car. Hatter and Shoe are here."

"That was quick"

"They were on leave."

"Do I want to know what for?"

"I didn't ask. They assured me it was just a formality. I'll run the record on it when I have time."

"Okay. So they're covering the car. Maybe we'll get some clue as to where Lavius and Ben might be."

"I don't think it's going to be that easy. Do you?"

"No."

"What did you get from Yancy?"

Ah. This wasn't going to go over very well.

"You don't want to tell me, do you?"

"Of course I do."

"Spit it out."

"It was a lot about how our choices change the future."

"He always says that. What else did he say?"

"Ben is alive."

She exhaled and nodded, as if a great weight had been pulled off of her chest. "Good. That's good. I mean, I know Than said it too, but it's good to hear it from a second source."

"He also said he's bound, in the dark, and can't sense time. He said I'd be the one who had to make the right choice to save Ben. That nothing of this world can save him. That he'd have to be given to us. Like a gift for something traded."

She stood there and stared at me until I finally shrugged. "It's what he said."

She pulled her fingers back through her thick, straight dark hair, and tucked part of it behind her ears. "Okay. That's... I don't like any of that. But fine. What did Jules say?"

"That I'm the Judgment card. That's neat, right?"

"I thought you were the Queen of Wands."

"Not today. Hey, let's go check on Jean."

"Delaney, no."

But I was already moving, and the room wasn't that big anyway, so it wasn't all that hard to slip past her and get the door open.

"Delaney." Jame stood on the other side, looking solid on his feet, arms crossed over his chest, like he was a bouncer guarding the entry to an exclusive club. "Answer her."

Stupid werewolves and their stupid hearing.

"Fine. She said I'm Judgment. That Ben will be freed through me. And also that I haven't been sleeping well and Death is a butterfly and that she'll smack me on the back of the head if I lose my heart."

"That doesn't even make sense," Myra said.

"Have you met her?" I asked.

"Yes. And she's very clear when she gives information like that. Was it a tarot reading?"

"Three cards. Nine of Swords, Death, Devil."

"What does that add up to?" Jame asked.

"I'm distressed, but through a death I will bind myself to a new devil."

"That's horrible," Myra said.

"Is it? I was listening, but half my brain just keeps replaying Jean getting hit by that damn car. I froze, My. I totally panicked and froze. She was lying there and I wasn't doing anything. Anything to help her."

"That's not true," Jame said. "You ran to her. You were almost there before she hit the ground."

That was impossible, so I didn't believe him.

"Speed. Not as fast as a vampire but." He shrugged. "The bite."

Oh, gods, I wanted to barf. "That's not what I wanted to hear."

"That you're fast?" he asked.

"That anything about me has been changed because of what that bastard did to me."

"A bite from a vamp that old? You expected nothing?"

I rubbed at my forehead. "I just…. Yes. I expected either all-out bat-transformation or nothing."

He sniffed, and I knew he was scenting me, probably smelling how much vampire was flowing in my veins.

I scowled. "Don't do that."

He raised an eyebrow.

"Don't smell-search me."

"I'm not searching. I'm being politely aware."

"Is there anything else?" Myra asked. "Anything else in her you can sense?"

Jame shook his head real slowly as if he were balancing a headache on his spine. Which he probably was. I wondered when he'd last eaten, knew he should be in bed resting, sleeping instead of hanging around the emergency room while my sister was looked after by doctors who would prefer Jame checked in beside her.

"Otherwise, she's the same," he said. "Now."

"Now?" we chorused.

He winced even though I was pretty sure we hadn't shrieked. Or I hadn't shrieked. Okay, maybe I shrieked a little, but at least Myra was calm.

"The longer that tie remains, the deeper it will become. Even you two know that."

I did know that.

I didn't like it, but I knew it.

"This day is almost over, right? Because I'm so over it."

Myra's hand pressed against my back and we were in motion, Jame waiting a few beats before he fell into place and followed us much more slowly.

Jules opened a door and motioned us into the little room. "She's doing fine," she said as we walked past her.

"I'm doing fine," Jean said, her words melting into each other. "Gave me pain meds. No consuss…condush…concussion. Hey, Myra. You look angry."

"I always look angry, Jee-Jee. I have resting pissed face." Myra walked over to her and brushed Jean's hair back so she could place a kiss on her forehead. "You are not allowed to scare me like that."

"Scare you? I was the one who got road raged."

"Good jump, by the way," I said, coming up on her other side and sliding my hand into hers.

She sighed and her eyes closed. "It was scary as fuck."

"I know."

"I didn't even see it coming."

"I know."

"S'fast."

"Yes."

"I'm tired now, okay?"

She'd said it like that since she was a little kid. Asking if it was okay that she was going to fall asleep.

"Go to sleep. We'll let you know when they're going to move you to a room."

"Night, honey." Myra slipped her hand into Jean's other

hand and looked around for a chair.

There was only one and it was filled with a very tired werewolf.

"He should get his own room," Myra said quietly so as not to disturb either of them.

"I don't know if you've noticed, but he doesn't really do what he should do no matter who tells him."

"Sounds like someone else I know."

"Hey. I'm trying. I really am, Myra. This whole vampire thing has me off my game. Do you know when that car headed for Jean I didn't even think about pulling my gun–which I wasn't even wearing–and I didn't even try to stop it. I just…" I rubbed at my eyes with my free hand.

"I think I'm tired."

"You are," she said gently. "You were assaulted, then pretty much threw yourself into organizing a hunt for your assailant."

"We're not going to find him in twenty-four hours, are we?"

She stared at Jean, who was sleeping deeply enough her eyes were moving behind her eyelids. "It can happen, but it's not a lot of time. Yancy said we'd find him, right? Because of a choice you would make."

"Yes."

"Ryder and I haven't come up with any leads through the DoPP. Rossi's so angry he's gone silent, which I hate, and the Wolfes haven't made progress either. I think we're going to have to meet him with that book, Delaney. Maybe even give it to him."

"No."

"He sent a zombie vampire to kill Jean."

"She's not dead."

"He won't let Ben stay alive much longer. There was never any guarantee he'd keep him alive as part of the deal."

"We're bringing Ben home. We're saving him."

"Listen." Her word was a low, harsh hiss. A whisper that she didn't want either Jame or Jean to hear. When she turned her eyes to me, I could see the gloss of too many sleepless nights. "I almost lost you. I almost lost Jean. We are not going to solve this problem with a little elbow grease and police work and a can-do attitude. The only way to deal with that evil is to lure him in with what he wants and then eradicate him. Period."

I held her gaze for long enough, the flush on her cheeks cooled some.

"We have to attack, Delaney. Defending isn't working."

"We'll attack. But we'll do it the smart way. He does not get his hands on that damn book. We do not give darkness weapons with which to hurt us even more. We do not answer danger with fear. We do not respond to pain with pleas. We are going to find him, and Ben. No book. Do you hear me?"

"I hate this," she whispered softly. She wiped a hand over her eyes, pressing with her fingers. "Okay. I hear you. I know you're right. But I've got jack squat to go on, Delaney and it's killing me."

"We've only been at this for a few hours. We still have time."

She looked over at Jame again. "He needs a bed. And painkillers."

"I know. He's not leaving me, so where I go, he goes."

"Maybe you should get some rest too."

I nodded. I needed some sleep. Even an hour sounded like heaven. But I knew I was in for a long night. Either staying here beside Jean, or going back to the station to pick up on the research Myra was not getting done.

A soft knock rapped on the door, and then the doctor was there. She smiled. "Good news. It's just a break and a sprain and some scrapes and bruising. No concussion, no other damage. We'd like to keep her overnight, so we're going to cast her arm and move her to a room."

And just like that, it felt like things were looking up.

It took some maneuvering to get us out of the room, and then Jean awake and situated so that there was space for the cart with the supplies and the doctor.

Jame was leaning against the wall, his eyes slit, arms crossed, mostly asleep on his feet.

"I'll stay with Jean when they move her to her room. You take him home and make him sleep." Myra said.

"Not tired," he mumbled.

Liar.

"I'm staying here," I said.

"She'll be sleeping and I'll be here watching after her. Get Jame home. Make him rest."

"Make me." He huffed.

"Delaney, just let me take the first shift with Jean. Get some food, and a half hour nap, then check in with me."

"I don't like leaving you here alone. Both of you alone with all these people."

"Are you listening to yourself?" The smile she gave me was a wry twist of her lips. "I'm going to check in with Ryder. See if he's got Hatter and Shoe squared away. I'm going to follow up on the list of possible places Ben might be held."

"Yancy said it was dark and cold and 'near to us but oceans away'."

"What are you thinking?"

"Ship maybe? Boathouse? Somewhere on the other side of a bay? Something that would make the 'oceans away' comment make sense."

"God angle?"

I nodded. "I'd thought about that. Oceans away makes me think Poseidon, but seriously, would Poseidon throw in with that monster against us?"

"Maybe not willingly."

"Okay. Sure. He's usually making some dumb decision or another. I'll check with him after I get Jame settled."

"Jame will not be settled," he said.

Myra and I exchanged a long look. Yeah, I was going to have to wrestle the werewolf to make him get some sleep before he passed out on me. Taking him home made the most sense. Which meant Myra was right. Again.

Darn it.

"You suck," I whispered.

She beamed.

"Okay. Come on, Jame. We need to get you home."

"I'm not sleeping."

"Fine. But you're going to need food, and I am too, and we both have blood on us, and we both need a change of clothes."

He held still, and I wondered if I really was going to have to threaten him with mace or handcuffs. Then he shifted his weight and rolled forward to balance squarely on his feet before he walked toward me.

"Check in with me," I reminded Myra.

"Check in with me," she replied.

The waiting room was nearly empty, just a mom and dad with a kid who was red-cheeked but otherwise pale. They had a barf bucket beside them, but didn't look overly worried.

"Delaney?"

A man stood from the shadowed corner of the room and strode our way.

He was tall, fit, dark-skinned and gorgeous, although I didn't think I'd ever seen him frown like that.

"Hey, Hogan."

"Is she okay? I heard, Jesus, I heard she was hit by a car? Is she? Delaney, is she all right? No one would tell me anything."

I reached out immediately and pressed my palm on his arm. I could feel the tremble running through his tense muscles, running through his body. Hogan never seemed to wear anything other than a T-shirt and shorts, even in winter. His skin beneath my hand was cold and clammy.

I was this close to making him sit down so someone could make sure that he wasn't in shock.

"She's fine." I held his searching gaze and tried to project as much comfort as I could. "She jumped out of the way, but was clipped. She landed hard and has a broken arm, sprained ankle, bruised ribs and shoulder. She's not going to be up and dancing tomorrow, but she's conscious, no concussion, and on some really good painkillers."

He swallowed hard, gaze shifting back and forth across my face as if he were waiting for the bad news.

"That's it. She's going to stay overnight. Myra's back there with her now. She'll be released tomorrow. How about you sit down? Here. Here's good." I sort of steered him toward one of the chairs and he didn't even seem to notice where he was going, just followed blindly.

"Jesus." He folded down and covered his face with both of his hands.

And then, heartbreakingly, face hidden, wide shoulders hunched, he started to quietly cry.

"Oh, now. It's okay." I sat down beside him and wrapped one arm across his back, my other hand on his shoulder closest to me so I could rub comforting circles there. "She's fine. She's really, really fine, Hogan. I promise she's fine."

His tense, cold body seemed to unwind, loosen, going hot and sweaty. I held on, made soothing sounds and waited for his shaking to ease, his sobs to quiet into measured breaths that finally changed from what sounded labored and focused to something a lot more natural.

I looked around for a tissue and found a box held in front of my face by a werewolf who looked like he could not be bothered to care about this guy's pain.

"Sympathy," I suggested.

"She's alive." Those two words carried anger, and pain, and a truth that made me want to squirm. And those two words said more. Jean was alive, and being looked after by people who loved her. Ben was lost and alone. We had only the word of a vacationing god and a donut-loving seer to know that he was still breathing.

Jame had every right to be grumpy.

I took the box and offered it to Hogan who finally lifted his face out of his hands. He used several sheets on his face, then eyes, sniffing, and finally, blowing.

Then he just sat there, the wadded up tissues in one hand, his arms lax on his thighs as he sort of stared in the middle distance.

"Can I see her?" His voice was almost even, almost steady.

"Yes. She's going to be moved to a room. Let me talk to someone and see if we can't get you to that room to wait for her."

I walked over to the reception desk to make sure that could happen.

CHAPTER 7

"I SAID no."

I turned off the engine and gave Jame my stern-but-fair cop look. "You have blood on your clothes and need your pain meds, which you left at home. We're now at your home. I don't care if you don't like it. We're getting changed, medicated and maybe even fed. Let's go."

I got out of the Jeep and he followed. I didn't care how much swagger or scowl he threw my way. He was hurting and exhausted and it showed in every line of his body.

He unlocked the door and stepped into the house he shared with Ben.

I'd last been here for their housewarming, a gathering that seemed to have pulled half of Ordinary through this modern two-story that overlooked the waves.

They'd lucked out on lot placement and how the house was built. The curve of the bank it stood on gave the illusion of a lot more privacy than there actually was from the houses on either side of their property.

The interior was not what I expected out of a couple of guys who fought fires for a living. I expected bare brick, leather furniture, and mismatched art.

Instead it was cozy. Welcoming. Soft, without feeling overdone. It was like walking into a warm cabin retreat with thick blankets and pillows stacked on the couch, recliners positioned for a view of the sky and the TV that took up one wall, and throw rugs positioned to soak up the echoes of the wood floors.

There were a few hanging plants, a scatter of mail on an end table and something that looked like a half-finished carving project on the coffee table. A ridiculously comfortable-looking rocking chair with a bright green lap quilt draped over the back was set into a nook that was lined with shelves filled with a selection of books, carefully wrapped comics, scrolls, and little trinkets, some that looked like they were gathered from all over the world.

Everything about the house spoke to comfort, rest, ease.

It was Jame's den, Ben's sanctuary.

It was the home they had made with each other, for each other.

Jame didn't bother turning on other lights as he stalked into the house, crossing the living room before going down a hall toward their room.

I supposed being a werewolf meant you didn't need light to navigate, and having a vampire for a boyfriend pretty much meant the same thing.

I was not a werewolf or vampire (no matter what Jame thought) so I flicked on a couple lights as I walked into the main room.

"Delaney?"

I froze, my skin cold. The air had dropped to freezing. I could see my breath.

Ghost. There was a ghost here. And not just any ghost.

"Dad?"

The word came out in a puff, and I wrapped my arms around myself to hold heat to my body.

I heard the shower turn on down the hall where Jame had gone. If he was in the shower, he couldn't hear me unless I yelled.

Okay, let's hope I wouldn't have to yell. I wasn't afraid of my dad, not as a man, a parent, or a disembodied spirit. But I was worried for him.

My hand cupped the worry stone in my pocket and I rubbed my thumb across the smooth warmth of the rose quartz. The motion and sensation calmed and centered me.

This was just my dad. Just his ghost. Just him.

"Are you okay, Dad?" Nothing. "Are you here to talk to me?" More nothing. "I felt you at the lighthouse. Saw you there. I'm worried about you. Can you show me where you are? Can you tell me you're okay?"

A thump of something heavy hitting the floor made me jump. "Shit. I mean, shoot. I mean, cool. Good. So, over by the mantle?" It was still cold in the room, but I wasn't going to cower away from my father.

"I don't know why you had to knock something off their mantle, Dad. If you broke one of Ben's antique knickknacks, you know he's going to be upset."

No sign of him. No sound of him. The room was still cold, but other than that, and the overwhelming feeling of knowing that had been his voice, his presence, there was nothing to prove that there was a haunting going down.

"Why Jame's place anyway?" I scanned the floor beneath the mantle. Spotted a fist-sized green stone lying near the table. It was big enough to have made the loud thud when it fell. I didn't know Ben collected rocks. Or maybe that was Jame's hobby.

"What was the lighthouse all about? I understand you checking in on me, or Myra or Jean. But these other places?"

I bent. "Well, at least it's not breakable." I had never seen a stone like that before. It was pale green and almost translucent with shots of black and red jagging through it, sparking deep fire that I was more used to seeing in opals.

"So let's put it back where it belongs." I picked it up and straightened.

"No." A soft sound. A plea. My father's voice. Too late.

The stone in my hand blazed hot, too hot to hold. My fingers clenched around it and I could not let it go.

The heat rolled into a vibration, a thrumming of music that poured over me, too loud, too strong, plucking me like a string against a sounding board.

It wasn't god power. I knew those songs, knew the dizzying sensation of god power loose and wild and fierce. Knew how to hold it, how to carry it across my nerves and muscles and skin, knew how to direct it to a place of holding, away from the god's body, but never far from their reach.

But this song, this roar was bone-deep and tore into me with teeth and fang. I'd never felt this power before.

It was darkness.

It was heat.

It was desire.

I couldn't force my hand to drop the stone, couldn't move, couldn't even blink. My body was not my own.

Cue the fear.

The room around me fogged out, going green at the edges. There was someone yelling, there were hands on me, but I sensed that at a distance.

All I could hear were the churning tones, all I could feel was the heat tearing through me.

And then everything went cold.

My father stood in front of me, solid and tangible and breathing, every detail clear. He was wearing his uniform, and look a little rumpled, his hair sticking up at the crown like it did when he rubbed his palm over the back of it or when he pulled all-nighters at the station.

I could smell the spice of his cologne, the slight hint of tobacco and coffee that was so familiar, so him.

But his eyes, oh, how I'd missed them. Not the color, which was a soft blue that tended toward gray, but the kindness, the intelligence, the light of the man who had known me and loved me and protected me for my entire life. Right there. Right there in front of me close enough to touch.

When I'd never thought I'd see him again.

"Dad?"

"Delaney, you need to step back. Drop the stone. Run."

I tried. Really I did. I struggled to open my fingers, turn my hand over, lift my feet.

Didn't get anywhere.

"I. Can't." Even my words were strangled, locked down. Impossible to push through my lips.

"Well, well. Delaney Reed. All tied up with a bow. I like what I see."

I couldn't turn my head to see who was talking but I had never heard that voice before. It was smooth, low, like honey and whiskey.

A man walked into my line of vision, coming out of the green foggy edges to stand beside my father.

Dad's eyes went hard, his jaw set. Whoever, or really knowing my life, *what*ever that was, Dad didn't like him.

"Demon," Dad said.

Oh.

Oh, shit.

The man—demon—was taller than my dad and wide enough in the shoulder, it made the rest of his body look lean, even though he appeared muscled under the lightweight button-down shirt and business slacks he wore. His tie was loosened at the neck, and matched his eyes, which were a stunning green, almost as light as the green fog around us.

And when he smiled, it was like the sun had finally decided to shine down on something so beautiful and wicked, it was impossible to cast light anywhere else.

I hated the hitch of attraction in my gut. But this demon had that level of once-in-a-lifetime Hollywood leading-man gorgeous that could turn anyone's knees to jelly.

Demon.

Handsome, conniving, amoral, selfish, cruel.

Even knowing that didn't take the thrall off his beauty.

So, whatever. I was attracted to a gorgeous image. Most humans were. It didn't mean I was going to act on it. Or rather, not in the way he probably wanted me to, if that smirk and wink he gave me meant anything.

"Why is he here?" I asked Dad. "Is he keeping you here, trapping you against your will?"

Every word came out steady, like I was bored with this whole thing already and willing to throw my authority around to get my way. I was good at this. I'd been taught by a master.

The corner of Dad's mouth quirked. I saw the pride in his eyes, the love.

Damn right, Dad. You and I can totally take this joker down.

"Not against my will."

That surprised me.

The demon chuckled. Yes, it sent happy shivers over my skin.

I turned my "ignore" up to eleven.

"I don't understand."

I wanted to touch Dad. To hug him, feel him solid and real again. But he was holding still in a very careful way, as if a line had been drawn between us. A line he couldn't cross.

"Your father gave himself to me," the demon said. "Willingly." The demon's eyes flashed red for a second, then faded to watery green.

"I'm sure there's quite a story behind that. Do I have to figure it out in three questions or are you going to fill me in?"

He paused, his lips parted as he considered me, then his smile came back in full force.

The handsome. It burned.

"I like the idea of making you work for it, Delaney Reed, but as time is sliding away, and I have needs to be fulfilled, we'll make this quick. Your father traded his soul to protect you."

"You did what?" I nearly shouted at the same time Dad said, "It wasn't just you, honey."

I glared at the demon. "You, shut up."

The demon opened his mouth, that same surprised look crossing his features before he smiled and pointedly pressed his lips together.

I glared at Dad. "You, talk."

"I was driving back from picking up a package from the casino. The package, a small padded envelope was addressed to me, just my name written across the front. I thought that was odd, but it wasn't the first time it had happened."

If I could shiver, I would. That had happened to me too. I'd picked up an envelope addressed to me, and it had warned me about Heimdall's murder.

"I opened the envelope and a stone fell out. A green stone with cracks of black and red."

"The one I'm holding."

"Yes. I didn't know who it was from or what it was, so I put it back in the envelope. I was going to put it in lock up. Make sure it was warded. The car...I lost control of the car." He frowned. "I don't remember it very well. The moment, the reason.

"I remember falling. Falling over the side of the cliff." He paused and tucked his hand in his front pocket, shoulders tilting sideways. Such a familiar gesture, my heart hitched.

"I knew, this was it. The end. My end. I'd hoped I'd get more years with you, Delaney. With all of you girls. Wanted to see you all build your lives, fall in love. Maybe have a chance to be a grandpa."

He shook his head, and his smile was sad. "But I knew. I was done."

Everything in me hurt. For him. For me. For our family. I didn't know what to say.

"So, you traded your soul?" Okay, it wasn't what I wanted to say, but I needed to know.

"I died."

We just let that truth pull on the ties between us, knotting our sorrow, our loss together so tightly, it was an aching bond we shared.

I exhaled and it was shaky. "I miss you. We all miss you, Dad. I love you so much and so do Myra and Jean. Nothing is the same without you. But we're trying. We're all working at the station, the town voted me in as chief. I still expect you to come through the door when people call me that."

He smiled, and it was soft and a little pleased. The kind of smile he always wore when we talked about his job being the bridge for the god powers in Ordinary. The job I'd inherited that made me the one and only person who could tell a god that he or she could or couldn't set down their power and stay awhile.

"I love you, Delaney and I love your sisters too. I never wanted to leave so soon."

"This is oh, so touching," Beauty McJerkface said. "I'm on a schedule, so I'll bring us to the punchline. I was trapped here. In this stone. Not of my own choosing, but because of a rather unfortunate dealing with a creature you'd rather not hear about. When the chance to change my fate fell in my lap, I took it."

"Dad's soul?"

"That, he offered. As I've said before. My chance, Delaney, is you."

If I could sit down, shake my head, press cool fingers against the back of my neck to clear my brain, I'd do any one of those things. But since I was still stuck in a thrall of some sort, all I could do was blink and wait for that to make sense.

"No." Dad turned to square off against the demon. "She isn't any part of our agreement."

"You have no say in our agreement now, Robert Reed. Those bones have been cast, cards turned. There is only the future at hand and all the ink upon it has dried."

"She is not a pawn in your game, Bathin. Let her go."

The demon held my father's gaze, his face utterly

impassive. Nothing Dad said made any difference to him.

"That is true," Bathin said. "She is not a pawn. She is my rook. And I will use her as I please."

"My soul—"

"Your *soul*," the demon shouted over my father's words. "Is mine. As such, you have no say over what is or isn't done with it."

Dad's jaw locked. His fists closed. I was pretty sure he was going to punch the demon in the face.

"Please." That one word, from my father's mouth almost sent me to my knees.

The demon's expression didn't change. "Better," he said, as if my dad were a dog that had remembered to heel.

Now *I* wanted to punch him in the face.

"This has been fated. When you agreed that your soul could be used to keep Ordinary safe. To keep me trapped here, in this stone. You knew giving me your soul meant I had full control of it."

Dad didn't say anything. And that scared the pants off of me.

"But I am a reasonable man." The demon turned to me, and I knew he was neither reasonable nor a man.

"You will come to understand that I always have my best interest in mind. Always, Delaney Reed. Therefore, you now find yourself in the unique position of my services. In exchange, of course, for your services."

"For my soul." I didn't have to ask. Hello, this was a demon I was dealing with. Souls were the only thing they traded in. The only thing they wanted.

"Yes. For your soul."

"No," Dad said again.

"Let her decide. If she refuses to give me her soul then I will do nothing more to take it from her. I am self-centered. I'm not unfair."

"Don't do this, Delaney," Dad said. "He wants more than his kind are allowed."

That—the 'his kind' comment—struck hard enough that Bathin's mild expression slipped into a scowl.

"I want what is owed to me. Nothing more," he snapped.

"This: your father gave his soul to me. In exchange, I agreed not to enter into Ordinary, nor to allow any of my kind to enter. Have I not lived up to the agreement?"

When neither of us spoke, he raised the volume. "I have lived up to every syllable of our agreement. And more. Because this, this is what I'm offering you, Robert Reed. I am offering you one more chance to trade your soul in a way that will bring good to your town. To your daughter, whom I can see you must love."

"Out of the kindness of your heart," I said.

"Out of my own best interests. We both know I have no heart. I took your father's soul and promised to keep it in exchange for an absence of demons in Ordinary. And now, as part of the trade with you, I will set his soul free."

Dad exhaled, a small sound that somehow carried both desire and sorrow.

"His soul for my soul," I repeated.

"No," Dad said again.

"Not just a soul for a soul. In what way would that profit me?" Bathin asked. He took a breath and for the slightest moment, something else seemed to shift in his eyes. I'd say it was curiosity and maybe need mixed with an urgent hope, but that would be too weird. This was a demon we were talking about here. No heart.

And I knew enough Demon 101 to never, in no uncertain terms trust one.

"I will free your father's soul, and I will grant unto you a single favor for your living soul, Delancy Reed."

"Don't do this, Delaney."

"What are his powers?" I asked Dad. "Myra would know, but I don't. What can Bathin do?"

"Nothing," Dad said.

Bathin sucked air through his teeth. "Falsehood, my dear man? I thought that beneath you?"

"Nothing is beneath me when my family's threatened. You of all things should know that."

"Yes, yes. How desperately you made your agreement with me. How terribly you wanted to ease the burden your daughters bear in your absence. So humanly *thoughtful* and earnest and…."

He stuck one finger in his open mouth as if he were going to gag.

Ass.

"What is his scope of powers?" I asked again, wishing I could reach my TASER and dial it to disintegrate.

Dad's eyebrows shot downward as he tried to recall his demonology. I could only imagine it was harder now that he had been dead for over a year and didn't exactly have reference material handy.

"Stones," Bathin said. "I know stones, and herbs, ways in which they can be used. I can move people in both physical and astral forms."

"That's it?" I asked.

He widened his eyes before narrowing them again. "That is so much more than you can imagine and all that I will tell you."

Bathin obviously knew how to keep demons out of Ordinary. Or maybe he didn't. It might simply be a coincidence that there were no demons in the town. A coincidence he took credit for.

Never trust a demon.

"You'll set my dad's soul free for my soul and a favor?"

"Yes."

My heart was thrumming a heavy beat. I didn't know where, exactly, we were physically right now. I mean, I remembered coming to Jame's house, but the green fog around me made anything more than a few feet away hazy enough I couldn't make it out.

This was either some kind of spell I'd triggered when I'd picked up the stone, or I'd fallen into some kind of between space. Time did weird things when it collided with supernatural happenings. The world around me might be running either really fast, or really slow, or not at all.

None of those possibilities made me happy.

The only thing that made me happy was seeing Dad. Even though he was scowling, angry at the demon and maybe a little angry at me too, for considering the demon's offer.

But then, he'd done more than just consider the demon's offer. He'd taken him up on it.

I suppose the one big difference was that Dad had been dying.

And in his dying moments, he hadn't used a deal with a demon to save his own life. He'd given up his soul to save Ordinary. To keep us safe. The people and the place he loved.

I understood why he didn't want me to make a deal. I would forbid Myra, Jean, and anyone else I loved from making any deal with any demon.

But right here I had a choice. I could set my father free or leave him trapped. Tied to this demon for all time.

The bite on the side of my neck burned cold, shivering down deeper beneath my skin.

"Delaney," Dad said, "you will not do this. Please. Your life. Your heart. You can't do this, baby."

"He won't have my heart. Just my soul. Is that right?"

The demon inclined his head. "It is what I said."

What was worth the price of my soul? My family's safety? The safety of my town?

Ryder.

I could ask him to break the tie between Ryder and the god, Mithra who had claimed him. I could ask him to bring my father back to life, although I thought that was probably outside his scope.

"Can you bring the dead back to life?"

"Can I?" He opened his hands. "I could make it happen. It would be...messy."

"No," Dad said firmer now. "That I absolutely forbid. I've made peace with my decisions, Delancy, and I will not have you throwing away your soul for my life."

That hurt, the ache turning in my chest. The need to bring him back to life was the need of a child who didn't want to face the hard decisions alone anymore. Still, it was very, very tempting.

"Ask," the demon whispered. "You know what you want. You know I can give you your desires."

Wow. When he turned on the charm, it was sort of stunning.

"He won't," Dad argued. "That kind of resurrection, this long after my death would take the agreement and direct involvement of gods and demons. Of Death, at the very least. And convincing him that I should be breathing again…. He won't do it, baby. Not for me. The favors between us are too great."

But would he do it for me?

For a fleeting, wild moment, I thought yes. Thanatos seemed to be, if not fond of me, at least amused by me. I might be able to talk him around to seeing my side of this, to maybe even team up with a demon to save my dad.

"How messy?" I asked Bathin.

"Gods and demons…." He grinned, full-blast charm. "Oil and water. There is no good way to mix us without a lot of agitation, and even then the mix is temporary. Imperfect."

So that was off the table. I exhaled, shaky. Fatigue was setting in, though it shouldn't make me tired to just stand there with a stone in my hand.

"What about vampires?"

"Explain."

"Do demons and vampires mix?"

He pulled his head back and the grin was gone. He considered me with those pale green eyes, as if trying to read the text inside my brain.

"Demons care not for vampires across the long dance of eternity we've shared."

"Can you kill one?"

"Most."

"Lavius?"

His eyes shot to the bite on my neck. From the heat in his gaze, and the dark expression, it seemed he was acquainted with the evil in question.

"With consequences, yes."

"Consequences?"

"If I killed him, you would die, and I want you living, Delaney."

"Why?"

"It would be so much more pleasant for me, and I am all about my own pleasure. I told you that."

"Terrific. Look, can you break the tie between me and Lavius, then kill him?"

"That would be two favors, Delaney Reed. I have only offered one."

"Delaney, say no. Don't bargain with this being. You know he's darkness. An end, not a beginning. Not even a weapon you should use."

I gave dad a soft smile. "He's the only weapon I have."

Bathin made a happy little humming sound. "I live to serve."

"Bullshit," Dad said.

If he couldn't bring Dad back to life, or kill Lavius, then there was only one other thing that I wanted, needed that badly.

"Can you find Ben Rossi and bring him back to Ordinary alive before midnight?"

Bathin's nostrils widened, as did his pupils. "This. This you desire. You are in pain. I can taste it, oh. I can taste it." He swallowed as if he'd suddenly shoved something succulent in his mouth. "Why have you misplaced that particular vampire?"

"My reasons are my own. If you can free my father's soul and find Ben Rossi, and return him to us, alive, breathing, whole—every finger, toe, and scrap of flesh he currently possesses, including his soul and sanity before midnight tonight, I will give you my soul."

"Delaney." My name left Dad's mouth in a hush that sounded like something heavy had struck his chest.

It made tears push at the back of my eyes.

Yes, I was frightened. Yes, I knew I was selling my soul to a thing of darkness. A thing that as Dad had said was an end, not a beginning.

I knew how stupid this was. How risky.

But I knew other things too. How much Jame loved Ben. How much Rossi loved Ben. How much it was my job, my *responsibility* to keep the people of my town safe. And that if I hadn't been the one to directly cause Ben to be taken, that I was absolutely the one who could right now, right here, directly bring him back.

Safe.

Whole.

And I knew this wasn't my end. I was bargaining my soul, but I was betting on the people who loved me. There would be a way to break this, a way to change it, to get my soul back. There were too many gods and creatures who had my back. There were too many mystics, and books of magic, and indomitable, clever sisters to think that my soul being in a demon's hands was going to be anything but temporary.

I could do this. Take this hit and save Ben.

It was no different than taking a bullet in the line of duty.

This was my choice. Maybe even the choice the seer and witch had known I'd have to make. And I was making it.

"Oh, Delaney, how you spin and twist. So very prettily."

I was back to wishing for my TASER again.

Bathin folded his hands in front of him, thick fingers slotting neatly in place. "You don't have to work so hard to convince yourself. You made your decision the moment I brought you here. See?" he said to Dad. "I told you she'd come around to see things my way. You underestimated her."

"I have never underestimated any of my daughters." Dad raised a hand and rubbed at the back of his neck, then shook his head. "Give us a moment, Bath, you owe me."

To my utter astonishment, Bathin nodded, gave me a wink, and then moved out of the range of my vision.

He might be standing right there listening to us and I'd never know since I couldn't move my head to look around. But Dad's gaze followed him, somewhere off behind my right shoulder, and he seemed satisfied with where the demon had taken himself off to.

"He owes you something?" I asked.

Dad shrugged. "We've been together for over a year. All we've had to do to pass the time is talk. He's…he's not quite like most of the demons I've met. That doesn't in any way mean I trust him. But he is unusual among his kind."

"Would you let him into Ordinary if he asked?"

"And have to clean up after the messes he'd continually make?" He chuckled, a dry sound I had forgotten and missed. "I'm not a masochist."

"So, here's what I can tell you: don't trust him. Always question his good will. He's not a trickster, not like Crow, or Odin, or the others. Not defined by his power like a god, not bound to his nature like a creature. All demons can be bound and controlled. All demons can be used by those who wield dark magic, blood magic, shadow rituals. Demons and gods do not suffer one another's company, he is right about that. Many other creatures won't suffer the company of a demon either.

"I can't tell you what losing your soul will feel like, honey. I don't know what it will do to you. I was dying when I gave him mine, so it was painless, a relief. And in all the time we've been locked here together, he hasn't caused me pain I couldn't bear.

"But this I can tell you. He can't be killed, not easily or without a price. He can be bound and contained, again there is a price. A sacrifice. There are rites. Talk to Rossi. He knows. He has books, ancient things, spells that will lash a demon down and hold them for eternity. But you must retrieve your soul before you bind him, Delaney. Living without it, living with your soul at the whim of a darkness like him will also come at a price you will pay every second of every day."

I expected to see Bathin again. Expected him to want to stop my dad from telling me all the things he knew about demons. Specifically how to take him down. But he didn't show up.

"There are rumors of how to steal a soul away from a demon. I've never put my hand on any of those things, but the books, the old books would give you a place to start. I know you can find a way. If not you, then Myra. She's always had a head for these kinds of puzzles."

"She loves you," I said. "She misses you. She loves the books you left to her. It makes her proud to know you believed she should have them."

He smiled and I could almost feel the warmth of his love on my skin. "Good. That's good. And Jean?"

"Misses you like crazy. She loves you too. She's dating a baker."

His smile turned into a grin. "She's always had a thing for men who work with their hands. Is she happy?"

"She loves the job so much. You know how she's always sort of rolled with whatever has come her way. The dating thing…I've never seen her so mixed up over someone. Mixed up in a good way. And he's a great guy. I know he cares for her."

"Tell her I love her and I approve of whatever makes her

heart happy. Tell them both that. Myra and Jean."

"I will."

"And you? Are you happy?"

I felt the blush rush to my cheeks. "Ryder and I are dating."

"Ryder Bailey? It's about time you two came around." He nodded. "I approve. I've always liked that boy. Always thought you two made a good team."

"Thanks, Dad." I exhaled, feeling a sort of loose happiness from hearing that. I knew he had liked Ryder, but there was something comforting hearing it directly from him."

"I like the work too, both policing and bridging, but filling your shoes has been...hard. I've made some dumb decisions. Bad mistakes."

"I've made my share."

"Not like this."

"Is Ordinary still standing?"

"Yes. But people have died on my watch. People who I should have kept safe."

"People died on my watch too, Delaney. There is a limit to what you can do, what any of us can do," he said gently.

"You are the law and the bridge for power, but you aren't a god who can bend the world to your desires. You aren't a creature who has influence over a man's thoughts, or the flow of time. You're human, Delaney. Maybe a bit more than, but human just the same. There are events beyond your control. A whole wide universe of them."

"I know." And I did. I didn't like it, but I understood my limitations compared to so many who stayed here in my sleepy little beach town.

"Are you sure I can't talk you out of this?" he asked. "You are giving away your soul."

"Ben was beaten. Kidnapped. Lavius broke his bond to Jame and nearly killed Jame. Before that, he murdered another vampire, and we're pretty sure he killed four vampire hunters who had rolled through town. He..." This part wasn't going to be pretty. "He sent a zombie vampire to run Jean over with a car."

"What?" Dad yelled. And that I could feel. His fury hot and stinging as if it were my own deep in my gut. "Who the hell is

Lavius? How does he know our town? What does he want?"

"He's a vampire as old as Rossi. Turned at the same time. He wants something Rossi has. Look, Dad. Jean's fine. She broke her arm and twisted her ankle. Bed rest and a cast, and she's going to be okay. But I can't…."

My voice gave out on me, caught up on a mix of grief and anger that clogged all sound.

"You're not going to try to kill him, are you Delaney? A vampire that old isn't something you are equipped to deal with. Promise me you're not going to try to kill him."

I wasn't going to make promises I couldn't keep. "Rossi is first in the kill-him line. I've never seen him so angry. Lavius hurt Ben, and you know Ben is…"

"…his son. Yes. Yes, of course." He was silent a moment. "I've seen Rossi kill. Have you?"

"No."

"It will change what you think of him."

I huffed out a choked laugh. "That's been happening an awful lot lately. I think I can take it."

"I wish…." His eyes clouded and sorrow settled into the shadows of his face. "If I could have stayed with you, with all of you, you know I would have."

"I know, Dad. We know."

"I didn't…it wasn't suicide. I don't know how I lost control, but believe me when I say I was trying to come home, honey. I never meant to leave you all so soon."

"We know. We know."

"Isn't this sweet?" Bathin was back, standing beside Dad even though I hadn't seen him approach.

I hated that smug smile on his face. I wanted to smack it off of him.

"You've had your private time," he continued. "Now we seal our deals. Delaney Reed, I swear to release your father, Robert Reed's soul unto the afterlife he has chosen, and grant you one wish in exchange for your soul. Is that acceptable?"

"Yes."

Something thrummed, like a great bass string being strummed somewhere in the universe, rolling out one note, deep and long and eternal.

"Name the favor."

"You will find Ben Rossi and return him to Ordinary, alone and alive, in as complete health physically, mentally, emotionally, spiritually as he is found before midnight tonight. You'll bring him to Jame Wolfe and give him to him freely into his open arms with no deals or bindings, contracts, or debts outstanding."

His pupils, which had been wide before were now so dark, they swallowed up all of the green of his eyes except for the faintest halo ring. He licked his bottom lip once, catching it in his teeth, then nodded. "Yes."

A second note plucked and joined the first in strange harmony that seemed wrong at first and then slid into something not pleasant, but intriguing.

"Say goodbye to your father, Delaney."

I turned my gaze to Dad.

He stepped forward, arms out, and I wanted to hug him, to feel him so much, a small sob escaped me.

Bathin *tsked*, and suddenly I was free. I could move.

Dad's eyebrows rose and he smiled. I launched myself at him, and he wrapped his strong arms around me, his left hand shifting up so he could press his wide palm against the back of my head and press my face to his chest, holding me tight, familiar and right.

"I love you so much," he said. "I'm proud of you. Of all of you. I always will be. Remember at every end is a beginning. Remember that. Ends are only the beginning."

"I love you too," I said. It seemed to be the only thing I could say. Over and over again as my heart soared and broke, caught between joy and sorrow, loss and love.

I squeezed him as tight as I could, memorizing his presence, the dimensions of him, the scents of something deep like cedar, coffee, and tobacco.

I never wanted to let him go. Never wanted to leave the warmth and protection of his arms.

"That's all," Bathin said quietly as if he were in a library and didn't want to disturb anyone. "That's all I can do, Robert. I'm sorry."

"You promised me," he said to Bathin. "Our deal."

"I have never broken my word. I will not break it now."

Something about that seemed to put a brief, wild hope in Dad's eyes.

"Delaney. I love—"

He was gone, the air in front of me empty and cold, without even a lingering hint of his scent, of his presence.

I pressed my hands against my face to wipe at my tears, and tried to pull it together. My heart felt like it was made of rice paper that was being squeezed tighter and tighter into a painful crumpled ball.

Bathin strolled over to stand next to me, so close, our shoulders brushed. "I can take that pain away, Delaney Reed. It is a small solace, but one you will know."

He pivoted so that he stood in front of me, dark eyes inches from my own, breath close enough I could feel it on my cheek, could smell the slight cinnamon of his words.

"His soul has gone on to the afterlife of his choosing. As we agreed. And now yours is mine. As we agreed."

He didn't touch me. Not a finger. He simply held my gaze. I thought I could look away, turn away from him.

"Yes, you could." He waited.

There would be a price to pay if I backed out on our deal.

"Yes, there would." He was apparently reading my mind.

Jerk.

His eyes glittered with something like delight and I hated him for it. Before I could stop myself, before I could even register what I was going to do, I wound my fist back and punched him in the face.

His head jerked back and he grunted.

I knew how to throw a punch.

He stumbled back two steps, his hand over his nose. And then he laughed. *Laughed.* It was loud and deep and full of dark joy.

"You punched me! You punched me in the face! Oh, you Reeds. Always so surprising!" He was still laughing, squeezing the words out between bouts of glee.

"You took my father's soul, you dick. You used it as some kind of a bullshit bargain for over a year. I should do more than punch you."

He pulled his hand away and glanced at his palm, looking

for blood or whatever passed as blood for demons. He nodded as he dabbed at his nose one more time. "I took his soul, true. But the deal we agreed upon was very real. There have been no demons in Ordinary in the time since his death."

"There have never been any demons in Ordinary!" Yes, I was yelling.

He narrowed his eyes. "That is not…true. And not what I meant, exactly. You do know that the vampire who has penetrated your borders isn't doing it on his own, isn't getting his own hands dirty."

My fingers automatically flickered up to the bite on my neck. He watched, and nodded.

"Yes, he attacked you—outside of Ordinary. But the other attacks, inside? How do you think he has been facilitating that?"

I'd assumed he was using vampires, or humans, or some kind of blood magic. But I knew, then, that moment, what Bathin was getting at.

"Demons?"

"We come in every shape, every size. We are very difficult to detect. We possess bodies of humans, of creatures, animals, inanimate objects. We are, in every way, an invisible army. Infinitely mobile, undetected and destructive. Who can say how many of your friends, family, have been possessed? Who can say how many mortals filling the stores, the streets, the beaches are possessed?"

I swallowed, my throat suddenly dry. It made sense in a way few things had lately. Ryder's boss Frank, was he possessed? The vampire hunters? Sven? The hit-and-run zombie vampire?

"I thought you just said there were no demons in Ordinary."

"No demons in their own form. No demons under full power. No demons who were not beneath their own control. No demons who were beneath anyone's control. I will admit there were some…issues in my guarantee."

"Issues?" I was back to yelling. It didn't seem to bother him one bit.

"The vampire? Lavius is very old. And…." He scowled. "He has powers I was not aware of. Once I had taken your father's soul, he insisted we remain trapped here. His idea, not mine. It limited my ability to follow through on every level of my commitment. That vampire."

A flicker of hatred so hot it left a burning impression behind my eyelids flashed over his face, as if for a moment, he had been nothing but fire and pain and anger. "That vampire nearly caused me to break my word. I find it…unacceptable."

He didn't like Lavius. He might even hate him. I wanted to take comfort in that, to hope that if he had to be the possessor of my soul that he would at least be the enemy of my enemy and all that.

"Now, you have given me your word. I will have your soul. As we agreed. I will not be denied."

This time it wasn't a burning flash of hatred filling his eyes. It was fire, hot and hypnotic, rising from his entire body, shaping him, changing him as he strode the few steps toward me again.

When he stopped he was three times as large as he had just been, his legs bent at the knees and powerfully thick, his chest bare and brutally muscled, his neck thick enough to support his head and the massive ebony horns that curled like a ram's downward along the sides of his face to either side of his shoulders.

Fire licked over every inch of his skin, rattled and hissed like electric snakes dripping down his blackened horns and lit his eyes to a bloody red.

The demon's true form

"Very dramatic," I said.

He paused, half a step closer to me. "Dramatic?"

I waved a finger. "Do you think that shape frightens me? Do you think seeing a creature in a natural state is something that would make me swoon?"

"I…it is imposing. I am imposing."

"Not sure I agree. You're the first demon I've ever met, so I have nothing to compare you to. But trust me, buddy." And here I dropped my eyes to between his legs, where he wore a carefully twisted loincloth of some kind. I shook my head. "I've seen better."

His chuckle was low and slow and licked somewhere deep down inside me. I didn't like it. Didn't like that he could touch me in those deep places. In the places where no one else could touch, where no one else could find me.

In my soul.

"I see," he said. "I knew I was trading up. Your father is a complex and interesting man. You must know that. His soul at my disposal, even though he was dead…that was an exquisite thing." He took a step closer to me, and another.

I could move. I thought I could move. I just didn't seem to have the energy to do anything more than stare at him as he advanced on me with hunger and need so clearly evident in every movement, in the glint of darkness in his eyes.

It wasn't the physical beauty of his body that held me so still. It was the beauty of his power.

Demons were from the underworld, yes. Demons were not to be trusted, and like he'd taken the time to explain to me, they were easily used, natural to betrayal, selfish, cruel.

They were chaos. But just like the gods who walked our beaches, just like the creatures—many who had reputations of being bloodthirsty monsters, boogiemen, evil—demons could not be painted with one brush.

Rossi didn't let all the vampires in the world live in Ordinary for a reason. A lot of them were horrible people. Same thing applied to demons.

While I would never trust a demon, I knew they were not, could not all be horrifying evil.

There was no denying I was drawn to Bathin. No denying that my father's soul had seemed whole, unharmed, though that could have been some sort of trickery.

And there was no denying my father and the demon seemed to have come to some sort of understanding between them, that was not jailor and jailed, and not friends. It was, if I had to put a name to it, more like they respected each other's nature and reason for the contract they had entered into.

That last thing Dad had said to him, that Bathin had a promise to keep, floated to the front of my brain. I wondered what that was all about.

"Delaney."

All thoughts froze and fell away like brittle snow on the wind.

He wanted me, he wanted my soul in a way that made me

tremble, that made me want to turn and scream and run. Or made me want to step into him, into that fire to know what it would taste like on my tongue.

As if.

I wanted my gun, a rocket launcher, a bomb. Anything that would kill him, stop him, make him, and the nightmare promise of his smile, go away.

"Breathe."

I breathed.

"You'll want to hold very still now." His hand extended, fire swaying at the tip of the three fingers he extended. It was warm, that fire.

A fire that did not burn.

"Why?" I shivered, suddenly too cold.

Three fingers stroked down, slashing from my left shoulder to my sternum. There was pain—out there at a distance. A scream.

And then the world exploded.

CHAPTER 8

SOMEONE WAS squishing me. I blinked and moved my tongue around in my mouth. It tasted weirdly of burned herbs and cinnamon. Sounds filtered into my awareness. Sights. Sensation.

My back was pressed against a wall, cold, and something dug in the back of my hip a little painfully, not that it seemed to matter much.

My front was covered by the back of a muscular, very pissed off werewolf. Jame.

He was still kicking off a fever, but from the tension in him, I knew he was in full protective mode. There was a threat.

Well, that was probably something I should deal with. I was the chief of police, after all.

"Hey, Jame? You wanna give me a little breathing room, buddy? Let me in on the situation?"

He growled.

Okay, not really helpful. I twisted a little so I could look past his shoulder.

A man stood there in front of Jame's fireplace, dressed in a leather jacket, t-shirt and jeans. No, not a man. The demon, Bathin.

"Tell your friend I am not a threat to you, Delaney." His voice was just how I remembered it. Low, whiskey smoke, heat and amusement.

"Nah, I don't lie to my friends." I patted Jame's arm. "This is Bathin. He's a demon. He had Dad's soul trapped in that stone on your mantle. He and I made a deal, and now he has my soul. So I think he's going to be sticking around for awhile. Do you have any coffee? I could really use a cup."

Jame twitched in that way only werewolves who were paying complete attention to every living thing around them could.

"He's a demon."

"Right. How about you sit down, have a chat, and I'll get

the coffee."

Jame moved to the side so he could glance at me over his shoulder. "He took your soul?"

I nodded. It was weird that it didn't bother me, wasn't it? Or was it? Was that weird?

"It's a long story, but there's some really good news." I wriggled enough, he finally got the message and leaned away so I could move off of the wall.

"News?" Jame pulled his cell out of his pocket and hit dial without even looking at it. I wondered who he had on speed dial.

"Yes. Let me just get coffee and we can talk about it. Coffee?" I asked Bathin as I started toward the kitchen.

He was leaning one elbow on the mantle watching me with a tolerant curiosity. "Yes. Two sugars."

"Got it. And do you want—" My words were cut off, because Jame was suddenly, silently right behind me, still putting his body between me and Bathin, but also talking on his phone.

"She's right here, conscious, but acting strange. She sold her soul to a demon." Pause. "Yes." He glanced at Bathin. "It's here." Another pause.

I stage-whispered, "Do you want coffee too? Or maybe tea? I'm not sure what you've got in the kitchen." I marched in to investigate, my were-shadow following on my heels. "And the cupboards say…coffee! Powdered lemonade."

"Strange-strange, not shock strange," he said.

"Refrigerator has… no surprise: beer and tomato juice. So?" I waved my hands at the fridge then cupboard.

He leveled a very serious gaze at me. "I will. Yes." Then he pocketed his phone, closed the refrigerator even though my hand was still on the handle, and physically guided me over to the coffee-making area.

"Make the coffee." He had his back to me again, close enough I had to brush against his shirt as I reached for filters and grounds.

He was in full protection mode, which I knew I should either consider sweet of him, or terrifying since I'd never, not once, been in the kind of danger that any werewolf had treated me like a part of their pack.

I paused, my finger over the coffee machine GO button and

wondered at that for a second. I seemed awfully calm about selling my soul. Was that like me? Was I always so calm when crazy stuff happened?

Maybe?

But at the back of my mind, doubt niggled. I had sold my soul. I had just spoken to my dead father. Shouldn't I feel more...more?

Huh.

I pushed the button. "Okay, Big Bad, you can walk me out to the living room so we can all sit down and wait for whoever you called to get here." I pushed at his back gently so as not to disturb his injuries.

Man was made of brick wall. He didn't even budge.

"We'll wait here."

I rolled my eyes. "C'mon, Jame." I took his hand and led him into the living room. "We can sit down and wait. Coffee's going to take a couple minutes to brew."

He pulled his hand out of mine and draped his arm instead around my shoulders. Instinct just wasn't going to let him do anything else.

"Maybe the couch?" I suggested.

I was herded to the couch and sat. I pulled him down toward me, but he didn't shift from his standing sentry position.

"Introductions, perhaps?" Bathin said.

"Jame Wolfe, this is Bathin, the demon who possessed my father's soul in trade to keep demons out of Ordinary, which he was only relatively successful at doing."

Bathin's mouth quirked. "So much attitude."

"Just telling the truth."

"Hush," Jame said. "Don't speak. Either of you. We wait."

Bathin's eyebrows lifted, but he remained silent, leaning on the mantle as if he had all the time in the world to waste here in Jame's living room.

"We might want—"

"No."

Okay, then. Jame wasn't having any of it. Fine. I was tired, but also weirdly full of energy, like that second wind you get in the middle of pulling an all-nighter. I tapped my fingers on my thighs, and then decided a few calming breaths would be good.

So I breathed calmly, thought calm thoughts, and rolled the kinks out of my shoulders and neck.

Jame was a solid wall of not-having-it, and Bathin seemed smug and satisfied and content to watch the two of us like some weird uncle at the dinner table who'd just been introduced to relations he'd never met before.

The knock on the door was followed by the door opening. It was fully dark out, which meant I might have lost some time, but it wasn't dawn yet.

That was good. That was positive. I hadn't lost too much time dealing with the demon.

"Hey, Myra." I should have guessed that's who he'd call. "And Rossi. Come on in. We have coffee."

Myra entered the room, her gun in her hands currently pointed at the demon by the fireplace. "Give her back her soul. Now."

"Mymy," I said. "There's more to it. You need to listen."

"Now." One clipped word.

I glanced over at Bathin and was surprised at what I saw. He was still a thousand gigawatts of gorgeous, but his lips had parted slightly, his eyes softened, but also sort of intense.

He looked like someone had just stopped his world and sent it spinning too fast and upside down. Totally gobsmacked.

I glanced back at what he was looking at. The furiously dark and sleek vampire?

Nope.

Just my sister, her pale skin showing off a few of her seasonal freckles now that we'd actually gotten some sun, her dark hair a thick wedge of black over her startlingly light blue eyes, her lips which I knew were fuller than mine and looked good in pale lipsticks, pressed in a unforgiving line as she faced down what she thought was a threat to someone she loved.

A threat to me.

"No, Myra don't. Don't shoot him, don't make any deals with him."

"You be quiet, Delaney," she said with more anger than I'd expect from her. "You don't get a say in how this goes down now. Not anymore."

Rossi hadn't moved yet, but I knew him. I knew how fast

131

a fanger could close the distance between him and the demon.

This was about to become a bloodbath.

"He can find Ben!" I blurted. "He's going to get Ben. He's going to bring him back before midnight, right to you, Jame. Whole and alive and sane and with no other bindings on him. He promised. That's what I did. That's what I sold...." I swallowed, couldn't say it as shame filled me so hard and fast I lost my breath for a second before that shame was washed away on a numbing, cool breeze.

"That's what I made the deal for." I looked at Myra wondering if she understood. Wondering if the words that came out of my mouth made sense or if she was looking at me like that because I was suddenly talking in some language she'd never heard before.

"Dad was there," I said, softer, not because I felt...well, anything. But because I wasn't convinced my words were reaching her.

I saw how those words impacted Myra. Saw the flicker of surprise, then fear, then anger. All of which she covered up as she lowered her gun. Though she did not, I noted, put it away.

"Go through it again. All of it."

I nodded. "I will. There's coffee. Let me pour some." I stood and walked out of the room. It occurred to me that every gaze in that room was on me, and then it also occurred to me that I was leaving a ticking time bomb behind me.

"Don't kill anyone. Any of you. We are going to work together on this, understand?"

I could see a slice of the living room through the wide doorway to the kitchen. That angle revealed only Jame's back— he still hadn't moved—and Bathin over by the fireplace.

He must have known I was looking at him. He tipped his face my way and winked.

What*ever.*

I pulled out enough mugs for everyone, including one for Rossi, and filled them all with coffee, except for Rossi's which I filled with the instant-hot water at the tap and a bag of breakfast tea.

I fixed them the way I knew everyone liked, then carried the whole parade back into the room.

"Two sugars," I handed Bathin his cup.

"Jame, Myra." They took their cups with matching scowls. Huh. Maybe they'd settled down after a little caffeine.

"Rossi, breakfast tea?"

He stood very still and unbreathing as only a vampire could, his eyes laser-tight on Bathin's every move.

"Tea?" I waved it in front of his face to break the stare-a-thon and he flicked his gaze to me.

"No, Delaney." His voice was soft and carried a kindness that I hadn't heard much of out of him. Like he was talking to a child. Wait. Was he treating me like a child?

Irritation pushed at the back of my mind and then just sort of fizzled out. It didn't matter. I wasn't a child, but it was too much trouble to get worked up over that.

That was normal, right? That was the adult response? Let it all roll off my back, no problem, no worry.

Rossi lifted his hand toward my face, his eyes still on me, peering into my own. It should be uncomfortable to be stared at like that. I found I didn't care.

"Careful, old one." Bathin's tone was even, carrying the roll of authority. "What's mine is mine."

Rossi ignored him and placed his fingers, gently at my chin so he could tip my face to better stare at me.

"Can you wrap it up?" I asked. "We need to all get on the same page here so Bathin can find Ben."

"Ah, child. If only your father knew."

"He does. He was there. His soul, his...spirit. He knows."

"Where?" Myra demanded. "Where were you? You just left the hospital an hour ago. How did you find Dad, get tangled up with a demon, and lose your soul in an hour?"

She made it sound like I'd lost my lunch money between putting it in my pocket and walking out the door.

"Talent?"

Oh, that was not the right thing to say. I didn't know why she was so riled up. Everything was fine. This was fine.

Plus, we were going to save Ben. That was more than fine, it was great. Maybe I should be a little more excited or anxious about that, but even though I wasn't jumping up and down with joy, I knew saving Ben was a happy thing, a good thing, and was going to be a huge relief.

Because then we could kill Lavius, no book of magic involved.

"Where," Myra said in a flat tone. "Were you?"

"Here. I drove Jame home for a shower and change of clothes. While he was doing that, I felt Dad's ghost."

"Here?"

"Weird, right? Yes. Then a rock fell off the mantle and I picked it up."

"What rock?"

I looked at the mantle, didn't see it.

Bathin held up his hand, the rock between his fingers. Instead of green with cracks of black and red, the stone was now this beautiful tone of clear blue with fractures of pale pink sparkles and a shatter of pure, solid silver shot through it like a forked lighting frozen in time.

It didn't look the same, and the reason for that flooded my mind. The stone had held Dad's soul. This one held mine.

I shivered and rubbed at my arm absently. "That's the one," I said. "Hey, you sent it to Dad on the day he died, didn't you?"

"I did not," Bathin said.

"Huh. I had just assumed you were behind that. Anyway, that doesn't matter right now. Here's what matters: Dad traded his soul to Bathin, who is a demon, in exchange for Bathin keeping demons out of Ordinary. Which he mostly followed through on, except for the demons that Lavius controlled and sent into Ordinary to do his dirty work."

"Possessions." Rossi sent that toward Bathin, waiting for the demon to corroborate my story.

But I wasn't done talking yet. "Yes, possessions, or so Bathin tells me. And while I will never trust a demon's words, it does all fit into place. So. Bathin offered me a deal. He would release Dad's soul in return for a favor he would grant to me. All I had to do was give him my soul."

"Holy shit, Delaney," Myra shouted. "All you had to do? *All?* And you went through with it? I cannot. I can*not* believe you did this! Ever since Dad died you've been…no, you know what? No. You don't get to throw yourself in the way of this bullet. Not again."

"Myra. Hey, Mymy, it's okay."

"Shut up." She slammed her coffee down on the table near her, and it sloshed. "You," she pointed at Bathin, "are coming with me, asshole."

She pulled the handcuffs out of her belt. Not the zip ties we used with humans, not the handcuffs we used with gods, but the brassy-copper colored ones that were intricately scrolled with spells and hexes and blessings and made in such a way that they could restrain any creature.

Though we'd never tried them on a demon.

I wondered if they'd work on him.

While I was lost in a moment of idle speculation, Myra stormed toward Bathin, gun in one hand, cuffs in the other.

He slipped the stone into his front pocket, his long fingers moving slowly as if he were putting on a show for her. As if he hoped her gaze would follow his fingers. His eyes were all pupil, his breathing a little shallow. Desire rolled off of him in waves.

I couldn't be reading this situation correctly. He didn't want Myra. Couldn't be lusting after her. He was just turned on because she was going to manhandle him. He probably liked any kind of physical violence that came his way. Because he was a demon.

Or maybe I was stereotyping again.

"Turn around, hands behind your back." Myra lifted the gun so that it was pointed right at his head. She was a crack shot. There was no chance she'd miss at that distance.

"Myra?" I said again. "Uh, he has my soul, so maybe don't shoot him?"

"Hands behind your back."

Bathin licked his bottom lip and then his mouth curled up on one side. "If you detain me, I will be unable to fulfill my contract with your sister. Every moment, Ben bleeds."

Jame jerked, muscles in his body going tight—fists, shoulders, back, stomach—as if Bathin had just punched him.

Myra didn't budge. "What I'm going to do to you won't take long."

He lifted his hands slowly as if he wanted to touch her, then paused and turned. "Isn't that a pity?"

I knew that's what he said. Just: *isn't that a pity?* But

somehow it sounded like *why aren't we having sex?*

If Myra caught the subtext that was more like domtext going on, she didn't so much as offer a flicker of interest or amusement.

She pressed the barrel of the gun against his head, then flipped the cuffs open and snapped them shut around his wrist, only pulling the gun away so she could cuff the second wrist.

Bathin grunted softly. It didn't sound like pain.

"Walk." She tugged him, then shoved him toward the kitchen.

He moved way too easily for a man with both hands tied behind his back. Myra paced him, her shoulders square, her jaw set.

I wondered if she was really going to shoot him.

Jame shifted on his feet, then silently followed.

"I probably should go make sure this doesn't fall apart," I said to Rossi.

He was still looking at me with that strange mix of kindness and sorrow. It made me uncomfortable, but the moment I thought that, the discomfort washed away.

Rossi sighed. "There are very few ways to force a demon to release a soul. But now, before his favor is served, before the contract is sealed with his action, will be our best chance."

"No."

He blinked and it was the eyes of a predator staring back at me. "You are not a part of this decision, Delaney. Not anymore. You've proved your inability to keep yourself out of harm's way."

Okay, that. That pissed me off. Nobody told me I wasn't doing my job right or wasn't making good decisions for myself or my town.

"Screw you, Rossi."

But even as I said it, the anger that had built into a hot ball of rage in the middle of my chest sputtered out, faded and was gone, leaving the cold and numb and stillness.

"Do you feel it, Delaney? The hole where your soul belongs? The absence of that which holds you centered, makes you human? That hole isn't going to heal. It is going to grow. Until it cannot be stitched over, cannot be closed, cannot be filled. And then you will hunger. Hunger for anything to put in its place. And the only things that can fill that hole are the things that will make you no longer human."

I inhaled, exhaled, knowing I should be terrified by that description, but only feeling the distant flicker of fear.

"That's grim."

"The truth often is."

"Is coffee one of the things I can fill the hole with?"

"Delaney."

"Or sleep? No? Well, then I'll just have to fill it with the satisfaction of freeing my father and saving Ben. How's that sound? Good? Sounds good to me."

"You aren't listening to me and this is not the time to make jokes."

"I am and it is. You know why? Because we win this one, Rossi. We get Ben back and we don't have to give away the dark magic book, *Rauðskinna*. Lavius doesn't get his hands on dark magic, doesn't get to use it against us. Plus, we now know he was using demons, which means we can put protections in place. I can't see how this isn't winning."

"It isn't winning if we lose you."

"I'm right here."

He didn't say anything.

I strode into the kitchen. "Please tell me none of you are naked."

None of them were, but they all looked my way. Bathin was the only one who smiled. He was sitting in a chair that had been turned so the back of it was against the small table in the corner. Still handcuffed.

Myra had put her gun away and held a clear seashell in her hand. I knew what it was, even though I hadn't seen it in years. It was a token Dad used to keep in his pocket. He said it let him hear the truth.

Coupled with the spell-worked handcuffs on his wrists, that little shell was going to let Myra know if Bathin was lying or not.

"Delaney," Bathin said. "Your sister seems reluctant to believe our agreement was entered into willingly by each party. Would you care to tell her?"

"No. Just because you have my soul does not make you my boss."

He laughed, loud and deep, and yeah, somehow that made him even more handsome.

Myra's expression softened into something near confusion or maybe curiosity. Her mouth even lost that hard line and sort of tipped up at the corner.

Bathin was a good-looking guy. Even Myra couldn't miss that.

He shook his head. "I cannot begin to tell you how enjoyable you are."

The little seashell glowed a soft green. The truth.

Myra made a frustrated sound. "You don't need to be here for this, Delaney." She hadn't even looked at me yet. "I'll handle him."

I could hear it in her voice. Worry. Anger. She was standing in the middle of a nightmare and thought it was her sole responsibility to wake up us all.

Forget that. I walked over to her, and put my hand over her hand, covering the seashell so that it was in both of our hands. Then I turned her toward me so she would stop looking at Bathin like something she wanted to shoot.

"I know I made a bad decision." The seashell glowed a kind of purple. Okay, not the whole truth. She raised one eyebrow.

"I know I'm going to regret my decision." Soft green. Better.

"You're worried and angry. So are Rossi and Jame. No one who loves me is going to think what I did is right." All green.

"But I trust us. I know we'll find a way to get my soul back. That isn't what frightens me. What frightens me…" Lavender. "What I know frightened me *more*, is losing Ben. When I went to see Yancy, he said Ben would be returned to us through a favor given by something that does not walk the land of Ordinary. As far as I can see, we're gold. Bathin owes me a favor and he's something that doesn't walk the land. He can bring Ben home."

Green, green, green.

"I might be wrong, might have made the wrong decision, and I'm sorry for that, if I did. But we need to put that aside and play the cards in our hands while we have them."

"You think I'll just do what you want now? Now that you've…now that you're…that?"

Ouch. Even though emotion was sort of at a distance right now, I felt her words like a sharp stab in my chest.

"This is too far, Delaney. You've gone too far for me."

"For you to what?"

Love me?

"Trust me?"

Finally she nodded.

Green.

That should hurt too, knowing my sister didn't trust me, but there was no sensation other than the need to see this through, to bring Ben home. Trust could be earned. I could earn it back from her. I'd have time.

"Then don't trust me. Make sure you put someone on me to keep me on the level. Or have someone brew up a spell or something to make sure I don't do anything crazy."

"There will be no spells," Bathin said.

"Not your property," I reminded him.

"Not true."

"You have my soul, not the rest of me. Not my body, mind, spirit, abilities, consent, or free will."

"Semantics."

"Do you hear that, Delaney?" Myra asked, obviously at the end of her patience. "Do you hear him? He thinks you're his *property.*"

"Yes. He's wrong. And kind of an ass. But he's our card to play for Ben. So why don't you uncuff him and let him do what he promised me he would do."

She didn't want to. I could see it in every line of her body. In the tension rolling off of her.

This might be the time I'd finally pushed it too far. Just because I was the oldest and her boss did in no way force Myra to blindly follow my lead or do what I wanted. We were all stubborn, us Reed girls. And for all I knew, she was planning on tying me down, locking me up, and launching a get-Delaney's-fool-soul back campaign.

She drew her hand from mine. "Will you immediately leave

here to find Ben?"

Bathin nodded. "Yes."

Green.

"Will you bring him immediately back to Ordinary, whole as per the agreement you entered into willingly with Delaney and she, stupidly, entered into willingly with you?"

"Yes." He wasn't smiling, wasn't pouring on the charm. He calmly met her gaze, and if I knew the guy, which I didn't, I'd guess he was being very serious and very sincere.

Green.

"Will you ever entertain giving Delaney's soul back to her?"

He didn't say anything for long enough, I knew the pause was uncomfortable.

"Not even I know the future."

Green. Not helpful, but truthful. Also, not a flat out refusal. It was something. It was more than I expected at this point, frankly.

"Myra," I said softly. "Let's get Ben back. Let's put this horrible mess to an end before we throw ourselves into a new one."

She pocketed the seashell, and motioned for Bathin to stand so she could unlock the cuffs.

"Turn," she ordered.

He did, quiet and complacent. But when her fingers skimmed against the inside of his wrist, I could see the slight shiver that ran through him.

She keyed the cuffs, tugged and latched them back onto her belt loop. She knew better than to stay in arm's reach, but Bathin was quick.

He turned and for a moment, just a second, they were close, bodies aligned in a dancing stance, waltz, or perhaps the tango, his tall and strong and intense, hers shorter and made of curves and edges of strength.

She looked up at him, her lips parted in a breath that was not fear, was not anger, was not pain.

He looked down, those pale green eyes saying yes to the question in her eyes.

It was a second, less than that.

And then the connection, the draw between them was

broken as she stepped back, scowl in place, whatever softness she'd shown gone as if it had never been there.

Bathin stepped back too and tucked both hands in his pockets, as if he were making a conscious effort not to touch her.

No. No, no, no. This demon was not going to touch my sister. Not now, not ever.

"Hey," I said, too sharply. "That is not happening, hear me? You stay away from my sister."

Myra looked at me like I'd lost my mind along with my soul in some kind of two-for-one deal, and Bathin just blinked at me and tipped his head like he hadn't heard me right.

Then he laughed, that deep chuckle again. "Your sister? Really, Delaney. Where do you come up with this stuff?"

Myra blushed, a hot slap of red over her cheeks. It was not embarrassment. It was anger.

Great. I just could not seem to do anything right.

"Stop being a dick," I told Bathin.

He raised both eyebrows.

"Go find Ben. Bring him home to Jame's arms like you promised. Don't drag anything, or anyone along with him."

"Now, now. There are no modification clauses in this contract."

"There are gods and other creatures who would be more than happy to put you in a jar and shake you into ash and atoms, Bath. I have them on speed dial."

"Nicknames and threats, like an old familiar tune."

"Go." Myra said.

"As you wish." He gave her half a bow, that wicked glint in his eyes making him look rakish and kissable, which was weird that I noticed because the only man who I found kissable was Ryder.

But before I could parse that, or Myra's stony reaction, he disappeared.

I exhaled and it felt like I'd been doing a lot of work just to hold myself up through all that. "I need a nap. Or a massage. Or both."

"Is there a place where she can lie down?" Myra asked Jame.

"Spare room."

Myra took me by the arm, her fingers a little more firm than necessary.

"You're still mad."

"Yep."

"I don't really need a nap."

"I think you do."

"You'll wake me up when he comes back? I mean, it's only a couple hours until midnight. He might be back any minute."

"I'll let you know if he comes back."

"When."

She opened the guest room door, flicked on the light, and guided me in to the bed which was covered with a fluffy blanket and a few mismatched pillows.

"If. He's a demon, Delaney. They aren't to be trusted. Ever." She pressed me down toward the bed, then knelt and started untying my shoes.

Like I couldn't be trusted to untie my own shoes.

"Dad trusted him."

"You think he did."

"I was there. I know he did."

"You were caught in some kind of a spell and under duress. You weren't reading the situation clearly. Otherwise you would not have been so stupid as to trade your soul away. Not even for Ben. Not even for Jame. Not even for Dad. You know better."

She was wrong. I knew she was wrong. Spell or not, I would have traded my soul in a flat second if it meant Dad and the people I cared for were okay.

But there would be no convincing her of that right now, and probably no point to even try. She was angry and hurt and scared and I was really, really tired.

Exhausted.

I leaned down onto the bed, the blanket having been pulled back for me, the cool press of the sheets against my skin a kind of bliss worth sighing over.

So I sighed over it.

And slept.

CHAPTER 9

THE BED dipped and someone bigger and heavier than me settled on the mattress behind me.

I knew, even without opening my eyes, who it was.

"You are killing me, Laney," Ryder whispered as he wrapped an arm around me and molded the front of his body to my back. "Couldn't you have called for backup before you put your soul on the chopping block?"

"Myra talk to you?"

He hummed and brushed his hand, warm and heavy, down my arm. I shifted around and he did too until we were both lying on our sides facing each other. It was pretty dark in the room. Hopefully not morning yet. Hopefully still before midnight.

"Are you angry at me?" I asked.

He spread his fingers over the rise of my hip and pulled me a little closer to him. "In the last few days you've been attacked and bitten by a vampire, and goaded into selling your soul to a demon. Neither were your idea. Not sure there's anything to be angry at you about."

"I wasn't goaded."

He moved his feet, catching my ankles between his. He wasn't wearing his boots, but still had on jeans, T-shirt, and kind of adorably, his socks.

"I can see contracts. It's my new superpower, remember? You were goaded, given a choice that left you no room to negotiate for an equitable outcome. You were railroaded, baby."

Warmth spread through me at his words, at his calm faith that some of this, at least the circumstances if not the choices, were not in my control. I tried to hold onto that, the warmth, the faith, the fondness that filled me, but it was sucked away by a cold wind that scrubbed me clean.

"So far I don't recommend the experience," I said.

"Selling your soul?"

"Walking around without one."

He waited, his feet tangled with mine anchoring me not to this room, not to this life, but to him. To us. To what we'd agreed we were to each other before there had been demons or vampires or gods involved.

"Does it hurt?"

"No. But that's the problem. Nothing hurts. I know it should. I know I should feel pain and anger and fear. I get waves, sort of glimpses of those things, but then they're gone and I just don't really care that I don't have them."

"Not such a bad thing to be insulated from pain and fear." His thumb stroked up my arm, painting a warm trail from the delicate skin of my inner wrist to my elbow, then skipping up, over my T-shirt, my shoulder.

"It's not just the bad emotions. It's everything. Even love."

His thumb paused, just a second, then continued the path to my jaw, his fingers dragging warm and gentle behind as he cupped my face. He rubbed his thumb at the edge of my chin.

"Can you feel me?"

"Yes."

"Can you feel this?" He pressed his thumb at the corner of my mouth, gentle, firm.

"Yes."

"How about this?"

He leaned in, filling the air between us, the space, the cold, the doubt. His mouth slanted, his palm and heel of hand guiding me to where he wanted me, my lips to his, open, willing, wanting.

I closed my eyes and melted into him, the only thought in my mind: *yes*. I wanted to feel him, to hold this building heat, the electric velvet sensation of his body sharing this space, this soft darkness with mine.

For a moment, I was alive. I was real. I was me.

And then the cold wind lifted, reaching out as if I had a hole in my center. The memory of Rossi's words returned, hard and bright: *That hole isn't going to heal. It is going to grow. Until it cannot be stitched over, cannot be closed, cannot be filled. And then you will hunger. Hunger for anything to put in its place.*

I had an emptiness where my soul had once been. Where my soul belonged.

That emptiness hurt.

I realized there, in my lover's embrace, that it wasn't that I couldn't feel pain. It was that being separated from my soul meant I was in so much pain I could not process it, could not comprehend the enormity of it.

And so I had twisted away from that agony. Somehow, I'd disengaged from it so that the pain was masked behind layers and layers of numbness.

If I thought about that hole inside of me a second too long, I'd be screaming, frantic, lashing out to find anything to ease that pain. To replace what I'd lost.

Including using something as beautiful and good and strong as the man I loved.

Hunger flared in me. Hunger and one very clear thought: take Ryder's soul, rip it out of him and use it to pack the wound inside of me that I could not endure.

No!

I pulled away, scrambled back, frantic in my need to get away from him, to save him from me—from *me*.

"Whoa, hold on, hey, easy." Ryder made a grab for me, but I was still moving. I flung myself away from him, my legs tangled in the blanket bunched at the foot of the bed.

"Don't," I begged, breathless, and as close to afraid as I'd been able to feel for what felt like hours, days, years. "Don't. I can't let you. Let me. Can't hurt…" And then I over-corrected and fell off the bed.

Ouch.

Everything went still. I sprawled on my back, staring up at the ceiling. They had nice crown molding. Also, I'd hit my funny bone. My arm was prickling.

Footsteps on the hardwood came near me.

Ryder stopped next to me, stared down.

"Reflexes like a cat."

"Thanks."

"Want to tell me what that was all about?"

"I'm…it's the soul thing. Rossi told me the longer I go without it, the more I'll miss it. And eventually I'll want something to replace it so bad, I'll do bad things to get them."

"Uh-huh."

From that lackluster response, he so wasn't understanding the problem. Of course the whole demon-and-soul thing was even newer to him than it was to me.

"You made me feel good," I said.

"Funny. That's what I was going for."

"But then I thought maybe your soul would fit nicely in the hole where mine used to be."

He bent and then folded all the way down so he was sitting crossed-legged at my shoulder. "You know that sounds kind of dirty."

I shut my eyes and shook my head.

"I think my soul would fit very nicely in your soul hole." I could hear the laughter in his voice. I didn't need him to poke me in the shoulder, but he did anyway. "Get it?" he asked. "You know, because we've already figured out that we fit pretty great in a lot of other ways."

"Shut up."

"I've got a really big soul, Delaney, all the ladies say so. Happy to share."

"This is not funny."

"It isn't. But you're smiling."

I was? I drew my fingers up to my mouth. Yep. Opened my eyes.

He was leaning down over me his grin pressing lines at the edges of his eyes. I wanted to touch him. Kiss him.

"If you want a little piece of my soul, I'm all for it, but we'll have to be quiet. Vampires and werewolves have good hearing."

I shoved at his arm and he moved back so I could sit, crossed-legged facing him, our knees touching.

"You have to promise me you won't let me eat your soul."

"We're talking about soul-soul here, and not sexy-soul, right? Because I can think of all sorts of sexy things involving your mouth and my soul."

"Ryder. I'm not joking."

He took my hands in his. Mine were cold and a little clammy. I wondered if my body went through the emotions I could no longer feel, or if I was just clammy because this whole no-soul thing was making me a little sick to my stomach.

His hands were warm and dry and calloused at the thumb

and bases of his fingers. He had working hands, capable hands.

"I'm right here with you, Delaney. Soul or no soul, it doesn't change my feelings for you. If sharing a part of my soul with you makes this better, then that's what I'm going to do. At least until we get your soul back, because make no mistake, this is temporary. There are ways out of your contract with that demon. There are ways to get your soul back. I am not going to let you live the rest of your life missing a piece of yourself."

"You know how to get my soul back?"

"No. Not yet. But my boss is the god of contracts. He also knows all the ways to break one."

"He doesn't like me."

"That won't matter."

It would. I'd known Mithra for most my life, and he not only didn't like me, he didn't like my family much either. He knew how to hold a grudge that lasted through the generations and had always wanted to be the overseer of Ordinary's laws and rules instead of the Reed family. It was why he'd made Ryder the warden. Mithra was looking for a way to control this town, and the gods and creatures within it.

I didn't like the idea of giving him power over the state of my soul, but didn't say that to Ryder. Maybe it was a possibility I'd have to consider. Maybe being soulless would get bad enough I'd make a deal with anything just to change it.

"Awful lot going through your head," Ryder said softly. "Want to talk about it?"

"No. Just." I huffed out something that might have been a laugh, but was really just a random sound. "I want this to be done. Want Ben home and safe. And want Lavius gone. Permanently."

"Dead, you mean?"

"Yeah. If we can kill an ancient like him, however we kill a monster like that, yes. Dead would be best."

"I've sent some feelers out to the DoPP."

"And?"

"Kept running into walls. But there's one agent who sent me a file."

"And? Does it show Lavius is involved with the agency?"

"It shows there is a lot of money coming in from a shell

corporation that is a shell corporation of someone very entrenched in old money."

"Could be a lot of people."

"Could be a vampire."

"Anything that could lead us to him?"

"Not that won't take some time. Do you think that demon is going to find Ben?"

"I kind of bet everything on it."

"Not everything." He leaned a little and planted a soft kiss in the middle of my lips. "And it's more of a temporary loan than a bet."

"Who knew you were such an optimist?"

He shifted and pulled his feet underneath himself so he could stand, then held his hand down for me. "I'm more of a realist, but my "real" has been expanded upon recently."

"Finding out gods are real?"

"Still not sure I completely believe in that. But no. That's not what I was talking about."

"Finding out creatures and monsters and angry ancient vampires are real?"

"No. Finding you. Just. Finding you."

I smiled for him. I knew I should be smiling for what he said, and for how it should make me feel: loved, cared for, all those other nice things. But since I couldn't feel the impact of his words, I went with what I knew I should do.

Fake it 'til you make it.

"You okay there?" he asked as I started toward the door with him, our hands still linked together.

"What?"

"What are you doing with your face?"

"Smiling reassuringly?"

"Well. Okay. How about you don't do things you don't feel like doing?"

"Because right now I don't feel like doing anything."

"Breathing?"

"Meh."

He opened the door. "So what you're saying is if I gave you a suggestion or two of what you should do, you wouldn't hit me?"

"I'm still trying to get my feet under me on all this. I'd like to at least appear as normal as possible. Suggest away."

"Did you have dinner?"

I thought back. Popcorn for breakfast, soup for lunch. A stop by the donut shop, but no donut for me. I stuck my hand in my pocket and found the warmth of the worry stone there. I rubbed my thumb in the smooth indent. It might be my imagination, but that action really was soothing, calming.

"I had some weird witch tea in the hospital that might or might not have been spiked. But no. I think I skipped dinner."

"I'd like to note that things like 'weird witch tea' no longer sound strange to me. Burger? Pizza?"

"Don't care. Whatever you want."

"That new Thai place?"

I hated that new Thai place.

"Sure."

"With the extra fish sauce?"

I extra-hated the fish sauce.

"I hate that stuff. No Thai."

Ryder smiled. "Good to know you didn't trade away your brain. I was beginning to worry your soul hole had gone to your head."

I smacked him on the shoulder with my free hand. "I'll order food."

Jame and Rossi were still in the living room, Jame in a recliner that looked like it had been built to fit him like a glove, and Rossi slouched against the arm of the couch, his long legs propped up on the coffee table.

Myra was in the kitchen, or at least I thought the sounds of cups and spoons banging around in there were her.

The men in the room watched my every move. "I thought I'd call in some food. Jame, is there anything you want. To eat?"

"No."

I looked at Rossi. "Nothing," he said. "I am curious as to what you'll order."

Vampires. For a race that really couldn't eat much at any one time, they sure were curious about other people's appetites.

But the question was: what did I want? Nothing sounded good, but that could be the results of it being nearly midnight, not that I didn't have a soul. I pulled out my phone and scrolled through the list of places open this late.

Just the Blue Owl out on the edge of town. Everywhere else would have closed for the night.

Not helpful for narrowing down my choices. There wasn't anything the diner wouldn't cook.

I dialed, got Piper on the line.

"What can I get you, Delaney?"

Piper was a demigod—a child of a god, namely Poseidon, and a human. She was old enough to be my grandmother, but only appeared about thirty. She'd also been involved in the god powers being stolen, used as bargaining chips by the god who had claimed Ryder as his servant.

That was old news though. It'd happened a whole week ago.

"Maybe a couple specials?"

Since Piper also had a knack for seeing the future, I went with it. "Enough for four, maybe five," I said. If Bathin made it back before midnight, he might want food too.

If demons ate.

I'd have to check in on that.

"I'll send out our delivery boy. He'll be there in a jiff."

"You have a delivery boy?"

"We do tonight."

"All right. I'm at Jame and Ben's place."

"I know."

Of course she did.

"You have my card on record?"

"Yes, Chief. I got you covered."

"Great. Thanks."

"Oh, and Chief?"

"Yes?"

"Hope is born from ashes and love yields to no other power. Return to your heart."

A chill washed over me, even though I couldn't quite muster up the dread that came along with it. Yancy had said the same thing to me.

"What?"

"It's what I wrote down. It came to me just before you

called. So I thought you should hear it. Did it mean something to you?"

"Not in any way I understand."

"Well, shoot. Sorry about that."

"No, it's good. Thanks, Piper."

"Sure. And stop worrying about if you should have come to me before Yancy. I can't see the possibilities of the future as clearly as him, I don't think. I just get specific glimpses of things that are sort of hard-wired."

"Hard-wired?"

"Like I see the knots in fate's strings, and he sees the whole loom on which fate is weaving. Maybe the whole tapestry."

"That's interesting. Are there any knots I need to know about?"

"Nothing except that thing I told you. Gotta hop, Chief. Movie just let out and I'm about to be swamped in pie-hungry people."

I said my goodbye and let her get back to work.

Myra walked in from the kitchen. Her hands were damp, and her eyes were a little damp too. Washing dishes and crying? Or maybe she was just tired and had been rubbing her eyes.

"You okay?" I asked.

She shook her head. "Compared to what?"

Okay. She wasn't in the mood to share. "Is Jean okay?"

That seemed to thaw her a little. "Yes. She's knocked out on the good meds. Hogan stayed until Hatter and Shoe showed up."

"Hatter staying with her overnight?"

"Shoe. Hatter's on patrol tonight."

I pictured the two officers. Hatter, tall and lanky like a cowboy doll someone had brought to life, and Shoe short, wide, and tough as a bear.

Dad had always liked the two of them, and trusted them. I'm not sure why he'd decided to tell them about Ordinary, but his instincts had been right. Hatter and Shoe were pretty terrific people.

"I ordered food."

She shook her head again. "Sure. Blue Owl?"

"Yeah. Piper seemed to know what we'd want, so I just

went with that."

"There better be pie."

"There better be pie," I agreed.

That got a small smile out of her, and I liked it. I wanted to see her happy, even though I knew I'd disappointed her. "Myra, I'm sorry."

"Don't." She put her hand on my shoulder and rubbed it a little. "I know you are trying to do the right thing here. I just…I can't agree on this one. So apologizing is just…yeah, not going to fly with me."

It was strange to have this distance between me and my sister. Over the years we'd gotten into plenty of arguments, but this was more than that. This was a huge life decision that she did not agree with and would not agree with.

There was nothing I could do at this point. But she watched me, like she expected me to do something. For the life of me, I didn't know what it was.

What would normal Delaney do? Smile reassuringly?

Ryder walked over—he'd put his boots back on—and draped an arm across my back.

"You two ladies doing okay here?" It sounded casual, but maybe there was more to what Ryder was saying. More Myra, or a person with a soul, could hear.

"This sucks," I grumbled.

"What?" he asked.

"I hate being treated differently. I'm still me."

"I know." He deposited a kiss on my temple.

It was nice, but I wasn't talking to him.

"Myra, do you understand that I only traded away a part of me, not the whole shebang."

"Your soul is an awful lot of you," she said.

"But not all."

"No," she agreed. "Not all."

The knock on the door got me moving.

"Nope." Myra blocked my path. "Stay. I got it. It might be someone looking for organ donation. Can't have you giving away your spleen before dinner."

I rolled my eyes and tried not to let any more of my frustration show. Turned out I didn't have to worry about that.

As soon as it hit, my irritation sort of fizzled out.

Super annoying.

Which I didn't care about either.

Rinse. Repeat.

The delivery guy turned out to be Mykal, our friendly vampire EMT.

"Didn't know you'd taken on a night job," Myra said as she let him in with the box he was carrying and directed him to place it on the coffee table.

"Just got done eating at the diner when your order came in. Told Piper I could drop it off."

He acknowledged Rossi with a short nod then set the box down and approached Jame who had been focused on him since before the door opened.

They worked pretty closely together since Jame and Ben were firefighters and Mykal was a paramedic. I thought they were friends. But Jame was a werewolf and Mykal was a vampire. Despite Rossi faking his relaxed and comfortable vibe on the couch, there was not a lot of love stretching between the two races right now.

"Hey, man. Any word?" Mykal held out his hand and Jame clasped it.

That was a good sign.

"Not yet. There is a demon looking."

"A...really? How did we score a demon on our side?"

"Gave it a soul."

"Well, that's a bummer. Who was the victim?"

"Delancy."

Mykal looked over at me, just a little of his fang showing when he smiled. "Protect and serve doesn't mean serve up parts of yourself to lying, cheating, underworld assholes, you know."

"That's a pleasant thought," a whiskey-smooth voice said. "Would you care to repeat it to the lying, cheating, underworld asshole who just saved this vampire's life?"

Bathin.

Bathin was standing in the middle of the room, just to one side of the coffee table.

In his arms was a very thin, very bloody, and very wet Ben Rossi.

Vampires are fast. Rossi and Mykal both made a move toward him. They would have reached him first if Jame hadn't roared.

"Do not touch him!"

That, like a slap of thunder, stopped all of us in our tracks except Bathin and Jame.

Jame was on his feet, moving toward the demon. Bathin carried Ben like he didn't weigh more than a box of chocolates, then transferred him, carefully into Jame's arms, blood and wet included.

"Into your arms. Breathing, as whole as I found him, with no ties I am able to break attached." Bathin looked over at me, met my gaze. "As we agreed."

For a second, just three heartbeats, it felt like time stopped, the world stopped, and everything, everything finally clicked into place, was going to be okay. Was going to be normal again.

I knew there was nothing but gratitude in my eyes. I knew Bathin saw it, because there was, for the briefest flash, a clear and sincere *acknowledgment* in his gaze. Almost as if it had actually been his pleasure to save Ben, to bring him home, to do this good thing.

And then the world seemed to begin again. Jame moaned, keened. It was a gut-wrenching sound, a mix of raw grief and relief and anger. A sound I hoped I'd never hear again.

He was bent, shoulders bowed in as if to protect Ben. Then he rolled the unresponsive Ben into his chest, as close to his heart as he could get him, his head tipping down so that he could place his lips over Ben's mouth.

"Is he breathing?" I asked. Stupidly. Vampires didn't breathe and I knew that. "Is he alive?"

And, yeah, that wasn't quite right either, but it was close enough.

Mykal put his hand on Jame's shoulder. Jame snarled at him, his body responding with just enough of a shift into wolf that his arms and shoulders and legs bulked up and his eyes flashed yellow.

"Easy," Mykal said. "Keep him there. Keep him in your arms. Hold him close. I need to check his vitals. Jame, let me see if he's okay."

It struck me then, as I watched Mykal, Jame's close friend who just happened to be the one person who Jame might trust to give Ben medical attention, that Piper sending Mykal here, on this little delivery-boy trip, wasn't a coincidence.

Piper has seen this knot in the string and made sure that we'd have the help Ben needed when Bathin brought him home.

Mykal touched Ben's face, then his throat, then pressed his hand on the back of his head, as if he could sense some kind of vital statistic through his hands that only a vampire could feel.

"He needs blood, Jame," Rossi said. "You need to get him to the hospital. Now."

Jame must have only heard half of what Rossi said. Must have only heard him saying Ben needed blood.

"The ambulance is right outside," Mykal said.

Jame wasn't listening to him. He shifted his hold on Ben and tore into his own arm with teeth and fang, biting off a big enough chunk of his own flesh that even, I, the soulless one hissed in sympathy.

"Jesus, Wolfe," Mykal said. "Sit down before you bleed out." Mykal was no longer being tentative and consolatory with Jame. He took hold of him by the elbow and back, and steered him to the couch. He forced him to sit, and then helped arrange Ben across his lap so that Ben's mouth could reach the bleeding wound Jame had created.

Jame looked both fevered and shocky, but at least he'd stopped growling. He couldn't look away from Ben. Not even when Rossi reached down and pressed his own fingers, which were dripping a thick, dark fluid, into the corner of Ben's mouth.

Mykal nodded. "Keep doing that. If he's going to make it, it will take both your blood."

"Can we help?" Myra asked.

Mykal looked away from Ben like he'd forgotten we were in the room. He made a quick assessment of all of us, including the demon, who he lingered on the longest, and then he nodded. "I might need to draw blood. I have some in the back of the ambulance, but he's critically low."

Myra was already rolling up her sleeve and so was I. "Will we be enough?" I asked.

Ryder disappeared into the kitchen, which, yes, was odd. I

didn't think he usually ran from needles. Or vampires.

"If not, we have more at the bank. I can get someone to bring it over."

"Fresher is better, is it not?" Bathin asked.

"Yes," Mykal said tightly, like it pained him to agree with the demon. "But we have rules in Ordinary."

"You taking it out via an I.V. line?" Ryder asked as he walked back into the room.

He was carrying two boxes of mint Girl Scout cookies and a jug of lemonade. I wondered if Ben or Jame liked Girl Scout cookies enough to keep them stocked.

"Needle and tube," Mykal said. "We don't put fang to flesh."

"Mores the pity," Bathin mumbled.

"Then let's do it fresh," Ryder said.

He set the lemonade on one of the side tables and opened the cookies, then went back into the kitchen for cups.

"Look who's taking charge like a boss," Myra said.

"I know," I agreed. "It's kind of hot."

She frowned, but a smile quickly replaced it. "You like a man who's going to push his way into making the rules around here instead of us? Seriously?"

"I'm not making them," Ryder said, cups in hand. "Just enforcing them. Think of me as the muscle, not the brain. You Reeds are the brains."

He winked at her, and she turned to me with wide eyes. "It's like when he was captain of the baseball team in high school. Thought he owned the whole school."

"That was my barn, don't you deny it. And trust me, I can back it up." Ryder rolled up his sleeve before pouring lemonade.

Yes, I was staring at him. Yes, I knew he was being insufferable and sexy as all hell. I knew I wanted to jump him, to kiss him hard until all that heat and arrogance was under my hands, just to see if he'd give in and give me the key to his barn.

Two things stopped me. One, there was a vampire possibly dying three feet away from us, and two, as soon as I thought those things: taking off his clothes and mauling him until he was sweaty and undone, the need for those things were washed away by a cool wave of numbing.

Dammit!

I glared at Bathin, who was watching all of us with a kind of grudging interest as we willingly got ready to bleed for our friend.

"You did not tell me it would ruin my sex drive. Ryder and I have barely had a chance to do the good and plenty with all the explosions and bites and power grabs going on." I was talking about the troubles I'd had to deal with lately, but said that way, it came out kind of dirty. I didn't care. I plowed onward. "No demon is going to get in the way of me getting laid."

Everyone in the room stopped. Stared at me. Well, except Jame and Ben.

Apparently not having a soul also removed my filter.

I did not care.

Much.

Okay, it was getting kind of awkward.

Bathin's eyes were wide and his grin matched. "*So* embarrassing for you," he breathed. "If only I'd gotten it on video."

I flipped him off and he laughed.

"Shove it, Bath." Then, to Mykal, "Just get the gear. Whatever Ben needs, we'll do it."

Mykal was out the door before I had finished the last word.

Vampires.

He was back before I'd even had time to take a drink of lemonade or interpret that look Ryder was giving me. Exasperation? Fondness? Horror? Glee? All of the above?

He mouthed, *good and plenty?* And raised both eyebrows.

"You first, Myra," Mykal said, setting things up on the table in front of the couch, and then pulling the comfortable recliner closer to the table.

"Why her? Why not me or Ryder?" I asked.

"You're soulless, Ryder's tied to a god. Myra's the most pure mortal out of all of you here." He didn't even look up. "Rossi, can you get me a blanket?"

Rossi didn't look like he heard Mykal.

"Rossi?" he said a little firmer. Then he said a fluid word in a language I didn't understand.

Rossi finally ticked his gaze away from Ben. He answered

in the same language, one low soft word.

"Blankets. They're going open vein for him."

That pulled Rossi into a straight line. He removed his finger from the edge of Ben's mouth, which was still latched to Jame's arm, though I couldn't tell if Ben was actually swallowing or if all that blood was just pouring out of Jame to soak the couch cushion.

What I did know was that Jame still wasn't well enough to offer unlimited refills.

Myra sat in the recliner and Mykal leaned it back, then prepped her arm. He was good at placing a needle. Vampires always were. Myra didn't even flinch.

Mykal rolled out the tubing and got it all hooked up, finally inserting a thin shunt into Ben's arm.

"How long for each of us?" I asked.

"Just a few minutes." He sat back and fiddled with the tube to make sure everything was in place. "His body should take over and draw on the blood."

Rossi reappeared with a fuzzy blanket in a disturbing electric orange, which he draped over Myra's lap.

"I don't—" she started.

Rossi tucked it in on either side of her. "You do."

She leaned her head back and winced. "Is this supposed to hurt?"

"It might sting." Mykal glanced up at Rossi, who placed his fingertips on Myra's shoulder, his thumb touching the side of her bare neck.

She sighed and closed her eyes.

Bathin exhaled with a little growl.

I glanced at him. His eyes were narrow and he was glaring at Rossi's hand on Myra like eye contact alone could make it catch on fire.

Rossi looked his way and gave him an unconcerned blink before looking back to Ben.

"Bathin," I said, "could I speak to you in private?"

"Where you going, Delaney?" Ryder asked.

"Just out on the porch."

"How about I come along?"

"Not necessary."

"Not negotiable."

Bathin folded his arms over his chest. "Not interested."

"Out," I said. "Both of you."

I shoved at Bathin's shoulder and it was like pushing a boulder. Holy heck, he was solid.

"You don't want to stay here while your sister bleeds?" he asked me.

"She's in good hands." He moved, walking toward the door, his tread a little heavy against the hardwood floor, which made sense if he was as solid as he felt.

Ryder slipped his hand into mine and we followed.

Just before Bathin stepped out the door, Ryder dropped something over my shoulders. It was Ryder's flannel jacket. The jacket was warm and smelled of him, and I wanted to burrow into it and leave everything behind.

Instead, I stepped out into the quiet night.

Bathin was leaning on the porch rail, smoking a cigarette. It suited him, the cherry fire of the cigarette, the thin waifs of cinnamon scented smoke coming off the tip curling around his wrist before snaking up his arms, the heavy stream of smoke he exhaled through the corner of his mouth.

He looked mysterious and dangerous and pretty much like a demon in man's clothing. The subjective side of my brain could see he was rocking the whole bad-boy thing big time.

"You want my sister."

He leaned back and lifted his chin, inhaling smoke again. "And?"

"If you touch her, I will slice your soulless carcass from brain to balls and feed you piece by piece to the angels."

Ryder's hand tightened on mine. Maybe surprise, maybe approval.

I didn't look away from Bathin because I wanted him to understand just how serious I was.

"Poetic," Bathin noted. "Put it on my birthday cake."

"You have my soul in your hands. You know I'm not lying. You touch her, you play with her, you make her want you, you hurt her, you make a *deal* with her, and the very short remaining minutes of your life will be agony."

Bathin's nostrils flared as he held in another lungful of

smoke.

"You can't tell me who I can and cannot touch, Delaney Reed," he rumbled, that whiskey-rough voice of his low. "I am walking this land now, accepted inside of Ordinary, by you. I am the owner of your soul. What I do, is not yours to decide."

"Like hell it isn't," Ryder said. He was a warmth behind me, a strength, and stood at my back, so close I would only have to lean an inch to touch him. His hand was still tightly in mine, making it very clear we were a united front.

"Don't be so quick to encourage her, warden. You don't know the steps to this dance."

"I know exactly what song is playing," Ryder said. "You took her soul, because without it you are nothing, powerless, weak. Without it, you can't even gather enough power to walk across our border."

Really? Was that right? Also, how had Ryder found the time to research into demons when he'd just found out about them this morning?

"You really don't see what is right in front of you," Bathin said. "The contract that you agreed to? Well, there is some fine print you might want to read."

"No. There is no fine print." I looked over at Ryder to see if he agreed with me.

He was frowning.

"A little awareness of this kind of exchange between our species. How it affects both of our lives."

Bathin lifted the cigarette one last time and sucked it down until the cherry burned against his fingertips and then turned to ash. He flicked the ash to his feet.

"Got it yet, contract boy?"

Ryder stilled. "Shit."

"There you go," Bathin agreed.

"What?" I asked. Bathin just exhaled smoke and stared at Ryder so I turned to Ryder. A scowl carved shadows into his face before his features smoothed. He didn't take his eyes off Bathin, didn't make any move.

"If he dies, you die with him."

"Seriously?" I asked. "Well, that sucks. What if I die first? Will it free me from our deal?"

"He has your soul, Delaney. He had your dead father's soul before that. You'll be dead, but your soul will still be in his hands."

"Got it." I speared Bathin with a smile that probably looked a little crazy. "If you touch my sister, I will kill you anyway."

"You won't."

"I will. It would be worth dying to know she will not be hurt by you. And hey, it's not like I'd feel any regret over it, right?"

He licked his bottom lip, then tipped his head. "And here I thought your father played hardball." He grinned. "You are just so much more entertaining than him. I definitely traded up."

I sort of hated him. A lot. Unfortunately, the emotion drifted on past leaving me with nothing but the faded awareness of it.

This was getting old fast.

"You should go in." Bathin nodded at the door behind us. "Your sister's tapped."

I didn't ask him how he knew that. Could be that about five minutes had passed. Could be that he was tuned into blood things. Or Myra things.

I didn't want it to be Myra things.

"They'll call us when they need us," I said. "Tell me what happened tonight."

"You are under the mistaken assumption that I will do what you tell me to do, Delancy. That's not how this story plays."

"You're a part of this town now," I said. "I'm the chief of police here. If I want you to give me evidence, you give me evidence. If you don't, I can kick you out."

"Still have your soul."

"Don't care. You won't be here with it. And I can lock this town down so you can't get back in."

"Yes," Ryder said, "she can."

Bathin flashed a sharp grin. "Definitely traded up."

The door opened. "Ryder, you're next." Rossi didn't spare Bathin so much as a second of his time, ignoring him like he was nothing more than a dead gnat.

Bathin's grin stiffened. More teeth, less smile.

Ryder squeezed my hand and didn't let go. He wasn't going to leave me out here on the porch alone with the demon.

"I'll be right in," I said.

He paused, and then he and Rossi exchanged a look.

Rossi stepped out on the porch and Ryder stepped in.

It was starting to feel like I was under constant surveillance. Like they didn't trust me alone with the demon or something.

Of course last time I'd been alone with the demon, I'd lost my soul. I did not regret that choice. We had Ben back. And if he could survive this, if he could recover, it would be worth it.

"How's Ben?" I asked.

Rossi's glittery ice eyes did not soften or waver. "Critical."

"Can we do more for him? Is there something or someone who could heal him?"

"No."

Bathin grunted, and it sounded like a muffled laugh. "You are brutal."

"What?" I said, but they were caught in a staring contest and I'd been on the sidelines of enough of those to know where that was going to end up.

"Nothing," Rossi said, his nostrils flared like something close to him needed to be bitten, decapitated, killed.

"Afraid?" Bathin taunted.

"Where is your king, Bathin?" Rossi's voice was cold and flat, like a slab of marble shoveled down into frozen soil. "Shall I guess? Shall I guess why you seek Ordinary's refuge?"

For the first time, I saw something like fear cross Bathin's face.

It scared the crap out of me. For a second. Then I was left with no fear. A shiver of cold slipped over my skin. I wrapped my arms around myself.

"That is not your concern," Bathin growled.

"Just as those under my protection are none of yours," Rossi replied.

"Her soul is no concern to you."

"Test me."

The air, cold with the wind coming down from the north, even though it was summer, suddenly heated up here on this porch like someone had lit a bonfire.

"No," I said. "Enough. You're done, both of you. This isn't about my soul. This is about keeping Myra out of your grubby mitts, and you telling us where you found Ben and if you know where Lavius is holed up."

"Is that what this is about?"

I hated that smug tone.

"Damn right it is." I knew I was angry, but since I couldn't feel it, my words weren't delivered with the strength I usually mustered.

"What do you want to know?"

"Where is Lavius?"

"And what's in it for me to tell you?"

"You live." That, was a new voice. I jerked and scanned the shadows below the porch. At least a dozen werewolves stood there in the dark, most of them in their human form, a few in wolf, all of their eyes burning yellow.

CHAPTER 10

GRANNY WOLFE stood in front of them all. Smaller than the rest of werewolves, with wide swaths of silver hair, she did not give the impression of being weak in the slightest.

Rossi and Bathin didn't even move, nor did they break their staring contest. I wondered if the demon and vamp had sensed the Wolfe family's approach a while ago since they didn't seem surprised at their arrival.

"Nobody's killing tonight," I said. "Not here. Ben's inside. Let's take a break from the bloodletting."

Bathin's mouth curled up on one side.

"The non-voluntary bloodletting," I added.

"You think I don't know this thing that's with you?" Granny said. "This demon dug a hole through you, child. You just letting that stand with you, *strigoni?*"

"He has no say over her," Bathin said.

"Push me, demon," Rossi suggested.

I stood between them, and turned my back on Rossi, because I knew him and trusted him.

"You aren't my friend, Bathin," I said. "You aren't my boss, you aren't my owner. You are an unfortunate circumstance that I have to live with. Nothing more. Like some kind of soul STD. Don't assume you can call the shots here."

He finally looked away from Rossi. "Maybe you need a history lesson, Delaney."

"All I need is for you to tell me what you saw tonight." I held up one finger. "Where was Ben?" Held up a second finger. "Where is Lavius?"

"Ben was bound and tied in a crate."

"Where was the crate?"

"Sunk beside a trawler about a mile out."

Well, that explained the water covering him. It also explained the cold and darkness that Yancy had seen around him. And that he was alone but also looked over and not near, but near.

I couldn't imagine what kind of hell that had been for him.

"Who was on the boat?"

"Two mortals, and a vampire. They're dead now. You're welcome. I'll put it on your tab."

I blinked. I hadn't told him to kill anyone, but it made sense he might have to in order to free Ben.

"She owes you nothing," Rossi said. "Who was the vampire?"

"I don't keep track of half-souls."

"All demons keep track of us," Rossi said. "Always have. Who was it?"

"Giorgio. Do you want to know how he died? Do you want me to explain how I tore him into strips?"

The weres growled.

"No," I said. "What did you do with the boat?"

Bathin leaned back on the porch rail. "Uh…left it adrift? What was I supposed to do with the boat? Bring it into the bay? Tow it into an iceberg?"

"Shut up. We'll deal with it later. Did they tell you where Lavius is?"

"They didn't tell me." From the way he said it, I knew he was being cagy about it.

"Tell me or I will let these werewolves take out their frustrations on you."

Four of the Wolfe boys stepped forward and the other four in wolf form snarled.

Bathin watched me with keen interest sparking across his features.

That's right, demon. I have friends and my friends have claws.

"I dug through their minds," he said. "The mortals and the vampire. The mortals knew nothing of interest. The vampire, however, was working directly for Lavius."

"Did he know where Lavius was?"

"No. If he once knew, it had been removed from his mind. Brutally. But Lavius left a message behind for you, Delaney."

A chill rolled over me, and dread flickered and died.

"By now he knows what I took from him. He knows you're the one who sent me to take it from him. He's coming for you,

Delaney Reed, and he is going to torture you for fun."

"He will not touch her," Rossi hissed. "This is your last warning, demon. If I find that you have colluded with him to bring Delaney, her sisters, or this town into any kind of danger, I will draw war upon you, your lands, and your people."

"Wouldn't that be an interesting thing," Bathin mused.

The door opened and Myra stood there. She took in the situation, her face pale, and—even though she might be trying to hide it—one hand trembling.

"Problem?" she asked.

"Not yet," I said. "You okay?"

She nodded. "It's your turn. For Ben."

"We're not done with this, understand?" I said to Bathin. "Don't go anywhere."

His body language had shifted, his chin lifted and tipped so that he could better see Myra over my shoulder. The heat coming off him spiked like he either couldn't hide his reaction to her, or didn't want to.

"I wouldn't dream of leaving," he said to Myra. Then, "Ben's waiting for you, Delaney. For your delicious, delicious blood."

Myra rolled her eyes like she couldn't believe his nerve and I widened my eyes in an *I know* sort of response. She pushed the door open the rest of the way and stood aside so I could walk past her.

Even though she was pale, I knew she could handle the demon, vamp and wolves.

Ryder sat in the extra chair, his elbows braced on his thighs, head hanging, the glass of lemonade in one hand. He seemed pale and worn out too.

Donating blood directly to a critically injured vampire was a lot more taxing than doing a regular blood drive. It's why we didn't handle feedings this way.

I made my way over to the recliner and Mykal gave me an encouraging nod. "Ready?"

"Absolutely. How's he doing?"

"He's stable, but still not conscious." He wiped the inside of my elbow with a sterilized pad, then sat on the coffee table and leaned forward to tie off my arm.

Granny and the rest of the Wolfes streamed into the house, crowding around Ben and Jame, each of them taking a turn to touch both of them. Some of his family moved off deeper into the house, and I got the feeling they were making sure the house was secure and setting up guards at the back door. Granny settled in the other chair.

Fawn, in her beautiful sable wolf form, lowered herself and curled up at Jame's feet.

So I didn't have to worry about Myra dealing with the weres. Good enough.

Jame wasn't looking much better. He hadn't once looked away from Ben, his eyes unblinking.

His arm had healed enough that he wasn't bleeding anymore, but he hadn't pulled it away from Ben's mouth.

It was like he could do no more than breathe in short, shallow pants and wait for Ben to wake up. As if he were incapable of speech, thought, action, his whole existence hanging on Ben's survival.

The needle was a tiny pinch as Mykal guided it into place. He messed with the tubing, and made sure everything was good to go.

"Do I need to do anything?"

"His body will draw it at the rate it can absorb. Just try to relax. Let me know if you experience anything stronger than a stinging sensation."

I leaned my head back against the recliner. I wanted to keep an eye on Bathin, Rossi, Myra, and everyone else who were now in the room.

But the stinging sensation of blood being sucked out of me was a little distracting and more than a little painful. It wasn't more than I could bear, but it was still uncomfortable. I closed my eyes, hoping to gather my energy. Soon the mumbling of voices in the room started to fade and a warm hand, Ryder's, linked with mine.

I soaked in his presence, his strength and warmth, and nodded off.

CHAPTER 11

I WOKE, my mouth too dry, my eyes too sticky. I stared at the ceiling trying to figure out where I was.

My bedroom, the blinds pulled closed, just an edge of light fingering in around them.

I didn't remember coming home. I rubbed my face, and the lump of cotton taped to the inside of my arm pulled tight.

That was the last thing I remembered—giving blood. I searched for how I'd wound up in my own bed. Nope. Nothing.

The sound of someone moving around in the kitchen leaked through the door, along with low voices and the smell of bacon and coffee.

Bacon and coffee was good.

My stomach growled in protest. I hadn't gotten a chance to eat the dinner Mykal had delivered to us, though I had a vague recollection of gagging down some lemonade and chocolate mint cookies.

Which were, note to self, a terrible combination.

I pushed blankets away and found I was in the same T-shirt I'd worn yesterday and panties, but no longer wore a bra or jeans.

Probably Myra. Hopefully Myra. If not Myra, Ryder.

I rubbed at my face again then dug in my dresser drawer for jammie pants and a change of clothes. Someone was in my house. I figured it had to be someone I knew since I had all those fancy locks in place now.

I slipped into my jammie pants and walked out of my bedroom down to the bathroom.

Bathin sat on my couch, wearing black slacks and a white dress shirt that glazed his chest and flat stomach and was unbuttoned three below the collar. He flipped through one of the Hellboy comics Jean had let me borrow and I'd forgotten to return

I didn't think I'd made any sound, but his eyes flicked to

me, his fingertip pinching the edge of the paper. His gaze roamed. It could have felt creepy or like he was checking me out, but instead it seemed more like he was gauging if I was steady on my feet, and if I was injured.

Not caring, exactly, but maybe concern?

"Morning, Delaney Reed," he said in that whiskey-and-fire voice.

I nodded. "You and who else?"

"Your boyfriend's in the kitchen. He's on the phone with your sister."

"Myra?"

"Other sister."

Okay, Jean. Bathin hadn't met her yet. I wondered how he knew I had another sister.

"I was trapped in a rock with your father for over a year." I didn't know if he had read my mind, or just knew what I was thinking. "We bonded. It was beautiful."

"Right. I'm going to shower."

He went back to reading the comic, flipping the page to pause, then shaking his head as if the comic had gotten important details wrong.

The bathroom was small but bright and clean, and the door locked. I started the water so the old pipes would have time to warm up before I got under the stream. I shucked out of my clothes and caught a quick glimpse of my reflection.

Pale, thinner than the last time I'd taken a good look at myself. The black circles that were the only sign of my vampire bite seemed darker, a thin line of red skittering from them like threads of caught lightning running under my skin toward my heart.

The bruising on my arm from the blood draw was purple edged, but already going green, and I had a serious case of bed-head.

But it was my eyes that sort of freaked me out. They were usually an ocean wave blue—not as dark as Jean's, not as icy as Myra's. Sometimes they sort of shaded green-ish in the right light.

Here, in the bathroom, they were a dove gray, with very little blue chipped into them.

It was freaky. Weird. Like I was faded, fading. The lack of color in my face somehow washed me out even more, as if I'd lost something.

And I had. Well, not lost. Traded.

My soul.

"Ben is home," I told my reflection. "Ben is safe."

Because that was worth it. That made my choice the right choice. The hard one the seer said I'd have to make. The right one.

I looked away from my eyes, looked away from the bite marks on my neck, looked away from my pale skin.

I didn't plan to study myself in a mirror again for a long damn time if I could help it. Choices made were choices done. No room for regret.

I ducked into the shower and scrubbed, letting the hot water and vanilla-smelling soap clear my head. What I needed was a plan.

We had today to come up with how we would kill Lavius. Today to find him, trap him, then do whatever kind of thing needed to be done under the full moon when Lavius was at his weakest.

Rossi had said he knew how to kill him. Would it involve an air strike? Ancient rituals? Tiddlywinks at ten paces?

I needed specifics.

I wanted to check in on Jean today too, find out how her arm and leg were healing. And I should see that Hatter and Shoe were settled. Just because I'd done a deal with a demon and was hunting an ancient vampire didn't mean that I could walk away from my job as a cop.

I rearranged the list in my head. First, check on Jean. Next, go to the station to touch bases with Hatter and Shoe. Last, pin Rossi down and make a plan for taking Lavius out.

I had the feeling Bathin could find Lavius if he wanted to. For a price.

I poured shampoo in my palm, then worked it to suds through my hair.

I felt like I was missing something. Like there was more going on that I couldn't put my fingers on, or something that was right in front of my face that I'd missed.

Bathin had said there were two mortals and a vampire on that boat. He'd also said he'd killed the vampire. I assumed he'd killed the mortals too. I should ask.

I wondered if the mortals had been willing or unwilling participants in all this. They could have been on the DoPP's payroll, or they could have just been unlucky enough to have had a boat available when Lavius had decided to crate and sink Ben.

Fourth thing for today: check on Ben and Jame.

But first, I wanted some of that bacon.

I dried, dressed in jeans and a tank under a light over-shirt, then made my way to the kitchen.

"Can't this wait?" Ryder's voice was lowered like he was trying not to be overheard by someone in the living room. Or maybe someone coming out of the shower.

I shouldn't eavesdrop.

I stopped just outside the kitchen and glanced in.

Totally eavesdropping.

He was on the phone, his back toward me. I caught my breath at the width of his shoulders under that soft gray T-shirt, and the narrow taper of his hips. He had on a pair of faded jeans with a hole in the back pocket and they clung to the muscle of his thigh and the tight rise of his butt, making his legs look long, strong, and hard.

"No," he said, "I'm not telling her that. You deal with it. Fine, put someone else on it. She doesn't need one more thing. No. You are more than capable of taking care of this." He reached up into my cupboard and retrieved a plate, onto which he stacked bacon and then tipped half a pan of scrambled eggs. "Threaten all you want. I don't give a damn. Right. Good? Fine." He pulled his phone away from his ear and stabbed the button.

I raised my eyebrows. Had no idea who he was talking to. But even without a soul, I was curious enough to want to find out.

"Should I guess?" I asked.

He had picked up the plate and a cup of coffee. At my question he paused, but finished turning toward me.

"You get some sleep?"

I walked into the room. "Redirection? Not really your style,

171

Ryder. Want to tell me what that call was about?"

"Nope. What do you think about bacon?"

"It's the most magical of pig parts."

"Want to eat at the breakfast nook?"

"Here's better."

He gave me the plate and I leaned against the counter, putting the plate in front of me so I could eat standing. He watched me, and I could tell he was tense. It sort of rolled off him in waves.

"You eat?" I asked.

"Over an hour ago. How'd you sleep?"

"Hard and dreamlessly."

"Good," he said on an exhale. "Feel any better?"

"As compared to when?"

"You were pretty out of it last night. After you gave blood, you passed out. Then…well, we brought you home."

It sounded like something was missing in that statement. I bit into the bacon, chased it with eggs. Breakfast was hot and seasoned with more pepper than salt, just how I liked it. Who knew Ryder knew how to cook?

"This is fantastic." I sipped coffee. Hot. Strong. "What's it gonna take for you to cook breakfast for me every morning?"

He paused, every line of his body stilled.

What had I just said? Was it something weird? I didn't think it was weird.

"You'd have to come over early." I finished another strip of bacon.

"Or stay late," he suggested. Casually. Oh, so casually.

"Right. Or that."

"Stay the night."

"Not like there's not room in my bed. Oh." I put my fork down, smiled. "Wow. How long was it going to take me to get that hint? Did I just ask you to move in with me?"

"Technically or accidentally?"

"Both?"

He picked up a tea towel hanging on the oven handle and wiped it through his wide hands. "I'd say yes."

"Yes that I asked you to move in, or yes to doing it?"

"Yes."

I smiled and the warm stutter in my chest that was part excitement, part desire thrummed good and strong before fading away. I knew my smile slipped, because his did too.

"Gods, I hate this." I took another swallow of coffee, wanting the heat from it to dig deeply into me and fill the cold I couldn't seem to melt.

"Hate asking me to move in?"

"Hate not having my life where I want it to be. Knowing what I am, what I really want. I'm…I'm not in a great place for figuring this out. For figuring us out."

"Uh-huh. Is this your way of saying it's not you it's me?"

"No. But it's not you."

He came up so close in front of me, he was crowding me with his body. He propped his hands on either side behind me, caging me in.

I inhaled the warmth and scent of him, something deeper and spicy that mixed with the scents of breakfast clinging to his skin.

"This isn't just about you, Delaney. This is about us. About what we are. Together."

Even without a soul, even without emotions, I knew I never wanted to cause Ryder pain. It used to be I thought keeping the secrets of this town and my job away from him would do that. But not knowing what might hurt him hadn't stopped him from wading in and getting hurt.

He had been claimed by a god who didn't like me, my sisters, and our town. A god who would rather pin Ordinary under his thumb. He'd traded his life away to that god just like I'd traded my soul away to the demon currently muttering to himself on my living room couch.

I couldn't keep the secrets from him, but what I should have done was stayed away from him myself. It wasn't the secrets of town that had hurt him, changed him. It was me.

And all of Jean's worry about hurting Hogan by telling him about Ordinary seemed like a repeat of what Ryder and I had been through.

If I'd never let him touch me, if I'd never wanted to touch him, if I'd walked away and let him live his life, and let me live mine, he wouldn't be here in this mess.

Just as screwed up as I was.

"Where did your mind go just then?" he asked. "I can tell you're thinking awfully hard about this."

I searched his hazel eyes, the warmth and sparks of brown and gray. I was pretty sure I loved him, when I could feel it. When I had a soul.

I hadn't said it, the L-word. We'd agreed we both felt it for each other, but neither of us had said it out loud to the other.

Maybe there was a good reason we were hesitating on that commitment.

For all that he was convinced I'd get my soul back, that was not a likely outcome of the situation. It wasn't even a probable one.

The very last thing I wanted to do was make him commit to me and then fake my feelings for him for the rest of our lives.

That was the worst kind of lie, the worst kind of harm.

Which meant…if I did love him, I needed to let him go. Get him as far away from me and the tangle of gods and demons and creatures and monsters that made it so I could hurt someone as good as him.

We'd had our beginning. Maybe it was time to have our ending. Dad had said that all endings were just the start of beginnings. Maybe we should slow down our relationship. Maybe we should step back until I had a soul. Until I was all me again.

The rightness of that stuck somewhere deep in my belly, and suddenly I wasn't hungry anymore. I pushed my plate away.

"I need some time to think. About this. About us. Being…together."

"That so?"

"I'm not kidding, Ryder."

"I can see that." He didn't move. Neither did I. Whatever he was searching for in my face wasn't there to be found.

"I need to think about stuff. What I want. What I need now that I'm different."

"You're still you, Delaney." Soft, a caress, his faith in me.

"This isn't…I'm not breaking up with you."

"I know."

"I'm just trying to be smart. Make good decisions. Logical

decisions."

"I know."

"I think we should take a little break."

"Nope."

"It takes two of us to continue this relationship."

"So let's continue."

"I…can't. I need you to be patient."

His lips pressed tightly together into a thin line and he finally leaned back away from me.

I missed the heat of him, of his body, his life crowding all up in my space.

"I don't want you to…." I lifted my hand, wanting to reach out to him, to pull him to me, but gave up on it halfway through the motion.

"What?"

"To give up on us."

"You just told me you want a break."

"I do."

"You want me to wait. Give you room to figure out how to deal with having no soul."

"Yes. That. Yes."

He shook his head. "I am good at a lot of things, Delaney, but living without you isn't one of them."

I didn't know what to say to that. What to say to the truth in his eyes.

All that came out was, "I need to check on Jean."

I hadn't meant to say that. But it was all I could manage.

He tipped his head in a sort of shrug. "So redirection is your style now? Come on. Even I won't fall for that." He moved away from me, across the kitchen toward the door. "Let's go check on Jean."

He strode out of the kitchen. The pain of pushing him away swelled hard and hot behind my ribs.

And then it was gone.

CHAPTER 12

"WHAT ARE you doing here?" Jean demanded. She was sitting in Myra's rolling chair and using mine to prop her braced foot leg upon, one crutch at her side like an oar.

Roy, behind the counter, took one look at me, the pissed off boyfriend behind me, and the sardonic demon behind him, and pushed up onto his feet. "I'll go put on the coffee." He lumbered off to the back room where he could fill the pot with water, giving the other two officers in the room a nod.

Hatter and Shoe. They were a study in opposites. Hatter was tall, all arms and legs, and dusky skinned with sharp, light brown eyes and short close-cut hair. He was lounging against the edge of Jean's desk, chewing on sunflower seeds he popped in his mouth out of a thin plastic tube, and looking like he should have on a cowboy hat to accessorize his uniform.

His deceptively lazy gaze took us all in. I didn't know what conclusion he came to.

Shoe, on the other hand, leaned against the back wall that separated my desk from the rest of the front room. Thick, lighter-skinned, red hair bright enough to give off its own heat, and hard dark eyes, his muscular arms were crossed over his chest and his gaze did not waver from my face. As if Ryder and Bathin weren't the thing he saw as a threat in the room.

That was weird.

"I wanted to check on you," I said. "Guess how surprised I was to find out you were here at the station working instead of home resting? Like the doctor ordered."

"Pshaw," she slurred. From the happy glitter in her eyes and slight flush on her cheeks, she was still riding the good ship Percocet.

"I told her to stay home," Roy said from over by the coffee pot.

"Traitor," she said with a loopy grin. "I brought you donuts to buy your silence. 'Cause donuts get stuff done."

So that would explain the three overfilled boxes of Puffin Muffin baked goods spread out across the desks.

"Hogan?" I asked.

She sighed dreamily. "He got up early to make sure I had two of every kind they make. Isn't that damn sweet of him? Damn sweet. Don't tell anyone, but I like him. And his butt."

"Did she take a double dose of the happy pills?"

Hatter swallowed the sunflower seeds. "Don't know. She just showed up. Like all that." He gestured at her. "Baker brought her in. He says he's not her boyfriend, and also that it's 'complicated' because she's 'pig-headed' and 'relationship-stunted'."

Wow. That was. Wow.

Jean just grinned. "Oh, yeah. I'm the stunted one. Psssssh. I don't hold the family record of staying out of a relationship that was right in front of my face, do I, Delaney?"

I ignored her.

"It was Hogan," I said. "He's her boyfriend."

"He doesn't know our Ordinary secrets. Shhhhh." Jean carefully lifted her crutch and sort of waved it at Shoe and Hatter, almost knocking everything off her desk.

I strode around the front counter so I could grab the crutch away from her before she bulldozed her collection of evil wizards.

"Hey," she complained. "I'm really gonna need that thing."

I propped the crutch against the desk and took her hand. "I know. But you should be in bed, honey, not here trying to work."

"Can't sleep. Too many monsters." She frowned like she had just realized what she said. "You know. The killer. Wait." She reached out with her good hand and grabbed my wrist. "Myra said you did something bad. With a demon."

Said demon chuckled a low, sexy sound. "She did. Very bad."

"I didn't do anything bad."

"Now, now," Bathin said. "It's not nice to lie."

I glared at him, even though I didn't feel the anger behind it for long.

"That's him?" Jean shifted so she could get a better look at

177

Bathin. Her eyes went wide. "Wow."

And yeah, he was all kinds of good-looking in the suit slacks and white shirt which somehow hadn't gotten dirty even though he'd carried a bleeding vampire in his arms. Or maybe he'd changed into a new shirt. Did he keep a wardrobe in some kind of magical bag I couldn't see? Or maybe he had a portal through time that opened on a dry cleaners.

"I manifest as I choose," he said, his voice a low roll through my mind. I wondered if he'd said it out loud or only in my head.

That made him chuckle again. He strolled forward and paused in front of the box of donuts on the counter. He took a moment to decide, then picked one coated in cinnamon and sugar.

"That's Bathin," I said, answering Jean's question. "And yeah, he's a demon."

Shoe, still leaning on the wall grunted. I suspected he was recording everything about the demon with that incredibly photographic memory of his.

Dad told me once he wouldn't trade his life with Shoe's for all the money in the world. Said it was a mercy to be able to forget certain details of life.

The older I got, the more I agreed with him.

Ryder pushed past Bathin, knocking his shoulder into the demon as he passed behind the counter.

Hatter reeled himself up off the desk and offered one long-fingered hand. "And you would be?"

"Ryder Bailey. Reserve officer."

"Pleased. That's Shoe."

Ryder released Hatter's hand and crossed over to the other Tillamook officer. Shoe offered a hand and a grunt, but didn't move away from the wall.

"Anyone want to fill us out-of-towners in on the demon sitch-u-ation?" Hatter asked in some kind of drawl that I knew was wholly put on.

"Delaney Reed traded her soul to me for three magic beans. It's a beautiful story full of giants and talking harps and 14-karat water fowl."

I flipped Bathin off. "It's a bit of a mess, but it all boils down to Bathin being in town for a while. Until we get a handle on things."

"And your soul?" Hatter asked.

"Oh, I have a handle on that." Bathin was staring at Ryder when he said that.

I didn't know if he was trying to make every person in the room glare, but he'd succeeded.

"We'll take care of that," Ryder threatened more than stated.

Bathin smiled, then his tongue flicked out to catch at the cinnamon at the corner of his mouth. It was very pointy, and very red.

"Wow," Jean said again. She was a little flushed and breathing a little hard, which only made Bathin chuckle, and that just multiplied all his heat and sexiness. She made another sound, one that didn't really form into words.

"Okay then," I pushed the corner of her chair so she swivelled my way and couldn't see tall-dark-and-douchey. "He's a demon. We don't like him."

"Oh." She nodded. "Right. Demon bad. I think I need some sleep, okay?"

"Sleep sounds like a great idea, honey. You need to go home and curl up in your bed."

"Yeah." A cloud fell over her and she went sort of tense. "That would be great."

It was clear she didn't want to go home. "Maybe I'll just hit the cot? That way I'd be here if you need me."

I was about to tell her the cot wouldn't be very comfortable with her bum leg and hurt arm and ribs, but didn't get that far.

"I have had quite enough of this, Delaney Reed." A voice called out from the door.

Bertie, our one and only Valkyrie, stormed into the room. Short white hair, sharp bird-like features, and a spring-tight compact frame, Bertie looked to be somewhere in her eighties, but was immortal. She was rocking a lightweight beige tank top with a silken over-sleeve that glittered with gold and matched the bright drape of blood-red jewels dripping from a chain around her neck. Her slacks and open-toe heels completed her look.

And by look, I mean it made her look like both the battlefield warrior and community coordinator she was.

"Bertie," I said, just as Hatter said, "Ma'am," and Shoe straightened up off of the wall and slipped into parade rest. Oh, yeah, they'd met her before.

"Tell me you haven't gone willingly into this travesty," she went on as if there were no one in the room but her and me.

"You're going to have to narrow that down. There's been a lot of travesty around here lately."

She paused in her march, and then surveyed the room as if looking for bones with enough meat left on them to pick. She squared off against Bathin.

"Hell-spawn. You have no place in this haven."

"I don't believe it's your place to say so, Valkyrie."

"There is a reason he denied you entrance."

"Ancient history. We had our time and made amends."

"Did you?" Her eyes got even sharper, and I thought I saw the hard glint of gold there.

"Yes."

Silence, while they weighed the truth of whoever they were talking about. I had a feeling it was my dad.

"He knew," I said, breaking the silence that was starting to get uncomfortable. "If you're talking about Dad, he knew that I traded my soul in exchange for Ben's rescue and Bathin's ability to be in Ordinary."

Bertie didn't even glance my way. "Did you deliver on your promise?" She sounded eerily close to a disappointed schoolmistress.

"Have I ever gone against my word?"

"Many, many times, as I recall."

He blushed. Or at least I thought that was a blush. For a guy who could choose his appearance, he seemed to have decided on scolded student. Wasn't that interesting? Bathin could be what? Ashamed? Flustered? Guilty? Whatever it was, he looked uncomfortable and I totally loved Bertie for cracking that cool facade he carried around.

Loved her enough I might even buy her pie.

"Yes." He cleared his throat. "Well."

I was so going to pin Bertie down and make her tell me

every detail she knew about Bathin because this was too good of a show to only see once.

"Hey, Bertie!" Jean waved. "Wanna sign my cast?"

Bertie broke the stare-off she'd been having with the demon and it was not my imagination that Bathin exhaled. Oh, he recovered quickly, but it had happened and I'd seen it. He'd been cowed by a little old lady.

"Of course I'll sign it, dear." She walked around behind the counter where no one went unless they worked here or were escorted by someone who worked here.

None of us told her she wasn't allowed behind the counter because all of us knew better than to tell Bertie what to do.

"Ma'am." Hatter sprang forward all legs and lank, and produced a red Sharpie out of his back pocket.

"Thank you, Officer Shoe." She took the pen from him, oblivious or not caring that the rest of us were still watching her every move. "Delaney, I need to speak with you even thought Ryder told me on the phone earlier that you were unavailable."

Ryder just sighed.

"Sure?" I said.

She tipped her head to either side, and considered Jean's cast as if it were a canvas that needed attacking. "I see that you have several irons in the fire. But I am going to insist you address yet another." She bent slightly and signed Jean's cast, adding a little heart with wings and claws. It was kind of cute.

"I can multitask and I have good backup. What do you need, Bertie?"

"I need you to stop the war before the first blood is drawn."

Pause. "Okay?" I'd been hearing there was a war brewing for months now, so this wasn't really surprising. "Details?"

"They've come together today. At the Starbucks. In the grocery store."

Since we didn't have another Starbucks, she didn't really have to define that for me. "Who? Now?" My thoughts raced. Was Lavius in Ordinary? Had he sent more undead, demon-possessed vampires into town to take us out?

If so, why would they stop at Starbucks? Did demons prefer a frothy latte before battle?

"Flat white, usually," Bathin said. "Froth makes me bloat."

I hated that he was reading my mind. "I hate you reading my mind."

He just smiled because he knew that as soon as I said the words, my hate was gone, leaving cool and nothing behind.

Stupid face.

"How many demons are there?" I asked Bertie as I catalogued what kind of weaponry we'd need to take with us, and whether we needed to lock down the area or evacuate.

"Demons?" Bertie frowned. "No. You misunderstand. I'm wholly unconcerned about bottom-dwellers."

Bathin coughed but it sounded like *racist*, and Bertie ignored him.

"It's much worse than demons."

"Vampires?" I asked.

She pressed her lips together, disappointed in my mental abilities.

"How about you just tell me, Bertie so I know what kind of weaponry to pack."

"It's the knitters. They've declared war. And the crocheters are geared up for the siege."

Pause.

"What now?"

"The knitters. You know. The K.I.N.K.s and C.O.C.K.s."

Jean barked out a laugh and set off into a howling giggle fit.

"Uhng...huh?" was the only thing I had to offer.

Ryder coughed, and then laughed, a deep, warm sound that made me want to press myself closer to him so I could wallow in the joy there.

Even Shoe and Hatter chuckled. Roy, just shook his head. "You're all children."

Bathin wasn't laughing, but he intently took in our reactions. He almost looked pleased. Which, okay, I hadn't known him for even a day yet, but I would have expected him to be sort of into pain and suffering, not a bunch of people laughing over a couple acronyms.

"Delaney," Bertie scolded. "This is serious."

"Right. Yes. Serious. Okay. So the knitters, that's the

K.I.N.K.s?"

Bertie nodded.

"The K.I.N.K.s have threatened the C.O.C.Ks?"

"Woulda' thought they'd be into that," Hatter delivered deadpan.

"Did they forget their safeword?" Shoe asked.

Jean's howl turned into a hissy wheeze.

Both men grinned at her reaction. She waved at them, trying to make them stop.

Bertie arched her eyebrows. "Perhaps we should head to the engagement before the members get out of hand and things take a turn for the worse?"

Nope. She'd started this. And Hatter wasn't going to miss a chance to make Jean choke on her tongue.

"If you're hard up, Shoe and I can whip those C.O.C.Ks into shape. Shoe's got lots of practice. He can whip C.O.C.K. with one hand tied behind his back. I hear he likes it that way."

Shoe nodded, his serious expression unyielding. "Hatter has a lot of experience with K.I.N.K. He's a master at dominating those kinds of situations."

Jean wrapped her good arm across her ribs and whispered. "Hurts. Stop. Oh, gods."

Ryder rubbed at his face and wiped at the corners of his eyes. His grin was wide and bright, and I wanted to feel that. To smile with him, to laugh at all these stupid jokes, to feel the heat and rub of emotions moving and pressing against my chest, my ribs, scrubbing beneath my skin.

But I was wind and emptiness, chained to the open sky, anything but free.

And I apparently also had a fiber war to deescalate.

"You two jokers will stay here with Jean until one of you can bully her into going home and getting some rest."

"Wait," Jean managed.

"Or," I amended, "help her get comfortable on the cot for some sleep."

She nodded as she wiped at her eyes. She calmed her giggles, then glanced up at Hatter who waggled his eyebrows. She snorted and leaned her head back, her hand covering her face.

"Gonna die."

"Roy, you're working your shift?"

"That's the plan."

"Good. Bertie and I will go deal with the knit and crochet problem." Shoe snickered and I leveled a glare at him that did absolutely nothing.

"Ryder, can you go check in on Ben and see how he's doing?"

"We could call."

"I'd rather get eyes on the situation. We don't need the vamps and weres going after each other."

"Ben was taken to the hospital early this morning," Hatter said.

I gave Jean's shoulder a quick squeeze. "Listen to the boys while I'm gone. You can sleep here. No monsters under the cot. I promise."

I stood and started toward the door. Bathin fell into step next to me, but Ryder muscled his way up and all but hip-checked the demon. He used those long legs and stopped in front of the door, blocking my way out.

"Hey, boss," he said. "I could use a second of your time. Are you listening?"

Bertie made a little *tsk* sound between her teeth. "Mr. Bailey."

And, oh, the look he gave her.

"You have my attention," I said, dragging his back to me. I did not need a pissed off Valkyrie in my station. "What?"

"Is he going with you?"

I frowned. "Who?"

"The demon."

"Where else would I go?" Bathin taunted. "I own her soul, and I find her interesting. We're tied at the hip, Ryder Bailey, and will be for years and years and years. I'm quiet enjoying the sensation of knowing your woman so intimately."

Oh, shit.

Ryder did two things simultaneously. He pushed me to one side and punched Bathin in the face.

"Whoa!" Hatter yelled, rushing forward.

I was rushing forward too, grabbing Ryder's arm and

pulling him back before he could settle in and pound the salt out of Bathin.

Not because I was friends with the demon. Because I wasn't sure what the demon would do to Ryder.

"Back off!" I forced Ryder out the door, which was no easy thing, then spun on Bathin who had been surprised enough by the hit to the face that he'd lost his footing.

"You will not retaliate. This is your fault. You pushed him. You were trying to make him angry. Well, congratulations, asshole, you did it. If you touch him, if you hurt him, I will find out just how deep this tie between us runs and I will make you pay."

His eyes flashed red. For a second, I could see the ghostly after-image of horns curling toward his shoulders and fire licking across his skin. In a blink, that vision was gone and he appeared to be just a guy in business casual kneeling on the floor of a police station lobby, with hatred in every line of his body.

I heard the engine to Ryder's truck growl to life as he gunned it out of the parking lot.

Great. He'd cut and run before I could call him on this.

"Isn't that what you wanted, Delancy?" Bathin practically purred. "You told him you needed time to think. You told him you don't want to be with him. You want space. And now you have your wish. You're welcome."

"I hate you." I knew it was true. Even if I couldn't feel it. I knew I hated him.

He rose fluidly to his feet, gaze locked on me. He closed the distance and stared down.

"No. You don't." His words were hot against my skin and I felt like I was frozen, caught
in a blizzard, and he was a fire beckoning, burning brightly.

He leaned in slow, smooth, fitting us together even though we weren't even touching.

I wanted to move. I needed to move. I didn't want him any closer. Didn't want him this close to me.

"You know I'm a necessary evil. Everyone loves a man with a little evil in his soul." He pushed forward, and I shoved his chest and backed up fast. Thought I'd hit the door, but the door was open.

Because he'd pushed it open when he was crowding me.

He deftly took my shove like it was nothing, and from the rock-hard feel of his muscles, it probably *was* nothing, and stood to one side, a parody of manners, holding the door open for me and Bertie.

"Ladies."

Well, the one good thing about not being able to feel any emotion was that I didn't blush at the fool I'd just made of myself.

I wanted to hit him until my hands were broken. Instead, I turned around and walked out that door, the Valkyrie on my heels.

CHAPTER 13

FOR A little town, we had a large grocery store that was part of a national chain. Since it was the biggest market and served not just the locals, but most of the tourists, it carried everything from flip-flops and beach towels to one of the largest wine selections on the coast.

It also had a staffed deli counter with plenty of hot lunch and dinner options, a full-service bakery, a pharmacy, and a Starbucks kiosk. Next to that kiosk was an open dining area decorated à la high school cafeteria, with uninspired fiberglass chairs and tables and mediocre lighting. But it had free Wi-Fi and air conditioning, which made it weirdly popular.

At full capacity, the little dining area could hold about two dozen people.

Even though there were at least twice that number of people in the space right now, it didn't feel all that crowded.

That probably had to do with the relative size of half of the people, which was small, and the average age of those same people, which was ninety.

It was an eclectic group of septuagenarians. A few white hairdos in tight curls, but the majority had died their plumage in neons and pastels, a virtual who's who of Manic Panic on display.

The preferred clothing of the day was a mix of stretchy slacks and long skirts and sleeveless tops.

That was probably why all the tattoos caught my eye. The tattoos. So many.

Some were a little hard to distinguish through the wrinkles and sags, but the K.I.N.K.s all had some version of yarn, knitting needles and a banner of words across it on their shoulders, and the C.O.C.K.s all had similar ink on their arms, except there appeared to be a red rooster and hook theme mixed in.

The remaining members of the crowd were a mix of ages, men and women, mortal and monster. The youngest on each side was a girl about ten years old brandishing a neon yellow crochet hook and half of a crocheted turtle corpse, and a boy about twelve gripping two slick silver knitting needles that carried an almost finished Pink Floyd THE DARKSIDE OF THE MOON flag.

As a matter of fact, everyone was not only standing and yelling (except the kids, who were sitting and watching it all with wide eyes), they were also all shaking handfuls of whatever craft they were crafting at each other like two armies banging swords against shields.

The K.I.N.K.s and C.O.C.K.s were about to rumble. They'd even drawn a line in the sand, which was a ball of yarn rolled out to divide the two halves of the dining area with one fuzzy strand of blue.

The group on the left all had needles, the one on the right all had hooks, so K.I.N.K.s to the left, C.O.C.K.s on the right.

Bertie marched up on one side of me, and Bathin lingered behind, looking overly interested in a stack of fire starter logs and bags of organic coffee beans.

It was hard to tell, even as I paused on the edge of the dining area, exactly what was being argued. But it was clear that there was no backing down on either side, and the volume was steadily growing.

Mob violence. Finally. Something easy.

"I want everyone to settle down." I pitched my voice to carry over the argument.

All heads turned, all eyes landed on me and the badge I'd stuck on my hip. They knew me, I knew them. We all lived in this little town together. Went to all the community events and fund raisers Bertie forced upon us, slogged through the four Oregon beach seasons of cold rain, freezing rain, windy rain, and raining tourists.

We even all shopped here in this big, overpriced, under-friendly supermarket.

We were a team. A town. A people. We weren't going to let a little whatever-they-were-arguing-about push us apart.

"I need one person from each side of the yarn to step over here and tell me what's going on."

Two sturdy looking ninety-year-old women who were all

nose and big watery eyes behind heavy plastic-rimmed glasses broke off from the front of each group and chugged over to me.

They looked like twins, because they were. The Macy sisters, Willie and Chester (their parents had planned for boys, and didn't let a little thing like daughters divert them from going forward with their plans) wore bright tank tops, loose skirts and striped socks. All of their clothing was knit (Willie's) or crocheted (Chester's).

It should have looked tacky and old fashioned. Instead they wore those clothes with a sort of vintage mod style that made it look trendy.

And yes, they each brandished a shoulder full of ink with the acronym K.I.N.K. and C.O.C.K. emblazoned brazenly over the lion's share of their crinkled real estate.

"What seems to be the problem?" I asked.

"This," Willie jabbed a needle with the softest gray gossamer lace floating off of it at her sister, "harridan swooped in with her jolly band of hookers and took our meeting space."

"It's a free country!" Chester warbled. "Those tables are first come first serve. We were first."

"You know we meet here every Thursday. This is K.I.N.K. territory and the lawman, well, woman, is here to drag you away."

"On what charges? Making better looking scarves with luscious drape?"

"Oh, you did not just say that. My scarves have drape for miles!"

"Crocheting is faster and easier than any snooty travesty you stab to death with those needles."

"Fast and easy. There's two words you've heard a lot over the years. Some things are more enjoyable done slowly—not that you'd ever know."

"Oh, blow it out your bonnet you two-needle hack. A real yarn thrower doesn't need two tools to create her craft. All she needs is a hook and her own two hands."

"Tell that to my slim, perfectly fitted socks and lightweight fitted sweaters you single-stitch derelict. Two needles are better than one."

"Ladies. Let's get back to the problem at hand," I said.

"A crochet hook won't get you kicked off an airplane. Do you remember what happened to your monogrammed Signature needles in LA?"

Willie blanched a little paler, which I wouldn't have thought possible with our recent lack of sun. "My babies." Her voice wobbled and her eyes actually watered. "I can't believe you brought that up. You monster."

Chester looked momentarily chagrined, and she stuck out her free hand to pat her sister's shoulder. "That was a bit below the belt. I apologize."

"Aircraft quality aluminum, Ches, aircraft."

"I know dear."

"Stiletto points and teardrop end caps."

"There, there."

"They were hand-crafted. By hand. And monogrammed!"

"Steady now, Will. You know, I think maybe it's time you replace them with a new pair."

Willie sniffed. "But the roof needs some patching and that back fence is on its last legs, and you always say I have too many needles already."

"Oh to hell with the fence. We have enough to deal with the roof and get you an entire new set of Signatures with savings to spare."

"And circulars?" Willie sniffed, but there was a glint of something in her eyes. Something wily.

"Of course we can—wait. Did you just try to hornswoggle me?"

"What?" Willie's eyes were comically large. "What are you saying?" She tapped her ear like her hearing aid had just kicked the bucket.

"You did! You tried to play me." Chester's face closed in like a shriveled walnut. "Forget the needles. We're putting in a new fence. All the way around the house! Twice!"

"You wouldn't."

"You bet your teardrop end caps I would."

"Ladies," I said sternly. "That's enough. What you do with fencing and monogrammed needles is your business, but your groups are going to be pulled in on disturbing the peace charges if you don't disassemble and move your gathering to a venue with appropriate capacity."

"We're not moving," Willie said. "We meet here every week at ten o'clock, and we've been doing it for six months."

"Well, we're meeting here at nine o'clock," Chester said. "You'll just have to find somewhere else to go. Bye-bye."

"There are other meeting options," Bertie said. And she would know.

"With coffee and pastries?" Willie challenged.

"There's the Perky Perch. It has a loft you can reserve for a small fee."

"We can't," they chorused.

"Oh?" Bertie asked.

"We were kicked out," Chester muttered.

"And banned," Willie said.

"Why?" Bertie asked.

Willie mumbled.

"I'm sorry, could you say that again?" Bertie asked with extra sugar on top.

"We were throwing balls of yarn at each other and broke a display stand."

Bathin barked out a laugh from where he stood next to the sunglasses display.

"There are other coffee shops in town," I said.

"Banned." Chester nodded.

"Same reason?" Bertie asked.

"Some variation of it, yes," Willie said. "The details aren't important."

"Then you have two choices." I gave them each a hard look. "You can either move your club meeting times to different days so you can both use this space and enjoy the last coffee and pastries available to you in this town, or you can both move your operations to a different space."

"But we were here first," Willie said. "We should get to keep our time, keep our place, and they should just get out of our mohair for once."

"Is that a possibility, Chester?" I asked.

"We always meet at nine o'clock," she grouched. "Some of us have things to do later in the day."

"No one wants to hear about your genealogy research,

Chester. Find somewhere else to meet. Like the library."

"Can't have food and drink there. Crocheters need coffee too. And we tip higher."

"You don't even drink coffee. You use the same tea bag and reload hot water for four hours."

"Like you know anything. I drink the chai tea now, so get off my feathers, Wilbur."

"Oh, shove off, Cheater."

"I'm not going to stand here all day, ladies," I said. "Make a choice. Either you change the day the C.O.C.K.s meet up, or you change the time the K.I.N.K.s get together."

They glared at each other for long enough, even their gang members behind them got tired of waiting and started working on their projects again, needles and hooks and fingers and thread.

Seriously, why couldn't they get along?

"I could move our bowling time to later in the day on Friday," Willie offered. "You could get all the C.O.C.K. you needed in the morning and have time for a nice nap before we met up with the girls."

Chester was still frowning, her face pinched and doughy, but the offer seemed to ease her scowl, though it would take an iron and steam to tell. "You said bowling is sacred time. You haven't changed our alley time in the last twelve years."

"Fourteen."

"So Friday. I could do C.O.C.K. *and* balls?"

"What more could a woman ask for?" Willie said with a smile.

Chester snorted. "All right, then. Fine. You can have Thursdays. It was interfering with my hair appointments anyway."

"Stubborn goat," Willie muttered fondly.

"Pushy mule," Chester replied. Then she turned to the group behind her. "All right, C.O.C.K.s, we're going to have to move our meetings to Friday at nine."

"Like it's always been?" someone in the middle of her crowd asked.

"Really?" I asked. "*Really?*"

Bertie just sighed and *tsked.*

I wondered if Chester had been angling for the bowling match time change all along. "Anyone have complications with that time?" she asked.

"Classes start soon," another voice said, this time a man.

"We'll make sure we adjust our meeting time for the autumn when that happens. Now, let's pack it up and roll it out. I'll see you all here tomorrow, soon as the cock crows."

That, apparently, was the signal for everyone to break out their best rooster-doodle-doos.

"Astounding," Bathin, behind me, close enough I could hear his near-whisper. "Although I would have had more fun if a war had broken out."

"This isn't about you and this isn't about fun."

"Oh, that's right. You can't feel those kinds of emotions any more. Isn't that sad?"

I considered throwing an elbow at his head.

"Is that a solution you can live with?" I asked Bertie instead.

"Yes, thank you, Delaney, but there is one more issue I need to address with the clubs. Have you noticed the yarn bombings around town?"

"Bombings?"

"Knitted and crocheted decorations in public areas?"

"Oh. Yeah, I've seen a couple."

"I need to know if you're going to allow those to remain."

"It's not like you to beat around the bush, Bertie. What are you angling for?"

"I'd like to encourage the C.O.C.K.s and K.I.N.K.s to explore their rivalry in a more public and useful way over the remaining weeks of summer."

"A contest?" She must have noticed the fleeting horror on my face. I'd gotten roped into judging the annual rhubarb rally and had not enjoyed it.

While judging fiber craft might not make me want to wash my mouth out with sand paper, the participants were basically gang members armed with pointy and hooked weapons.

Nope. I wasn't going to willingly incite violence among the fiber fiends.

"Yes, a contest. I'm shocked you feel that strongly about it, considering your condition."

"Is there any other way you could have phrased that?"

"Yes. I chose not to. My proposal is that we challenge the C.O.C.K.s and K.I.N.K.s to decorate the downtown area along the main road. I'll of course set boundaries. Anything I deem in bad taste will be removed immediately. Nothing will obstruct the flow of pedestrians, nothing will obstruct access to businesses or parking. I'll vet it with the businesses too. Those that wish to opt out will remain untouched."

"You've put some thought into this, I see."

"It's been on the back burner. But since they've already declared war on each other, I thought we could use the battle to Ordinary's advantage."

"I think we just ended the war."

"Not the tussle over their meeting space, the yarn bombs. It started with the C.O.C.K.s making beautiful little bracelets for their members and allies."

"Allies."

"Once the K.I.N.K.s saw what was happening, they began recruiting their own allies with knitted bracelets."

Okay, yes. I'd seen those on a couple of people in town. "They're asking people to fly their colors?"

"Show their support."

"Right. That's so much different."

"Out of bracelets came door handle wraps, bike stand cozies, and tree sweaters."

"I saw the lamppost flower. It was cool."

"Yes!" Three of the knitters said in unison. They high-fived each other, then went back to furiously working yarn between needles.

"Yes. It is lovely, but required an extension ladder under the cover of darkness. I'd like to establish some safety measures. Perhaps borrow a few of the city workers to help install the art?"

"I thought you called them bombs."

She rolled her eyes. "I didn't make up that term, Delaney. It's an international phenomenon and it's time Ordinary staked its claim and become a part of it."

"It sounds like you've got everything in place to go ahead with this. You know the forms you need to fill out and file. I'll tell my officers not to drag anyone in on graffiti charges if they catch them in the act of installation."

"Good. Then at the end of the summer season, let's say Labor Day, we'll have a nice little ribbon ceremony for the most original, a few other categories, and maybe give a walking tour to anyone who wants to see the creations in a sort of art on the lane."

"You sure you're not jumping in on this a little late? This stuff usually takes months to plan."

"In this case, I think striking while the iron is hot is more the way to go."

Several of the crocheters were done packing their gear and were making their way toward the exits. Bertie kept an eye on Chester, following the Macy sister's slow but steady shuffle.

"There are a details I need to sort. Delancy, don't wait for me. I'll catch a ride from someone here."

"Are you sure?"

She gave me an arch look. "Why don't you get a cup of coffee before you go patch things up with Ryder?"

I blinked. Not because she'd guessed that I was thinking I should find Ryder and make sure he wasn't angry, but because I wasn't. That thought hadn't even crossed my mind. And it should have. I should have felt worried and maybe even miserable about him storming away from the station.

About me telling him to leave. That I needed time and some space and he was angry about it. Probably justly so. Was I making a huge mistake pulling away from him? It seemed like the right thing to do. I didn't want him hurt, and there were too many things in my life that weren't under my control that could hurt him.

This was the smart thing to do. For both of us. Because I cared about him. So it made sense to step back, make sure the choices I made didn't negatively impact, or worse, actively harm him.

For a second I was absolutely frozen with the terrifying notion that this would be my life. I'd drift through it, nothing making me happy, or sad, or excited, or terrified. That I'd live every day with a sort of blank, steady progression from logical thought to expected action, to logical thought, over and over again.

I couldn't just drift like that, a tourist in my own life. Not for long. It would drive me crazy. It would tear me up inside, even if I couldn't actively feel it. And then what would happen? Would the next logical step be that my life was pointless? My life wasn't worth living? Would I just give up my badge, walk away? Would I even have the strength to end my life if I was living it while dead?

Did I just seriously just map my remaining days out to the inevitable conclusion of suicide? And was that the only thing I had to look forward to?

I couldn't be overreacting, since I didn't even have the emotional energy to fuel a panic attack.

Although this felt like a panic attack, minus the panic.

"Breathe." Bathin held out a cup of coffee. "One, two, three. Exhale."

I stared at him. "What?"

"She told you to go after your man."

I did not have enough brain cells available to figure out what that hot look of his really meant, much less the words he said. He pushed the coffee out again and half nodded toward Bertie. "She's expecting you to say something."

The coffee was in my hands now, and I looked back at Bertie. "Okay. Thanks. Keep me in the loop with the, whatever this whole thing is." Did that make sense? I was having a hard time corralling my thoughts as they slipped through me too fast and liquid.

Her stern gaze caught my attention. Anchored me somewhat, a rope thrown out into the storm of my thoughts. "I think you have enough on your hands without dealing with the yarn crafters. Yarn walk, Yarn amble, Y'all?"

"Yarn Y'all? That's what you're going to call it?"

"I don't know yet. But I'll have it decided before the end of the day." She waved a gold tipped hand at me. "Go. Have your coffee. I have work to do." She paused halfway through turning away from me and gripped my wrist, her fingers strong and pointed and surprisingly tight. "Don't jump to conclusions. I saw you go pale as a sheet just now. Ryder isn't a lost cause. Neither are you. Just don't lose hope in the ashes. Love is a power that does not yield as long as you return to your heart."

There it was again. Those words. "Who told you to say that?"

"No one tells me what to say."

"'Love is a power that does not yield?' That's not something you just rattle off in farewell."

She frowned. "I think it perfectly suits this situation."

"Does it?"

"Doesn't it?"

"I don't know. I don't even know what it means!"

Understanding clicked on behind her eyes. "Just because the demon has your soul, doesn't mean it isn't yours."

That made less sense.

"Careful," Bathin murmured. "Tell all my secrets and I'll tell all of yours."

"There are none I regret." Steel in those words, an absolutely uncompromising confidence.

"Oh, I'm creative," he said.

"I can see that. And I see so much more. All those within you."

Bathin did that uncomfortable thing where he sort of blushed. What was it with Bertie? What dirt did she have on him? I really wanted to know.

"Couldn't hurt to let me in on some of his secrets," I said.

Bertie winged me a tight smile. "Let's have lunch then. Soon."

Bathin scowled.

I smiled, even though the feeling didn't last long enough for my mouth to get securely in place. But still there was something so normal about this. Bertie being her typical overbearing self, my vampire-bitten, soulless, demon-bound, break-up filled life making little to no impact on her plans and her busy schedule.

Plus, she was never one to shy from the opportunity for a good gossip.

I liked it. Liked knowing that I wasn't the center of the universe. That the people of our little town were going forward with fences and bowling leagues and yarn bombings all without any input from me.

"Good. I'll call." And with that, Bertie was off, taking the straightest line to intercept Chester before she made it past the cage of plastic bouncy balls near the doors.

All in all, that had gone a lot better than I'd expected.

I lifted the cup to my mouth automatically, but paused to stare at the plastic lid before it
could touch my lips. "What is this?"

"Some call it coffee."

"From the Starbucks?"

The look he gave me.

"What kind of coffee?"

"I'm assuming the kind made out of roasted coffee beans and hot water."

"No, seriously, what did you order for me? How do you even have money anyway? You spit in this, didn't you?"

"I'm beginning to wish I had. It's a vanilla latte, Delaney. I told the barista to give me what she thought Chief Reed would want and she gave me this. If you don't like it, dump it out."

He wasn't angry. As a matter of fact he was grinning pretty widely, and had pushed into my space a couple more inches like he just couldn't get enough of me right now.

I couldn't tell if he just loved getting a rise out of me, or just loved getting a rise out of everyone.

"What did you pay her with?"

"She comped it because she appreciates the law, or maybe just wanted to thank you for getting rid of the gray-haired screaming rumblers."

Good name for a rock band.

"They didn't have gray hair."

"I like your attention to the details that don't matter."

"I like you getting out of my space."

"And your spunk."

"You're about to find out if you like my fist, my knee, and my can of mace."

"What, no TASER?"

"Why waste the charge?"

"Ouch. Still, that's a lot of effort you're promising."

"No effort at all. I feel like punching something right about now."

"Isn't that grand? I'm right here." He waited, daring me.

My phone rang. "Step back. Now."

He paused, then stepped back and slurped at his drink. The store, the sounds of shoppers, beeps of the checkouts, smell of coffee and maple glaze and rotisserie chicken all surrounded me again. I hadn't realized it had all faded away, hadn't realized all my attention and every sense I owned had been tuned to one thing only.

Bathin.

Why? I didn't even like him. Was it a soul thing? A demon thing? Was he making me see only him? Or was it just because he had my soul tucked away somewhere I couldn't feel it anymore and I wanted it back that I couldn't look away?

My phone rang again. I glanced at the screen. Ryder.

I swiped my thumb across his image—a picture I'd snapped of him with the face paint mask he'd worn at the Cake and Skate. He didn't look like a business owner, or a reserve officer, or a secret agent for the DoPP or a lackey for a god in that picture. He looked like a guy who had gone a little nuts and let his considerable artistic talent go wild with a fine point brush and a box of carnival paint.

He looked happy, alive.

"Ryder?"

"I'm at the hospital. You need to come down here."

I was already walking to the door. "Ben?"

"He's awake."

"That's good, isn't it?" The tone of Ryder's voice wasn't giving me a lot to go by. "Is that not good?"

"He says he knows where Lavius is."

"Holy shit. Okay. That's great. Why don't you sound happy?"

There was a pause, and I rolled my comment back through my head. It didn't seem like a strange thing to ask and didn't seem emotionally tone deaf. I was starting to be uncomfortably aware of that now. Like every time I opened my mouth, I had a chunk of parsley stuck in my emotional teeth.

"He said he doesn't want to say anything more until you're here."

"I'm on my way." I unlocked my Jeep and climbed in,

Bathin following like a coffee-slurping shadow.

He was also eating a candy bar. When had he paid for that? There was no way the barista had comped him a Butterfinger.

"I don't think you should come."

Right. I was still talking to Ryder.

"What does that mean?"

There was a shuffling sound and I imagined he was moving out of hearing range of someone.

"He's insisting he talk to you. It's all he'll say."

Okay, that was a little weird, especially if Jame was there for him to talk to. But trauma was a trip and a half and I was more than just a cop. I was also the person who made it right for the creatures who lived in this town. The person who made it right for the gods to vacation here.

It wasn't too much of a stretch to think he wanted to give me information and that he thought I would be the best person to receive it.

"Like I said, I'm on my way."

"Delaney." The pause while he gathered his thoughts and I listened to him breathe.

Inhale, exhale. Inhale, then exhale on a sigh. "Let's look at this from another angle. Ben was kidnapped. Lavius found you on the beach and bit you to send a warning to Rossi. Which you did. Then you just happened to pick up the rock with your dad's trapped ghost or whatever in it at Jame and Ben's house where it's been for the last year or so.

"You don't know who sent that stone, who planted it here," Ryder said. "And it just so happens to contain a demon in it who just so happened to know where to find Ben."

"He's on our side," I said.

"Is he?"

"I...I don't know."

He grunted as if I'd just proved his point.

"We know Lavius sent demons in vampire bodies to Ordinary to hurt Jean," he reminded me like I hadn't been there when she'd been run over.

"Maybe not Jean specifically." I was playing devil's advocate, trying to poke holes in the theory Ryder was unpacking.

200

"That was not a luck-of-the-draw hit-and-run, and you know it."

True.

"Do you think Ben is possessed?" I asked.

"It's possible. Isn't it." Not a question.

I answered him anyway. "I don't think he's possessed."

His theory that Bathin might not be playing for our side was pretty strong. I could take it one step further and wonder if Bathin had also been sent by Lavius. It wasn't inconceivable that vampires could play a long game. Immortality had to have some perks.

Dad didn't know who sent that demon-infested rock to him.

It could have been Lavius.

It could have been Bathin.

It could have been anyone.

"Is Rossi there with you?" I asked.

"Yes."

"Have you asked him?"

"If Ben is possessed? Do you really think he would be objective about that?"

"He's old, Ryder. When it comes to stuff like this, he is stone cold solid." Or at least I hoped he wouldn't let his affection for the man he considered his son make him blind to something as serious as demon possession. "You can tell him and you can trust him. I'm on my way. I'll meet you in the lobby."

I hung up because even if Ryder's theories were correct, and Lavius wanted me to see Ben because it was a trap of some kind, I'd need to be there to deal with the fallout. I considered calling Myra, but she'd stayed up even later than I had last night, poring over old books for "answers" according to the curt text I'd gotten when I'd pinged her this morning.

"Trouble in paradise?" Bathin asked.

"This isn't paradise," I said as I merged into traffic toward the hospital.

"Every man's paradise is another man's hell."

And I didn't know if the yearning in his tone was a good thing, or a bad thing.

CHAPTER 14

RYDER WAS pacing inside the lobby, his stride slow and easy, and more of a prowl. He saw me coming before we were in speaking range, his eyes shifting to Bathin, who walked stride-in-stride with me.

I could see the anger on Ryder's face, and just shook my head. I didn't know how to tell him that I didn't like Bathin and that we were not friends or friendly no matter how much he walked at my side like he belonged there, or how many free lattes he scored for me.

"He's not my friend and I don't like him." Hey, look at that. The direct approach. Go, me.

Ryder's eyebrows went up. "Who?"

"Bathin. I know what he is. I know what he's done to me, and the first chance I get, I'm going to fix it, or make him fix it."

"You really shouldn't tell your enemy your plans you know," Bathin noted. "Takes all the pop out of it."

"Then why don't you tell him to back off and leave you alone?" Ryder said, ignoring Bathin like he hadn't even spoken.

"I have."

"Have you?"

"You really haven't," Bathin supplied.

"Shut up," I muttered.

"Well?" Ryder asked.

"What?"

"How about you tell him now." It wasn't a question. It was a dare. "Tell him to get the hell out of this hospital where one of your friends is injured. Tell him to pound sand."

I knew how much Ryder wanted me to do this. I wanted to do it too. But I also knew Bathin would be more useful to us if I kept him in my sight.

I didn't trust him, didn't like him, and didn't want to set him loose on our town.

There wasn't much about this situation I had control of,

but I could darn well keep the demon on a leash.

Bathin chuckled. It annoyed me briefly until it didn't.

That annoyed me too.

"Friends close, enemies closer." It sounded lame even to me.

I'd never seen Ryder shut down so hard. Every line of his face settled into stone, unmoving, unemotional. Only the fire in his gaze gave away what he thought about that old chestnut.

And what he thought was that he hated I was going with the easy out. He might even think that I had fallen for Bathin's overpriced charms.

What would the whole-soul Delaney do in this situation? Hug him? Smile? Tell him I was scared, determined, clear-headed?

I wish I knew what whole-soul Delaney would have done, because all I did was nod. "I know you don't like it. But it's not going to change right now."

The pulse of silence beating between us was miserable.

"I don't agree with you, Delaney. Not at all. Ben's this way." Ryder turned and walked away so quickly, I could feel the warmth of the space between us disappear like a draft up a chimney.

I started after him, and Bathin, wisely, followed at a bit of a distance. My emotions were a muddle—anger, fear, hope, sorrow—and they each hit me hard, like silver spikes hammered into my chest. Spikes that were yanked out again so quickly I was left breathless from the pain of impact and removal.

I stopped halfway down a hall and pressed my palm against the wall to catch my breath. To steady my reeling mind and body.

This no-soul thing wasn't just hard, it was exhausting.

"Now, now," Bathin murmured from behind me. "We aren't giving up already are we? Your father assured me you Reeds are stout stock. I had his soul for more than a year. I've had yours for less than a day." He made a clucking noise with his tongue.

"He was dead," I said, steadying my breathing and pushing away from the wall.

"Yes, well, let's not have you go there just yet." He pressed his palm between my shoulder blades and oh, gods, the heat that bloomed there was almost enough to buckle my knees.

Because with that heat came more. So much more.

I felt worry, real and full and centered around Ryder's still retreating figure. I felt love, thick and heady and so big it stretched my skin and made me moan softly in wonder that I could carry something so totally consuming and still have room for my flesh and bones. Skating on top of those two mammoth surges of real, solid emotions was sorrow. Because I knew this wasn't going to last. These emotions would be snatched away and I'd be hollowed out again. Empty.

"There," the devil on my shoulder whispered. "All better now?"

My inhale hitched. I stifled the sob caught in my throat and pressed my lips together before I made any needy sounds.

Before I begged.

"We can be good together, Delaney. For a long, long time."

The heat of his palm shifted as he stepped even closer to me.

I wanted to burrow into these emotions. Dive in and breathe, drowning on the feelings that had been just outside my reach for so long.

Less than twenty-four hours.

And already the craving for this, for being whole and filled with the decadent textures and flavors and sensations of real emotions was terrible.

This bright moment was a hook on the line of lies Bathin dangled through his clever, hot fingers.

Dad was right. We were made of sturdy stock.

Sturdier than the promises of demons. Sturdy enough to make the right choices.

I wordlessly took a step away from Bathin. It felt like my ribs were being ripped out of my chest.

I took another step.

Bathin's hand slid away. The emotions—love, worry, sorrow—all tumbled down like leaves lost beneath the cold moonlight.

"Such a thing you are," Bathin whispered.

He didn't move to follow me.

Two steps turned into three, three into four until I was striding after Ryder, the dense air of the hospital cooling the tears on my cheeks I hadn't felt fall.

BEN'S ROOM was larger than I'd expected, but was made small by the six wolves, three vampires, one nurse, and one reserve officer who filled it.

Three of the wolves were sitting on rolling doctor-office stools and were plastered against one side of the bed, leaning arms, hands, heads against Jame's feet, hip, shoulder. Covering him in a blanket of limbs, of family. Pack.

Jame lay on his side, his arm crooked over the top of Ben's head, his other arm carefully lined along Ben's side, fingers splayed on the patch of intact flesh on Ben's hip bone.

Ben lay on his back, his eyes closed and every bone in his body looking too large and sharp for the skin that covered it. He had a variety of machines hooked up to him, blood on an I.V. drip, and the blanket pulled up in lopsided bunches across his chest.

Granny Wolfe sat on Ben's side of the bed in the easy chair that seemed to come standard with the room.

To the right of the room was a built-in couch tucked against a wide window across which the blinds had been drawn. Two vampires lounged on the couch, and Rossi stood in those shadows, arms crossed, eyes on Ben, like he owned everything and everyone in the room.

It was an odd allegiance, especially since just a few hours ago, I was pretty sure the weres and the vamps were about to give the K.I.N.K.s and C.O.C.K.s a run for their money with who could throw down in this town.

Ryder was near the foot of the bed. He shifted so that his back was to the vamps and he could keep an eye on me instead.

What did that say about the level of trust he shared with me?

"Hey," I said softly, because even with the whiplash sting of having felt my emotions and lost them again, I knew this was a sacred space, a healing space.

I knew the werewolves curled around Jame were giving him

strength and calm. Strength and calm that would in turn be transferred to Ben.

Jame didn't glance my way, his eyes steady on Ben as if he were his whole world.

There was an ease to Jame's body language. He might still be in pain, but it was no longer agony. I didn't think that had anything to do with his physical wounds. I think it was all different because of the bite mark, still red and a little ragged that showed so sharply on the side of his neck.

They were joined again, had claimed each other. I didn't know if Ben had been conscious for that or if Jame had used Ben's mouth to puncture Jame's neck. But they were together. Tied tight.

Something in me unwound knowing that, and I let myself savor the relief that only lasted long enough to tantalize and torture, like saltwater on a thirsty tongue.

Ben's eyes snapped open, wide and fever-glossed. "D'laney?"

I crossed quickly to the head of the bed, Ryder stepping out of my way like he didn't even want to risk the chance of touching me.

It bothered me. Until it didn't.

Ben didn't quite track my movement. I stopped beside him, where he wouldn't have to move his head to see me.

I was aware of Ryder stepping in closer, the tension of his body. But I didn't hesitate to touch Ben's hand. Ben was strangely hot, and since vampires usually ran cold it threw me for a minute.

"Hey, Ben. I thought I told you not to get into trouble on your little fact-finding mission."

He tried to smile, half his mouth lifting. "Not my boss," he whispered.

"Yeah, well, you're going to be fine," I said, even though I had no idea if that were true or not. "You just need to rest, and let Jame and the doctors and nurses take care of you, okay?"

"He knows."

Chills ran over my body, terror bypassing emotional conduits and riding ancient lizard-brain instincts instead.

"Lavius?"

"Yes."

"What does he know?"

"The moon. The book."

"Full moon?"

"He will be there. You. You have." Ben moved his mouth, the muscles at his neck straining, tendons popping.

Jame leaned in, placed his mouth over Ben's shoulder, then neck and just breathed there, a soft growl that sounded almost like a purr rising up out of him.

Ben's eyes were wild, frantic. I pet his hand gently. "Easy. Give it a minute. Just relax and feel that man of yours."

Ben swallowed repeatedly, and Jame just kept on purring, or maybe he was talking in a low grumble. Whatever it was he was doing, it worked. Ben relaxed by degrees, his body, his face, and finally his eyes, which fluttered shut.

I waited. There had to be more Ben wanted to say. More than Lavius knows we had the book because that was old news.

After a full minute, I glanced over at Granny. "Does he need anything?"

But it was Rossi who answered me. "Wait. He's gathering his strength."

The vampires in the room all shifted, and it sounded like wings against silk. Only Rossi held perfectly still, a tower in the shifting wind.

I missed Rossi's laidback hippie, free love vibe he usually strolled around with. But I couldn't deny that the granddaddy badass vampire thing he was rocking was a not only a better fit right now, it was also totally hypnotizing.

So I waited.

The silence wasn't uncomfortable. Jame kept making those low, growling sounds. Then finally lifted his head and pressed his forehead to Ben's temple, his eyes closed.

Ben stirred again, opened his eyes.

I smiled encouragingly. "So far you've told me Lavius knows we were planning to meet him at the full moon tonight. You said book, and I know Lavius wants the book. He knows we have it. We're not going to give it to him."

Some of the panic drained out of his eyes. "Mansion. Portland. Power. But here…" The words locked up again, as

Ben stiffened to silence.

Jame stroked Ben's arm, easy, steady contact. It seemed to help.

"Weak here. Demon. Possess." Ben stuttered, then worked his mouth, no words coming out. I could see the pain it caused him. And the frustration, so close to panic.

"He has vampires working for him who are demon-possessed," I said.

"Wanted me."

"Wanted to possess you?"

"Marked."

I looked over at Rossi. "Demon-marked?"

Rossi finally stepped out of the shadows and stood behind me where Ben could see him.

"Benoni, son of my sorrow, see me," Rossi commanded gently.

Ben's eyes stuttered upward and fixed on his maker.

"There is no demon who could take you. No mark I can't break. You are mine."

Was that true? I noticed that Bathin had settled into the corner of the room, silent enough he hadn't disturbed the wolves.

I sent him a questioning look. He shrugged and flicked his eyebrows. A "yes" sort of look. Rossi was that powerful for the one vampire he'd turned.

On the one hand I was relieved that Ben couldn't be possessed. On the other hand I was annoyed Bathin hadn't told me that when I was arguing with Ryder earlier.

But then, Bathin wasn't really on my side here. He had gotten what he wanted: a soul, a person to torture, and access to the forbidden lands of Ordinary.

I didn't know why he wanted to be in Ordinary, but it wasn't hard to guess the answer to that wouldn't be anything good.

"He will kill you." They were the strongest words I'd heard Ben say so far. I thought he meant Lavius would kill Rossi. But Ben wasn't looking at Rossi, he was looking at me.

"I know he wants to. He already told me that." I meant it to be comforting but it came off sort of dismissive. Not what I had intended.

Ben's body seized with that panic again.

Jame leaned in, the wolves behind him moving with him, pouring out comfort. Rossi's strong fingers wrapped around my arm. He pulled me away from the bed and into the shadows.

"It's a compunction," Rossi said.

"What is?"

"Ben is being forced to tell you Lavius's message. It's all he's been trying to say since he's been conscious. I had hoped that bringing you here and letting Ben deliver the message would break the spell."

"Spell. As in real magic and real spell?"

"Death isn't the only *Ichor Techne* spell Lavius knows how to cast."

"Can we break it? Can we neutralize the spell? Wash it off or something?"

"I did. This is deeper than the surface." His eyes flicked to the blood dripping down through thin tubes to feed Ben's emaciated frame.

"He injected the blood spell *into* him? It's inside Ben?"

Rossi's eyes glittered in the shadows. "Yes."

Oh, there was so much hatred in that one word, so much need to savage, to kill.

"Will the transfusion erase it?"

"No. It has eased it, diluted the strength, but the spell remains."

"How do we break it?"

"There is a counter spell."

"But?" There had to be a catch if he hadn't just cast it yet.

"It is written in the *Rauðskinna*. If we cast it, Lavius will know. He is waiting with a counter spell. One that could bring the book of dark magic to him."

"How do you know that?"

"It's what I would do."

"To save Ben we have to use the book. If we use the book, Lavius will what? Zap it to him and use it on us?"

"Yes."

"What's our counter move?"

"Kill Lavius."

"I'm all in on that plan, but we'd have to find him first."

"Ben said he's in Portland. A mansion."

"He also said he's locked away and powerful. I am not going to authorize a full scale attack with nothing but planted information to go on."

"I'm not asking for your permission to kill him, Delaney. It's time you remove yourself from this fight, and let me put you somewhere safe, where Lavius can't use you against me."

Oh, hell no.

"If you think locking me up is even a slight possibility, you have lost your mind, Travail. I'm the law here."

"You are compromised. In more than one way." His eyes drifted to the bite on my neck, then the demon over my shoulder. And maddeningly, to Ryder.

"Look, if you want to be the guy with your finger on the trigger, I'm all for that. This is your old history crawling all over my town and hurting my people. I know I'm no vampire slayer, but I have skin in this game, you understand?

"He killed Sven. He killed the vamp hunters who rolled through town. He beat the crap out of Ben and Jame, and attacked me. He ran my sister over with a car.

"*Ran her over.*"

I paused to take a breath and lower my tone. I was furious, I could feel it boiling up, hot and thick before cooling under that weird soulless wind that raged through me.

But it wasn't just anger that was fueling my protest.

I had taken the responsibility to protect this town like so many Reeds before me. My father had died doing so. I wasn't about to walk any other path than the one I chose, no matter what damage I'd taken along the way.

"This is my town. My people. My fight. We do this together, or I will use the authority that is rightly invested in me to tell everyone, every single creature, exactly what I expect them to do in this situation. Do you understand me?"

For a moment, more than a heartbeat, more than three, I thought I'd finally pushed Rossi past his fondness for me and my family.

Because for a moment, standing there in front of me wasn't the easy-going live-and-let-live guy I'd known all my life.

I was staring down the badass granddaddy vampire who could break me, literally, in half with his bare hands.

When he didn't say anything, I filled the silence. "We counter his moves. We out-think him, we out-plan him, we do this smart, and we do it together as a united front, me, you, the Wolfes, the gods, and demons and anyone and any*thing* else we need to call on to hit hard and fast. I want this one and done. We draw Lavius to the battlefield of our choice. And we end him."

Rossi looked past me to Granny Wolfe, and they seemed to have some kind of silent conversation I did not understand.

Ryder shifted behind me. I wondered if he would stand with Rossi, or if he was going to try to drag me out of the room. I hadn't seen his rule-following compulsion under full power and wasn't sure where it would land in this situation.

I wasn't breaking any rule that I was aware of, but I was pretty sure I was forging new ones.

"Delaney's right," Ryder said. "We do this together and we wipe him out. Locking her away won't keep her safe. He's already marked her. He'll know where she is."

I was glad he'd taken my side, but not thrilled with his casual assessment of how compromised I really was.

"What's the smart move?" I asked.

Rossi finally blinked, and my heartbeat stuttered. I didn't realize I'd been standing there with my fists clenched, stiff, as if I were trying to stand up against a slow-motion bomb blast coming at me from point blank range.

I was sweating and all my muscles were fatigued, like I'd just run a short marathon.

Rossi was old. Ancient. He had a lot of power, a lot of sway. I'd just been treated to a taste of that power and he hadn't lifted a finger against me.

Lavius was just as ancient and powerful as Rossi. We didn't just need to hit him hard, we needed to kill him with one blow.

"We need a plan. Bulletproof," I said. "I know you already have a plan in place and bringing me here to bully me to the sidelines was part of it. Tell me the rest."

"You are risking more than your life, Delaney." Rossi's tone was flat, without the warmth I usually detected beneath the surface. "You are risking Ryder's. Your sisters'."

"Yeah, because Lavius likes to make people pay by pounding their loved ones into submission. I understand that. My loved ones are tough as hell. We can take it. What's the plan?"

There was no arguing with that truth, so he didn't.

"I'll use the book to break the spell on Ben. Then I'll kill Lavius."

"Want to fill in the blanks, or should I just handcuff you to my side and give you a commentary of surprise and awe as things unfold?"

"Delaney." This, finally, said with the kind of exasperated tone I was used to. I knew right then, that he wasn't going to do this without me.

Ryder reached over, his fingers brushing against the back of my wrists. Reminding me it wasn't just me Rossi was siding with.

Us. Rossi wasn't going to wage this war without us.

"I'll buy you a cup of fancy hospital coffee," I wheedled. "We'll take over a conference room down the hall, call in the people we need and do this proper."

"We're not planning a battle in the hospital," Rossi said.

"Why?"

Rossi gave me a look like I was stupid. "Their coffee is terrible."

Right. That was a problem I could get on board with. "I hear the Perky Perch has a loft we can reserve."

He looked back over at Ben. This was why I had suggested the hospital meeting room. I didn't think Rossi was going to let Ben out of his sight.

"Go on now," Granny spoke gently for the first time since I'd gotten there. "I'll watch our boys."

Jame made a little humming sound that was both kind of a protest and also absolute contentment. Like an adult being told he was a good child. Like someone who had thought the man he loved had been beaten and killed, and now he had his family, no, *both* their families keeping him safe.

Our boys. That was good. Better than good. It might even be good enough that I could hang up my referee stripes because the fight between the Rossis and Wolfes had been called off due to lovey-dovey weather.

Of course, Rossi could tell Granny to shove it and this could all turn into a fist fight in a blink.

But Rossi nodded. "Call who you want," he said. "But the fewer we involve in this, the better."

Small meant less of a target and less chance for collateral damage. It did not mean less fire power. Not in this town. "Are you bringing anyone?"

"No."

I glanced at Ryder.

"If you tell me to stay behind, I'll have the nurse fit you with a chloroform drip."

Okay then. I pulled out my phone and dialed Myra. Because I knew what kind of hell I'd catch if I didn't let her in on the plan.

"Myra Reed," she answered.

I drew the phone away from my face and stared at the screen. She knew I was calling, I didn't know why I'd gotten the formal response.

"Hey?" I ventured.

"What's wrong?" I caught it then, the burr in her voice. She'd been sleeping and had answered on automatic.

"You okay?"

"I'm fine."

"I woke you."

"It was a power nap. I overslept the alarm. What's wrong?"

"Nothing." I paused. "Nothing new. But we're meeting at the Perky Perch to go over tonight's plan. Meet us there in a half hour?"

"Where are you now?"

"Hospital. Checking in on Ben—he's conscious, but under a spell we need to break. Jame and the pack are staying with him. Rossi's going to the Perk. Ryder and me too."

"And Bathin?" The way she said it, like she knew the answer and wasn't judging the outcome totally made it sound like she was judging the outcome.

Thing was, I couldn't be sure she *didn't* want him there.

"I don't think leaving him behind is going to do us any

213

good."

I didn't look over at him but I could feel his smirk. *Feel it.* Creepy.

She sighed. "Have you called Jean?"

"No. She was stoned on painkillers and catching a nap at the station when I saw her earlier. Before you say anything, I tried to talk her into going home, but she didn't want to be alone. Roy's with her. And either Shoe or Hatter said he'd stay too. She's covered."

"Hogan might be there too."

"Maybe," I said.

"Who else should I call?" she asked.

I sifted through the people, creatures, and gods in the town. Whose strength did we need? Whose life did we dare risk? Death might be handy to have on our side. If Lavius was going to be killed, it stood to reason that the god Death would be the most direct route.

But he was only a few months into his first vacation. If he wanted to wield his power, he'd have to pick it up from where it was stored in the beer growler in Odin's travel trailer, and then he'd have to leave Ordinary for a year.

Maybe as a last resort, I could ask Than to do that. For now, having him as a consultant on the issue might be all we needed.

"Than," I said. "Maybe Aaron, if you think the god of war would want to give us a few pointers."

"Do we need Bertie?"

"She's overseeing her own war."

"Come again?"

"A bunch of C.O.C.K.s and K.I.N.K.s. are going to bomb the city. She's got this."

The pause was longer, then I heard air blown out in a stream. "The knitting groups?"

"One's crochet."

"Is there a difference?"

"I've been told."

"Yarn bombs?" She really was a good cop. Smart. Determined.

"Bertie thinks the tourists will like it."

"Okay. I'll call Than and Aaron. If we need someone else, we can call them from the coffee shop."

"Good." I ended the call and then looked around. I didn't realize I'd been walking while talking. I was almost to the lobby already. I hadn't even said goodbye to Jame or Ben.

I rubbed at my forehead then pinched the bridge of my nose.

This had been a long day already and it hadn't even begun.

An arm wrapped across my shoulders, warm, strong and heavy enough to make me feel grounded, centered in my own skin. Yes, I said I wanted space. Yes, I should be pushing him away and demanding that space. So he wouldn't get hurt, so I wouldn't get him killed.

But I couldn't do it. Couldn't even gather enough energy to try.

"I thought you were mad at me."

"I am," Ryder said easily. "It doesn't mean I don't love you. Anger and love are not mutually exclusive. Especially when someone is being a full-time disaster."

"Part-time disaster at the most, thank you," I said haughtily. I leaned into his heat, wishing I could feel him, really feel him, but thankful he was there just the same.

"You forget I've known you a long time."

"What does that have to do with this?"

"You don't do part-time anything. If you're into something, you're in it all the way."

Well. I couldn't really argue with that.

He gave me a smile, pleased with himself. "Come on. You know I'm right. And I'm driving."

If he thought I was going to fight him on either point, he was wrong.

CHAPTER 15

"STUPID ISN'T a strong enough word to encompass this conversation," Aaron declared. "I thought you wanted me here to make sure you didn't get yourselves killed. Was that the goal? Or did you just want me to take notes for your tombstones?"

I swear, every time he opened his mouth it was the verbal version of throwing a gauntlet.

Maybe inviting the god of war to our planning session wasn't such a good idea.

"If you'd like to come up with a better plan, we're right here waiting," Ryder said through clenched teeth.

"I'm not here to plan." Aaron leaned back in the secondhand office chair and adjusted his wire-rimmed glasses, his eyes sharp and happy. "I'm on vacation, remember? No war for this guy."

I tried and failed to stifle a snort.

I was pretty sure Ryder was going to hit our local nursery owner in the face. After all, Ryder had recently proved he was wound up enough that he felt fists were a viable strategy for conflict resolution. So had I, come to think of it.

Rossi spoke up. Again. "He is coming for us. That we know. He knows Ben was taken right out from under his nose. He knows his lackeys were killed. He knows it is us.

"We choose our battlefield, here, inside Ordinary where we are stronger and he is weaker. We take the book to a void magic node, which might buy us enough time to use it to break the spell on Ben. Lavius will attack as soon as he senses the book is within his reach."

"And when will it be within his reach?" I asked.

"As soon as I break the wards that mask it from him."

"Can you do that after you cast the spell for Ben?"

"I can't cast the spell with the wards on the book."

"So," Ryder asked. "How many minutes are we talking between you breaking the wards, and completing the spell casting?"

"One."

"And how fast can Lavius be on our doorstep?"

"Seconds."

"Someone else needs to cast the spell," I said. "We'll break the wards, you'll meet Lavius's attack and someone else casts the spell."

"No one else can cast this spell." Rossi's eyes tightened. "It is...difficult. It is in the blood that flows through his veins. And it takes an ancient, a man of my making."

"A vampire?" Ryder asked. Behind the word was the hint that there were a lot of vampires in the town.

"The maker who turned Ben."

Oh. Well, we only had one of those and he was right there on the other side of the table glaring at Ryder.

Goodbye plan A.

"We'll attack him, keep him occupied while you cast the spell. What do we hit him with first?" Ryder said, quickly moving on to the salient points. I liked that in a man. A knowledge of when to get to the violent stuff.

"There are weapons at our disposal," Rossi said. "Some we should choose not to use."

"Like Delaney?" Bathin asked. He'd kept his mouth shut for the last half hour, so I was sort of surprised he'd chimed in now.

"No," Myra said to the demon. "Delaney is not a weapon and not going to be used as one." Then to Rossi: "You said the bite wasn't something we could use to kill Lavius."

"It isn't." Firm. A challenge.

Bathin sighed. "For want of a nail, a kingdom is lost, old one."

I thought I could hear Ryder's knuckles crack as he tightened his fist. "You have something to add?" he asked the demon.

"This is not my sad little carnival. You don't want my opinion."

"Then keep your mouth shut."

Right. Growling at the demon was going to shut him up. Why hadn't I tried that?

"But since you asked so sweetly, Mr. Bailey," Bathin said with a beatific smile, "that bite and the tie to Lavius it planted in Delaney can absolutely kill him."

"No," Rossi said. "It cannot."

"You're afraid of shadows, ancient one," Bathin said. "And you'll let every person in this town fall just to keep your promise to a man long dead."

"Be silent," Rossi snarled, "or I will cut your tongue out before your heart."

"Whoa." I stood up, hands extended, as if I could separate the demon and the vampire more than the table between them already did. "There are rules we follow here, Rossi. You know that. There is no killing allowed. Not between creatures, not between humans, not at all."

Ryder was also standing, his hands loose at his sides like he was ready to pull a gun and start pointing it at someone.

I hoped he wasn't armed because I was not prepared for this discussion to dissolve into a discharge of weapons.

"The demon is protected under the laws set into the very soil of this town," Ryder said in that odd drone that happened when Mithra's power was pushing hard on his willpower. "That we even have laws, rules, tenets to harbor a demon pisses me off. But if you break that law, Rossi, it won't just be Delaney dishing out the consequences. It will be me, and the god of contracts through me."

Rossi didn't look even slightly cowed by either of our threats.

Aaron leaned forward in his seat, looking like he wished he'd brought popcorn for the show.

"Don't add another layer of crazy to this cake," I said to Rossi. "I'm already juggling all I can handle and I need death-of-the-demon-who-has-my-soul to be off the plate right now."

I thought he heard me, his stance easing an infinitesimal amount, though his killing gaze never left Bathin.

"Delaney," Bathin cooed staring right back at Rossi, stone to his fire. "Would you like to know what your father made Rossi promise him before he died? What he promised him about you?"

Rossi shot up out of his chair. I sprang forward at the same time, and so did Bathin. I leaned out in front of the demon, throwing myself between them.

And yeah, sadly, I was fast enough to do so before Rossi started around the table.

"Sit. The hell. Down," I said.

A sliver of the murderous lust in his eyes seemed to cool. But if I didn't know Rossi, if I hadn't been around him since I was a kid, I would be terrified of him.

He chewed on that anger, the muscles at his strong jaw clenching, the meat of his lips stretching against the protrusion of his fangs. He wanted to kill the demon, right here over this cheap conference room table.

I didn't blame him. The table was awful.

And so was the demon.

Instead, Rossi straightened and sat back in his chair.

I turned on Bathin, who in five minutes had caused more trouble than the literal god of war at the end of the table.

We didn't have time to play games, didn't have the luxury to squabble or fight or commit homicide.

"Leave." I told the demon. "You are not helping and I don't have time for your shit. You serve nothing but your own desires and I do not have time to coddle self-absorbed monsters. Leave. Now."

Bathin raised one eyebrow. "Are you sure you want to set me free on this succulent little town? Are you sure I won't feast on all the sweet treats?"

"You do, I kill you."

"Then you and I will be locked in death together. For eternity. Much more enjoyable than with your father. Perfectly cozy."

"Gonna give you to the count of three," Ryder drawled. He pulled his gun out from the side holster I had foolishly hoped he wasn't wearing, and placed it on the table in front of him. "One."

Bathin didn't even bat an eye at the gun.

Myra reached into her pocket. Seriously? Had everybody brought guns to the conference room?

But she didn't draw a gun. She withdrew a piece of chalk.

Okay...that was...weird.

Bathin instantly stilled, gaze, body, and breath focused on that slender white tube in her fingers.

She didn't even look at him, but instead sketched something on the table top, quick sure strokes mapping a design, her dark hair tucked back behind her ears and swinging softly at the curve of her neck with each motion.

"What's this?" Bathin asked, not even glancing at what she was drawing, but enraptured with her face. He leaned forward, fingers spread, fingertips pressed against the cool table top to hold his weight. The look on his face wasn't fear. It was curiosity, humor.

And it was hunger.

"Do you think you have the leverage over me to complete this spell? You, a mortal woman? Do you think anyone does?"

She didn't answer, so he just kept taunting her.

"You have been a clever little girl, haven't you? I haven't seen that form of rune in centuries. It didn't work then, and the one who used it was a master spell worker who I had a vested interest in paying attention to. You could say I was mildly obsessed with him. You, though. What worth are you to me?"

"Hey," I said, though it was actually better if Myra wasn't something he thought was worthy. But still, he had insulted my sister, and I couldn't let that stand.

She never once looked up, her eyes narrowed and shoulders set as she continued to draw.

"What is that?" I asked. "Myra, what are you doing?"

"No one has successfully thrown that spell on me," Bathin continued. "You are going to be terribly disappointed in yourself when you fail. Do you think I want you—that you are something I want—that you could really send me—"

Myra finished her drawing, looked up, and met his gaze.

"How sad for you. It won't—"

She snapped the chalk in half.

Bathin disappeared with the sharp bang of a popped balloon.

One minute he was standing there smoldering and smack-talking my sister, the next he was gone, leaving nothing but an empty seat and a hint of his aftershave behind.

Aaron gave her an admiring slow clap. "Nice."

Myra leaned back against her chair and stared at the broken chalk in her hand for a minute. A pink blush washed up across her cheeks and down her neck. Then she straightened and pulled herself together, all business again.

She wiped her palm across the table top, erasing what she'd drawn and pocketed both pieces of chalk.

"My?" I asked, stunned. "What did you do?"

She smiled, and the smile turned into a breathy laugh. "I popped him out of here." She snapped her fingers.

"I didn't even...how did you know...was that magic?"

"It was. Found that little trick in an old journal Dad had in his stuff. The journal belonged to a dwarf who retired here. He didn't like demons much."

"Sindri," Rossi supplied.

"That's right." Myra looked around the table. It was just me, Aaron, Than—who had been even quieter than Bathin— Ryder, Rossi and Myra here now. It felt so much more peaceful and friendly, now that Bathin was out of the picture.

"Now." She turned to Aaron. "Don't make me throw you out in a more mundane manner."

Aaron lifted his hands in mock surrender. "I'm here because you wanted my opinion on your plan. I'll give you my opinion, even if I think your plan is stupid. Which it is."

"We already heard that," Ryder said. "Suggest an alternative."

Aaron shrugged. "I don't get involved in the mechanics. I'm on *vacation* which means nothing you do will get me involved in the mechanics."

Myra rubbed at her eyes, her hand covering her face for a moment.

"Hey," I asked. "Did doing that magic do anything to you?" I knew all magic came with a price. I didn't want Myra to be giving up something important when we could have just pushed Bathin out the door, or duct-taped his mouth shut and tied him to the table leg for a little peace and quiet.

"Other than make me happy to finally get him out of my sight?" she asked. "Not really. I'm a daughter of Ordinary, a Reed. I'm connected to the land via the will of the original gods who created the place. All I had to do was make sure I was grounded to the town and my place inside it. Ordinary kicked him out. I just drew the doorway and pushed it open."

"Will it work on all demons?" Because that could be useful. I was already pulling together a plan for dealing with the possessed vamps I figured Lavius might throw at us. If we lured them to an area we had chalked up with that spell, we could get rid of them.

Myra opened her mouth, but Rossi answered.

"No it won't work on all demons. Not in a broad stroke, as you're thinking. It takes…the spell is counter-weighted by the demon's own desire. He has to want something about the person who is casting it, be invested in them in some significant way. A desire to kill them, to make a deal with them, to possess them, to love them."

Myra startled at that last thing.

I didn't like where this was going.

"It's not those," she said firmly. "It worked because he knows how much I hate that he has Delaney's soul. He wants to watch me squirm."

Rossi studied Myra, a slightly quizzical look on his face. "One could assume so."

Which was about as vague an agreement as I'd ever heard. I looked at Myra, trying to see what Rossi saw in her, what he suspected.

She looked satisfied, like a cat who had just finished a bucket of cream. She also looked a little flushed, her eyes glittery. All I saw was that my sister was happy. And victorious. She had enjoyed pulling that little trick. She had enjoyed tossing that smug know-it-all out on his ear.

"How long will he be gone?" I asked.

"I don't know," she said. "Long enough for us to finish our plans. Rossi, is there some way we can use Delaney's tie to Lavius to our advantage? If not to kill Lavius to trap him? Trick him?"

"Nothing that wouldn't kill her. And that," Rossi said, giving me both barrels of his attention, "is what I promised your father. That I would protect you and not willingly allow your death by any hand."

"Oh," I said, because that was all I could come up with. If

I could still feel emotions, I was pretty sure I'd be touched and overwhelmed. "Thank you."

"So we stick with the original plan?" Ryder asked. He'd retrieved his gun from the table and secured it in his holster.

"The original plan is wholly uninspired," Aaron grumbled.

"It is clean and concise," Rossi said.

"Tonight at moonrise we summon Lavius by breaking the ward on the book and casting the spell on Ben?" I asked.

"At the Party Putt Putt," Rossi said.

"The mini golf course?" It was such a weird request. That little indoor mini-golf course and party space was, well, well-used was the most polite term I could come up with. It had been in Ordinary for years, and hadn't had an upgrade since opening day. "Why there?"

Old Rossi looked a little exasperated, but Myra was nodding.

"Because," Rossi said, "The magic void which will hamper his ability to access the power stored in the *Rauðskinna* is deep beneath the sand trap." Rossi said that like he was explaining that the sun rose, the moon set, and evil vampires always had a backup plan.

"Right," I said. "Of course it is. Than, will you be there?"

Death had been silent through most of the conversation, watching us with that calm attentive manner. He didn't get worked up over the dramatics of the living, which I supposed made sense. He did seem interested in this particular scuffle with Lavius, and had readily agreed to be a part of this meeting.

He sipped his hot cocoa, which I knew was so delicious, it could make angels trade their wings in for whips. The cup looked delicate in his long fingered hands.

Than looked, well, not at ease, but like he was getting the hang of both the being mortal and vacationing thing. He seemed well-rested and comfortable in his Hawaiian shirt that featured pink flamingos melted à la Salvador Dali surrounded by bubbles so numerous and small, the remaining shirt looked like it was covered in googly eyes.

His shirt was staring at me.

Creepy with a tropical flair.

"Do you want me to be at the Party Putt Putt?" he asked.

"Yes?"

"You understand better than any that my power is at rest, Reed Daughter. Vampires linger in the gray places outside of Death's reach. It has always been so."

"I don't want you to kill anyone." Well, I did, but I understood he wouldn't. Not without having to leave Ordinary and stay away for a year.

"I just…when we kill Lavius, which is the only acceptable outcome of this plan, I don't want any surprises. I want him to be dead-dead. Declared dead by Death. All the way dead and not to rise again like some kind of nightmare in a striped shirt and fedora."

"Did you marathon Friday the 13th movies again?" Myra asked.

"No."

Yes.

"But I want zero Freddy Krueger action going on. I'd like a promise from you. From your power. Anything that dies tonight stays dead."

"I see." Than stood. "You will have no such promise from me for my promises are already given." And then he walked out of the room, without looking back, without a single additional word.

"That was…what just happened?" I asked.

"I think…" Myra frowned. "I think you hurt his feelings."

"Me? How? I wasn't saying he was bad at his job. I just wanted him there. Even on vacation, he's got a better handle on death than any of us at this table. I don't think him standing on the side and declaring the time of death breaks the rules. Does it?" I threw a look at Ryder.

"No. He wouldn't have to access his stored power to know if someone was dead. He's got good eyes for that."

Aaron huffed. "Please. He told you he doesn't want to be a part of your little fist fight, Delaney. This isn't important to him. Vacation is important to him and you're ruining it. Now you made death sulk before your big showdown. Smooth, Chief."

"It's fine," Myra said. "Than doesn't have to be there. It will be fine. We know how to kill Lavius, right?" She looked expectantly at Rossi.

"Oh, yes," he said, low enough it made me shiver. "We do."

Okay, even though I was worried (fleetingly) about disappointing Death, I knew the granddaddy badass vampire was on our side.

And that was good enough for me.

CHAPTER 16

RYDER AND Rossi walked me out into the salty warmth of sunlight and calls of seagulls scrounging for early dinners. The wind was just enough to keep the heat from being too much, and the little parking area was filled with cars.

Myra was at her cruiser, having what looked like a very serious conversation on her phone. Aaron had stayed behind as soon as he spotted a couple people from the K.I.N.K.s and C.O.C.K.s sneaking into the joint.

For a god who insisted he was on vacation, he sure did get his kicks watching people get into fights.

"There is one thing I want you to carry." Old Rossi reached into the inner pocket of his jacket and withdrew a slim silver dagger in a sheath. He held it out to me.

"I don't do knives." What I was really saying was I didn't want to get close enough to Lavius for a knife to be necessary. If I was close enough to stab him, he was close enough to bite me.

Or break me.

Vampires were strong.

"Take the dagger, Delaney."

Vampires were also stubborn.

"Don't need it."

"You very much do need it. The blade is poisoned. If you strike Lavius, it will slow him. It isn't enough to kill him, but it should be enough so that you have a chance."

"To kill him?"

"To survive long enough to get away from him."

He didn't sound all that sure about my chances. Fear fingered at the back of my throat, but didn't stay long, dragged away by my missing soul.

Maybe having no fear, or at least not feeling it, would give me an advantage against Lavius.

Or maybe it'd just get me killed.

"What kind of poison?" Ryder asked as he came up behind us.

"It's a spell. Nothing written in any book you would ever read."

"Is it written in the *Rauðskinna*?"

"No."

I groaned. "So we have more than one dark magic book we have to deal with?"

"Not every book of magic is dark, Delaney."

"Is this one?"

Rossi looked like he didn't want to answer that. Then: "Yes."

Great. It was a dark magic dagger. Still, if I had to fight Lavius, I'd need more than a gun at my disposal.

"Does everyone get a magic dagger?" I accepted the knife, getting used to the weight in my hand. I didn't take it out of the sheath.

"No. Only those who he is connected to."

"Neat." Since I wasn't wearing a jacket, I stuck the dagger, sheath and all, in my back pocket.

"You'll be there tonight?" It came out sounding a little small. Needy. I tried to feel ashamed about that, but couldn't have managed it even if I still had full-access to all my emotions.

"Yes," he said immediately.

Good.

"So now we wait?"

"I have a few matters to deal with. Preparation. For now, you rest. Go home, Delaney. Get some sleep. This will not be easy."

"Is there anything else I should know? I don't want to be surprised here, Rossi. If there's something...uncomfortable you don't want to tell me...whatever Bathin was hinting at, I'd rather hear it from you than be surprised."

He paused, there in the sunlight, an anomaly in this world, but no less beautiful because of it. The weight of his years seemed to gather around him, stretching across the many things he had been, the many things he had done.

All the choices he had made, good and bad.

He nodded, just once, and I knew he had made another

choice. Maybe even his final one.

"There is nothing more you need to know, Delaney." His gentle voice. His kind voice. The one I'd known from childhood. "We'll meet at the Putt Putt at eleven and then all this will finally be done."

He reached out to me, his cool fingers brushing across my cheek so faintly, it could have just been the wind. "All things come to an end." There was sorrow in his words, and forgiveness.

Then he turned and walked away, across the parking lot and down the narrow footpath toward the cliffside that would lead to the beach. He was pulling his shirt off over his head as he went, baring that impossibly pale skin that should not endure the sunlight to the wide judgmental sky.

I wondered if he was going to strip everything off, as he so often did. Wondered if I should follow him and either give him comfort, or write up another indecent exposure ticket for his collection.

Decided, instead, to give him his time.

It didn't escape me that he was going to kill a man who had been a soldier beside him, a man who had been a brother. I didn't care how old you were, or what that person had become as time tread through multiple lives. Killing someone who had once been at your side, at your back, had to be a hell of a thing to get right with.

"How about I drive?" Ryder asked.

"I don't want to go home and just wait."

"What do you want to do?"

Good question. "Patrol. Check in on Jean. Write some traffic tickets."

Be normal.

"Hey," Myra called out. "We have a situation."

"What is it?" I crossed the parking lot to her.

"Brawl at the wayside off the Easy. Wedding party gone bad. Someone got thrown in the drink and came up punching. Hatter and Shoe need backup."

The wayside was a large parking area with access to the beach and the smallest river in the state of Oregon. There were restaurants and hotels nearby and the parking was obvious from the main road through town. Locals really never hung out there, but it drew tourists like honey drew badgers.

"Go," I said. "I'll be right behind you."

"Nope. You are off duty. You got that? Until tonight is over, that vamp bite is gone, and that demon gives you your soul back, you are done for now."

"Are you telling me I can't do my job? I'm your boss, Myra, not the other way around."

"I am telling you that Ryder and Shoe and Hatter and I can handle a couple of people in a shoving match, *and* we're not going to get bit by a vampire or possessed by a demon in the process."

I couldn't help it, I laughed. "Rude. I am not possessed."

She squeezed my shoulder. "I'm not calling Jean in on this either."

"Duh. Jean's injured."

"So are you."

And okay, yes. I hadn't stopped long enough to think of trading my soul away as an injury.

It had just seemed like taking actions, any actions, was a better use of my time. Especially if it meant staying one step ahead of, or gaining control of the chaos in my life.

"Going home is the best thing you can do right now," she said a little softer now that she could see that the lightbulb had clicked on over my head. "I'm going to take care of this and get all the backup we need together for tonight."

"Backup?"

"You know we're not just going to rely on Rossi and a book of spells, right?"

No, I did not.

"Uh…"

"I've got this. You go home. I'll send Ryder to pick you up tonight."

"You want to jump in on my side here and tell my sister I know how to do my job?"

Ryder shook his head. "I know better than to get in between you two. But just so you know, I think Myra's right on this one."

I was torn between wanting to argue, and not actually

caring enough about getting my way. If I wasted any more time fighting with them, they'd be too late to back up Shoe and Hatter.

"Fine. Go." I waved them off.

Ryder caught my arm, tugged me to him. "It's going to be okay. Everything. We're going to make it all okay."

I wanted to believe him, but I knew nothing was that simple. "You bet your ass we are."

He grinned, shook his head, and reluctantly let go of my arm.

I stood there and watched as he hurried into the passenger side of the cruiser, was still standing and watching as my sister and my boyfriend drove away, red and blue lights flashing.

CHAPTER 17

"DRINK, DARLING?" The demon in my kitchen smiled innocently and offered me a glass of red wine. "Or would you like me to fetch your slippers for you?"

"Go to hell, Bathin."

He sucked in a breath and pressed a hand to his chest as if shocked at my language. "But I just got back. Didn't you get my postcard? *Wish You Were Here?*"

I tossed the dagger down on the coffee table by the couch and stood there with my hands on my hips. He was still holding the wine. Two glasses in one hand.

"Is that where she sent you?"

He shrugged, and the innocent housewife thing he was pulling fell away. Leaving him tall, dark, and dangerous, in slacks and white shirt, and smiling at me like he knew where all my guilty pleasures lay beneath the layers of me.

"Does it matter? It won't happen again."

"You underestimate my sister."

He gave me half a nod. "Yes, I did. I promise you I won't repeat that little oversight."

"She's smart. If you challenge her, she'll be the last Reed you'll ever tangle with."

"Is that so?" He looked even more interested in her now.

Dammit.

"Give me the wine."

He handed it over. "Bad day, pet?"

"Go away."

He chuckled and then walked around the furniture so he could sit.

"Tell me all about it." He lifted his glass in a kind of salute and then took a spare sip of the liquid. He settled into the most comfortable chair in the room and tipped his head toward the couch. "No, I'm serious. Have a seat, and tell me about it."

"Maybe I'm going to bed."

"Doesn't sound like you're too sure about that." He sipped, patient, implacable.

Not warm, but easy? Welcoming? And I found myself wanting to do just that: sit here and spew my troubles all over him.

Maybe it was because he wasn't anyone who mattered to me. I didn't care about his opinion on my messed up life. I could say anything I wanted and what was he going to do about it? Tattle on me?

No one would believe him. Because he was a demon. Two-faced, conniving, self-serving and everyone knew it.

I sighed and dropped down on the couch, careful not to spill the wine. "You know what bothers me about all this?"

He waited, sipped.

I turned the glass between my fingers, scowling at it and not really seeing it. "He hasn't made a move."

"Lavius?"

I nodded.

"He sent a demon-possessed vampire to run over your sister."

It was my turn to be silent.

"He kidnapped Ben. Tortured him. Yes," he said at my glance, "I know torture when I see it. Cast a blood spell so dirty I wouldn't touch it with a lead-coated pole. Used it to kill a vampire who was also one of Ordinary's citizens."

He sipped again. "Not enough? He broke the life-tie between the vampire and werewolf. That's…difficult. He had those vampire hunter idiots drowned. Well, killed then dumped in the ocean." He shrugged as if the details of their gory deaths didn't matter.

"All that seems a bit pedestrian for an ancient vampire, doesn't it?" I asked.

Bathin was quiet long enough I wondered if he had an opinion on that.

"It depends on how you measure his efforts. Getting the *Rauðskinna* from Rossi may have just been his most recent goal."

He was calm, talking through it as if this were all supposition. But I was a cop. I knew when someone knew more than they were saying.

"You might as well share with the class," I said. "Nobody here but me, and nobody out there is listening to me anyway."

That got a small amused expression out of him. "Not like you to be so maudlin, Delaney. Where's that Reed spine made of steel and tougher stuff?"

"What aren't you telling me, Bathin?"

"Oh, so many things." He pressed his lips against the rim of his glass, drank again, the thick red liquid leaving a shiny coating behind on the inside curve of the glass.

"What aren't you telling me about Lavius that will help us kill him?"

"Better question," he approved.

I waited. Thought about drinking the wine, but really, wasn't thirsty. Still, I kept it in my hands, because that was normal and it gave me something else to focus on besides his wicked hungry eyes.

"Rossi will be angry if I tell you," he said.

"I can deal with him."

He pursed his lips, then set the glass down beside him and folded his hands together. "How much do you know about vampires?"

"More than most."

"How much do you know about the ties they inflict?"

My hand went to the bite on my neck. "Like this one?"

"Exactly like that one. He bit you once. Just once. Did you stop and ask yourself why?"

"I didn't have time to ask myself anything. He told me. He told me he did it to bring Rossi to his knees. To make Rossi give him the book."

"And Rossi told you what about that?"

"That we could use the tie to hunt Lavius down. Use it to kill him."

"Then why haven't you?"

"He said…." I frowned. "He said it wouldn't work."

"Either it works or it doesn't. Which is it, Delaney?"

"He lied." It wasn't a question.

Bathin nodded. "He lied."

"We can use the bite, the tie to find Lavius?"

"A vampire could."

"But he didn't want to because…is he on Lavius's side?"

Bathin raised his eyebrows. "Do you think Rossi would betray you? That's not really in his nature is it?"

Betrayal wasn't something I'd ever seen from Rossi. He was about as straight a shooter as anyone in this town. Clear about his wants, needs, goals.

Clear about his laws, rules, and punishments too. He was a steady hand and presence who dealt with all the vampires in this town. If someone crossed him, if someone broke his laws, he just killed them. No betrayal necessary.

"He's trying to protect me," I said, putting it together. "He promised my dad he wouldn't let anyone kill me, and he won't use the bite to…deal with Lavius because it might harm me to do so."

It felt right. Even if I didn't know the exact details, it felt right.

"He made that promise. Your father told me as much. It's the truth."

"If I believe you."

"If you believe me."

"How can the bite harm Lavius? Could we use it to…lure him into a trap? Slow him down? Chain him up?"

"We can use it to kill him."

I frowned. There had to be more to it than that. "How?"

"First, you have to die."

I didn't have a clock in my living room, so the silence that followed that statement wasn't broken up by anything except the push of wind scattering a few fir needles across my roof.

"Theoretically?" I ventured.

"Literally. He has tied you to him with only a single bite. There is a reason vampires turn their victims quickly or kill them quickly. Turning is final. Killing is final. But a single bite? That is a transient state."

"For him or for me?"

"For both of you. If you are killed, if you die while still being tied to him, he is vulnerable. For a very short time. Minutes. But just long enough to strike. He would be caught, tangled in your death, mortal, killable, no special spells required."

Chills rolled down from my scalp to my knees. This wasn't exactly good news. I understood why Rossi hadn't wanted to tell me. For one thing, it was a vulnerability in vampires I hadn't known existed. For another, I'd have to pay a pretty big price—the biggest price—for it to work.

"I'm not seeing this as our opening volley," I said.

"Which is why it would be so unexpected. Rossi won't know you have this information. Lavius won't think you'd be stupid enough to act on it."

"But you think I'm stupid enough?"

"Clever. Clever enough. Because you have me."

I raised my eyebrows.

He sighed. "And I have your soul. You won't die, well, not completely, as long as I hold your soul. I can keep death, or any other god, from taking you."

"And I trust you to do this?"

"Do you want to trust me?"

"Are you saying all this time you were holding my father's soul he wasn't really dead?"

"He was dead. His body died, and then we came to an agreement, before his soul passed into death. And after a year of being dead, unless the body is very carefully preserved, there is no going back.

"But for you, with this. It would take seconds. You'd would be back in your body before brain damage could set in."

"Way to sell it."

He shrugged. I felt like the sucker reaching for a dollar bill on a fishing line.

"How?"

"Some of that could be up to you. You'll need someone to kill you, and someone to bring you back from death. Since your pal Death seems fond of you, I'd start there."

"He's not fond of me," I said distractedly while my brain ran through this option. Who did I know who would kill me because I asked them to?

"Have you looked at his face when you're in the room?"

"Kind of hard not to," I said. "It's not me he's fond of. It's the very idea of humanity."

"Hate to break it to you, Butter Brickle, but he's been

staring at humanity, at the very idea of it for a long, long time. And not fondly."

"He won't kill me while he's on vacation."

"You're so sure of that?"

"After you left the meeting—"

"After I was rudely relocated by your heartless sister?"

I stopped and stared at him for a minute, taking in the details. Sure, I'd heard his words, but it was the tone that threw me.

He sounded...not angry. Anger, I'd expect. He sounded relaxed, content. The kind of tone someone would take after they'd had a great first date that ended with some front-step snogging.

"You liked it."

He rubbed his tongue behind his top lip and gave me a droll expression. "You're not listening to me. She attacked me. Jumped me. Impinged on my freedom of movement. I believe there are rules against that sort of thing in this town. I might want to file charges."

"She's a cop. The rules are different for her when she's operating in the best intentions for all citizens in question."

"Maybe I'll ask your boyfriend if her attack against me is in the rule book."

"She didn't attack you, she removed you from the premises because you were about to cause a riot. And you don't even hate her for it. You like it. Like that she figured out a way to out-smart you. How did she do that anyway?"

"It's a common enough spell." He took a sip of the wine. Even with all this sipping, he hadn't managed to take even a half-inch off of the level of liquid he'd poured.

"No, I really don't think it is common. Rossi said it wouldn't work on all demons. Care to float a theory as to why he told us that?"

"Not at all."

"Could it be because he mentioned the spell has to be counter-weighted by a demon's desire? That the demon has to want something from the caster for there to be enough leverage for the spell to actually work?"

"Vampires are not experts in magic or demon kind."

"What is it about her that you desire, Bathin?"

He sipped wine. Said nothing.

"If you're falling in love with her—"

His sharp laugh cut my threat short. "Hardly. A mortal woman, *any* mortal woman would never be enough to...maintain my interest."

"So you'll keep your hands off."

He nodded. "You're the only Reed for me, Delaney. And I find you very satisfying."

"Again with the not making me want to trust you."

"I don't need your trust. I've told you the truth. If you are killed, Lavius is vulnerable. The details of arranging your death and subsequent rebirth are up to you."

"Rebirth?"

"Oh, I'm sure you don't want my input on that. I might be lying. I am a demon, you know."

I set the wine glass down with a thunk. "Shut up and tell me."

He stared at me for a moment, his silence pointing out my stupidity louder than words. "Rebirth, as in coming back to life, resurrection, reanimation."

"It would be a temporary end?"

"It would be an end. But if you had someone powerful enough on your side, it might be temporary."

"And there are no side effects to...I'd still be...I wouldn't come back as a zombie, right?"

His mouth curled in a smug smile. "Have you ever met a zombie?"

"Answer the question."

"If you were brought back to life, you would still be you. Soulless, because, obviously." He waved a hand down his body as if I'd forgotten he was currently in possession of my soul. "But still you. Your life force, your spirit," he winced as if it pained him to say the words, "that could never be lost."

My pulse was sort of erratic and my skin was damp and cool. If I'd had emotions at my disposal, I'd guess I was both terrified and kind of hopeful. If I could take out Lavius without risking that the book fell into his hands when we broke the spell on Ben, then this chance might be worth it.

237

But I knew Myra, Jean, Ryder, and probably a pile of other people would not agree with me on this. They also wouldn't trust it would really work with nothing but a demon's word to vouch for it.

I stared at Bathin, and he returned my gaze, easy, direct, clear. As if he was showing himself to me, letting me look past his nature, or maybe past the disguise he wore for everyone else, all the way down to the realness of him. The bits that made him tick. The stuff of him that was, maybe still not good exactly, but not cruel, not evil, not toxic.

"We do it fast," I said. "We do it now. And we do it with people who will trust me, because no one will ever trust you."

"Hurts so much," he said airily. "And yet I go on."

I closed my eyes and worked through what I'd need. Worked through who I'd need.

"Okay," I said opening my eyes a few minutes later. "I have a plan. And you're going to do everything I say."

"At your service." His words were smooth and calm, but his smile was wicked and dangerous.

Was I making the stupid choice? Maybe. But this plan had a lot going for it: surprise timing, hitting a vulnerability Lavius wouldn't expect us to use, while protecting our own vulnerabilities: Ben and the book that could not fall into Lavius's hands.

And if we could keep this fight out of Ordinary, or at least away from all the people and creatures Myra was currently corralling for backup, so none of them were risking their lives?

So my sisters weren't risking their lives?

That was more than worth the choice, stupid or not.

CHAPTER 18

BATHIN MADE some kind of excuse of not caring who I dragged into our plan, since he didn't really know anyone in town and no one would trust him anyway. He told me he'd rather hang around my house, prying open my old diaries and laughing at my angst.

I left him to it (I'd burned all my old diaries when I'd turned twenty-three and spent a night reading them in embarrassment and horror).

If we were going to pull off a preemptive strike we'd need to have everyone on board and the plan set in action before midnight.

I'd thought about asking Myra to help me do this, but she would have cuffed me to the holding cell bars until next year.

Jean was in no state to pull off something like this, nor would Hatter or Shoe be up for the whole murder-your-fellow-officer I was going for.

I briefly considered Bertie because she was a Valkyrie, and familiar with war, death, and delivering spirits to specific places. But I'd have to listen to her lecture me about how stupid the plan was and if, by some remote chance, I actually talked her into it, she'd would force me into indentured servitude of rhubarb contest judgings and whatever other horrible community events she dreamed up.

Rossi had already told me where he stood on the idea of using my death against Lavius, and I guess Death had weighed in too since he'd just up and walked out on me when I'd asked him to make sure all sales were final as we punched Lavius's last ticket.

Aaron was too hungry for conflict, and honestly, I wasn't going to ask any of the gods to give up their vacation by picking up their powers. I'd done that once already. And while it had been worth it to save Ordinary, it felt weird to ask them to pick up their powers just to save me.

But I knew who wanted to kill Lavius more than was worried about me being temporarily dead.

I just had to convince him to do it.

The hospital hallway was quiet, lights lowered to give a false feeling of peace and comfort. I knocked softly on the door to Ben's room, but I hadn't needed to. The werewolves inside had amazing hearing and smell, and I'm sure they'd known I'd been headed their way since I hit this floor.

Fawn opened the door and tipped her head, sending her walnut-colored hair shifting from one shoulder to the other. "They're sleeping."

I nodded. "I need to say something to Jame. I wouldn't ask if it wasn't important."

She blinked and leaned a little forward to...sniff me? Okay. Weird.

"You stink like demon."

I laughed, one loud bark that made me slam my palm over my mouth before I woke anyone up. The joy of that true but disdainful statement slipped away into the breezy freezy no-soul hole in me, but for a moment, I'd enjoyed her snark.

"I could talk to him out here."

The look she gave me. "He's not going to go that far from Ben. Come in."

And, yes, that was possibly the only thing that would keep Jame from joining in on my little murder plan.

The room was much the same as I'd last seen it a few hours ago, except Jame and Ben were curled up alone in bed, the wolves who had been draped over Jame lounging in chairs they'd scrounged up from somewhere. The vampires who had been tucked away on the bench by the window were gone, replaced by two more of the Rossi clan who were playing a game of cards for a prize pot that appeared to consist of sour gummy worms and cigarettes.

Granny Wolfe was there, her eyes granite behind those big glasses, watching my every move.

"Jame," I said quietly. "I need to speak with you."

Jame opened his eyes, rolling his head enough so that he could see me without jostling Ben who was cradled into Jame's warmth as much as his wounds would allow.

"Speak," he said in a whisper that sounded like it covered a voice gone too long screaming.

"Outside this room would be better. So Ben can sleep."

That was it. My only shot. He'd either be curious enough to leave Ben behind and come with me briefly, or he wouldn't.

If he wouldn't, I'd find the next person on my list.

"You can talk here," Granny said. "What he hears, we all hear."

"Not this. It's private."

Granny pursed her lips, then sucked on her teeth, contemplating what to make of me.

Not having any emotions does wonders for one's poker face.

Jame didn't wait for Granny's decision. He shifted carefully, and by tender degrees, untangled himself from the man in the bed. Ben didn't open his eyes, didn't move. I glanced up at the bag of blood steadily dripping into him and wondered how many drugs it had taken to knock him out.

Granny's hand came to rest on Ben's shoulder so that he wasn't alone in the bed, wasn't without contact, but she did nothing else to object.

I stepped outside the door, held it open for Jame. He followed me down to the end of the hall to the first unused room. His movements were stiff at first, but strength and fluidity replaced sore muscles with each step.

This was stupid. Stupid to ask a man bent on revenge to be a part of a very logical, one-shot plan.

What was I doing?

I checked that the room was empty and shut the door behind us.

"We can kill Lavius before midnight. Which means we can break that spell on Ben. And Lavius won't be able to get his hands on the book."

"When can we do it?"

I searched his face. He looked more like himself. His eyes still burned with pain and anger, but his body remained solidly human, his stance that of the firefighter I knew.

"Now."

"I'm in."

"You'll have to leave Ben here and come with me to do it."

"I wouldn't let that filth here. Near him. Never again."

Right. That made sense.

"There's one more thing. Something that a lot of people won't be happy about."

He waited.

"The bite." My fingers fluttered to my neck and his eyes flicked to that point, then back to my face. "It ties me to Lavius. And when I die, he'll be vulnerable for a short time, mortal for long enough, we can kill him."

He was holding his breath. I could tell because I could feel the warmth of it as he exhaled, long and slow.

"No."

Huh. Maybe it had been more of a long shot than I thought.

"Okay. Well, I'll let you get back to Ben." I walked by him. His hand shot out and caught my elbow before I reached the door.

"Did you just offer to die so we can kill Lavius? Is that what you just did?"

"Temporarily die. Not like...not forever dead. You could revive me, right? You have paramedic training."

He growled softly. "That is the most stupid...don't do this, Delaney. Your death is not the answer. Where did you even get an idea like that?"

I didn't say anything.

"The demon." He sighed. "That demon isn't to be listened to. He took your soul. Now he wants your life. He wants your pain. Remember that. He will always want your pain. Don't kneel down and give it to him so easily."

"I don't. I won't." I wasn't even going to try to talk him into seeing it my way. "We still have a good plan. I just thought it was worth the risk if it meant we had a faster way, a more clear line of attack. I want Ben to be better. I want Lavius out of our lives. Permanently."

"Not like that. Not for that price." He lowered his head until he was sure I would hold eye contact with him. "You are important too, Delaney Reed. Important to Ben and me."

I nodded, wishing I knew what emotions I should be

feeling.

He let go of my arm.

"You're staying with Ben, right?" I asked.

"I'll be there when Lavius comes to die. I'll be there to watch him bleed."

"But until then?"

"Here. Keeping Ben safe."

"Good." I opened the door.

"Don't do it," he said again.

"I won't."

It was a lie. I wondered if he could hear it in my voice, smell it on my skin, see it in the movement of my body.

From the sigh he let out before he fell into step beside me, the answer was yes.

ONE WOULD think the advantage of living in a small town is that there is always at least one person who secretly, or not so secretly, wished you were dead and would be more than happy to make that wish a reality.

I hadn't thought it would be hard to find someone to kill me, temporarily, but Jame telling me he wouldn't do it sort of put a wrench in my plans.

If my friend wouldn't kill me for revenge, I'd just have to ask an enemy to kill me for fun.

"You want me to do what?" Brown asked, his voice a little too loud. I pulled my phone away from my ear. I could either go all police chief and demanded he do this for me, or I could try to tug on his heart strings.

Who was I kidding? Elves' hearts were little blobs of wickedness mixed with bad poetry stuffed behind their ribs. I turned my Jeep toward my house, heading up the gravel drive to the top of the hill.

"This isn't a favor," I said. "It's not a request. This is an order. You need to kill me tonight." Yeah, I'd gone with the police voice.

"I don't know what you're smoking, but no thank you, Chief. I'll just continue to live my life not behind bars."

"Do you remember that evil you felt, the…" I tried to

remember what he'd called it. "The ancient horror? We have a way to kill that. It involves me being temporarily dead."

There was a pause on the other end. I didn't even hear him breathing.

"Temporarily," he repeated.

"Just long enough to kill the bastard."

"That works?"

"I have it from a reliable source."

"And your sisters are waving the pom-poms and cheering you on?"

"No. I haven't told them, and I'm not going to. Because it sounds…"

"Crazy? Are you listening to yourself, Delaney?"

"You can tell me no. I'll find someone else, Brown."

"I didn't say no. I just don't know why you picked me. What about me makes you think I am capable of killing anything, anyone?"

"We aren't friends."

"That would be my point. Why ask me?"

"Unlike my friends, you aren't falling over yourself to protect me like I'm made of glass. You can be trusted to do a job, do it right, and step away. You have slightly shady morals. This is a job. And I'm asking you to do it. Not as a friend, but as a citizen of Ordinary who has a chance to help make this town and the people in it safe again."

Another pause.

Brown had said elves set down roots when they found their home soil, and I knew he'd chosen Ordinary as his home. He was a locksmith and security expert, so I knew he liked keeping things safe.

This should be something he wanted to do.

I waited, the cheery bright afternoon feeling wholly wrong with so much death and pain looming on the horizon.

"Fine," he said. "I'll come over to your house. We'll get it done."

Relief washed over me for an instant, soothing and clean before it was gone. "Good. Thank you. I'm here now."

"I'll be there in fifteen. I expect the door to be locked when I arrive."

"Promise."

I parked the Jeep and sat there for a few minutes, just thinking.

Myra and Jean would kill me when they found out about this. I knew that. They were already angry that I'd been attacked—not my fault—and even more angry that I'd traded my soul for Dad and Ben—totally my fault. It had been my choice and I still didn't think it had been the wrong thing to do.

But this?

Shit.

I lowered my head until it banged softly against the steering wheel.

This was wrong. Not telling them was wrong too.

And all the justification I was talking myself into, all the logic that pointed out it *wasn't* wrong, that powering through and taking action was the right course to follow was falling apart the more I thought it through.

Bathin was a demon. He'd tricked Dad into giving up his soul, tricked me into giving up mine. Jame wasn't wrong. Bathin liked pain.

But he'd saved Ben for me, for Jame. He'd brought him back as whole as he could. That had to stand for something, didn't it?

He could be playing a long con. He might want something more than just my soul and the freedom to walk around Ordinary.

Hell, he might want me dead. And he might have just found a way to talk me into helping him kill me, by making me arrange my own death.

Holy shit, that was slick.

I pulled out my phone, stared at the screen, then thumbed through my contact numbers. I needed to call smarter people who had souls and could trust their instincts and their minds better than me right now. I needed Myra's calm logic, Jean's sharp insight. I needed Ryder's decisive confidence.

I needed my family.

I hovered my thumb over who to call first, then pressed the picture of Ryder in his painted mask.

The phone rang once. "We got this." It was a weird way to

answer the phone.

"Good? What do we got?"

"Whatever you're worrying about."

"Who said I'm worrying?"

"I know that look on your face."

I closed my eyes for a second, and sighed. Then I looked out the window. "Where are you?"

He stepped up and tapped my side window. His phone was held up to his ear. "Roll down the window."

I could hear him on the phone and through the window. It was silly. And made me smile.

That made him smile, easy and warm.

I wanted that Ryder. Wanted to be the one who put that look on his face. But in order to do that, I'd have to be able to feel things. To have a soul. To have emotions.

Also, it'd be helpful if I weren't dead.

And if I weren't trying to push him away for his own good.

Why was my life so complicated?

I rolled down the window. "Officer," I said.

"Chief. Nice afternoon."

"It is. How was the riot?"

"Not as colorful as I'd expected. By the time we got there, Shoe and Hatter had it mostly under control. Myra stayed to help get some statements, mop up the crowd."

"So you decided to stop by?"

We were still talking into our phones, which wasn't necessary since we were just inches away from each other.

"I decided to find out why you're driving around town telling people you want to kill yourself."

And that, that was not joy, not love, not warmth.

That was pain.

I pulled my phone away from my face, and thumbed it off. Then I opened the door.

Ryder stepped back and I stepped right up into his space, my fingers gently on his hips, then, when he lifted his arms opening room for me, my arms wrapped around his waist so that I could press myself to him, tight, fitting us as if we had always belonged. As if he could be the heart that beat for the both of us.

"Talk to me, Laney. Tell me what you're doing. Explain…explain it. Because I can't understand this. Can't understand what you're thinking."

His mouth was pressed to my temple, and I could feel the softness of his lips, the scratch of his stubble as he spoke, so close to me, as if he could bury his words, his strength, his worry, deep beneath my skin.

As if he were trying to reach me.

"It's not as bad as it sounds. It's a way to take Lavius down without risking him getting his hands on the book. It's a way that will kill him. A way that he won't expect."

"By killing you?"

"Only a little."

His hand was pressed against my back, his thumb rubbing a slow arc.

"How'd you figure this out?"

"You are going to hate it."

"Bathin?"

I nodded.

We were quiet, and I counted his breaths, evenly spaced between the beats of his heart.

"Tell me."

"It's a vampire thing. An Achilles' heel. He only bit me once, so I'm not dead and I'm not turned. That in between state gives us an opening to kill him without risking the book."

"But we'd risk you."

I didn't answer because I didn't have to.

"How do we do it?" he asked. "Talk me through."

I hadn't nailed down the death part, hadn't wanted to think of how I would prefer it to go. "Bullet isn't my preferred, but I don't like knives either. Maybe suffocation? They say drowning doesn't hurt."

"Jesus," he whispered. "Just. Don't. I meant how do we kill him?"

"I thought Death could do it. If not him, Bathin. Maybe Rossi?"

"Beheading?"

"Rossi says it usually works."

Ryder was still, even his thumb stalling. I knew I should

move away. I didn't want to, but life was made up of lots of don't-wants that turned into gotta-do's.

"If we do this, we do it with Rossi right here at our side. And your sisters. Have you called Than?"

I eased back, took a step, but stayed close enough my fingers still rested at his waist. He shifted his hands to my hips.

"You'll do this? You'll let me get killed?"

"I'm not committed to it, no. But I can see the…rules of the tie you have to Lavius now that you pointed it out. It's fuzzy, but there is room in how the connection is implanted for the vulnerability to be exploited."

"So you don't think Bathin is lying?"

"Oh, I'm sure he's lying. But I think the connection could be a weakness for Lavius."

"That's…not what I thought you'd say."

"I heard Rossi. As soon as he breaks the wards on the book to kill the spell on Ben, Lavius is going to be all over us. The way I see it…we need to strike, without putting the book in his grasp, and without limiting Rossi from being able to kill him."

"Right," I said, disappointed that he hadn't put up more of a fight for me staying alive. "That's logical. The one thing Lavius wants is the book. If we can keep that out of play and still have a way of killing him, then problem solved."

"Problem not solved. I'm not going to let anyone kill you, Delaney."

I just stood there staring at him. Because what should I say to that? I'd just wanted to hear those exact words. But they were the wrong words now. They weren't the words that would solve our problems.

"I don't know what to do," I said.

There. That was the truth.

Ryder lifted one hand and cupped the side of my face. I leaned into that contact, his thumb stroking up the line of my cheek.

"We'll make a decision together and stick to it this time, okay?"

"You and me?"

"Well, and a few others."

That's when I heard the tires on the gravel approaching us.

I shifted away from Ryder, far enough we weren't touching and I could pull my gun if I needed it.

Two cars came up my drive. One was Myra's cruiser. No big surprise. The other was Rossi's VW bus in all its restored-to-original turquoise and white.

"You already called the cavalry?" I asked.

"Nope. You did when you went around asking people to kill you. Never turn to a life of crime. You'd make a really sloppy criminal."

I slapped his arm and he chuckled.

Myra got out of the cruiser, and so did Jean, who looked angry as a wet hornet with crutches and a cast.

Rossi's van opened and Brown stepped out, dimples and good looks fitting seamlessly with the summer day and plans of murder.

Rossi slid out of the driver's seat, stepped around the front of the van and then leaned against it, glaring at me.

"No one kills you." It was the kind of statement only a creature of power can really pull off. The kind that makes the words hammer down into your bones so that you feel them in the soles of your feet.

"I know what you promised my dad. But this isn't an end, it's an advantage. Lavius won't think you'd let me die because he knows you won't let anyone kill one of your own.

"You proved how you respond to your family being harmed with Ben's kidnapping. So let's use this advantage he's handily given us and take him down."

"Death is not a toy," Rossi said a little too loudly. "It is not a state of mind that can be entered into and out of like a room. It changes a mortal. Delaney, it will make you someone, *something* you are not."

"I'm already something I'm not. Soulless, remember? So yeah, I don't care about the changes death will force on me. After we kill Lavius, I'll get my soul back from Bathin. After *that* I'll find a way to deal with whatever marks death leaves on me, okay? I might be damaged, but this is not a permanent state for me. Not even close."

Even without a soul I knew I was a little more than mortal. I knew the limit of my own strength. I knew I could handle a quick death and quicker resurrection and come out of it still standing. I was a daughter of Ordinary. My roots, my blood, generations of Reeds chosen by gods sunk deep in this earth. Ordinary would hold me strong, just as I had held strong for it.

There was no storm we Reeds could not face.

"Could it work?" Ryder asked.

"No," Myra said, just as Jean said, "Oh, screw you, Bailey."

Brown had spent all this time staring up at my house, a look of confusion on his pretty face.

Bathin might be up there, watching us. The elf hadn't met the demon yet, but that didn't mean he couldn't sense him. He'd said he could tell when darkness and evil walked through Ordinary, and Bathin had those words written on the inside of his shoes.

"Could it work?" Ryder asked again.

He didn't need to ask Rossi that. Not really. He was all-powerful with the ability to see contracts, agreements, what would or wouldn't happen between connections. He had already told me he could see how the tie and my death could be used to gut Lavius.

Now he was just waiting to see if Rossi was going to lie about it.

I had to admit it was kind of hot.

"Do you really care for her so little as to ask me that, Ryder Bailey?"

Ryder clenched up, his muscles tight, and I could feel the effort it took for him to force his body to relax, to not just yell with the anger those words lit inside of him.

"I love her, you ass."

Holy shit. I think that was the first time I'd heard him say that word. Well, yell it, at a vampire, but still, it was for me. For us.

"Love her enough to know that this choice is hers. We can try to talk her out of it, we can offer other *better* options which is what I hoped we'd do.

"But her job is to keep Ordinary safe from all threats. And she is damn good at her job. Even when other people get in her way and keep vital information that could be the difference between her trying to do something on her own with nothing but a damn *demon* on her side, to doing something with the support of the people who *love* her."

Oh. Oh. I had not...I didn't think he'd see it like that.

But he wasn't done. "Not that I think death is the right option here. But if it *is*, if it is the path we walk, then I want to know every detail of how we're reducing the risks and getting her back. I will not be shy about writing this up and getting it signed in blood. Yours, if necessary. Understand?"

Something shifted in Rossi. He gazed at Ryder for a long, long moment, then back at me. There was judgment there, and sadly, disappointment. But there was also a sort of acceptance.

It wasn't like he was blessing our union, or even that he was agreeing with Ryder. But it was pretty hard to ignore the claim Ryder had just staked on me. On my capabilities.

His faith in me was humbling.

Things were going to be done, and however we went forward, it was going to be with full disclosure and a mountain of dotted i's and t's crossed in triplicate.

"Do you have a weapon that will kill Lavius?" I asked. "We're not going to go forward unless we have that, and a plan B in place, which could be our original plan A of making it up as we go."

"I have a weapon," Rossi said.

"Is it the book or a dark magic spell?"

"No. It is a blade."

"To cut his head off?"

Rossi reached behind his back and withdrew a dagger. It was short and wide, really no longer than his palm, and didn't look all that deadly. I thought it might be made of stone, dark and brittle, but when the light caught it, I realized it was made of clay.

"That's...that's it?" It looked small. Insignificant against an ancient evil.

"Yes."

"And you're sure it will work?"

He sighed and rolled his eyes heavenward. As if there was ever going to be any help coming from that quarter for him. "It will work. It is formed of the soil from the battlefield where he was originated."

And by *originated* he meant turned.

Oh. That gave that little knife a whole new level of killability.

"Like a stake to the heart," Ryder said.

"Better," Rossi agreed.

And I took a second, maybe three, to contemplate that Rossi had not only gathered up enough soil from the battlefield where Lavius had been turned to make it into a knife, but that he had also been turned on that very same soil.

Was that knife in his hands intended for Lavius, or had it been an option, a choice, a way out Rossi had kept for himself in case this world and existence became more than he wanted to endure?

I looked away from the knife and into Rossi's eyes. My answer was there, and that answer was, *yes*.

"Just the heart?" Ryder was asking, carrying on a conversation beyond the one Rossi and I were sharing.

"Any vulnerable point," Rossi said. "Through the eye, heart, neck, brain, groin. The same kill points one would seek for a human. Any other blade would not be enough, but this one." He stopped. And really, he didn't need to say any more.

This was a different kind of risk than giving up the book. This was risking Rossi's life. Because if the knife fell into Lavius's hands, it could be used just as easily and devastatingly on Rossi.

"If you do this, Delaney," he said, to me, and me alone, "we will both be risking our lives."

And if we didn't do this, if we waited and used the book under the full moon, it would be Rossi alone risking his life. The book would be in Lavius's control, and I was certain there were spells in it, dark magic that could be used to turn that knife on Rossi.

Rossi knew all that. Hell, he'd *planned* it.

"Is there a spell in the book we can use to kill Lavius faster than he can take the book from us?"

"No."

And that had been my last idea.

"Okay. We hit him with what we've got," I said. "Two plans. The first is using me as a weapon. Kill me, kill him, then find a way to bring me back. If that doesn't work, use the book to bring him here, endure whatever hell he'll unleash on Ordinary long enough to kill him. Then you all find a way to bring me back."

Everyone was quiet for a second. That promise, that agreement between Rossi and me solidified and settled. We were going to take his brother down. He and I. One of our deaths or both of our deaths given to protect the people we loved. To protect the home we loved.

We weren't going to do it alone. We were going to trust the people who loved us to dig us out of the hellhole we were about to bungee into.

Rossi understood that. I understood that.

He smiled, and it was the best thing I'd seen all day.

Then the quiet exploded into arguments. Everyone had an opinion, one they wanted me to understand, agree with, and accept.

But I only heard one voice. Oddly, it was Brown's.

"Uh, Delancy? Delaney?"

"What?"

That's when I noticed how pale Brown had gone, all the shadows of his face a sickly green, his eyes too wide and almost cat-feral.

"It's here."

He was staring up at my house. I turned to look, but it was just my house, up there. Nothing different.

Then pain hit me searing in a ripcord of through my chest and throat, burning too hot at the bite at my neck, exploding in my brain.

Come to me.

It was a whisper. It was a force that shut down every scrambling thought, every scrap of fear that fell useless through my grasping fingers. There was nothing. Nothing but that command.

Come to me.

I lurched, stumbled to keep my balance, blind with the need to follow. I would throw myself against walls, stone, broken glass to get to the one who owned me.

Not the demon. It was not Bathin's whiskey and smoke in

my mind.

It was snakes and oil, filth and hunger, rotted needs ambling through me, plucking, biting, sucking. It was Lavius.

Fight him.

The concept disappeared even as I thought of it. There was no world around me but his words, his needs.

I staggered up the stairs, my breathing too hard, everything hurting, and everything *craving*. I wanted him. Wanted him to want me. Wanted to throw myself at his feet, would carve a vein open for him and beg him to drink, to touch, to own.

Something in me was screaming.

Someone near me was yelling.

Someone was on the phone, I don't know why that detail stood out, but it did.

And then there was a hand wrapped around the front of my throat, a palm too cold to be alive.

"You are mine," Rossi said. The tiniest prick of pain flickered near the bite on my neck, and I struggled, fear finally huge enough to reach me even without a soul, even under Lavius's compulsion. The pain at my neck slipped away, was gone. I shuddered and sobbed.

Did Rossi just bite me?

"The hell, Rossi." That was Ryder. That was also the sound of a bullet being chambered. "Let go of her."

Things were not going well. Not at all. And I had no control over any of it, could barely track it all.

That, *that*, was enough to make me panic. But all my body could feel was the echo of panic, too far away, as it shook me and sent sweat down my spine.

"I didn't bite her," Rossi said. "It's a mark. With the blade. Her blood on my tongue a promise. Proof of what she is to me. If you want her alive by the end of this, Ryder put your damn gun away and follow my lead."

I couldn't see Ryder. Couldn't make my body move. I was caught there, at the top of my long stone staircase, staring at my front door, Rossi pressed close up against me, cold as marble, unyielding as steel.

And furious.

That, his fury, and his claim on me, protecting me with my

blood on his tongue, settled something in me.

Which, I know: weird. But he had always been in my life. A kind, if quirky figure. Loyal to keeping our town safe. Good to the people under his watch, and good to me.

His strength behind me, willing to see this through so that we could save this town, well …that was all I needed.

"Walk," he said near my ear. "Remember your soul is your own. Ashes can still hold hope and love holds power. Return to us. Don't get lost."

It was so close to the fortune cookie advice everyone else seemed to be giving me lately that I wasn't even surprised anymore. My soul was my own. Well, yes, and no. It was mine, but currently in Bathin's possession.

My heart. That belonged to Ryder.

I walked. I wasn't sure if I was doing it because I wanted to, because Rossi ordered me, or because Lavius had called me. My front door opened on the first try.

Brown made a frustrated sound, and I wanted to tell him I had locked it behind me and it still hadn't kept the bad guy out, but then I was in the room, in the house that had been my home for most of my childhood and almost all of my adulthood.

And I'd never wanted to turn and run away from a set of four walls so much in my life.

Bathin was there, I knew it from the tug in my chest, from the awareness of him that seemed to go along with him holding a part of me. But he wasn't who I was focused on. Wasn't who I felt myself dragged toward like a chain on a hitch.

Lavius stood in my home. In my living room, his back to the big picture window that looked out over the driveway, houses, greenery, and ocean below.

His eyes were on us.

On me.

"You have done well."

That made no sense. I hadn't done anything. Hadn't agreed to anything.

And that was when I realized he wasn't talking to me. He was talking to someone else.

Only a couple of people he might be having a conversation with. Rossi, which, yes, scared the hell out of me to think Rossi might be getting Lavius's approval and therefore might not be on our side.

Or Bathin.

"As we agreed," Bathin said.

That should not surprise me. But, hell.

Bathin was working with Lavius.

Bathin had betrayed me, tricked me. It made sense, how he so quickly found Ben when no one else could, how he had manipulated Dad into thinking he was the only demon who wanted a soul in Ordinary, how Lavius seemed to have access to demons to possess his vampires.

I wanted to be furious. So angry that even the briefest contact with the air I breathed would incinerate Lavius and his pet demon. But that emotion was beyond me, held at bay.

Bathin strolled over to stand next to Lavius. Not quite close enough to touch him, but near enough there was no mistaking that they were on friendly terms.

"Enjoying the sad little carnival now, Rossi?" Bathin smirked.

"Very much," Rossi said, his words like stone crushing the air Bathin dared breathe in his presence. "You will crawl for my mercy."

"Looking forward to it." Bathin batted his eyes.

"Silence!" Lavius demanded. "Kneel." He stabbed his finger and Bathin grit his teeth, then, as if a mountain were rolling over him, he buckled to the floor, breathing heavily.

Everyone else hit the floor too, except me, and Rossi, who still had his hand pressed over my throat.

Lavius wasn't even breaking a sweat, cool and put together in his sharply tailored suit, his black hair streaked with gray brushed back in a cut that spoke of money and power.

He didn't look away from me. "Did you bring me the book, *frater*?"

"No," Rossi said calmly, though I could hear an echo of old hatred behind the word. "You have stepped onto my land and harmed those who are mine. This is your ending."

"It is your weakness, this fondness for the animals we slaughter. Do you not know they are nothing but means to gain power? You have claimed this clump of dirt and the insects that crawl upon it. I have claimed all the rest of this world. And now this, too, will be mine."

He lifted his hand. In it was a gun.

Rossi stilled as only an unliving thing can.

Everything slowed for me. I felt the twitch of Rossi's hand where the clay dagger was still hidden, a small movement I might have missed if he weren't still holding me with his palm over my neck.

Since when did vampires use guns to kill each other? I thought only the knife or dark magic, or a beheading or stake through the heart would take out a vampire.

Hadn't Lavius gotten the memo?

I steeled myself for Rossi to shove me out of the way so he could stab Lavius. Instead, he whispered so that only I could hear him, "Forgive me, Delaney."

And then he shoved me toward Lavius. Toward his gun.

CHAPTER 19

I MIGHT be fast because of the bite, but I was not faster than a bullet.

It hit me, a bloom of heat and pain, right below my collar bone. The impact felt like someone had swung a sledgehammer at my chest.

Agony.

And then I was falling, the air turned to Jell-O, filled with screaming, yelling, and more gunfire.

I thought then—in that brief moment when I could no longer breathe, but couldn't bring myself to care about it—that Ryder was in that room. So was Myra, and probably Jean, who was totally stubborn enough to lump her way up the endless stairs to my front door.

I knew Brown was there too, and of course the demon and vampires. But I wished I could disappear, hide myself from my sisters and the man I loved. I wished they didn't have to see me die.

I also belatedly wished I'd done a little more research on how, exactly, someone was going to bring me back to life. As far as I knew not one of the people in the room had that power.

As far as I knew, a bullet to the heart wasn't something anyone had the power to bring me back from.

My body was too heavy to move, too heavy to pull air into. I exhaled, and it was a relief, everything foggy and warm and numb and good. I couldn't open my eyes, didn't need to. I was surrounded by comfort as if someone had just rushed in and wrapped the softest blanket around me, warm with sunlight, and fresh and clean.

I rested there, finally, happily forever.

"Ah, ah, ah. Not so quick, Delaney." Bathin's voice was a shock of cold water.

Everything spun away from me, and then…

…and then I was standing next to where Bathin knelt. No

time had passed, the stretch of forever in that sun-warmth comfort leaving no mark on this living world.

The room was slow-motion chaos. Myra ran toward me, firing at Lavius, but the bullets were taking years to cross the short distance of the room, and each fell just short of him, pausing before they clattered at his feet like kites suddenly crashing without the wind left to hold them.

Jean hobbled toward me, no gun in her hand, but the crutch braced in one hand so she could smash it into Bathin's head.

And Ryder.

Everything in me stilled when I saw him. He was looking at me. Not at my body, which lay in a curled heap, as if I'd fallen asleep in a messy knot, guarding my heart from my nightmares while the deep, red blood beneath me poured out in a growing pool.

He was looking at where I stood, his gaze just a degree to one side of actually meeting mine, his expression locked down and blank, a hardness there, an *inhumanity* I had never seen before.

Was this the face of the man who trained with the secret government department that hunted paranormal creatures? Was this the face of a man who slid into the position of law enforcement like a fish to the sea? Was this the face of a killer?

Yes.

His eyes ticked so that he was looking right at me. Right through me.

And I knew this was also the face of a man whose heart had stopped beating, and who had nothing left to live for.

"No," I whispered, my voice not carrying any farther than my own lips. "I'm here," I said, even as the echo of my words bounced back to choke me.

Ryder didn't hesitate, didn't pause. He swung toward the vampires, faster than anyone else in the room was moving. Lifted his gun, aimed it not at Lavius, but at Rossi.

Bathin was moving—hell, I was moving. I threw myself at Ryder, was flying, weightless, across the space between us, falling slowly, slowly, slowly.

Bathin lunged up off his feet, his face flame and stone as

the false mask of humanity he wore stripped away, melted from the inside out by the fire that ignited, exploded across his skin with each heavy, smashing step he pounded across my living room floor.

He ducked Jean's crutch, grabbed Myra and deposited her behind a chair without breaking stride.

Demon. Nothing moved with that kind of power. That avalanche of violence.

Then he lowered his shoulder and barreled right into Lavius.

The ancient vampire saw him coming. He lifted one hand, fingers tucked hard against palm, crooked out like hooks in a net.

Bathin grunted, and even though he was nearly bent at the waist, pushing forward, every granite fire-wrapped muscle straining, he could get no closer to Lavius.

"You are dust beneath me, blight," Lavius sneered. "Your service will be rewarded when I serve your head to your king."

I was still falling, caught in a slow motion that allowed me to see the rest of the room in close to normal time. Time enough to see Bathin's dark, unholy eyes go narrow with hatred. Time enough to hear the bellow of his snarl.

A flicker of pleasure rolled over Lavius's face. "Did you think I would ever trust you, princeling? You were nothing more than a means to an end. An entire kingdom of darkness is at my pleasure."

I missed what Bathin said, as I finally found my feet, so close to Ryder, all I would have to do is breathe forward to be pressed against his back. Ryder who squeezed the trigger and fired at Rossi.

"No!" I yelled again, the sound nothing but a whisper.

Rossi moved, fast. So *fast*. The bullets peppered the wall behind where he had been a fraction of a second before. Ryder's bullets useless against the vampire.

Lavius knew Rossi was here to kill him. Knew how fast Rossi could move.

Lavius turned, fired that gun, the one that had killed me, just as Rossi closed in on him.

That bullet snapped a hole below Rossi's left eye. Blood

oozed from it, so dark it was black. The smile on Rossi's face, spine-bright and full of bones, did not falter.

His hand rose and brought down the clay knife in a vicious slash at Lavius's face.

Lavius stepped back, smooth, easy, as if he had danced to this song a hundred times, a thousand times. He fired the gun again, Rossi dancing forward, closing the distance and taking the bullet in his chest as if it were no more than rain against his skin.

Rossi snarled, one hand flicking out to lock around Lavius's throat. He squeezed, nails digging beneath skin, foot hooking behind the other vampire's ankle.

Lavius countered, the gun now empty of bullets—how many had he fired—using the chunk of metal to slam upward on Rossi's arm trying to break his hold.

But Rossi would not let go. They tumbled to the ground, twisting and slashing, fast, fast, fast, cobras tangled in death throes.

They broke apart too quickly for me to see how, both of them bleeding in more places than just a moment before.

The clay knife was on the floor, kicked away by Lavius who pulled out a blade of his own. A blade like the one I carried, green and black with dark magic.

My blade! I reached for it, but I was insubstantial. I was nothing.

I was dead.

Even if I could use the blade it wouldn't kill Lavius, it would only slow him down.

Could that be enough to turn the fight to Rossi's advantage?

I ran back to my body on the floor, already in better control of my drifting state. Myra and Jean were there, Jean on her phone calling for an ambulance, eyes wide with tears, face shock-white, hand trembling. Myra knelt over me, trying to stem the bleeding on my chest with her jacket, her face grim, mouth moving around a single word over and over again: "please, please, please."

It was horrifying. I stumbled beneath the wave of guilt and fear and sorrow that crashed over me, threatening to drag me torn and tattered over the rocks of this moment, this pain.

I gulped air. Even though I was nothing but a ghost, I could feel that pain, could feel that bone-hollow sorrow.

I could *feel.*

It stopped me in my tracks.

Maybe a second went by, maybe a minute as I watched my sisters fighting for a life I wasn't sure I'd ever regain.

"The knife!" I yelled. "Myra, gods, get the knife. Stab him. Stab Lavius."

She couldn't hear me. She couldn't see me.

But Brown was suddenly there, his head cocked to one side as he stared at my body. "What? What knife?"

"You can hear me?" I rushed around so that I was standing next to him.

"Delaney?"

"The knife. Get the knife. It's in my belt. There. At my hip."

Brown frowned, and knelt, reaching for the knife while carefully staying outside the bloody pool. Myra didn't even say anything as he pulled it out of the sheath, didn't even notice him, her eyes too intent on my face, the snarl of her lips changing her chant to a curse.

Brown didn't move, just frowned down at the knife, glanced at my body and shifted his grip on the handle.

"No! Not on me. Don't stab me."

But it looked like that's exactly what he was going to do.

"Stab him!"

Brown's eyes flicked to my face, to Myra, back to me.

Damn it.

I grabbed his wrist, intending to point the blade at Lavius.

Brown shivered, but held very still. My hand had sunk all the way through his hand and sort of aligned with it, like I was pulling on a well-fitting, overly warm and slightly squishy glove.

Ew.

"Show me," he demanded.

Those two words were more than a demand, they were a path, an invitation, a compulsion.

I stepped forward, stepped *into* Brown.

A thousand sensations swamped me: a body, warm and beating around me, vision so sharp I could see the motes of dust in the sunlight coming in from the window, could smell each distinct kind of blood mixing in the air, could hear...

...everything. The trees hummed of wind and sun and deep, dark soil, the seagulls sang of food and sand and shells to crack, even this old house grumbled about the loose-fitted window pane and missing shingles.

No wonder elves—well, Brown—made good thieves. The whole world was yelling and whispering and pouring out all its secrets.

I could hear the knife too, a hiss of death, death, death, steady as a drip of acid.

"Stab Lavius. This will slow him down. Use the knife. Use the knife."

I lifted my hand, hoping he might feel it.

His hand lifted. He nodded. "Show me."

I didn't need to be asked twice. I ran, Brown's feet rising and falling as if this were my own body. His breath was caught, ragged and weird in his chest. This wasn't comfortable for him, might even be painful.

I hesitated.

"Do it," he breathed.

And so I did. I rushed up behind Lavius—silent as only an elf can be, a part of the world around me and leaving no trace behind as only an elf can be, and maybe most importantly, fast as only an elf can be—and plunged the knife deep between Lavius's ribs, angling the stroke upward toward lungs and heart.

Lavius jerked, yelled.

The impact of that sound of unholy pain threw me out of Brown's body, shuddering and raw, desperate for escape.

Brown groaned and dropped the knife like it was on fire, then bolted, stumbling over his feet, trying to get out of the blast zone of the ancient horror, the vile *thing* that Lavius was made of.

Rossi swung, his bloody fist gripping the clay knife again, his face drenched in thick black blood, one eye gone blind as he bared his fangs and shouted old words, old promises, old curses, old, dark magic.

The clay knife angled down, fast, too fast for mortal eyes to track, and somehow achingly slow.

The blade buried to the hilt, and still he thrust it deeper, fueled by his rage, into Lavius's throat.

Lavius threw out both arms and shook, shook, his body thrashing while speared in place as if a lightning rod had just skewered him from skull to sole.

The air filled with screeching, howling, darkness.

And then Death strolled into the room.

CHAPTER 20

"THAN," I said. "Help. Please, help."

His eyes flicked to me and they were endless, deep, and oddly, not unkind. It was Than, the god-playing-mortal in my little town-playing-normal. But it was more. It was Death.

His god power shifted and flowed around him like a cape of smoke and fire, flickers of light falling like ashes and snow stirred by the heartbeat of power.

"Every living thing ends," he said, a voice of forever, a voice of time echoing, song, shadows, and light.

No one was moving in the room; it was as if time had broken, the world stalled, the universe halted on its eternal pivot.

Only Lavius was moving, his mouth opening and closing around a silent scream, his eyes wide with terror.

I saw my friend, Than, the god of death, resplendent in his cloak of power.

Lavius saw his end.

"Death is patient," Than said almost softly. "But death always, always wins."

Than lifted one hand and that cloak of power unrolled from around him, wings of stars, of darkness, of something so good, it made me ache with wanting to touch it.

Wings that wrapped around Lavius, folded and cradled and covered and smothered until there was no more movement in Lavius's body, no more pleas on his lips, no more light in his eyes.

He fell, just as slowly as I had, landing hard and solid on the floor.

Death turned his gaze to Rossi, who stood, covered in blood—his own and his brother's—his expression anger, sorrow, hatred.

"Travail," Death whispered.

Rossi turned toward Death, met his gaze. Waited for his judgment.

"Beg me to spare you," Death said, and there was no longer anything friendly or human in his tone.

"Bring her back to us." It was whispered, I thought, in a language I did not know, but still understood. "I will pay her passage." Rossi fell to his knees, but did not look away from death, did not bow his head.

"Perhaps," Death said, "it has already been paid."

"No," another voice rang out.

I spun. Ryder crossed the room to stand before Death. He looked taller, wider, his body outlined in a hard yellow light. But it was his eyes that frightened me. That might be Ryder's body, but it was not Ryder looking out of that gaze.

That was Mithra, the god who owned him, the god who was using him as his vessel. The god who did not like any of us Reeds enforcing the rules and laws of the town.

The god who would be happier if I were dead.

"You have no power here, Mithra," Death said.

"My power resides in all laws of the universe," Mithra said, "Even in the laws of death." It was Ryder's voice, but colder, harder.

"You do not rule over me," Death intoned. "I am eternity."

"I rule over the contract Reed blood has made with the gods of Ordinary. Delaney's death must be final. The bridge is no more. The Reed guardians have failed to uphold their vows to the gods within its borders. They must relinquish their station to the standing warden. Ordinary will follow my rule. As it is written. As it should have always been."

Was that true? Was our status as guardians, my status as a bridge that allowed god powers to be set down when gods vacationed in Ordinary so tenuous? Was there nothing more that held us tight to this land?

"You are within Ordinary, Thanatos," Mithra said. "You must bide these laws."

Death's smile was frightening, cold, cruel. "Death is everywhere. Death is all. Beginning and ending. And within Ordinary's boundries, all gods can die."

He lifted one hand, his fingers long pale bones and claws.

Ryder stiffened as if a hook had sunk into his chest. He shuddered, convulsed, the light in his eyes fading.

"No!" I yelled. I threw myself between Mithra and Death. "Don't kill him. Don't kill Ryder. Please, Than. Please."

It took a breath, two, before Death relaxed his hand. There was blood at the corner of Ryder's mouth, but he didn't seem to notice it.

"Enough," Bathin said, his voice low, thick, and hot. "Delaney only dies and reliquishes Ordinary's guardianship if I say she dies. I hold her living soul, as has been agreed, a favor to Death."

I didn't look away from Death even though Bathin's words tumbled around me in confusion. He had my soul because of Death? A deal they had made?

"Lies," Mithra hissed.

Bathin strode forward, his true form clear to me in my ghostly state. He was huge, dark, fire and ash, powerful. But was he powerful enough to take down a god?

"Can you not see the contract agreed upon between she and I, Mithra? Has your power so dulled? Challenge my hold on her, god. It will amuse me."

Really? Was I going to have to stop a demon and god fight to keep Ryder safe now too?

"Not helping," I said to Bathin.

But Ryder's head snapped up, realization twisting his face with an ugly hatred I had never seen before.

"You are *nothing*!" he screamed at Bathin.

"I am demon." His nostrils flared and lightning flickered in his smokey eyes. "And my contracts, are rock-fucking-solid."

And there, next to Bathin, appeared my father. Hope from ashes. He wasn't as clear as he had been when I'd seen him trapped in the stone with Bathin, but there was no mistaking his smile.

"As is the law of Ordinary," Bathin went on unrelentingly, "when one bridge dies, another of the Reed family will rise and take their place. As is the agreement made with the previous bridge of Ordinary and Death himself," Bathin said, "Robert's soul has been here, within the borders of this town, housed within me. I am alive. And therefore Robert is very much alive. He can take Ordinary upon himself again, through me as his conduit, or he can give it to his daughter, Delaney when she returns to her body. You, Mithra, have always been too late to stake your claim to this land."

I blinked hard. Shook my head at my dad. I thought he'd died. When I'd made that deal with Bathin, I thought my father's soul had gone onto death.

Not so, my child, Death whispered in my mind. *It was not his time. But now...yes, soon.*

Mithra glared at the demon, at my father, at me. Then finally, at Death. "You allowed this?"

"A favor owed to a friend of mine."

He meant my dad, not the demon. I was sure of it.

"I could destroy this land," Mithra said.

"You would have to destroy the original gods who created it first," Death said. "One stands before you."

Mithra scowled. Then his face, well, Ryder's face, cleared. He nodded once.

"Checkmate, Thanatos," he said. "I concede this match to you."

Death is patient. And Death always wins.

The light in Ryder's eyes dimmed to the normal, beautiful hazel I knew and loved. He looked confused, pale. He couldn't see me. I wasn't even sure if he could see the room around him as he lowered himself to the ground, exhausted.

"Dad?" I asked, moving toward my father.

"Ah-ah. No." Bathin's words stopped me. "There is no more time."

Dad mouthed something, and I could hear it like a sigh on the wind, *"I love you."*

Death held his hand out. Dad's eyes were so bright. His smile became a grin as he accepted Death's hand. His soft laughter filled the air as he became a single spark of light in the swirling cape full of lights that surrounded Death.

"Oh," I said, because it was the only sound I could make. He was gone. This time, I knew, he was truely gone.

"Reed Daughter," Death said. "I think you've had quite enough of resting here. It is time for you to return to your heart."

My heart. Ryder. Myra. Jean. Ordinary, and all the people within it.

"Just so," Death agreed.

The world hitched, a giant machine catching on the gear that ground it forward through the universe.

And then everything began again.

"Wait," I said.

My words echoed back to me, time crashed on and on, seconds, minutes, all too fast, all too loud, and I inhaled a ragged breath.

Pain. So much pain.

"Damn it, Delaney," Myra sobbed. "Keep breathing. I'm going to kill you, so keep breathing."

There were sirens, voices, hands. Too many smells, colors, sensations. I tried to reach for them all, hold them all, cling tight to them all, because I knew it was life, this messy mix of pain and hope and joy and heat and tears.

I saw, briefly, Myra's face, streaked with tears, splotchy cheeks against paper-pale skin, eyes red and glassy. "You are such an idiot. Keep breathing. Just keep breathing." She tried to smile and it made it all worse. "Everything's going to be okay.

SOMEONE WAS watching me.

I opened my eyes, the unfamiliar ceiling and low light of the hospital room blurring for a few breaths while I blinked and blinked. My chest felt heavy, so I didn't even try to take deep breaths.

I did move my hand a little. Everything hurt in that distant way that let me know I had a wall of painkillers between me and my injuries. The sterile smell of oxygen explained the tube at my nose.

Okay. I was hurt. How badly?

Memories fell out of my head in one big clump. The gun, Lavius, Rossi, Bathin, Ryder, Brown, my sisters, Dad and Mithra and Death.

Lavius was dead. I'd seen him burn in Death's embrace. I tried to hold onto that as a crawling panic slapped hands all over my skin as if trying to make sure I was awake.

Had I been shot?

Had I been shot *again*?

I blinked some more, trying to focus on the room, and not my racing thoughts. Thoughts that felt an awful lot like fear.

I could feel again? Was I was alive? What exactly had happened?

"Easy, Delaney, you're okay."

Myra's voice, a little flat and tired, but there, right there. Then I felt her hand catch my hand and squeeze, saw her stand up and lean over me and wait until I could focus on her face.

"Hey," I breathed.

"They have you on some heavy drugs, so it's okay if you feel tired and weird. You were shot, but the bullet disintegrated. It wasn't made of metal."

Not sure I should be excited about that. "What was it made of?"

"Dirt and blood."

I felt the nauseating panic stick fingers down my throat.

"They've cleaned out everything they can. You're on some heavy antibiotics, and you ran a fever for a while."

The details—common, normal—helped me keep my footing as panic sluiced around me. "How long?"

"A week." She smiled at whatever look crossed my face. "Oh, you're going to pay for this, don't worry. I'm furious at you, but right now I'm just happy you're alive." She shook her head. "You're officially suspended from work for a month."

"What? You can't—"

"I can, and just did. You need to take some time and work on healing. And maybe...maybe you should talk to someone, figure out how you can guarantee you're not going to make these kinds of decisions under pressure again."

"You would have done the same thing." Panic was getting overridden by my indignation.

"No, Delaney. I would not have. I would have gone to you. We would have made a plan, and I would have followed that plan."

She waited for me to argue, even though she knew I wouldn't.

"I was trying to keep everyone safe," I started, my voice more unsteady than I'd like. "Ben was gone, Jame...he was in so much pain...and Dad...what was I supposed to do? This is my home. They're my family."

Myra reached up and silently wiped the tears off my face,

then tucked a tissue in my hand. "I know," she said, as she gently placed a kiss on my forehead. "I know, honey. You can sleep now. It's going to be okay. You're going to be okay."

I thought maybe she said something else, but time snapped, and when I opened my eyes, the room was much brighter than it had been.

"Hey, beautiful." Ryder.

I smiled and he smiled back. He leaned over me, his face close to mine, his hand coming up to cup the side of my face, thumb stroking my cheek. "It's good to see you awake."

I could feel the warmth of him, smell the clean scent of sawdust and sunlight that clung to his clothes, and the spicy undertone that was all him. There was nothing left of Mithra in him now.

"I'm sorry," I started.

"Shhh." He leaned down, hand still holding my face, and tilted his mouth to mine, kissing me softly. My lips were chapped, but that didn't seem to bother him.

"You're okay. We're okay. Your sister's a little pissed off, but me and you? We got this."

I swallowed back the tears that threatened to fall. Why was I always crying? Maybe not having my emotions for so long made a kind of backlog and now I was doomed to over-feel everything.

Or maybe I'd been shot, died, and had woken up here, in my town, with my family, and the man I loved.

"You're not mad?" I asked.

"I didn't say that." The slash of smile he gave me was teasing. "But unlike your sister, I prefer a fair fight. I'll wait until you're on your feet before I lower the hammer."

I huffed a laugh and that made him smile more. "Do you remember? Mithra?"

He frowned. "Back at the house? I called on him. I think. Asked him to help. I was desperate. I think I blacked out."

"Oh," I said. I wasn't sure how he was going to take being controlled by a god. Maybe it was a discussion that could wait until after I could think straight.

"There we go. Think you'd like to sit up a little? Maybe try our vast array of gourmet ice chips?"

His thumb was still stroking my cheek gently, his eyes holding my gaze, filled with warmth and love and comfort.

"You know I like to live dangerously."

That tightened the edges of his eyes, but only for a moment.

"Too soon, baby. But yeah, you've always been a troublemaker. I don't think one little fight with a vampire is going to change that. I wouldn't want it to."

"But?" I said, because I could hear it in his voice.

He turned away to fiddle with the buttons on my bed, and I missed his touch immediately.

"But we're going to set some rules, agree on some boundaries for how we all pitch in to look after this town and all the people in it."

"We already have rules."

"You have rules, which you ignore when it suits you. I'm thinking I'm a guy who'd like things written down with signatures signed nice and neat on the dotted line."

"I thought you said that wasn't who you were." The bed lifted, and even though I was still on pain meds, I wasn't too groggy, or too sore to enjoy the change of position. I didn't know how long it'd been since Myra had been here watching me, but she wasn't in the room now. Right now, it was just me and Ryder.

"I'm exploring the possibility that my new position as warden of this town might have its upsides."

Ugh. That was exactly what none of us needed. Another person, especially one doing the bidding of a meddling god, all up in our supernatural business.

"I see you are thrilled with the idea."

"Myra and Jean won't like it."

"Jean suggested it. Myra agreed to it so quickly, I didn't even have time to argue her into it."

"Traitors," I grumbled.

"Sisters who want to keep you around for a few more years."

"I know how to do my job without you setting rules for me to follow."

"I won't be setting the rules. Well, I won't be the only one.

We're going to all come to an agreement on rules. All of us who are here to look after Ordinary. All of us who put our lives on the line."

Just thinking of Myra and Jean putting their lives on the line in the same way I had pushed fear and then—even stronger—guilt through my veins.

"I really screwed this up, didn't I?"

He was done with the buttons and had straightened the blanket over my feet. Now he was moving around to the side table where I assumed the ice chips awaited.

"I'm gonna have to go with yes on that." He sat on the edge of my bed, then scooped out ice with a plastic spoon. "But we got through it. We all got through it." He nodded, and it sounded like he'd been telling himself that for a few days now.

I reached over and pressed my hand on his thigh. "I am so sorry," I whispered.

He nodded again, suddenly very interested in dumping that ice chip back in the cup and searching for a replacement. His shoulders straightened and he twisted, ice balanced on the spoon.

"I know." He waited for me to open my mouth for the ice.

I did and the sliver coated my tongue with clean, cool relief. I rolled it around, trying to coat every part of my sticky tongue and sore mouth.

"So. There are a few things that we'll need to take care of today. That's why we asked them to lower your painkillers. Are you too uncomfortable?"

I took a second to give my body a quick assessment. I was sore, yes. And there was no way I wanted to stand, or do anything else to put weight—even just a shift of gravity—on my lungs, but all in all I wasn't doing too badly.

"I'm good for now."

"There's a button that you can hit if you need morphine, okay? But if you're ready for some company, I can go get everyone."

"Everyone? How many? Who?"

"All the gods, your sisters, Hogan, Bertie, Shoe and Hatter. Probably a few more now that they know you're awake."

"And here I am, looking my best."

"You look amazing." He leaned down and kissed me again, and I decided I could live with that little lie between us if he kept doling out those kisses.

"Ready?" he asked.

"Why all the gods?"

He was silent a second, studying me. "Myra said you should know. You should feel it."

"I don't know what she's talking about."

He placed his hand on my leg, fingers warm, palm heavy. I wanted him to rub his hands all over my body and let him remind me I was alive, whole, me.

"You died, Delaney." He paused, letting me absorb that. "The bridge to Ordinary died for a very short time. The permission and avenue for all gods to vacation here, to set their powers down, died."

His voice wasn't quite as steady on the third repeat of my death, and I never wanted to hear him say it again, but braced for it anyway.

"When that happens…." His eyes went distant, as if he were reading text hanging in the air between us. "…the power of the bridge must be given to a new member of the Reed family."

That thumped me pretty hard, and I exhaled. "I'm not…I'm not the bridge anymore?"

"No. You are." His eyes focused. "There's a bit of a loophole for temporary death, reincarnation, and apparently favors from Death to your father."

"Yeah?"

"Yes. You weren't gone for very long, technically, not even dead. Your soul was not given to Death, nor your spirit. So while the bridge was absent from Ordinary for a short time, your dad's soul was housed in a living being, so he was able to hold it until you were back in your body. I still don't know how he pulled that off."

"Okay." Was this where I told him the demon had admitted I couldn't really die unless he wanted me to die? I didn't actually know what that meant in the long run, didn't know why all the gods were here to see me, either.

"Ready?" he asked.

No.

"Sure."

Then he got up, and opened the door for all the gods of Ordinary.

It had been awhile since we'd had them all together in one place. And honestly, the hospital room, though fairly spacious, wasn't quite up to the task of containing them all comfortably.

That didn't stop them. Every god and goddess of Ordinary filed into the room, uncomplainingly standing as close together as they could around my bed.

I couldn't see them all from my vantage, but the gods closest to me: Aaron, Than, Odin, Zeus, Frigg, were familiar faces.

"Hi," I said. "How are you all doing?"

Aaron was the first to speak. "You just cancelled our vacations. How do you think we're doing?"

"Don't," Ryder, who had somehow made his way through the crowd of bodies to stand at the head of my bed said.

And surprisingly, Aaron listened. I must really look a mess.

"We're leaving, Delaney," Odin said. He had the growler full of power hanging from the crook of one thick, scarred finger. "For one year, as we must."

"Leaving? But..." I looked at a few faces trying to make sense of this, "Why?"

"You died a bit." Odin scowled, angry at me for revealing that little failing of mine. "Enough that the bridge was gone, and so all of our powers returned to us. Since it was either pick them up, or forfeit them to some random mortal, we picked them up."

"All of you?" I said, still not following as quickly as I'd like. "All of them?"

He flipped the latch and uncorked the growler, then tipped it upside down. He didn't actually have to do that to prove to me that the powers were no longer stored there, were no longer in his keeping. I could, if I focused right, see the powers flowing through the flesh and bones of the people around me, could hear the songs, the rising chorus and sheer magnitude of influence, force, and will.

"All of us," Odin said, and that was when I realized it wasn't just my friend Odin standing there. It was Odin the god, wise and weary, his one eye already set on a distant horizon, the power drawing him forward into the world and universe as surely as a sail in the winds of a storm. "All of the powers."

Those words were final, a hammer on the stone of this moment, inexorable, inescapable.

And then all of the gods, all of the goddesses, people I had known all of my life, shopkeepers and artists, business owners and hermits, volunteers, almost-uncles and aunts, do-gooders, do-nothings filed past my bed and said goodbye. A touch of a hand, a brush of lips on my temple, a wave of power, power, power, moving and flowing like a river I could not stop, sliding through my fingers, racing toward the sea.

It seemed only fitting that when they had all left the room there was only one god remaining.

"Hi Than," I whispered. My chest was tight with the effort to not break down completely. Tears ran hot and silent down my cheeks, and the collar of my hospital gown was wet.

"Reed Daughter," he said as if this was the first time we'd met. "This was a most interesting experience."

I winced. "I'm sorry you only got a couple months here. I'm sorry you have to go. This is all my fault. I promise it will be better the next time you come back. Please come back." That last was so small, I wasn't sure if he'd heard it.

"Dear child." He reached out, his arms long, his fingers, slender like pale blades. He cupped my hand in both of his, and his touch was warm, comforting. "I did not say it was an unpleasant experience. Nor am I unhappy with how these events have played out."

He paused, those eyes, endless, cold, filled with the power of the ultimate end, flickered with something else. Warmth. Humor.

As if he had a say about how the events had played out.

Wait. Had he?

"All the gods leaving?" I asked.

He waited.

"Lavius's death?" The cables cinching my chest loosened. "You wanted him dead, didn't you?" My brain moved sluggishly, trying to put the pieces together through the muzzy painkillers. "You planned this? You came here...did you send that stone to

Dad? Did you…" The enormity of it, if it were true, knocked the words out of me.

Had Death sent Dad that demon-filled stone? Had he known Dad was going to die, and thrown his lot in on the chance Dad would negotiate with the demon, who would in turn negotiate with me?

But if that were true, Death would have had to have known so many other things would happen, would all fall in a row like black dots on white dominos—bones and holes manipulated by his hand.

He'd have to know that Heimdall was going to be killed. That Crow would screw up and allow the god Mithra to claim Ryder. That Lavius was on the hunt for dark magic and was making his move toward Ordinary. That Sven would be killed, the vampire hunters drowned in Lavius's bid to catch Rossi's attention.

That Ben would be kidnapped, Jame nearly killed, and me attacked.

And I wondered that anyone, even Death could have known all those things, could have so carefully planned each happening.

Or maybe he hadn't planned it. Hadn't planned anything. Fate was a different god power, after all, and so was destiny.

Maybe he just knew what was inevitable. Maybe he could see the beginnings of everything that was to happen because he was, ultimately, the end that allowed it to be.

I had wondered, back on that day he had called and met me at the casino over frou-frou coffee to negotiate the terms of his application for vacation, why he had decided to vacation in Ordinary now for the very first time.

Had he talked to my dad by then?

If he knew this was all going to happen, had he decided this was his chance to remove that one ancient evil out of the world, and claim a death denied to him for centuries? If so, then maybe this all made sense.

"You knew." It wasn't enough to carry all the nuances of my understanding, but it was all I had room for with the stunned shock and admiration filling me.

"I am sure I do not know what it is you think I knew."

"Everything. You knew everything."

A curl of his mouth—so *so* close to a smile, though a sly one.

"I am a very old god, Reed Daughter. I know a great many things."

"Lavius," I tried. "You wanted him dead. You knew he was making a play, would make a play. And you knew what he'd do. You've wanted him dead for years."

"Centuries." With that one word it was Death, grim and cruel standing beside my bed holding my hand, his skin gone smooth and cold as marble and steel. "Centuries," he hissed.

There was a burning hunger there, an anger at a war long fought, and slowly, there was the sense of a vicious victory.

"And Dad? Bathin? Mithra? You knew?" My throat closed around those words. Had this all been a move in his game against Lavius? Had he killed my father, all but sold my soul for this game?

"Ah, Delaney. Do you not know me better than that?"

I searched his face. I thought I knew him once. I was beginning to believe I should never make that mistake again. "Do I?"

"Yes," he said firmly. "You do. I would never bring a man to his death early just to satisfy my impatience." And there was more behind those words. He had not killed my dad, didn't make the deal with the demon to do so, didn't make *me* deal with the demon. Maybe he nudged things, allowed the options to unfold, offered his favors.

We made our choices. All of us. Dad, me, Bathin, and certainly Lavius.

Free will, baby.

I nodded. I'd known Than for less time than any other god who had stayed in Ordinary. I supposed it didn't make sense to trust him so much. But I did.

He'd brought me back to life, hadn't he? And he'd somehow made Bathin give me back my emotions.

"Thank you," I said. It covered a lot of things, but I wanted to make sure I specified a few. "For letting Dad stay, and for taking him gently." He'd told me once that when Dad had died, he'd had a lot of questions for Death. Now I knew those questions involved a demon, an ancient evil, our safety, and Death's favor.

"For killing Lavius. For letting me return to the living. And for making Bathin give me back my soul."

Both eyebrows rose and his eyes sparkled. "The demon still possesses your soul."

"He...does?" That was weird. Because I could feel. Like right now, I felt surprise. And confusion. "But I can feel."

"Ah. I believe you'll need to speak to your sister about that."

"Myra." I didn't even have to ask. I knew it would have to be her. And oddly, I knew she might be the only one who Bathin would listen to. But his deals never came without a price. If she had done something stupid, I was going to get out of this bed and kick her butt.

"Now. It is time for me to leave this quiet shore." Thanatos patted my hand, more like a fond uncle than the embodiment of death.

"It's only a year. That's the rule. Any god who picks up his power only has to be gone for a year."

"Yes?" There was curiosity in his tone.

"Please don't stay away," I blurted.

And then, right there in front of me, with Ryder as a witness, Death smiled.

"I wouldn't dream of it, Reed Daughter. I still have so many kites to fly." And with that, he turned and walked toward the door, straight and lean, head held high as he faded into smoke and gray and was gone.

I exhaled, and it came out on a shaky laugh. Ryder squeezed my hand and I realized he'd been holding onto my hand this whole time. I squeezed back, and watched the door, wondering if this was really over now. If this had all been about gods and ends, or if there was still a beginning for us, for Ordinary.

A beginning that didn't involve any more death, blood, or murder.

The door opened and Myra and Jean strolled in, followed by Shoe, Hatter, and to my surprise, Hogan, but not Bathin.

"Hope you ordered orange juice," Myra said. "This might take a while."

CHAPTER 21

SHE WAS not joking. Myra and Jean settled in for the long haul, bringing in comfortable chairs, tall cups of coffee and a tray of fruit for finger food.

Hatter and Shoe had stayed for just a few minutes. Gave me a hard time about how I'd obviously missed the class for how not to get shot by a gun twice in one year, and then they'd left to keep the streets of Ordinary safe for the tourists, creatures, and residents.

Not gods though. Because there were no more gods in Ordinary.

That was weird.

The demon hadn't shown up yet either. I'd expected he'd want to be here to see me get lectured by my sisters, but apparently he had other demon-y things to do. Or maybe he was gone for good.

Since he still had my soul, I wasn't sure if that would be better or worse.

Probably worse, knowing my luck.

Also, I planned to get my soul back. There was no way I was going to let him keep it a moment longer than necessary.

"Are you still listening to me?"

Myra had been going on about how many businesses had just been abandoned by their owners, and how many residences were now standing empty. It was a logistical problem we'd never had to address before: a mass exodus of so many gods and goddesses. It was going to be a huge pain on a practical level for security, ownership, upkeep and day-to-day routines.

All of the deities had been hands-on with their interests and hadn't left a lot of staff behind to deal with it all.

It wasn't really a problem if Odin wasn't around to make more terrible chainsaw art, and we could drive by his cabin once a week to make sure no one had broken in, but there were gods who ran much more vital businesses. Hades' popular bed and breakfast, Athena's surfing shop and lessons, Aaron's yard and garden nursery, Zeus's fashion boutique.

"I'm still listening," I said. "And I agree with the plan so far. We let the lead workers at each business step up into managerial positions, make sure they're compensated for it…that's in the gods-own-business rules somewhere isn't it?" I glanced at Ryder.

He looked up to the left, as if running through a card catalogue in his head.

"Yep. There's a pool of money set aside for this contingency. All of the deities have been contributing to it over the years. We'll need to find out how to access…oh, the Reeds are executors. So." He shrugged. "We're good to go."

Okay, so it was getting to be pretty nice to have contract man as my boyfriend.

"We'll check in on their residences, but otherwise keep them as is until they return," I said. "Let's say twenty-four months. We'll hire a service to air them out once a month."

"All right." Myra lifted her cup to take a drink, found it empty and stood to toss it into the little trash basket in the corner. She stretched, her hands pressed against her lower back before sitting back down.

I didn't know how long she and Jean had been here, but I was starting to get hungry. And tired. Also, I still ached, but didn't want to take the morphine boat into night-nightville.

"What else is important, Mymy?" I asked. "I'm fading pretty fast here."

She looked at me, looked over at Jean, then made a sort of half nod. "Are you sure?" she asked Jean.

"I think so. Yes. I am."

I glanced at Jean, who just raised her chin like I was going to challenge her about something. But I had no idea what was going on. Until I glanced over at the door and Hogan, who had been here earlier and gone out for some errand I'd missed, walked back into the room.

"My ass is numb," he said. "I thought you'd never call me in from the waiting room. And also, I've been listening in at the door."

I had a moment of my heart beating so hard it hurt. But

then Ryder squeezed my hand. "We got this," he said again. It was beginning to be one of my favorite things to hear him say.

"Have a seat, Hogan," Ryder said. "These women are about to blow your mind."

Oh. *Oh*. We were going to tell him. All of it. The rest of it. Bring him into our merry little band of life-on-the-liners. Bring him into our family.

It meant something. It was a big decision and a part of me hoped Jean wasn't making it just because I'd been hurt.

"You're up." Myra sort of waved at Jean, giving her the floor.

Jean took in a breath, let it out, then turned to face Hogan. He read her mood and pushed a stool over near her then dropped down on it. "All right. Go."

"Gods are real. They vacation here. They put down their god powers, and live like mortals. You know a lot of them. They've all left town recently because we've had some problems lately."

Hogan's eyes flickered to the brace on her leg, cast on her arm, then back to her. He leaned forward, arms across his knees, fingers laced, and nodded. "Go."

"Okay, so it's more than just gods. There are also some supernatural creatures in town. Um, vampires, werewolves. Valkyrie, gillmen, giants, elves, nymphs, gnomes, sirens, kelpies. Like a *lot* of different kind of creatures. They're not vacationing. They just live here because it's safe. Usually safe. Because we keep it that way. Us Reeds. And well, Ryder too, and a couple other people, but mostly us Reeds."

She waited. He waited. We waited.

"Speak," she said, exasperated.

"That it?"

"Yes?"

"Don't know what you want me to say."

"I want to know if you believe me. If you think I'm insane."

"I know you're insane, but that's a thing I like about you." His smile was bright white against the darkness of his skin. "You think I don't believe in that sort of thing? Gods and monsters and all that?"

"Nobody believes in those sorts of things," she said.

"Uh-huh. There's some churches that would argue with you on the gods. They're all about the believing."

"God. One."

"More than one kind of church, more than one kind of god gets believed in." He shrugged. "You say there's monsters, I say fine. So long as they come to my bakery, not that new one that doesn't even use real butter, and just so long as they don't try to hurt you."

"Hogan...."

"No. I don't care about what's in this town as long as it has you, Jean."

"Aw..." I accidentally said out loud.

Jean threw me a scorching glare and Ryder snorted.

"You're just going to take my word for all this?" she asked Hogan.

He unfolded his fingers, then strung them back together again. "I've seen some folk around town do things you'd think a person can't do. Maybe some of them were a little more than human, and I think that's okay. That's not such a bad thing, us being different but still all fitting together, don't you think? It might even be its own kind of beauty."

And yes, even drugged up and hurting, I could tell this was a continuation of a conversation they'd been having.

I pressed my lips together so another *aw* didn't escape.

"Okay," she said. "Okay. So that's what it is. The secret I've been keeping. And now you know it, and now you have to help me keep it."

He nodded. "How about I just keep treating everyone the same and keep my mouth to myself?"

"Well, not *always* to yourself," she said.

That got a big grin out of him, his entire body smiling, from relaxed shoulders to open hands, to bright eyes.

"Wouldn't want to be stingy," he agreed.

"Yeah." Jean was looking at him like there was no one else in the room, and that word came out mostly breath and want. I was pretty sure I was about to see more of my sister's love life than I'd bargained for.

"Maybe you two could go get dinner, or lunch, or whatever time it is meal," I said. "Talk it over, kiss it over, whatever, somewhere private where I don't have to watch."

Jean nodded, barely sparing me a look. "We're done with this for now?" she asked Myra.

"No," Myra said, "but you should probably take your meds and get off your feet for a while."

"Good idea. I need a bed. Breakfast in bed."

"It's dinner time," Hogan said.

"Dinner at the drive-thru, breakfast in bed."

He stood and walked over, helping her up onto her feet and handing over her crutches. "Your wish, my pleasure."

I opened my mouth, and slapped my hand over it again before any more sappy sounds came out of it.

They made their way out of the room and Myra waited a whole half-second before turning on me.

"This ends here and now, Delaney."

I fished around on the bed and made a point to hold up the morphine button so she'd clearly see it as I depressed it.

Click.

"We'll make some new rules," I agreed. "I've got my law-and-order boy right here to help us out."

"This isn't a joke."

I knew it wasn't, could see the cruelty of what we had been through, what my choices had put her through in all the micro-fine lines of her face, as if grief had been painted beneath her skin and had permanently changed her.

"I know. I hear you, really hear you, Myra. And it's not just the morphine talking." I smiled, but was pretty sure it came out goofy and didn't do anything for my case.

"You can't," she said, "you can't...the list is so long, I don't even know where to start."

"I can't put my life on the line like it isn't attached to anyone. I can't leave us like Dad left us, like Mom left us. I can't think my pain is a small price to pay for other people being safe. I'm required to live out as many decades as possible here, until you and me and Jean are old ladies in rocking chairs, smoking cigars and arguing over bowling games and fences.

"I'm not allowed to die again. Not for a very long time, and when that time comes, it will be because I'm ready for a new adventure, not because I'm cutting this one short."

She opened her mouth, shut it, sniffed, then blinked.

I opened my arms. "C'mere, Mymy. I'm gonna be fine, and so much not as stupid. Stupider, as I was." I made a face, my nose felt numb. Okay, maybe the morphine had kicked in. Didn't make my sentiments any different.

She finally got up out of her chair, and sat next to me on the bed. I was still sitting too. She carefully rested her forehead against my shoulder and let me pat her back.

It wasn't exactly comfortable, but we both needed it, so we stayed there for a long time.

I was getting sleepy, sort of fading in and out with the rhythm of her breathing and my own heartbeat and drifting thoughts, when one thing hit me.

"What kind of deal did you make with Bathin?"

"What?" She wasn't leaning on my shoulder anymore. As a matter of fact, she was sitting in a chair again, Ryder curled up with his back toward us on the sort-of-recliner thing they'd brought into the room, his coat over his hips as a blanket. I wondered where his dog, Spud, was tonight, who was looking after him. Wondered if he was home alone in Ryder's nice lakeside cabin or if maybe his next door neighbor the Jinn was looking after him.

"Delaney?" Myra said.

Right. I had a question. A question for her. "Bathin," I said. "He gave me back my feelings, but he still has my soul. I know he liked keeping them from me. And you, Than said you did something, made him give them back? My feelings back? What kind of deal did you make with him, Myra? With the demon."

"I didn't make a deal."

"Demon. You made a deal."

"No." She shifted in her chair and put down the tablet she'd been writing on. That was when I noticed she had several file folders, an accordion file, and a stack of paper spread out over the low coffee table in front of her chair. She was working at night in my hospital room.

We were going to have to talk about new rules for her too. Like there was a time of day when she was no longer allowed to work.

"I told him he owed us," she said. "Told him he owed you

and owed me to give your emotions back. Because selling off your feelings wasn't a part of the deal you'd made with him."

I sat there a moment, rolling that around in my head. "And he listened to you?"

"Yes, he did. I'm the law here, Delaney, and if he wants to stay in Ordinary, he's going to have to follow the law."

Huh. Funny how me being the law hadn't made a bit of difference to him. I was pretty sure him doing what she said had nothing to do with her badge.

"He likes you."

"Demon. Incapable of real emotions."

"Does it say that somewhere in a book?"

"Several."

"Maybe he's different?"

"All of them are different, none of them desire anyone for anything other than pain and manipulation."

"Right," I said, even though I wasn't agreeing. I wasn't disagreeing, either—I mean, Myra knew her beans. If she said demons weren't relationship material, I was more than willing to believe her. But I'd seen Bathin in some pretty key moments. Moments when he didn't think I was watching him watch her.

"I think we need to keep an eye on him," I mumbled as I felt sleep reaching up to draw me down again.

"It's on the To-Do list."

"Do you think he was working for Lavius?"

"He said he got jumped by Lavius. Agreed to his terms, to bring him Rossi. Said he played a part but never served him."

"You believe that?" I did, because I knew he'd been in cahoots with Dad and Death. I was just curious as to what she'd say.

"I believe he did what he had to, to save his own neck."

"And that's…."

"Typical. Never trust a demon. But he has your soul, and he's still here. That's something."

"Right." I nodded. "If only we knew why he was really sticking around."

She pretended not to hear me. I pretended not to see her blush. Then I closed my eyes, letting Ryder's soft snores lull me down.

286

WHEN I woke up next, it was to the scent of hot chocolate being waved beneath my nose.

I moaned, a soft, needful sound and opened my eyes.

"Hey," I started, then stopped. I had expected Ryder, or maybe Jean. Not Bathin.

"Morning, little trooper. How about some contraband cocoa?"

I looked around the room. Myra was gone, but Ryder was still there. He was sort of crunched up on his other side now, his arm over his eyes, one hand on his gun which rested in the holster on his hip.

From the sleek blue light and dark shadows filling the room, I could only assume it was the middle of the night, that in-between hour when it felt like time wasn't ever going to mean something again.

"He's out cold. Been up for a couple days, sitting with you, covering the police work, dealing with the exit of deities."

"Myra?"

He waved the mug of cocoa at me again. "What about her?"

"Where is she?"

"Why would I know?"

I just gave him a look. "Where is she?"

"At Jean's house. They're staying together again tonight. Oh, they say it's because Jean might need help in the middle of the night with her injuries, but we know why they're really clinging to each other like frightened children. Life is such a fragile thing, something you've reminded them of quite a lot lately."

"Don't be an ass." I moved the bed so I was sitting up a little more. "And pass the damn cocoa."

He handed me the paper cup, which had no lid but an obscene mountain of whipped cream on top. Just how I liked it, really.

"She's right. You're much more fun when you get all moody."

I sipped cocoa—well, took a couple bites of whipped cream and ignored the bait. I knew Myra wouldn't have offered my continued pain as a source of amusement to talk Bathin into giving me back my emotions. I knew my sister. She had threatened him, and I was pretty sure it was with more than just snapping a piece of chalk.

"Did you make her promise you anything? Did you trade her something for my emotions?"

"A gentleman never tells."

I tipped the cup, got down to the cocoa. It was rich, warm, and delicious. Actually, it tasted just like the cocoa from the Perky Perch.

"Good thing I'm not asking a gentleman then. Tell me, Bathin. I get that you don't like us, I get that you want to wind us up and watch us wobble around. What did you take from my sister in exchange for my emotions?"

He studied me for a moment, that uncommonly handsome man who was neither of those things. Finally: "Nothing. She asked, I returned them."

"Just like that."

"Do you believe me?"

"No. But I believe her. She said the same thing."

"Well then. Maybe I've turned over a new leaf. Changed my ways. Reformed for the good of Ordinary, for the good of all."

I took one more sip of cocoa, holding the cool whipped cream and warm cocoa in my mouth for a moment, savoring, before swallowing. Then I handed him back the cup.

"I liked it when you at least pretended to tell the truth. Maybe go back to that."

He grinned, a hot slash of teeth. "I'll see what I can do."

"You didn't honor our deal," I said.

"That doesn't sound like me."

"You said you'd let Dad die in exchange for my soul. But you kept him. In you." It sounded just as bad out loud as in my head.

"I promised you I would release him to the afterlife of his choosing. He chose to remain with me as a favor to Death, for a very limited time."

"That's a lot of risk and what-if's on my father's mortal soul."

288

"Or it's just fate."

"Know her?"

"We've met. I'm not a fan."

"Good. Free will's a lot more fun."

He chuckled. "Isn't it just?"

I closed my eyes, too tired to get in an argument with him, and not really seeing any reason to at this point. He had my soul. But I'd get it back.

I was a Reed, and a damn stubborn one.

"We'll see," he said as he rose. Right. He could read my mind. I pictured him doing some unlikely things with his anatomy.

He laughed, then walked across the room, and settled down in the chair where Myra had been sitting.

I didn't know why he was staying in my room.

I didn't know why it was oddly comforting either. But the nightmares that were my memories were waiting for me down there in my slumber, and I thought that maybe having a demon occasionally—well, mostly, okay, only when he felt like being—on my side wouldn't be a bad thing right now.

When I slept, I dreamed of fire and ash. All the flames were warm, and the ash that fell from the velvet sky melted against my skin with the sound of my father's laughter.

EPILOGUE

"THEY PUT locks on it," I said.

"Still not seeing a problem." Ryder offered me a French fry from his plate. We were sitting at a table at Jump Off Jack's, our local and award-winning brewery. It was where Ryder and I had gone on our first date.

"I didn't say it was a problem. Just. It's not. Not the same."

I'd told him about the whole Mithra take over I'd seen happen. Then I'd filled him and Myra and Jean and Hogan in on the death-favor with Dad and Bathin.

Ryder had been furious when he heard Mithra had possessed him. I knew there was going to be a lot more reasearch into what Mithra could actually enforce in contracts. Myra was on board for finding a way to make sure Mithra couldn't take over Ryder's body again. Even Bathin said he'd be happy to help. We told him no, but still, he offered.

Demon.

Chris Lagon, a gillman and brewmaster and owner of this joint, deposited two fresh beers and gave me a wink. "Town feels all roomy now. Wasn't sure I'd like it, but it's growing on me."

"They'll be back," I said, knowing he was talking about the gods who had left.

Now, a full two weeks after they had been forced to pick up their powers and pack up their bags, the town was both getting back to normal and still sort of holding its breath, waiting for the gods to return.

Like the ghost girl at the lighthouse waiting for her love to return from the sea.

Except we weren't going to pull any tourist dollars off our absent god situation.

"Beers are on the house. I'm working up some holiday brews and need the feedback."

"No rhubarb?"

He laughed, a liquid bark that sounded a little like a sea lion, something I would never say to his face, since I liked free beer.

"No rhubarb. Pumpkin, spices, coconut. Give it a go."

I lifted the deep, dark beer that had a shaft of red where light hit it the hardest, and sipped. Gods, that was good.

"Amazing," I said. "This is a winner."

Chris gave me a half bow, and then wandered off to the next table, depositing a sampler tray.

I took Ryder's fry and bit down into the heat and crunch and salt of it. My appetite was still off. So was my breathing and sleep schedule and range of motion.

Basically, getting shot with a blood and dirt bullet meant to take out a vampire left all sorts of lingering pains and weirdness.

I was recovering, and as far as the doctors, ancient texts, and witches could tell, I would be whole in the long run. But the short run was still sort of a day to day thing filled with pain and change, and hope for tomorrow to be better in small ways.

"Why don't you tell me why you don't want to go home." Ryder picked up his beer, took one drink, then pushed everything to one side of the table so he could fold his elbows down and watch me. See me.

I resisted the urge to rub at my neck, where the bite from Lavius had faded to soft red freckles I wasn't sure I'd ever be rid of. The tie between us though? That was gone. Blessedly so.

And so was he.

Except for when I closed my eyes, when I dreamed at night, or when a shadow shifted in my quiet house. Then he was everywhere, his hatred, his anger, his cruelty.

I heard the gun in every loud noise, and in every soft silence, Rossi's apology, *"Forgive me, Delaney"* right before he had shoved me into that gun, that bullet, that death. I hadn't seen Rossi since I'd come back to life. The scratch on my neck he'd given me to prove his claim was gone, healing like a normal scratch.

Leaving a lot of confusion behind.

"You can start by telling me where you just went right then." Ryder's voice was easy, gentle. The tone he'd been using an awful lot with me lately. A tone that reminded me that maybe I wasn't as whole and healed and strong as I hoped I was.

I was getting there, I just wasn't at the finish line yet.

I rubbed my fingers through the cool condensation on my glass, trying to pull up the nerve to tell him the truth. Oh, who was I kidding? I'd never been good at lying to him.

I lifted my gaze, and was caught by the green of his eyes, the smile that did not hold pity, only interest, only love.

How had I gotten so lucky?

"It's my home. I grew up there. I love it. I know I love it."

He waited while I fiddled with my napkin. I thought about stealing another French fry just to sort of lighten the mood, but had a feeling he wouldn't fall for it.

"A lot of my good memories, years of them are in that house. But since the fight. I just can't see past it."

"Move in with me."

And wow, that was not what I had expected. I thought he was going to offer to sleep over a few nights, maybe suggest I get someone in there to cleanse the vibes or smudge the spirits or make me buy a cat or some such thing.

He took the utter surprise on my face in stride. "It doesn't have to be permanent, but for a little while, a few days, a few weeks, move in with me. You can have the spare room if you want your own space. Your own bed." He paused, then carried on as if he didn't want to give me a chance to argue. "Spud loves you. Dog has good taste."

"Spud loves me, huh?"

"Head-over-heels for you."

I smiled and stole another fry. "Maybe I'll give him a little treat. To buy my way into his good graces since I'll be taking up some of the room."

"He doesn't need any gifts. Just you, Delaney. You being alive. Here. That's gift enough."

I knew we were no longer talking about the dog.

I crooked a finger at him. He raised one eyebrow, then leaned across the table. He was tall, Ryder Bailey, which was a good thing since bending forward wasn't anywhere near a comfortable position for me yet.

And he could read my mind a little, or maybe just my heart. Because he kissed me, and I kissed him back.

RYDER DROVE me home and helped me pack a bag, and boxed up the perishable groceries with the ice from my freezer so we could put them in his refrigerator. He even remembered to grab my pillow and my favorite Grateful Dead T-shirt of Dad's that I liked to sleep in, and my Chewbacca cup.

Then he drove me to Jame and Ben's house because I asked him to.

"I'll come in with you." He wasn't offering. He was stating.

"I can do this on my own. We don't have to be joined at the hip." I said this as he stepped out of the driver's side of his truck and came around to open my door.

"I know you can do it on your own, but I think I've earned a little attached-at-the hip time, don't you?" And that wasn't really a question either.

"I'm not going to do stupid things anymore," I repeated for maybe the hundredth time. "I promised Myra."

"I know."

"You made me sign a no-stupid contract."

He grinned. "I did."

We were walking to the door. "You don't believe me."

"I believe you, it's just this town has a funny way of changing a person's mind under the right circumstances."

He knocked on Jame's door. There was a long, long pause, and I wondered if Jame and Ben weren't home. That they'd gone back to the hospital to make sure Ben's remarkably quick recovery was still going well.

And then the latches shifted, the locks turned and the door slowly opened.

"Hello, De-la-ney." Ben's voice was a total wreck, a mix of ragged and whispers. I didn't know if that was going to heal fully or not—none of us knew—but he was standing.

He was pale, brutally thin, with lines of red as if he'd been burned by hot lashes across the skin I could see on his face hands and wrist, but there was a wild living heat in his eyes.

The smile he gave me was victorious.

"Come in." He shuffled back two steps, and Jame was there in the shadows, so close Ben couldn't have taken another step if he wanted to. Jame's hands found their familiar place on Ben's hip, his back, as he gently steered his boyfriend, who made a half-hearted protest, into the living room.

I followed along, my own boyfriend in a very similar support position with me. When Ryder had me settled in a soft chair across from Ben, who was on the couch and tucked between a pile of pillows and the fluffiest pinkest blanket I had ever seen in my life, I rolled my eyes at Ben and he rolled his back at me.

"Hush now," Ryder said.

Jame growled.

Ben and I grinned at each other.

And that's how I knew Ben was going to be okay, and really, so was I.

I THINK almost every person in town made time to come by and see me, either at Ryder's cabin where I rested in a chair out by the lake reveling in the last gasps of sunshine days as the cool of autumn crept into the night, or at the station where I snuck in with Jean to get some work done while Myra told both Jean and I that we shouldn't be there until we were healed.

I was practically buried in a landslide of casseroles, cakes, cookies, fruit baskets, coffee cards, get well cards and various bubble baths and weirdly colored stuffed animals.

It was nice. More than nice, it was really, really sweet, even if I would be eating casseroles until the end of time.

Shoe and Hatter had done more than stick around while we were short-handed. They'd asked to be transferred.

We were still waiting for all the approvals and paperwork to clear, but Tillamook was looking to reduce the force due to budget cuts, and Ordinary had enough room to take on two officers, especially once Bertie heard about it and got a bond passed through so quickly, there wasn't even time for the volunteers who had gone door-to-door to get signatures, then manned the phones for vote reminders, to organize a victory party.

Chris Lagon had thrown an impromptu bonfire on the beach and supplied the beer, so it all worked out.

The budget budged, thanks to the willing taxpayers of the

town, and we were all set for an increased police presence.

With the decrease of deities, I didn't really think we needed the extra help. Then Roy reminded me that he was going to be retiring soon, and that even with my sisters and I working full-time, there still was too much work to do.

He'd also reminded me that it was only the gods who had been vacationing in Ordinary who couldn't come back for a year. Any other deity out there could at any time decide to take a vacation.

And then he'd told me to take my antibiotics and threatened to make me watch the two-hour video of his golf swing practice he was supposed to review before his next class if I stayed at work with him.

So, yeah. We were going to get new people on the force.

Yay, us.

But in the constant stream of well-wishers, I had not once seen Rossi. I asked Myra about it, and she told me he'd gone back to his house after the fight and she hadn't seen or heard from him since.

He was probably licking his wounds. Dealing with the knowledge that Lavius was gone now. The brother he had once been, the enemy he had become. Gone.

The loss of a contemporary when one was many hundred years old, must be an odd thing. I'm sure I couldn't comprehend the vastness or complexity of it.

But turning away from the world wasn't going to make anything better.

On a morning that finally felt crisp around the edges with the promise of fall, I had one of my well-wishers drop me off at Rossi's house. Ryder was already on duty and had been called out to deal with Mrs. Yates's penguin. Someone had not only knitted, or maybe crocheted, it a full ballerina fairy ensemble, they'd also strung it with lights and suspended it over one of the intersections with a traffic light.

The incoming high school tricksters were thinking outside the box with that one, and I made a note to have Ryder shake down the younger members of the K.I.N.K.s and C.O.C.K.s to get a couple names, confessions, and if possible, a couple fines.

I mean, yes, it was funny and also adorable because those

kids could knit and crochet. But that penguin was concrete. If it had fallen on a car or worse, pedestrian, someone could have really gotten hurt.

So Ryder didn't know about my visit to Rossi, but it wasn't like I was going to see Rossi just to stir up trouble. This visit fell squarely beneath the don't-do-anything-stupid-without-telling-me-first deal I had going with Ryder and Myra and Jean.

That deal came with a clause that somehow dealt with actual police-business type dangers. Ryder had explained it to me, at length in bed, and I think he just did it so he could bore me to sleep.

Mission accomplished.

I shifted the gift under my arm—never say I was an inconsiderate caller—and rang the doorbell.

Leon answered the door, looked me over from toe to face, his eyes only catching briefly on the thing beneath my arm, and gave me a short nod. "He's in his office. He knows you're here."

Vampires. They could spot the uniqueness of a beating heart within a mile radius.

"Thanks." I took my time walking back to the room where I'd last talked to Rossi about the threat of Lavius over the murdered Sven's body.

Even though I knew there was a high chance there were no dead bodies behind the door, I hesitated on the outside and got my emotions in order. I was still jumping at shadows. Ryder held me tight and woke me gently each night (room of my own did not mean I wanted a bed of my own) and still the nightmares were inescapable.

This, though. This was daylight, a friend of mine. Someone who might be hurting in ways I couldn't understand.

I knocked softly on the door.

"It's open, Delaney."

I pushed the door and stepped inside.

The room hadn't changed much. There was no dead body on the coffee table (thank goodness) and the furnishings were clean line modern from a few decades ago, the walls a soft pastel and all of them lined with glass lighted shelves.

On those shelves were carved eggs, all of them powerful in their intricacies, commanding the gaze even though they were the most fragile of prisons.

Rossi sat on the couch, very still. There was something about the way he was just suspended in that position that made me think he had been sitting there, exactly like that, for a long time.

His hands were flat on his thighs, head level, and eyes...oh, his eyes.

"What happened?" The words were out of my mouth before I could think them through. Because I knew what had happened. He'd been shot too. In the face. With a bullet meant to kill a vampire just like him.

He'd been shot other places too. His chest, I thought. My eyes ticked down and I stared at his very crisp, very clean white shirt that was just loose enough it could be covering bandages, wraps.

"Death," he said, his voice rusty and deep. "Death happened."

A hundred years of sorrow rode those words. A hundred more of longing.

"Death might have happened, but life won. We won."

"I am not a living thing, Delaney."

"Well, not right now, apparently. You should go to the hospital and have your face looked at."

He turned his head just slightly, as if it weren't used to moving anymore. He stared at me balefully out of one eye. The other was covered in a black satin patch, the bands of which disappeared beneath his long salt and pepper hair. The wound on his cheek that rode at the bottom edge of the patch looked too raw, as if fresh skin could not find purchase there.

"There is nothing they can do for my face."

"Will you heal?"

I could tell he didn't want to answer me, but he did anyway. "In time."

The silence between us stretched out. The coast guard chopper rattled its way down the shoreline, enough I could hear it, not enough to disturb the precariously balanced eggs on glass shelves.

I wondered if this was what grief, what mourning looked like on him.

"I'm sorry for your loss."

His eyebrow rose. "My loss."

"I know he was important—"

"He was a blight that should have been burned out of the world years ago. A tumor I should have removed."

Ah. So it wasn't sorrow, it was guilt.

"Yeah, that would have been nice of you. But it's not what happened. Still. We're alive. He's not." I shrugged. "We win."

Again with the uncomfortable silence.

"I looked for a card that said, *sorry your brother was such a psychopathic dick* but they were all out. So, here." I held out the thing from under my arm.

It took him some time before he looked away from my face and down at my hands. Like I was suddenly speaking a language he had never heard before and he needed some time to process that.

"Why are you pointing a sheep at me?"

"It's not a sheep. It's a llama."

"It's blue."

"It's a sad llama."

"Why are you pointing a sad llama at me?"

"I'm not pointing, I'm offering." His lips twisted in doubt. "*Fine.* I'm giving. I'm giving it to you as a gift and you can't refuse because that's rude."

"Delaney, I shoved you into the bullets of a killer. I broke my vow to your father. I killed my brother without an ounce of regret. Being rude isn't much of a stretch for me."

"Take the llama." I jiggled it and it made this soft little snore-gurgle. We both stilled and stared at it. He looked panicked. Maybe a little disturbed. Like he really, really didn't want to touch it.

Oh, he was so going to touch the heck out of it now that I knew it made noise.

"You got me shot." I shook the llama and it gargled at him. "Which, really, was what I'd agreed to since I was the one going in there to die so we could kill Lavius. Yes, you made a promise to my dad."

Shake, shake. Garbly-squeal. The look of horror on his face was priceless.

"I made promises too," I said. "Promises to living people in this town. And I have gone against my better judgment—you might perhaps remember I gave my soul to a demon—to find a way to keep the people I care about safe.

"That's all you did, Travail. You went against your better judgment and knew I was willing to take a hit so you could kill Lavius. There wasn't any other way, I don't think."

My thoughts wandered over the tarot reading Jules had given me. Nine of Swords for worry, Death for change, and the Devil for chains that needed breaking.

"Wow," I said, realizing how it all fit together and how right she was. "Jules should really be charging more money for her readings."

Rossi made a sound that was a little like a sigh and a lot like frustration. Right. We were talking llama.

"Take the llama. This is the price I demand you pay for getting me shot. You must accept the blue llama of penance."

And that, *that*, got a small smile out of him. He was stiff, unbending as if the things inside of him were all edges rubbing together in the wrong ways, but he stretched out his hand and took the llama. He held it on just his fingertips, as if he were afraid to let too much skin touch it.

"You are a willful woman, Delaney. You always have been."

"Thank you."

"This toy is atrocious." He stroked it unconsciously with his other hand. It really was remarkably soft.

"You like it."

"I do not." It was out of his fingertips now and cradled in his hands. Both his thumbs were petting the long neck and flat back. Something in the way he held himself softened. He wasn't the easy-going love and peace and hippie-groovy Rossi that I knew so well, but he was on his way.

"He likes you."

"It's a toy, Delaney. It's not alive."

"Some of my favorite people aren't quite alive."

He huffed a laugh then and I grinned at him.

"Sit down," he said. "And let me pour you some tea."

299

MORE ORDINARY MAGIC?
YOU BET!

ROCK CANDY:
ORDINARY MAGIC - SHORT STORY

Coming Fall 2017

PAPER STARS:
ORDINARY MAGIC - SHORT STORY

Coming Winter 2017

SCISSOR KISSES:
ORDINARY MAGIC - SHORT STORY

Coming Spring 2018

ACKNOWLEDGMENT

THIS, I thought, would be the end of our adventures in Ordinary, Oregon. Three books seemed like just the right amount to tell Delaney's story. But then a demon happened and messed up my plans. So, I am happy to say there will be at least three more short stories set in this world, and very possibly two more books. Two short stories will come out late 2017 and then one in 2018. The two books will hopefully be out in 2018.

I'd like to think my family for putting up with me while I pulled this book together. You are all amazing, supportive, wonderful people. Thank you to Dejsha Knight for beta reading this under ridiculous circumstances, and Sharon Elaine Thompson for doing the same. I'm not sure I can express how much your insights helped make this book better. Big shout out and heartfelt gratitude to Skyla Dawn Cameron, copy editor and formatting genius extrodinare, who came to my rescue with flying colors. Thank you to the talented Lou Harper, for once again giving this world such a fantastic cover.

To the Deadline Dames and all the indie published writers out there sharing information, swapping stories, and plotting mischief—thank you for being a part of my life!

All my love and gratitude to my husband Russ Monk, and my sons Kameron and Konner Monk. The three of you make the world a better place, keep me encouraged, and always make me laugh. I love you.

And most importantly, to my amazing readers. You are the best! This book would not be here without you. Thanks for spending a little time in Ordinary, Oregon. I hope you enjoyed your stay and will come back soon to see what is in store for our heroes, monsters, lovers, gods,(yes, and that demon), and all the other extraordinarily ordinary folk.

ABOUT THE AUTHOR

DEVON MONK is a national best selling writer of urban fantasy. Her series include Ordinary Magic, House Immortal, Allie Beckstrom, Broken Magic, and Shame and Terric. She also writes the Age of Steam steampunk series, and the occasional short story which can be found in her collection: A Cup of Normal, and in various anthologies. She has one husband, two sons, and lives in Oregon. When not writing, Devon is drinking too much coffee, watching hockey, or knitting silly things.

Want to read more from Devon?
Follow her online or sign up for her newsletter at:
http://www.devonmonk.com.

CPSIA information can be obtained
at www.ICGtesting.com
Printed in the USA
LVOW11s1712201117
557024LV00003B/853/P